A WOMAN OF HEART

A Novel By

Marcy Alancraig

Ane - You are a woman of
heart. Thank you for
all your guidance
& wisdom!

Marcy

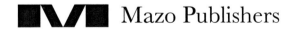 Mazo Publishers

A WOMAN OF HEART
ISBN: 978-1-936778-94-2

Copyright © 2011 Marcy Alancraig

Published by:
Mazo Publishers

Website: www.mazopublishers.com
Email: cm@mazopublishers.com
Tel: 1-815-301-3559

Cover and Page Design by
Prestige PrePress
prestige.prepress@gmail.com

Front Cover Background Photograph
© Fernley | Dreamstime.com

To
Cynthia Lasky, Sonia Margulis and Catherine Houston,
whose living and dying taught me so much.

To
Debra, with love

CONTENTS

Part I
TRUTHS YOU SHOULD KNOW

Part II
SECRETS WAITING FOR AN EAR

Part III
COMING TO TERMS

About The Author

Marcy Alancraig's writing arises from her love of California's many landscapes and the people who have been shaped by them. *A Woman of Heart* came into being after Marcy became intrigued by a community of chicken ranchers who lived in the rural town of Petaluma during the 1920s and 30s. After two years of research and interviews with their descendents, their joys and conflicts found their way onto the page.

A full-time English professor at Cabrillo Community College in Aptos, California, Marcy finds time for writing between grading papers. Many of her short stories and poems have been published. In 2010, she won the Hayward Award for Excellence in Education, a state-wide recognition of her long-standing commitment to students and innovative teaching.

ACKNOWLEDGMENTS

A circle of friends and loved ones surrounded me during my writing of this book. I would especially like to thank the descendants of the Petaluma chicken ranchers, George Nitzberg, Israel and Alma Tillin, Reva Tow and Ann and Herb Weitzman, whose tales gifted me with details of ranch life and the tenacious spirit of their parents and relatives. I gained more historical detail from Rebecca Beagle, Anna Cherney, Sherry Katz, Keiko Kubo, William Margulis, and Ed Mannion. Kenneth Kann provided me with invaluable transcripts of unpublished oral histories of Petaluma chicken ranchers. Jack Olsen set me on the right track in the very beginning with his usual humor and encouragement.

It took a long while for this novel to find its final shape. My immediate family eagerly read drafts and kept me encouraged. I was also helped by the interest of Patti Guyselman, Thelma Van Epps, Winifred Bear, Janice O'Brien, Paula Ross, Nancy Whitley, and the women of my Writing From the Heart class, especially Jessica Vandeveer. For their steadfast belief in me and vast patience, I thank Anne Fox, Frances Whitney, Donna Cummings, Beverly Wolfe, and Ruth Guthartz. Sherry Katz's weekly phone calls and Alice Bloch's gentle guidance always provided me with direction when I thought I was lost. The enthusiastic support of Rob and Julie Edwards and Tillie Olsen moved the book through its final revision. I could not have completed the novel without the scrutiny and inspiration of my old writing group, Annette March and Lynda Marin, who midwifed this manuscript. My current group, Connie Batten, Sandia Belgrade, Lorna Kohler and Sara Friedlander, have kept me writing during the novel's long journey to publication. Wendy Witt, Anne Fox and Frances Whitney were excellent copy-editors, and I am grateful for their attention and care.

Agent angel Gabriel Constans lived up to his name with his undying belief in the book. I'm also grateful to the team at Mazo Publishers for shepherding the novel into print. Finally, this book would never have been completed without the support of my partner Debra, whose presence in my life creates both possibility and joy. Thank you all.

Marcy Alancraig
Aptos, California

YIDDISH GLOSSARY

The characters in this novel speak English, albeit peppered with Yiddish. Below is a glossary of this vernacular to help the reader have a clearer understanding of their conversations.

Ai yai yai – my, my – it can be happy or sad depending on the inflection
Alter Kocker – old man or old fart

Bissel – a little bit
Boychik – a diminutive of boy used affectionately
Bubbe – grandmother
Bubchik – a diminutive of bubelah
Bubee – another diminutive of bubelah
Bubelah – a term of endearment similar to "darling," "sweetheart" or "honey"

Chutzpah – gall or brazen nerve
Cockamamie – mixed up, muddled, ridiculous

Dayenu – Enough
Drek – Trash, not worth anything

Famisht – confused, mixed up, "like a chicken with its head cut off"
Farfufket – befuddled, discombobulated, crazy and unhinged
Farpotshket – very messed up, famisht to a greater degree
Feh – an expression of disgust

Gevalt – a cry of astonishment such as "What happened?"
Gey gezunterey – go in good health
Gey avek – go away or get out of here

Kinder – children
Kvetch – to fret, fuss or complain

Macher – someone who has connections, an important person
Mazel tov – congratulations and good luck
Mensh – an upright, decent, honorable person
Meshuggeneh – a crazy woman

Meshuggener – a crazy man
Mishegoss – craziness, madness

Nu – so or well
Nudnik – a pest, a nag, an annoyer
Nudzh – to pester or nag

Oy – a lament, a protest, a cry of dismay or joy

Platke Macher – a gossip or trouble maker
Pogrom – massacre of Jews

Schmatte – rag
Sha – quiet, hush
Shayne Maydele – pretty little girl or lovely girl
Shepping Naches – gathering pleasure or special joy from
     the achievements of a child
Shirrup – be quiet!
Shlemiel – a simpleton, a constantly unlucky person, a sad sack
Shlep – to carry, drag or pull
Shmuck – literally, penis, but also a dope or jerk

Tsuris – trouble, woes, worries, suffering
Tuchis – buttocks

Vey – oh
Vey iz mir – oh my God
Zaftik – juicy, plump, buxom

Prologue
VOICES IN THE NIGHT

AUGUST 1980

Rheabie Slominski can't breathe. A slab presses on her chest, condensing her ribs, turning her lungs to flame. *"Vey,"* she moans, trying to get out from under the weight. She hears others crying – a worm, maybe a beetle or sow bug, one of the creatures that lives outside on what remains of her small chicken ranch – tiny lives that gasp and then succumb to the pressing. The smell of their deaths fills her chest. "No!" she tries to scream, but her mouth won't form the word.

Rheabie wrenches awake, her hands clutched around her blanket. "Such *chutzpah,*" she tells it, "thinking you could suffocate me. A flimsy piece of cotton – where did you get such nerve?"

Rheabie feels the quick drumbeat of her seventy-eight-year-old heart. "Slow down, already." She tries to take a breath. "Do your job," she tells her gasping lungs. "A dream we're talking. Nothing you should get excited. A dream – nothing true."

But she's not sure, still feeling the press of whatever was weighing on her while she was asleep. Her arthritic fingers won't unbend, holding tight to the dream. "A premonition you're not," she instructs it. "Enough already. Time you should go."

Rheabie shakes her head, making herself look around the shabby bedroom which has cupped her life for more than fifty years. Her clothes sit folded neatly on a chair, ready for the morning. Her bathrobe, in case she should need in the middle of the night, waits at the bottom of the bed. And then there's the photo of Jake, dancing at their forty-fifth anniversary party. "Such a fool, you," she tells the long-dead face in the silver frame on her dresser. Beside it, a glass of water glimmers in a stab of moonlight. "Yes," she nods. "What I need. A little drink."

Rheabie, be careful. One of the voices she's heard for years moves toward her from the shadows.

"Mamale?" But Mamale's been gone a long time now, lost first in 1917 and then again in 1937.

There's danger.

It can't be Shlima or Gitl, taken at the same time.

You won't be able to do it alone. This time you'll need help.

She tries to stand, to move toward the voice, but her legs have turned shaky.

"Who's there?" she calls. "Jake? Is that you?"

It's time for truth. Someone else needs to know.

Rheabie feels the breath of the night wind, leaves rustling through the gum grove that shades the eastern corner of her two acres. She hears it drift across the old chicken sheds, rotting boards turned white under the touch of the moon. The whole ranch – or what's left of it – seems to lift up into the silent breeze. Once, her entire road sang with the squawks of pullets. Most of the town too. "Chicken Capital of the World" they called Petaluma once – through its crowded years in the 20's and even beyond, as it limped through the Great Depression and then rebounded after the war. "Chicken Capitol" until big business came in the 1960's – all in the name of progress, a celebration of new technology. Feh – crowding the animals so close in cages they couldn't breathe. Destroying small spreads like hers.

Oy, and look at what the place has become – a bedroom community for the big *machers* who work every day in San Francisco. Such a downfall – a place once proud from feeding eggs to the people now just a suburb, houses everywhere, crowded close. Not that the wind cares. It touches everything, carrying what's left of her life into the night sky.

"Wait!" Rheabie calls and lunges forward, her hand out, trying to hold back the gust. Or maybe she's just reaching for the glass of water on her dresser, or wanting to hold the dream, in case there's something she should decipher in what it means. Whatever her hand wants, it comes up empty. Because the book of Chekhov stories, carelessly thrown down by the side of the bed when she got sleepy last night, trips her. Rheabie falls, fingers splayed open. Wind roars around the house as her hip breaks.

Danger, the voice says. *Time to tell someone.*

Rheabie doesn't hear. She's crying as she inches toward the phone, hoping she'll be able to reach up and grab it. And then what? Call Mimi? Too far away in Ithaca. Davy and Mari? How's Berkeley going to help, a good hour and one-half ride from here? Alone, too much alone. No Mas, traveling in Japan. No Nate, stuck in an office in Washington, D.C. Not even Shoshie, her what was promised, her most shining grandchild. Rheabie has only pain, the hip screaming. Only her elbows, digging in for each movement against the floor. "*Vey iz mir,*" she weeps, "I can't do this."

You can, the voice urges her. *You must. The time has come.*

The phone line shines in the shadows ahead of her. Dust feathers the section with the cord peeking out from under the bed. Rheabie tugs, then ducks when the Slimline falls from her night stand.

Tell. The house fills with whispers. *Danger's coming.*

She punches the buttons. 911. "Help, Jake. Mamale, come get me. Shoshie, it's time. There's something needs I should say."

Part I
TRUTHS YOU SHOULD KNOW

SEPTEMBER 1980

Chapter 1
UNEXPECTED STORIES

RHEABIE

Every morning the past week, a wolf wakes me up from the kitchen. The minute I open my eyes, I hear it, walking back and forth. Yes, Shoshana, it's you I'm talking, pacing like a caged animal. I know it's hard to be here, taking care of a sick old woman, but enough already! Maybe you should relax a little? Just sit down?

I want we should visit. Listen, how often do I get the pleasure? Three stays in twelve years – and never more than a week. It's not much.

Now, don't get huffy. Did I say it should be any different? I know from the restless in you, my woman-what-loves-the-road. That itch to travel – it's in those eyes of yours. Green – like the trees you love so much in Washington State. Seattle, Berne, Lydon – all the rainy places you've lived, they show in your face.

So listen, I understand how it must be hard, all this California sun here in Petaluma. September is the worst month, so hot and no fog. Still, we are trapped together in this little house, until my broken hip should get better, or I give up and die like your grandfather. You know the *tsuris* what happened the night I broke it. Giving up I don't do. So maybe we can pass the time, telling each other stories? The truth, I'm talking. The real business of our lives.

I don't mean the "everything's fine, don't worry" we both of us tell your mother and sister. I mean the big deal, Shoshana. All those surprising afternoons with a lover, for instance – I know you've had them – full of juicy business. Or those nights that broke apart in the sink maybe, like a tea glass whose pieces you couldn't find.

Yes, of course, I've known my share and more, those kind of moments. These stories I've been waiting all your life to tell. Why? Because it was promised a long time ago, you should listen. By who? Never mind. That's coming. And because even as a baby, the way you tapped your feet – so cute in those red corduroy booties – I could see you knew from restless. Only one year old and walking already. You lived with the same hurry and push what was born in me.

You don't believe? All right, I'll prove. Get out the photo album. The one what your grandpa put together – our early days on the ranch. You remember where it is? The left-hand book case, third shelf down. That's right. Ach, so many memories. Look. This one, taken five years after we started here. You see? Me, feeding the pullets, in a hurry to get back to the kitchen. So much to do that day, for the camera I didn't have time. "Enough already!" I swore at your grandpa. "The borsht is waiting!"

"Just one more," he begged. "Smile."

Notice the grin on my face, dolly, so strong and stubborn. Like I was biting back a curse, so much hidden behind those teeth. And did you ever wonder what I was seeing? Look at my eyes turned sideways, lost and lonesome. Hungry I was – for a glimpse of the Ukraine, a *bissel* of Terlitza, what I hoped might appear behind the barn. *Oy*, those were hard days. Like you, I was woman what did not know from home.

It's not an insult, lovey, only the truth about us. Take a look at this one. Bent over the garden, showing my *tuchis* to the world. I was bigger in those days, yes, by a good thirty-five pounds; you could see me coming. I liked having hips back then, curves what meant something. Afraid I never was of *zaftig* thighs. But sorry I am to say, all that weight – it wasn't all my body. Here's the truth, dolly: I was a woman made big from carrying the dead.

Ach, don't look so shocked. All your life, hasn't your mother told you I'm crazy? Well, it was *mishegoss* to her all right, the fact that in my body lived ghosts. Every day of her growing up, though she never knew it, the spirits of my mother and my two sisters, Shlima and Gitl, haunted our family. Yes, no kidding. And my spirits had opinions about my life, the ranch, and the way Jake and I were raising your mother and uncles. Such mouths they had on them, but no one else could hear.

No one else heard how it first began the winter of 1917, a dark evening. Picture the Ukraine. A *pogrom*. Blood on snow. Ukrainian soldiers, they'd burned our village. Shot most of us; by night time, there was hardly anyone left alive. Only a few, working in the cemetery. Chopping the frozen ground to dig graves. Finally it was over. I stayed behind after the burials. "I'll be all right," I told my uncle Yosl. "Time I want with them," I motioned to the mounds at my feet, "alone."

"Mamale!" I wailed when he left me. "Why didn't you run from the soldiers?" I pulled my hair. "I wish they'd killed me too."

Then I looked down at the graves and took off my coat, unbuttoning my blouse with shaking fingers. "So long, goodbye. It's over." My skirt fell against the muddy snow. I looked around to make sure that no one was there and then I stood up, naked. We're talking January in Russia. "Gitl! Shlima!" I called. I was too full of tears to know from cold.

"So *nu*?" I opened my arms. "What's the matter? This is not a good enough invitation?" The stars above me heard a whisper, and then a gasp, as my dead family began to laugh. A great wind came from the north, eager and lonely. It only took a moment, and then the spirits of Mamale, Shlima and Gitl climbed up from their graves and into my bones.

I couldn't see them, but I could feel how they'd come into my body. Stretched my arms; my joints, they started to swell. I was bigger, surprised and comforted, but like a balloon, a little swollen. I'm telling you, dolly, it was crowded under my skin.

And so I dressed, heavier by another ten pounds at least, in the ruins of a town torched by the Ukrainian Nationalist Army. My poor Terlitza – completely destroyed. A horror, yes, but also an opportunity. Finally, to America I could go. Uncle Yosl had been good enough to give me his blessing. "Tell your cousin Yonkel in New York to do right by you as you have done right by me." I picked up a small bag what was all I had left in the way of belongings. Then, I slipped into the woods and ran.

Too young, too upset I was to know the danger. Such *chutzpah!* Only fifteen and never before had I mixed with ghosts. Back then, running between fields, I couldn't see the crime I was committing. It's no small thing, *bubee*, to steal a spirit from its grave. The ground, it holds all what the dead need in order to grow.

Well, you don't think that at the end of life, that's it – kaput – it's all over? Ai, Shoshie, this "eternal rest" business – a nice idea if you're tired maybe, but all wrong. The dead have work to do, learning what they never knew before and holding a place what's special to them. They are busy, binding and guarding, making things grow again.

The minute I left Terlitza, I robbed my mother and sisters of this business. Trapped in my body, poor things – no place they could stretch. No piece of ground what could teach them how to get over who they'd been in life. A prison my ribs became – the more I hid and bribed and traveled. Each time I crossed a border, tighter my ghosts got locked into the cage of my bones.

Two years later – crossing the Atlantic – I was used to them talking inside me. Such *kvetching!* Always whispering, jerking me from dreams. Mamale was worried. *Do you hear what your neighbor, that Levy, was saying, the terms of the peace treaty? Such a busybody and not even seasick. Who can believe him? Ai, if only we were back home in Terlitza, then I'd know...* She wanted we should turn back. This new Soviet Union, how could it go forward without her? What she was missing, now that her beloved Bolsheviks had won!

If I got bored by politics, I could sip a slow cup of water and listen to my sister Shlima. *It's too cold, this boat, and it rocks too much. Do you think that captain knows where he's going? Rheabie, such a stink in here! Get up and wash a little. So what, you're sick? A girl should never smell from vomit. We raised you better than that.*

"These cries are love," I said, "bringing light to this awful darkness." I thought my ghosts whined to keep me company or bring me pleasure. Whole candles I lit from the suffering of my dead.

Don't misunderstand, Shoshana. Me they adored, my dear departed family. A thousand blessings they showered on the girl smart enough to get to New York. Sponsored by cousin Yonkel, who'd done well in the needle trades. *That boy,* Gitl hoped, *knows what's what. He'll help us find Papa. Fifteen years since we've seen him – Yonkel will know what do.*

Who needs Papa? Mamale scoffed. Not for her, a reunion with a long-forgotten husband. *Turn this ship around, Rheabie. I want to go back. No matter what that Levy says, a glorious fight for freedom still rages in our land.*

They picked and pecked, bickering the long sweep of water to Ellis Island. I smiled in the dark, grateful not to travel alone.

So America, New York, a crisscross of nightmares – the stories you've heard so many times you must know them by heart. Remember how Yonkel met me after Ellis Island and helped me find Papa, thrown into a grave by typhoid? Eleven years he'd been dead, and we never knew. Then work in the garment shops, walkouts, the excitement of building a union. So busy I was in those organizing days. Sometimes, walking home after a strike meeting, Mamale would kvetch, *Enough already! It's too tiring, this strange country. Vey iz mir, I want to go home.*

But home, Gitl reminded in a sad voice, *is just some marker in a forgotten graveyard. Terlitza is no more, but here we have Rheabie. When she talks, the whole world listens to what we have to say.*

I don't care. I have to go! Mamale insisted.

Wait, I urged her unhappy spirit. *I need you. Don't you want to see what kind of life Jake and I make on the land?*

For by that time, I'd met your grandpop, and already we were saving our pennies to come to Petaluma. Moysche Blumberg, his friend from the union, had read a flyer and gone west to start a chicken ranch. "We can do it too!" Jake declared after reading Moysche's letters. "So, it's hard work, yes. But a man is his own boss. Raising eggs – what matters for people – not sewing topcoats. Chickens, a house, garden. Rheabie, we'll plant seeds."

He practiced planting at night in the thin bed we shared and grinned in his arms he held a mystery. "A man could spend a lifetime," he gasped, "learning all that you are."

A smart one, that Yakkov Slominski, even with his famous temper. I could not bring myself to tell him that in me he got a bargain – four laughing women for the price of one.

And so we carried our story across the country to California. This Petaluma chicken ranch founded on socialism and free love.

Don't laugh! Your generation is not the only one to carve a life from principles. In Petaluma, during the twenties, by our principles we lived strict. A whole group of us, one hundred families, mostly communists and Zionists. A few anarchists and socialists got thrown into the soup.

None of those comrades noticed how I grew larger during loud Jewish Center or Party meetings. They never guessed that I plumped up with the opinions of my ghosts.

"Such a lucky man, your Jake!" Moysche Blumberg would say, filling his plate at the weekly potlucks. "What I wouldn't give, Rheabie, for a *zaftig* woman like you, not afraid of a little meat on her bones."

How could he know that the meat I carried was made from spirits with loud voices, *kvetching* and homesick? Blind as Grandpa, he and our rancher friends saw only the smiling face of Jake's wife, Mimi's mother. The woman kind enough to adopt those poor orphans, your uncles Davy and Nate.

The big truths in me I hid, Shoshana, behind that life of *kinder*, eggs and politics. By 1929, it had become a regular misery, what went on between me and my ghosts.

By then, they'd found a way to escape from their prison. Popping out of my body first thing in the morning, they floated the whole day near the ceiling. Like hawks circling a tasty pullet, they commented about every single thing I did.

Mamale would scrunch up her face and make her lips like she was sucking on a lemon. *Rheabie, what kind of mother are you? Hard-boiled eggs and beets, such a breakfast you're fixing. And maybe you noticed how the floor needs mopping. What, you're going to ignore the mess? No woman back home would let it go another day.*

Shlima, my middle sister, a jumble of bones from the time she was ten, would float above me in a rumpled black dress as I was working. *You call this a clean washing? What's the matter, the bleach didn't like you? In Terlitza, hanging out clothes with such stains, I'd die from shame!*

Even Gitl, her with the sweet nature, would scold me. She'd pop up in the garden and call, *Davy just woke up from his nap. He needs you. How come the weeding is so important you can pretend not to hear?*

They never stopped, not even when the sun went down and the *kinder* were settled. Forced back into my body by nighttime, they wailed Russian songs from the small of my back. And I tossed and turned, pleading they should be quiet. Sometimes I sat straight up in bed and shouted, *Shirrup, already! A crazy woman you're making me.*

Jake would pull me back down. "*Sha*, it's just a nightmare." But what did he know? Your grandpop was the kind of man who slept without dreaming. Besides, this unhappy haunting, from it I could not wake.

In the morning, I'd make tea and feel Mamale leave my body. She floated over the stove, never saying a word. *Whatever I said last night,* I apologized, *I'm sorry. I didn't mean it.* She wouldn't answer. *Talk to me,* I begged. *You can't leave me here in America, this life, all alone.*

Then one day in March, right through that very kitchen door, stepped a little, red-haired neighbor woman. This one, grinning, there on the left in that snapshot. Mae Cherney. The comrade what helped your grandmother make a little peace for her ghosts. Listen, this is not a struggle written in the history books. Not politics and eggs, Shoshana, the tale of my life you maybe expected to hear. But probably you know already, dolly, that in this life we are not always given the expected stories. From my heart, that tired and beating muscle, this is the truth I need you should know.

Chapter 2
WHAT TO BELIEVE?

SHOSHANA

"The truth?" Mom used to sputter in the middle of getting ready for a visit from Grandma Rheabie. She'd slap down her dust rag on the dining room table and glare. "Don't count on it. Your grandmother wouldn't know the truth if it hit her over the head."

"But she said in her last letter…" I sneaked a glance at my sister Aviva and smiled. The quickest way to stop one of Mom's tirades about the sloppy way that we did our chores – "Is it too much to ask that you stack the forks in the drawer? We are not animals. We have hands, not paws" – was to mention something about one of Grandma's stories. Nothing distracted Mom more than a question about her childhood on the chicken ranch out west.

"Your grandmother exaggerates. She twists things around and makes it all sound fun. I thank God for the day that your father took me away from that place. Don't believe her lies."

It was hard not to believe Grandma when she came swooping in the door of our house in Ithaca, opening her arms to give us noisy hugs. Mom never let us go to the train station with Dad to meet Grandma and Grandpa when they arrived from California for their annual Thanksgiving visit. "You girls will just be in the way," she said.

Grandma started waving from the moment that Dad's car pulled up in the driveway. She hurried up the brick walk, never mind if it was slippery with snow, blowing us kisses as she came. "Here, dollies." Before Mom could squawk, she opened her suitcase right there in the foyer and distributed our presents like she was a fairy queen with a magic wand. "So, *nu*, what's the harm?" she asked as we ripped open the faded wrapping paper that covered books or balls. Mom stood beside us, frowning. "Isn't Thanksgiving a time to appreciate?" Grandma would ask. "My beautiful granddaughters, such *bubchiks*, only once a year do I get to see them. This I appreciate from the bottom of my heart."

I loved the disorder that my grandparents brought to our house for the two weeks of their visit. Late at night, I could hear the rumble that was Grandpa Jake's laughter rising up through my floorboards from the kitchen downstairs. A low thud meant that he'd slapped his water glass down on the table. He and Dad were arguing politics again. Grandma cooked and talked, turning even dishwashing into some kind of adventure. "The dishes are on strike, making solidarity with the union. Line them up nice in the drainer, Shoshie. They are marching like we did during the Great Strike in San Francisco. What was it, Mimala, 1934?"

"I don't remember," Mom muttered. "And no one from our family did any marching." She rolled her eyes and sighed loudly. "Don't you start telling lies."

The fairy tales that Grandma told in a dramatic whisper at bedtime when I was very young never seemed like lies, their magic so real that my feet tingled in the exciting moments. I'd listen, breathless and tense, holding tight to Bernie-the-bear, while Grandma invented witches who granted wishes or gave away poisoned apples, but she always made everything turn out right in the end. Afterwards, she leaned back against the headboard and asked, "So *nu*, this story you liked?" I nodded, trying hard not to ask for another. Mom made Grandma promise only one tale a night, and I knew, as well as I knew anything at five, that soon Mom was going to open the door, hallway light flooding the room, so she could come in and check. Grandma sighed and then opened her skinny arms to gather up Bernie and me, cooing a Russian lullaby. The song, lilting and lonesome, was her way, I thought, of sneaking me another story. I fell asleep on her chest, listening to what I called "the magic music," convinced it was the language of the fairies and that the wild horses or enchanted castles she spoke about in that Russian accent of hers had to be real.

Later, it was the tales she spun about growing up in the Ukraine that were full of magic. "The houses in Terlitza were so tired, they leaned this way and that, resting on each other." Grandma pulled me into her shoulder. "Yes, like this. And inside, *bubee*, such noise, each family in their own way. I was the baby, like you. Your great aunts, Shlima and Gitl, they bossed me like you wouldn't believe. That's where I think your mama gets it from," she whispered, "but that's our secret. Don't tell."

I never revealed the truths that Grandma spoke at night, but by the time I was fourteen, I loved to startle the dinner table with some tidbit that Grandma had dropped during the day. "Candling eggs to see if there's a chick inside sounds like fun. It'd make a great biology project."

Mom looked up from her plate and frowned. "Absolutely not. Besides, the only eggs in this house are sterile and used for cooking."

"But I can get some fertile ones. Make an incubator. You know it's not hard. You took care of them on the ranch every day."

"Don't remind me," Mom snapped. "And I said no. Absolutely not."

"Are there anymore mashed potatoes?" Dad asked, pretending that Mom wasn't really angry.

She didn't even stop to look. "You've had enough."

I hadn't. "But Mr. Cooper will love the project," I protested. Aviva nudged me under the table to shut up. I pinched her leg. "Please? It'll get me an A."

Grandpa Jake leaned back in his chair and smiled. "It's not a bad idea, Mimala. We're talking science here. Mixed with history. For a good college, she'll need the grades."

Mom stood up and began to clear the table. She snatched Grandpa's plate first. "No offense, Papa, but Abe and I have worked hard so that these girls don't have to live like we did. I'm not going to have them start now."

"It's who you are. What made you." Grandma shook her head, but spoke gently. "A different way of living than now, yes, but what's the harm they should know how it was?"

"You don't tell how it was," Mom's voice rose. "We worked, every minute, and for what? Hand-me-downs to wear to school. No trips, because the chickens had to be fed. So much worry. And those damn birds stunk to holy hell."

Grandpa wasn't smiling anymore. Grandma looked as if she'd been hit. "It was more than that," she insisted.

"For who?" Mom turned her back, carrying a stack of plates into the kitchen. They clattered into the sink. "The plain truth – we never had more than two pennies to rub together," she called.

"All right, yes," Grandma admitted. Then she shrugged, but Mom couldn't see it. "A penny isn't everything," Grandma whispered, patting Grandpa's arm.

When Mom returned, gathering up platters and bowls, Grandma tried again. "So you remember hell and I think paradise. So what? We're both the old generation now, Mimala. It doesn't matter what we think." Then she winked at Aviva and me, sending comfort across the lace tablecloth. "But you, dollies, like the pennies you mother wanted, but so bright and new, with the future to make in front of you. Your inheritance, this is. The truth in it you have to find, what you want to believe."

Sixteen years later, walking across what's left of the old ranch to the vegetable garden, I'm not sure what I want to believe. Surely not Grandma's latest tale, this strange story about *pogroms* and *kvetchy* ghosts that she surprised me with in the kitchen. Look at me, I demand of the rustling eucalyptus, one of a series of shedding trees that she calls the gum grove, leaning into the wind on the edge of her property. Do I look five or even fourteen? How could she think that I'd swallow this haunting business about her mother and sisters, even if she swears in her best fairy tale voice that it's the truth?

The garden is quiet, and I want to drink its stillness: water beading the cucumber leaves, tiny pools gathered at the bottom of squash blossoms. Maybe a swallow of dew would quiet me too, let me shake off Grandma's questions and stories that follow me around the house as I tend to her broken hip. I bend to cut a few chives for our breakfast omelets. Isn't it enough that I interrupted my life in Lydon to come to California to nurse her, loaning both my job and cat to my neighbor Lillian? All right, so maybe I was just about to quit the Kitchen Kupboard anyway. I'd been in Lydon almost eighteen months, and it was getting old. But still, this crazy story she wants me to believe?

I look up at the bare brown hills behind the ranch, a series of soft arches that run west, eventually tumbling down into the Pacific Ocean. But they're so dry, a sea of dead grass punctuated by a few oak trees. All I can see is the same unvarying golden brown, broken every once in a while by a twisted shadow of dark green.

I long for the sharp mountains I left behind, thick with cedar and Douglas fir, so tangled by undergrowth that they are hard to walk through. Why did I trade them to shop for groceries and cook Grandma's meals?

Because she needed me.

But, I argue, was it worth it to walk away from Mark, one in a series of indifferent logger boyfriends, just to *shlep* Grandma back and forth to physical therapy? He's probably shacked up with someone else by now while I weed and wash dishes, put her down for naps and get her up again. And even if he were not, I was going to leave him anyway. But for this?

A crow cuts the sky above me with its cry. "What do you want?" I ask, sounding as sharp and angry as Mom.

It's only been two weeks, and already I am as mad as my poor mother used to get whenever Grandma came for a visit. I'm tired and restless, hungry for solitude. But there's dusting and vacuuming yet to get to this morning, plus tying up her newspapers into bundles for recycling. Grandma even wants me to do her monthly stint next week at the Ecology Center, sorting glass and aluminum cans. Isn't that enough? Do I have to believe her story too?

"Of course?" Rheabie Slominski would answer if I was bold enough to sass her with such a question. I hear her words, even though she doesn't say them, when I bring all the vegetables back to the kitchen, "A little belief, what's the hurt?"

I didn't realize how much that belief hurts the woman that I've grown to be. I crack the store-bought eggs into a mixing bowl. "No more keeping chickens for me," Grandma told me when I first arrived, watching me react with shock at the sight of the empty coop. "So many years, the layers. With this finally, I am done."

I approved the change – "so much less work for you, Grammy and what is your money for, anyway? You can afford to buy eggs" – surprised to find that at thirty, I've turned as practical as Mom. And I've come to understand her impatient point of view: sometimes Grandma's truths are ridiculous. Or too wild and involved, interrupting bedtimes, chores and appointments. The tales are disruptive, with no relation to what's real in the world. As I turn over the omelets, I am disappointed in myself for taking Grandma's ghost story so seriously. Mom would ask, "By now, shouldn't you know better than that?"

I do. I set Grandma's plate down on the table and then flip my hand, turning the palm face up. Grandma smiles to see me make the same "here's your feast" gesture that Mom used to mark the beginning of Thanksgiving dinner. I am my mother's doubting daughter. There is nothing in Grandma's tale about ghosts and the red-haired Mae Cherney that I want or need to know.

Chapter 3
WHO'S THERE?

RHEABIE

When you were little, Shoshana, your favorite fairy tales always began with a mystery. Something happened – a feather fell down from the sky and at the front door came the knock of a stranger. Our hero answered and suddenly, her world turned over; the adventure began.

Bubelah, as far as I'm concerned, the mystery here is the heart between you and me. So *nu,* what kind of friendship can we grow from knowing each other? About your grandma, so much you don't know! About my beautiful granddaughter – a zillion truths I've been waiting all these years to hear. Believe me, between us we'll make some crazy story. I promise you, just like a fairy tale, upside down the world will seem.

But first, you got to knock on the door of yourself. A little tap, a little answer. Like those jokes your grandpa liked to tell. He'd hit the wall, remember? "Knock, knock. Who's there?"

For me, it was Mae Cherney all those years ago come into this very kitchen. Her knocking, it turned my world on its end. I know you don't want to listen, but *bubbe,* why not indulge a sick old lady? You got anything else better to do today? Listen, from this story, maybe something about yourself you'll come to understand.

So picture it: a summer afternoon in 1929. I was tired from fixing lunch for her, my new neighbor just moved here from Los Angeles. A big meal for her and that string bean she lived with – Art Katz. Like you, in those early days we didn't marry. The first ones, we were, to call it "free love."

But your grandpa and me – we did it legal, worried that immigration might poke their nose in and send us back to Russia. Most of our friends, they had more courage to live from their beliefs. And Mae and Art were American-born, so what did they have to worry? Their union, it was something private between them that whey told to the stars. Besides, for reasons we never knew, they seemed to have money. Bought the one fancy house on Chapman Lane, the Victorian, where now those nice O'Dells and their dog, they live.

You remember Art – all those Thanksgiving dinners in San Francisco before you moved to Ithaca. The man with the cigars. The one what told stories about the war in Spain, we should all be spared from listening. How many times did you look up into his lonely face and hear the same tales?

Well, dolly, this you haven't heard: how after lunch, Mae got down to the real business of their visit. "So we hear you are the experts on eggs. We could use a little advice," she declared in Yiddish. In those days, when we got together, no one spoke English, not even at Jewish Center meetings. Being born here, Art and Mae knew the language of America backwards. And Jake, he could do business with the *goyim*. But to be polite, to make things easy, Yiddish we talked at home. And a little Russian, when we didn't want the *kinder* should understand.

"We need help," Mae said again. From Glendale our neighbors had moved only the week before and, like us when we started, what did they know from chickens? No Farm Bureau pamphlet could teach how to succeed with those uncertain hens. One bird with the pox or an unexpected freeze and months of work – gone, before you could finish sneezing. Talking with each other – sharing ideas, vaccines, worries – was the trick what kept the banks from foreclosing on a ranch.

Across the table Art smiled. "If it's all right with you, I'd like to see your setup." He licked some sour cream from a spoon. Maybe the man didn't eat enough. "Moysche Blumberg said you had the best ranch, except for his, this side of town."

"Such a bragger, that Moysche." Jake winked at me, reaching for the last piece of honey cake. "You want to come with, Rheabela?" Some crumbs he brushed from his beard and said to Art, "She reads those chickens like a book. One look and she can tell feed, water, kale – whatever they need." In his chair, he leaned. "It's Rheabie's eye what makes the ranch."

"Not true." I blushed, surprised by your grandpop's compliments. If we were alone, die he would before saying such a generous thing. In those days, Jake was proud, meaning stubborn in the mouth, full of his own big efforts. About how hard everyone else worked around him – even the *kinder* with their chores – he never said a word.

Still, I don't want you should misunderstand, dolly. Just because your grandpa was a miser with praise didn't mean nothing. In the tender department, Jake could be as wild as the Russian River when it floods.

But not in public, not to strangers and not about ranching. So *nu*, Slominski, I thought, what is this? The look in your grandpa's eye told me: he was making a competition with Art for the best ranch, and already he was sure he was winning. Never mind, they had the better house. How could Art succeed with Mae, so slim and fashionable, at his side?

A store-bought dress she wore – talk about pleats, talk about gorgeous! But for ranch visiting? *Oy*, the manure. She'd be sorry soon enough. Jake thought Mae's dress meant she couldn't work, would melt in the heat maybe, and the Slominskis would come out better. Ignorant man. How could he miss the look, so firm and mean, in her eye?

"Rheabie and I will settle up here first," she said like she was the boss of the business. "Take notes, Art, on what we need to do."

But so bashful I felt when it was just the two of us alone in the kitchen. I wanted Davy, only six then, to hurry and wake up from his nap.

"A good sleeper, your boy," she said as I snatched the serving fork from the pot-roast. Before I knew it, it had dripped on the brand new oilcloth.

What's wrong with you? Mamale wanted to know, floating near the ceiling in her silk company dress. *Get a rag to wipe up.* She sighed and shook her head. *And what's the trouble with this Mae Cherney person? Can't she see you need a little help?*

Maybe she doesn't know from dishrags, Gitl offered, perched on the kitchen counter near the teapot. She pushed a tangle of brown hair back from her sweet face. *Look how smooth, her hands. Hot water they must never touch.*

The last thing we need on Chapman Lane is some kind of Rockefeller, Shlima sneered from the top of the icebox. Such bony ankles my middle sister had, kicking out from under her dark skirt. *If she and that Art want to make a life from chickens, work she's gotta do.*

I stood up and spoke silently. *Have a little patience with a stranger.* Then I looked up at the sour face of the woman who raised me. *I don't notice you, Mama, rushing down to help.*

We can't, Rheabie. Mamale drifted like a cloud above the table. *You know the rule. Spirits cannot take part in the world.*

A meshuggeneh law, I declared as I stacked the soup bowls. *A little cleaning, a little mopping – what's the crime you should help?*

"I'll get that," Mae said, and she carried my stack to the sink – a short, graceful movement. Then she turned, giving me the evil eye. "So, Rheabie Slominski, I've been waiting all these weeks to meet you. The minute we thought of moving, Sarah Goldstein at the Educational League started in, 'You'll love my friend Rheabie, the best woman in Petaluma. Here, read these letters.' She even showed me pictures from parties at their old ranch. Well, you know Sarah – hours of talk, and she made me curious." Mae folded her arms and leaned back against the counter, her green eyes looking right at me. "So who are you really?" she had the nerve to ask.

Such a question! Mae was smarter than our old neighbor Goldstein, who thought nothing lived beneath the surface of a person. The troubles with my ghosts or worries over the *kinder* – from Sarah these I could always hide. And when Jake let go with his bad temper, she believed my stories about his yelling. "The letter in yesterday's paper about the woman question," I explained when she mentioned hearing him roar last night. Not Davy's glass of spilled milk or Nate denting the water bucket. "Such hard work, this ranching. A man needs to let off steam."

After only one lunch, already I could see Mae was different. No easy story would stop her from sniffing out the truth. Such tales she'd spread about the Slominskis – all over town. So, I folded my arms and got stubborn. "Who I was really" was nothing she needed to know.

Good girl, Mamale nodded. *That's how we raised you.*

Shlima agreed. *Mazel tov. For once you show some sense.*

Mae watched my face, like a kitchen door slammed shut, and looked disappointed. Then the woman gathered up her breath to knock again on the screen. "Are you gonna tell me what I got for a neighbor?" She stared at me as if looking through mesh. "It's important since our properties are so close. Who lives here, anyway?"

Who does she think? The Czar? Mamale spat.

Mae continued, "I mean, what kind of woman? Even Moysche and Luba rave about you. 'A kind heart, good organizer. Whatever you want, she gives.'"

Like this meal, Shlima hissed, tightening the pins what held her bun. *All that work for nothing. I'm telling you, send this woman home.*

Mae had no notion of going. She stepped back from the table and looked at me – such eyes, the color of leaves. "I have trouble sometimes with women who live like fruit bowls – so generous, everybody gets a piece."

I didn't know what she meant but *oy*, the coldness in her words, like the church bells on Easter morning in Terlitza. Ding-dong dangerous – like April, Ukraine's Jew-killing time. Well, I thought, one *pogrom* in a lifetime is plenty. From Mae's questions, I turned away and started the water in the sink.

And then: a small voice, a "Please, comrade, forgive me." Mae sounded so sorry I turned back around to her. "My mouth is always too quick. It's just that we're so far from town out here, more chickens than people for neighbors. How do you live" – she was almost shaking – "with so much alone?"

"Like I always have," I answered, "ever since I came to this country. My whole family, except for my uncle and cousin, died in the Ukraine during the war."

Shlima screeched, *What did you tell her that for?*

Ai yi, Mamale moaned, hitting her forehead. *A newspaper headline from our murder you had to make?*

Is the world ending? Gitl asked, stepping in finally. *Sha! You two make such a fuss over nothing. Let's see what Mae will do.*

Mae sat at the table again, watching me. Such a look! Curious, but also kind.

But dolly, what I saw in her smile made me nervous. All right, so I got brave and told her a little truth. Why did her look make me blush?

And then I turned even redder – I hadn't mentioned Jake, *the kinder* or our comrades. What kind of wife and mother was I, making like I lived alone?

"Do you miss your family?" Mae asked gently. Then she shook her head, "*Ai*, what a question. Of course you do. It's me who's counting every glad mile from my mother in New York."

I almost laughed – from shock at her boldness. Among our people, such a thing you never said. Outside the family, no matter how much *tsuris* your relatives caused you, it was not for talking. But Mae spoke the truth, like from me she wanted. I thought: So *nu*, what would it hurt I should speak my own?

"I should be so lucky," I choked, hoping no one would understand me.

Shlima did, looking up quick from the rocker near the kitchen window. Even Gitl seemed shocked. And in the midst of their silence, came a scream from Mamale. *How could you envy her?*

My mother gave a wail and struck her chest in agony. *Out of my grave, I come all the way to America to help you. This is what I get for thanks? Rheabie, be ashamed!*

Ashamed I was, for being such an ungrateful daughter. How, I wondered, could I have said such a terrible thing? Everyone in the room felt the same.

Except for Mae, the stranger, who was now smiling. "I like you," she said, pressing her hands together like she'd decided something.

My ghosts shook their heads. What was there to like?

"Listen," my guest said, "can we be friends?" She cocked her head to the side. "Not like Sarah with all that flattery and politeness. I'm talking living true with each other as comrades and neighbors. Do you want?"

This, dolly, was the size of heart living inside Mae Cherney. She was bold enough, at a first meeting, to ask me for friendship, the kind without lies. But as I watched my mother's tears, I knew I didn't have it in me to be so generous. I didn't know what it meant, a living person to trust.

"What are you talking?" I shook myself and turned back to the sink, full of soapy water. Some kind of joke I tried to make from being a coward. "Maybe it's the chickens, all that squawking, but between me and my feelings, there's nothing you'd care to hear."

Mamale nodded. *Good girl.*

You have us, Shlima crowed. *What do you need from her?*

"Well, you are smaller than I thought," my new neighbor said, rising quickly from the table. She spoke louder. "Rheabie Slominski, proud owner of a thousand chickens, you don't have the courage to live from what shines behind your eyes."

Like a smack, those words, that brought my cheeks to burning.

For a nonsense not worth listening? Mamale sneered. *Didn't I raise you better?*

You tell this platke-macher where she can go.

But I couldn't. Something in Mae's voice caught at my chest and curled like a hand there. In her words lived a question I didn't know how to ask. So I wanted she should stroke what had turned my heart into a bird, beating and afraid of capture. I wanted a soft voice to smooth my feathers down.

Instead, I got eyes what made bold enough to look right at me. As if she held my wildness between her palms, ready she was to toss that bird into the air. Who knew if my wings would open and if I'd remember how to use them? Anything could happen in Mae Cherney's kind of world.

"What do you want from me?" I asked.

"Someone to talk to," she said, "a real person – not a reputation."

Ai, Shoshie, how she confused me. I looked at my feet.

Silence, with my spirits holding their breath, waiting.

Silence – until Mae shrugged. "All right, then." She walked to the door. "This is not such a big town you can't find me. Come over someday, when you get brave enough."

The screen slammed while I pretended to wash the dishes. After Mae hurried down the porch stairs, out the window I looked to watch her walk away.

I'm telling you, the light was the same as right now, this minute, a good fifty years later. That sunshine, it led me from her straight back to yours. I didn't know it then, but into my own future I was looking. So *nu*, now I'm going to ask you Mae's big question. Shoshana, granddaughter of my heart, listen up. This is important. When are you going to get brave enough already to talk to me?

Chapter 4
BORN SILENT

SHOSHANA

I have never talked much – not to Mark or any of the other loggers who've shared my bed, not to the women on my shifts in cafes as we balance orders for ham and eggs and BLTs on white. They've even made a joke of it at the Kitchen Kupboard, betting a free meal on any fool who's wandered in off the interstate if he can get me to say something besides "What'll you have? – Here you go – Thank you very much." My neighbor Lillian swears that my silence is what makes the regulars give me such good tips. They figure that a twenty for a three-dollar meal will make me ask who did it and spill the beans. I make a point to always slip the bills into the pocket of my brown apron, never looking at what I've got until I can put my feet up on my raggedy couch and count the cash at home.

Mom claims I was born silent, hoarding my words, making secrets where none needed to be. Maybe I only seemed quiet in contrast to all the chatter in that house, the way Dad and Aviva and Mom talked and talked, afraid of what the silence might say. I learned to listen out of self-defense, reading whatever lay beneath their talk. It was a matter of hearing the tones, so that I could get up and slip from the room – "Shoshana, where are you going?" – before something hurtful was thrown my way. My family, a whirlwind of noise, a carousal organ out of tune, made me a gift in their loudness. To survive in that house, I learned to hold my tongue and see.

So now I know what to look for when I bring my eyes away from the omelet pan and egg-crusted plates in the sink and turn toward the old woman who is waiting for me in her small kitchen. I peer at the reluctant patient who demanded help to get up this morning so she could fix her own breakfast. Grandma fussed when I wouldn't let her and made the food instead. So was her crazy story about ghosts my punishment for not following her wishes? The tones in her voice made it sound more like a reward – a tip, like the ones left under a plate at the Kupboard. Grandma is trying to bribe me, hoping for interest and questions. Maybe she just wants a little more talk to fill up her long days.

Poor Gram is a fragile bird now, imprisoned by the pin they put in her bones and by her walker. She's penned up, like the chickens she used to raise, by a fall which happened the day after my mother had surgery to replace her own arthritic hip.

I didn't hear about it until Mom called. "Stealing the show, like always," she complained in a weak voice from her hospital bed. Her words were slurred from the pain medication. "The very same bone too." But the anger was strong, like always. "Your grandmother's got to have all the attention. God forbid, it should belong to me."

I sighed, trying to listen sympathetically as the rain fell on the roof of my little house in Lydon, punctuating the irritation and worry in the request that I could sense was coming next.

"Shoshana, I wouldn't ask such a thing," my mother moaned, "if anyone else could do it. But you know the list: Aviva's due in a month, Mas is away, and Uncle Davy and Aunt Mari are useless." I pictured her left hand clutching the TV remote at the edge of her bed, the wedding ring she still wore all these years after my father's death shining beneath the fluorescent lights. "Darling, it's up to you. When she gets out of the hospital, go to California and take care of her." Mom took a breath. "Please? No one else can."

I think it was the "please" that made me pack my duffel bag, arrange for Lillian to take my place at the Kupboard and finally tell Josie, my boss, more than she had ever known about my family. "Glad you opened your mouth, sweetie," she said, sending me off after my last breakfast shift with everyone's tips and gas money as a bonus. Her slap on my shoulder, sticky and white with flour from making berry pies, shoved me out the door all the way south to this quiet kitchen. "Keep a look out," Josie said. "You know how to use your eyes."

So now I am here, the only person near enough to Grandma to notice the bits of pink scalp showing through her wisps of white hair. When I was little, her braid was thick and stiff as a broom. She had such long eyelashes. And now look at them. How did they ever get so thin?

If I had Mom or Aviva's ability to chatter about nothing, I could ask Grandma such mundane questions. I'd be able to sit calmly beside her while she talks about the past, instead of wanting to jump up and rush into the garden. A good granddaughter wouldn't feel so trapped in this house. She'd be able to answer cheerfully instead of snarling each time she was asked a personal question. She'd even have the nerve to tell some of the truth. "Listen," I'd say, borrowing her accent as I always do when I have visited for too long, "about you and your stories. I know you want to hear from me too, but I can't talk to you. This is not going to be a trade. I don't have the years on me or anything to tell."

Grandma would nod, understanding finally that I can't go against my nature. "So all right, already. It's okay," she'd whisper, content to leave me alone for once, to watch the breeze move the dying coleus on the windowsill.

A gust touches my cheek, lifting the hair off my neck and cooling the sweat that's gathered there already. It swirls the newspaper resting near Grandma's feet. She looks up as if she's heard my thoughts, and the morning grows quiet between us. Grandma hums a little, catching her breath on a folk song whose words, I remember now, used to send me to sleep at night.

I take up a brush and move to stand behind her, tugging at the blue twistie that holds her weak braid. And while she closes her eyes and bites her lip in pleasure, I work the bristles, brushing over and over. The ends of her hair, thin and broken, bounce against the knobs of her spine.

"This is what we have, Grandma," I want to say, "me in my silence, with my hands working, so now you are combed and braided. We have you, tied to your walker, but so full of tales that they're pressing to get out of your mouth."

I continue to stand with my palms, resting now, on the wings of her shoulders. I can feel the bones, sharp and pointed, through her cotton blouse. She reaches a hand to squeeze my fingers. "Such a pleasure you are," Grandma sighs. "Thank you, heart of my heart."

I am surprised at how pleased I feel at her compliment, and my lips open, against my better judgment, as I shape the beginning of a question. Looking out the window into the silhouette of the dry hills, my voice cracks as I break the habit of a lifetime and I ask, "So, are you going to tell me what happened next, between you and that Mae?"

Chapter 5
THE GUARDIANS

RHEABIE

What happened next? Magic, that's what happened! Shoshie, the day I met Mae Cherney, you wouldn't believe what came and put a finger on my life. Not pretend, not fairy tales and superstition. Real magic. A group of ghosts – Guardians they called themselves – later that afternoon, they appeared on the hill.

Don't look at me like that. You asked, so I'm telling. Would it kill you to believe your grandma just a little?

It's the truth and so yes, maybe it's a little scary. These Guardians, I admit, they frightened the meat right off my bones. *Oy,* the power what oozed from their fingers! And eyes what made me shudder, so soaked they were with time. Listen, this is for real, and I swear it on all the years of my living. In your short time on this earth, haven't you met up with something you can't explain?

No, I'm not talking the usual mysteries, love and how it comes and goes without asking. I don't mean the riddles of families or politics or wars. Such puzzles, they're only the regular business of living. The magic I'm talking was bigger and older than that.

Shoshie, this largeness – it was something you knew when you were little. When we'd take walks together, you'd point it out to me. "Grandma, look at the sun on the creek. It's smiling." One night in this very backyard you danced to a song from the stars.

Ai, what a crime, we grow up and close our eyes to the biggest story. Believe me, just like you I was until that long-ago summer day. Mae started the whole business – what with the ache she left after our first lunch together. The kitchen felt so close, I had to get out of the house.

But Davy was stirring from his nap, and soon he would cry out "Mama, come," wanting to tell his dream. Mimi and Nate were maybe an hour away from rushing up the porch stairs to shout about their day at school. I had no business walking somewhere. But with Mamale going at the rocker and Shlima frowning into the kitchen table, *bubee,* I thought I would scream.

For what? There's nothing you should be upset about, Shlima stated. *What do you need with Mae Cherney?*

And you, such a blessing for company, I should dance for joy? I protested, wiping pot roast spills from the kitchen floor. *What do you know from what I need?*

Shlima's fingers marked off checks in the new oilcloth. *What if this neighbor, proud of her smarts, gets sharp enough to spot us? You think she'll want a friendship, the day she sees you talking to ghosts?*

Oy, Shlima. Gitl walked toward her across the floor I'd just washed. Not even one mark her ghostly feet they made. *The world's not bad enough, you have to borrow trouble?*

Gitl always hurried to my rescue during family arguments but not strictly for my sake. It was an old story; for years now, she got pleasure from making Shlima mad. *Who's seen us, all this time? Even Jake, who should know better, doesn't guess for a second who shares his bed.*

Shlima hit her palms together in disgust. *What do you expect? The man shtups with his eyes closed.*

Stop with the vulgar, Mamale scolded from the rocker. *Be nice.*

I didn't know from nice as I slammed down the scrub bucket. To slap Shlima for her rudeness I wanted, but I'm sorry to tell you, Shoshie, that about your grandfather, she was right. He liked to adventure where you couldn't see, a bed always in the darkness. And about what he did and where, he refused to look.

So? Gitl scoffed. *What makes you think this Mae can see spirits any better than Jake?*

Such a sour look Shlima made from her face. *A red-haired woman has powers.*

Oy gevalt! My calm sister Gitl yelled loud enough to clean the ceiling. *Superstitious and backward! It makes you feel better, maybe – to think with your tuchis instead of your head?*

Stop it right now, you two, Mamale hissed.

Shlima lifted up from her chair into the air. *At least I don't have the mouth of a fishwife!*

Gitl ignored her and smiled sweetly. *Better such a mouth than shit for brains!*

Enough! I echoed Mamale's outraged cry as I threw the mop water over the porch into the roses. *You want to wake Davy with such badness? Ai yai yai, listen.* A wail and then sobbing was filling up the house. And so strong, I could tell he'd been going at it for a while. I hadn't even heard – because of my sisters and their squabbling. *It's your fault*, I yelled. *Listen to those screams.*

A thousand curses I flung at my family as I dropped the bucket and hurried to your uncle. I was fed up – to my neck – with all their noise. *What would it take*, I asked as they followed me through the kitchen, *you should shirrup for once and let me live my life?*

Your life is what we're here for, Mamale assured me, a ghostly hand patting my shoulder.

I shrugged her off. *By me, this isn't living.* Such a hurt silence behind me, but I didn't care. Words that I had not even let myself think hurried out of my mouth. *What I wouldn't give, you should go back home.*

Silence filled the house, thick despite Davy's crying.

Silence, the quiet I'd been aching for, but dolly, it wasn't right. Ach, all these years later it still hurts me, that meanness to my poor mother and sisters. The worst part: they knew it was one hundred per cent the truth.

All of a sudden, no one was beside me in the hallway. Arriving at Davy's room, I was alone. He'd stopped crying but was hiding under the sheets – a hand holding his blanket. "Who's in there?" I asked, pulling back the bedding and lifting him in my arms. "What is it, *bubee*? You woke up lonely, maybe? Is that why the tears?"

"My dream scared me, and then there were the shadows." Davy wiped his nose on my shoulder, then leaned back to look at me. "Can you see how they have eyes?"

My sweet son was right – the shadows did have eyes because Shlima and Gitl forgave me long enough to slink into the room, full of their own "I'm sorry's." Mamale, still mad, added her frown to the mess. All three crowded near the doorway, pressed like wallpaper against the clothes chest.

"No, over there." Davy pointed to the window, framed by thin blue curtains. Between them, I saw a group of quick faces – blue eyes, brown ones, smiles, a gray eyebrow – and then nothing. In a blink, the shadows were gone.

Who is that? Mamale gasped.

Strangers. Spirits. Shlima leaned her head out after them, shaking her fist. *Gey and gezunterey!* When she turned to face us, her face was grim. *All different foreign ghosts,* she reported, *six, seven, eight, maybe. Very old and not our kind.*

The dead, you're talking? I clutched Davy closer to me. *Ghosts I don't even know?*

Gitl sat down beside me on the bed, puzzled. *Maybe we're not the only ones come back from the grave to help the living.*

All right, fine. My heart tap-danced in my chest. *But you're enough for one family. What do they want, those strangers, to come here?*

Davy wriggled past my fear. "Did you see, Mama? The shadows pushed the bad dream away. They were nice to me."

"Really?" I smoothed back his hair, trying to calm my shaking hands.

Davy nodded, big eyes as round as Gitl's. "They winked and told me not to worry about the dog. They chased it. They yelled and made it leave the room."

"You had a dog in here?" I kissed his cheeks. Ah, now here was something I could understand.

Davy jumped down from my lap. "The dog bit me. Right here." He showed me the place on his leg where yesterday he'd been scratched playing in the blackberries. Such an imagination, that *boychik*. "That's what I'm telling you. My dream."

"Good," I stood up, relieved.

Mamale shook her head. *Just because he thinks they were a dream doesn't mean we don't know better. Bold enough to smile even, those spirits.*

Then she sighed. *Listen up, ungrateful daughter. What you said, it's tearing at my chest right now, and I can barely breathe from the hurting. To think I raised a girl with such an evil mouth. But we have to put it away, because there's a bigger misery to talk over. These strangers – ai yai yai, have we got trouble here.*

Well, trouble or not, Davy comes first, I insisted. *I want you should understand. From this day forward, I will not neglect my family for any ghosts.*

And then I bent to my son, not even waiting to see how my spirits reacted. "Such a long story from a small boy, maybe you need a cookie? I know an oatmeal raisin what's got your name on it in the kitchen."

"Three," Davy nodded, "one for me and two for the shadows. I want to find them."

Not without me, I thought, my heart banging. "So, let's have an adventure," I suggested to Mr. Big Eyes, hoping to steer him toward something different. "Just you and me – how about we take a walk?"

No! Mamale gasped. *Not out where those spirits can find you.*

"A long walk?" he asked, eyes brightening. "Up past the fences?"

Rheabie, be careful, Shlima warned.

But I ignored her. "Up enough," I promised. "We can look down on all the houses of Chapman Lane."

What are you doing? Gitl cried, as I followed my son to the kitchen.

Taking care of Davy, I answered, glad for the first time that long day.

Almost an hour it took to huff and puff up the big hill behind the ranch. "Hurry up, Mama!" Davy's eyes were fixed on a big rock at the very top. And nothing else would do, because from there, a boy could see all of Petaluma. In that wild country, what belonged to no one we knew, he could shout: "You are mine. I name you Slominski Rock!" Then Davy could sit and rest, waiting for me to catch up. He could laugh at the smallness of his brother and sister as they walked home from school.

"Like ants, Mama. Look at them. Aren't we tall?"

I didn't feel tall; I felt tired. All that way I'd walked listening to Mamale *kvetch. Oy vey,* she moaned, beating her chest with her hand, *such an idea, this walk of yours. Why don't you make Davy stop already? The Himalayas he has to climb?*

What are you complaining? I tried to pull a little more air into my plump body. *You don't have lungs that hurt.*

"Papa's pointing," Davy yelled. "He's showing Mimi and Nate where we are."

So wave, Shlima urged. *Maybe if they look hard enough they'll see we've turned into birds.*

In this sun, Gitl tilted her head up to the sky, *I wouldn't mind a pair of wings.*

Davy pulled at my hand. "So beautiful. Like one of my dreams."

Like a dream, the heat: rising up through the rock and warming our tired bodies. And then a hawk, circling, so close we could hear its wings. "Look at the tail," Davy pointed from my lap, "so red."

He squirmed, your uncle, gladness shouting from every corner of his small body. Then he jumped down, "Look!" and pointed. "Over there!" Davy ran across the hill, whooping. "The shadows are here."

"Wait!" I screamed. "No!"

Because he was right – coming towards us, the very same spirits what had smiled at me from his window. Tall, foggy, and – I screamed again – not like people at all. They were older than us somehow and, like wind or bobcats, full of wildness. Yes, they had human hair, bones, skin – all the regular business – but human wasn't who they were at all.

For instance, the thin woman, the one your bad uncle reached first because he didn't come when I called him. The way she swung him up in her arms, laughing and talking – like the Irish girls from the Shirtwaist Workers Union. Wispy hair, calico skirt, freckles. A nose so small you could miss it if you blinked.

Then your uncle laughed, and she threw back her head and shouted with him. *Oy,* how I shivered, Shoshie, at the terrible sound. Like all the grasses on the hill, suddenly they found voices. And her body, so misty looking that I could see through it. Little shadows, like redwing blackbirds, dipped up and down over what should be her bones. The month of June, so hot it could kill all the pullets in one afternoon, in a human shape – that's who stood before me. And that spirit had my Davy in her arms.

"Put him down!" I ordered in a voice I had never heard come out of me. So much muscle, low and growling. "Put him down right now."

The ghost smiled, a breeze whipping up an empty field. Davy she set back on the grass.

"Come here," I demanded of my bad boy.

"But Mama," he protested. "She was going to ride me piggy back."

We mean no harm, Missus, said a curly-haired man, brown as the backside of our barn. A gray robe he was wearing, worn and coarse with a rope around the middle. Worse – a wooden cross, big enough to make me shudder, hung from the side of his belt. Like a Terlitza priest, only with him there was nothing Russian. Still, I trembled, looking at this ghost. And worse, I know the man, he saw it. A nod he gave me and then his hand moved, palm up, making his body change. Instead of see-through, what I was used to already, he got solid. It should have made me feel better, yes? Except his muscles, they were made of clouds and rain. That spirit, he turned into the one of our wet winters right before my eyes.

Who are you? I asked, trembling so much I was worried I'd fall over. I grabbed Davy, and squeezed him against my legs. But your uncle wiggled away, unafraid to face that whole group of strangers. A grin, even, he had on his brave face.

We are Guardians, said the oldest. A wrinkled woman, she had blue tattoos on her chin and wore a skirt of reeds along with a shell necklace. Let me tell you, it didn't cover much.

Oy vey, I gasped, putting my hand over Davy's eyes. He was only six. The boy didn't need to see her bare breasts.

But then, like the priest spirit, she made a motion with her hand and started to grow solid. Her legs, they grew still and began to root into the dirt. And for a second, all that age in her, it seemed like wood rings wrapped around her middle.

Stop! Enough already, I begged.

So she got ghosty again. *Thank you,* I whispered. Better, I thought, Davy should see breasts than watch her turn into a tree.

The woman laughed, as if she could hear me, and it sounded like the breeze moving through the gum grove. A friendly noise it was, leaves rustling in the wind.

We are Guardians, she said again, with a wink and nod at Davy. *When I was alive, my people were known as Winamabakeya, People Who Belong to the Land.*

Okay, okay, so maybe you think your grandma is making this up, or like your mother, you want it should be the Alzheimer's. Poor Gram, you think, in her old age she's lost whatever sense she ever had. Listen *bubee,* I understand the comfort in pretending this whole business is some kind of fancy story. Back in 1929, I kept hoping to wake up from this *meshuggeneh* dream.

But no such luck, because no matter how hard I wished, the Guardians just kept smiling. The eight of them, the five of us, quiet and still on that hill.

Until Mamale croaked beside me, *What are you doing here? Why are you bothering us?* She looked so scared, I was worried a puff of wind should blow her away.

We came for you, the old one said, her head bowing. The rest nodded like her except for the wintry priest. He did them one better, going down on his knee.

For what? Shlima gasped, almost lifting off the ground with shock and a little anger maybe. *Get up, already.* She waved her arm at the religious kneeler. *We don't need anything from you.*

Don't you, now? asked the one who'd played with Davy. She folded her arms across her chest, studying Shlima. Her skirt swelled, got round and blowy, like lupines and poppies in a breeze.

Of course not, Gitl insisted, drifting to stand beside me. I was so glad for her, I almost leaned my head on her shoulder like I did when I was little. I wanted my big sister should make everything all right, send the danger away.

And you know what, Shoshie? For the first time in years, I realized maybe she could do it. I believed, like I hadn't since that terrible day of the *pogrom,* that everything might be all right. I blinked tears from my eyes, turning to look from her to Mamale and Shlima. In facing the Guardians, the four of us had come close enough to smell a little peace.

Davy's Guardian smiled and the old one humphed, her eyes like sun on leaves, shining. *Please forgive our interruption,* the priest one said.

And then they began to fade, like dew in the morning. In a minute, the hill would be empty, back to the safe place it'd been before they came.

Except not if your uncle could help it. "No! Don't leave," he cried. To me he turned. "Make them stay."

"But *bubee,* they have to go." I tried to hold him, but he wouldn't let me.

"No," he sobbed. "Come back! They promised to play with me."

"Shadows have business," I tried to explain. "You can't keep them."

"No, no, no!" he cried. Then from his mouth, a truth so strong it made me lose my breath. He looked up. "You're the one sending them away."

I was. Or at least, letting them leave, and glad I was about it. For myself, for Mamale and Shlima and Gitl, such a pleasure to see the Guardians fade. But what about this boy who, I had bragged earlier, should come first, no matter what, when it came to a ghost business? It hadn't been more than a couple of hours, but already I was breaking my vow? *Oy,* what kind of mother was I?

A smart one, Shlima answered my silent question. *Let these Guardians go and good riddance. They're don't belong here, and they mean us harm.*

Harm, just like Mae Cherney maybe? I asked, a little idea beginning to make a light in me. So much danger in this life, every minute – at least, that's the way my ghosts saw it. And I'd always believed them. Yet, for the first time, I started to wonder. How much, how many people, had I stopped myself from knowing because I was afraid?

I mean, these Guardians – so all right, yes, they were scary, but who couldn't see, with their wind and grasses and leaves, that they belonged here? And in how they spoke and treated us, so quiet and polite, there was nothing close to harm. So what was I worried, Davy should want to play with them? A little piggyback with the Irish girl, what could be so bad?

Wait, I called out and they stopped fading. In a blink, those spirits, they were back, strong and glowing on the hill.

Rheabie, don't do this. Mamale tried to poke me. *Foolish child. Do you know what this will mean?*

I don't, I answered, facing up to her for once, *and maybe I don't have to. What's the law says I need to be sure before anything I do?*

But things happen, Gitl said gently, the same voice she used to reason with me when I was little. *You have to be careful.*

I looked her right in the eye, a grown-up now, and asked a question I'd been holding for twelve years. *If we had been careful, that night, before the Ukrainian Army came, would it have been any different? The pogrom, could we have stopped it if we knew?*

Unfair! Shlima cried. *The nerve, you should ask such a question.*

Is it fair, I stared down my angry sister, *that now you want before anything happens, the future I should know?* Then I bent to Davy, who had stopped crying and was watching the Guardians, his bright face smiling. "One piggyback and then we have to get home to fix supper. When I call and say it's over, you promise to come?"

"Yes," he yelled, running with eager feet. With a swing and a yelp, as if all the grasses on the hill had started laughing, his piggyback ride began.

But what is going to happen, Mamale asked, *when he goes home and starts talking to his brother and sister? Such fighting you're going to have when him they won't believe.*

Oy, she was right and I could hardly stand to admit it.

See, Shlima crowed, strutting in front of me. *You should have thought first.*

Plenty of time I had for thinking as the Irish ghost carried Davy across the hill on her back like he was the king of the grasses. Such gladness in his face, the whole story he would have to tell. And yes, there would be yells and slaps, tears when the family thought he was lying. "Davy's usual fairy tales," Nate would shrug. Mimi would sniff, "Just a dream." And that poor boy would wipe his eyes, "Mama will tell you. She saw them." And what could I say?

So I looked at the old one, the tree, because she seemed the smartest. Straight out, with all the courage I had in me, I asked her: *What should I do?*

I heard Mamale hiss, and Shlima shook her head: *What nerve, wanting help from these strangers.* Gitl said nothing, just sat by my side. Then old one, Wina she said I could call her, beckoned, and the Irish girl came over.

"So soon?" Davy whined.

The spirit put him down on the grass in front of the old lady. Wina smiled at him, so warm, so knowing. Then she reached out and put her hand on his head.

What? Shlima rose up off the ground in a big hurry. *Stop that!*

A piggyback's bad enough. We don't need anymore, Mamale screamed.

Sha! I ordered. On Davy's face – such a sweetness, like I had never seen. He closed his eyes and stood quiet, almost dreaming maybe. Her hand patted his curly hair.

And then, the patting stopped, and the sun got brighter. That light, all gold, filled up the hill. I blinked at it, so shiny – and when I was done no more Wina. All the Guardians, they'd disappeared.

Davy opened his eyes. "Mama, I'm hungry. Let's go home."

"Enough playing you've had already?" I asked, looking at him closely. All right he seemed, nothing strange or bothered. "Done, you are, with the piggybacks for now?"

"What piggyback?" he asked, rubbing a scratched knee. Then he cocked his head, like a pullet trying to coax a little more feed, and sighed. "I'm tired. Will you carry me?"

All the way home, he got a ride, that *boychik,* such a wheeler-dealer. I piggybacked as much as he asked, amazed about the Guardians how he didn't remember a thing. That Wina, she made a magic on him, what made for peace in the house when we got back for supper. But you know, Shoshie, even then for Davy I felt a little bad.

Think about it. My boy I'd cheated of his first experience with a wild magic. Much later, after the war and his two years in that prison camp, I spent nights wondering – would he be any better if that piggyback ride, it had stayed close to his heart? But how could a piggyback make better what he suffered – forced labor, the beatings – from those Nazis? Still, I wonder about it – every time I look into his sad eyes.

And that's why, my dearest girl, when you were nine and Wina came down from the hills to meet you, I asked she should make it so you remember. Like a tree in the wind, she nodded, and put her hand on your head. "Yes," you said, looking up at her and then you smiled, so bright and happy. I was there. I saw it. Wina, the oldest of the Guardians, she leaned forward and kissed the top of your braids.

Chapter 6
LOSING A DREAM

SHOSHANA

"No." The word breaks from my chest, a rush of air that crashes through the screen door and spills into the tangle of my grandmother's roses. "Please," I whisper, balling my fists on the table, my throat blocked by tears.

I feel a breeze at my cheeks as Grandma Rheabie sits back and waits, her dark eyes watching. If I could talk, I'd force myself to beg, "Please. Don't take the dream away from me."

Because what she's been telling me was a dream, so vivid that I can still close my eyes and feel the press of those fingers from my childhood. To this day, I can see the yellow fields where I was standing, miles and miles of them, shivering in the wavering heat. And I was alone, except for the voice that promised, "Later, daughter, I will need you." It was my mother who spoke so softly for once and, in an unusual touch, tenderly stroked my hair.

I can still feel the way her fingers moved across my braids, pulling on one playfully. I remember how she leaned down and gave my part a little kiss. And then I woke, my neck twisted into the pillow I had made from a sweater squashed against the car window. We were in the Chevy station wagon somewhere in the desert, part of the long drive of our move from San Francisco to Ithaca. As Aviva slept beside me and Mom and Dad talked quietly in the front seat, I looked out into a sky full of stars.

I can touch that dream, the same way I have dug my fingernails into my twisted napkin. It's as real as the sigh that fills my grandmother's throat.

"I don't believe you," I tell her, looking past her stories out into the road where the Lubbock's Fairlane rumbles by, lost and dusty. If I had any courage, I'd run the length of the long driveway, flag it down and demand a ride north from Grandma's neighbors. Back to Lydon and the Kupboard, sharing jokes with Lillian and Josie; back to the cabin, Rasputin's meows, nights with Mark and the quiet of big trees. But the Lubbocks keep driving, and I am left alone here in this cluttered kitchen with a crazy old woman. I have nowhere to escape as Grandma tries to refigure my whole life.

I kept that dream like a favorite shell that I'd found at the beach to lighten difficult moments when I was in junior high school. I'd take it out and grip my fist around it as I sat hunched on my bed, trying not to cry. When Aviva and I fought over a new dress and Mom took her side, I told myself that it didn't matter. When Viva got excused from chores and I didn't, I tried not to care. Even though Mom crowed about how she and my sister were so close – "like two peas in a pod, and you are your father's daughter" – I knew that someday, some time, my mother was going to need me.

I don't want to think that it's some kind of joke, the way I've waited all these years for a real phone call or a long and teary letter. I thought it finally came, the day after her hip surgery, when weeping, with gratitude in her voice, Mom sent me here. Here, to this shabby house, full of someone else's life and memories. Here, to these dry hills, washed in the yellow of my dream.

"Shoshanala," my grandmother insists, her stern voice pulling me back to her plaid cotton shirt and the silver gleam of her walker. "Listen, *bubee*. Never once, your whole life, to you did I ever lie."

"But..." I begin, pulling the dream like a sweater around my chilly shoulders.

She shakes her head. "Right there, in the old cow pasture, you met Wina." Grandma purses her lips. "Such a sad day. She only had time to touch you before your mother called and two minutes later, you got in the car, packed to the brim, because you were on your way already, moving back east."

I don't want to believe any of it, not her brown eyes, filling with tears, nor the familiar smell of the pasture. It's not possible that what she says is true.

"Give it back," I want to shout, meaning my life, steamy days in Lydon where I couldn't see out of the Kitchen Kupboard because of the mist. Those afternoons when Harry or some other regular told a good joke, and I had to force myself not to laugh as I slapped his lunch plate on the table and waited for my tip. I want back the crazy kind of hope that got me through a bad shift, the dream I held as I mopped up coffee spills and pie crumbs, imagining that a letter from Mom, full of what I meant to her, might be waiting in my empty box at the post office.

"Come home," I wanted her to write in her wavy hand, "back to where you belong, where I can see you. Your place is in Ithaca. Aviva isn't enough for me."

I've been such a damn fool, waiting all these years for impossible words to be spoken. I can't believe that I've wasted so much time.

"It's not fair." I feel the words gathering in my chest, drumming on my sides, the thrust of a shout building. I clamp down my jaw, trying, as I have done all my life, to hold in the noise. But the tears are pressing on my tongue, and I shake my eyes free of them, biting my lip to keep from crying.

"*Bubelah,*" Grandma coos. She leans forward in her chair, her arms reaching to touch me. "What is it? Tell me quick, dolly, the truth. What's wrong?"

Like I'm nine and lost in a supermarket, I gulp and sputter. The words choke, but I manage to spit out, "Where is my mother? What's her part in all this?"

Chapter 7
SEEING MIMI

RHEABIE

It's all right, lovey, go ahead and cry. Want a Kleenex? Here: a glass of water. Sip a little. To tell the truth, it's a relief, hearing you sob. Sometimes – your face in the morning the past week – I was afraid from crying you didn't know. But I should have trusted more all the ingredients what make up the soup of your story. Your mother, after all, she was the one who taught *me* to cry.

And I can tell, it's Mimi burning your heart right now – such a big fire. But look, dolly, in the air around you. See her hands? Busy patting your shoulder, like she was here, wanting to comfort. Her fingers – here and there – moving like flying birds. And on her face – such tenderness. I swear, your mother's here this very minute. Such feeling in her, what she would die before showing in real life.

She's a mystery, your mother, such like jam and dill prickles mixed together. Her softness hidden, but still true, still full of so much buried love. Every Sunday night Mimi confuses me. Sweet and sour, like Chinese pork, when she calls full of news about you girls.

"Mother," she begins. Then her voice drops, and her hands, they fly around me. "Mother, are you eating enough? Why don't you let Mrs. Neilson come like I wanted? You're too old to take care of yourself anymore."

With Mimi, maybe you've noticed: you can't listen to what she says exactly. Pay attention, Shoshie, to what flies behind her words.

This Mrs. Neilson, for instance – for months your mother nagged how that good woman should move in – I'm so feeble. But the minute my hip breaks, who does she send? Yes, my darling. It's a gift from your mother, you're here beside me. She knew I needed you. So maybe, between the two of us, we can make from all her bristles a little sense.

But where to begin? Honest to god, I'm not sure when Mimi first hid the love what lived in her heart. Was it the day, sometime near her third birthday, when Jake and I indulged her in a little dancing? We sang – clapping hands in the kitchen – while Mimi twirled on the table. Such a wildness in her that afternoon, stamping her feet. And her face – the more she moved, the more she got older. A short, little woman she looked, with joy in her cheeks, a thousand years old.

And she would not let us stop, even though our voices were hoarse and the chickens needed tending. It was getting close to dark and too much work waited to be done. "Enough,"Jake said finally, leaning back in his chair beside the table. He smiled as he wiped sweat from his face.

Mimi frowned at me. "No!" She shook a stubborn head.

Just like Shlima when she was a baby, Mamale cooed from the ceiling. *Can't take "no" for an answer.*

I didn't play like that. Shlima shook her head. She tapped her feet as if we were still making music. *Look at that girl, so wild and fierce.*

You just don't remember, Gitl laughed and swooped to touch Mimi's hair with her ghostly fingers. *This darling – she's just like you.*

The darling was staring at me, wanting I should begin more singing. "No, dolly, that's all." Then I turned to the stove to give the borscht a little stir.

"Mama, don't!" Mimi screamed. She threw back her curls and began to cry. Such a noise, it scared from the hens a day's laying. It scared Jake and me – never before had we heard her make this kind of sound. In two minutes, her voice had grown up, so much sadness in it. Where had my daughter come to know so big a grief?

Stop! Stop! Mamale shouted, *I can't stand it*! Then she popped into the wall, taking Shlima and Gitl with her. The last I saw before the wall paper swallowed them up – all three weeping, hands over their ears.

I picked Mimi up and began to cry too, hearing a shovel chipping at frozen dirt in the Terlitza graveyard. Mimi gulped and hiccupped. Holding her stiff body, I smelled the smoke of my mother's death.

"*Sha*," I whispered into her neck, "it can't be helped, my poor *bubbe*." She rolled her head back and forth on my shoulder and cried some more. A thousand kisses I gave but they didn't stop her screaming. "That's enough," I said finally, making my voice stern. "Mimi – no more tears."

"*Sha!* These things happen," I told her after another tantrum when Nate and Davy came two years later. "The boys need us – both their Mama and Papa died – so we are their family now."

"I don't care. Send them away," she sobbed, stamping the floor of her new built-on bedroom.

"I can't, dolly." So much work we had put into that little room, as if it could make easier this adoption of Jake's nephews. What did we think, your grandpa and me – that painting and wallpaper would do the trick?

Not by Mimi Slominski. Watching me carefully, she stomped over to her dresser. Such big eyes as she pulled out a drawer and threw it on the floor.

"Stop it!"

Then she ran to the kitchen and began on a cupboard. Such a big noise the pots made, banging on the floor. "I hate you!" she cried.

I pushed past Davy, only three then, who watched her from the doorway. In his eyes, something hurt and tired, something afraid.

"That's enough, Mimi," Jake rumbled from his place at the kitchen table. Usually, his voice was enough to stop her, but that day she ignored him. Jake started to get up, a hard look on his face. "I mean it," he threatened, standing over her. "We got others to think of now."

"I don't want others," she wailed, tossing a lid toward her new little brother. I screeched as it just missed his feet and skittered against the door.

And then there was a smack, Jake's palm on Mimi's *tuchis*. The sound: so big, so sharp, it cut the kitchen in two. Never before had her father ever lifted a hand to her in anger. He yelled, of course – his temper was always burning. But a matter of principle it was with us for raising *kinder* – no hitting. Discipline we could make by what came out of our mouths. But that day, Jake made like his father and gave a good slap; Mimi twisted around to look up at him. On her face, the red shock of surprise.

So maybe this is the moment your mother's heart went into hiding. I watched Mimi's eyes get dark, turning hard as wood.

"Not another word," Jake demanded as he set her on the linoleum and refused to look at me. "I won't hear it." His beard he tugged, the spitting image of his father, the rabbi. In his eyes, such a look – like a Yom Kippur service, dark and musty and afraid. "You got a job to do here, missy," he glared at Mimi. "From the house you can't leave until you help Mama clean up."

"But..." Mimi began, the tears finally crowding her lashes.

"Now, Jake," I started, shocked at the way he had broken with our beliefs.

"*Sha*! Both of you!" The tone of his voice was dangerous. His rising temper – a sour taste what filled the room. Then he bent to the floor near Davy and tried to sound softer. "Mimi, your brother and I are going to bring Malka in from the pasture. If Mama says so, when you are done, come up to the barn and help us milk."

"I will not," she said, her mouth trembling.

"All right," Jake shrugged, hoisting Davy on his shoulder. "Suit yourself."

Mimi pressed her lips together and stared as the screen door slammed behind them. I swallowed, afraid of the coldness, like her father's, what I saw in her eyes.

Mamale hissed, *So what's to fear? Such a throw, she deserved that potch on the tuchis. Jake did right.*

You got to be harder, Shlima nodded, childless but sure she was an expert on *kinder. Mimi'd be a better girl if occasionally you should give her a slap.*

I shook my head. *Barbaric! Unprincipled! Oy, such a bad business we have here. Wait 'til I get my hands on that Jake.*

What, so you'll hit too? Gitl asked, standing near Mimi. *Talk about meshuggeneh. Better you should pay attention to your own kitchen. Someone here needs you right now.* She was right. I looked closely at my poor Mimala, her feet silent and twisted together. All that fire in her, the joyful dancing, it was frozen away. "You are all right?" I asked, kneeling down beside her. A spark I searched for in her sad face.

She hung her head and turned away from me.

"*Nu?* Then come." I stood up. "We got clothes to fold."

That night, Jake and I, we had a big argument. "Mimi needs discipline!" he screamed. "She's spoiled. Such a temper we got in that girl."

"Like someone else I know!" I spat back. "You make for her a good example. Just like your father, him with the hands, what made you run away."

Almost purple Jake turned. "Don't you dare say I'm like him! A little spanking is nothing close to the beatings I got."

"Mimi learns from your example." I tried to catch his arm. "What's right, what's wrong, from you, she sees how to be."

Jake turned to stare at me. "I won't have her hitting the boys," he declared, "like Papa hurt my poor brother. We have to do better by Nate and Davy since Avram's gone."

"Then teach her by keeping your temper," I begged. "Promise me you won't spank."

Some promise he made. It happened a thousand times in the next two years: Mimi's tantrums and Jake's spankings. The anger in both of them so deep, I lived everyday afraid. Afraid of the tears and the yelling, those potches on the *tuchis*. Plates and pots thrown on the floor. Once, a glass. Poor Mimi – in an agony, feeling orphaned. Poor Jake, wanting order in the house. At the time, I didn't understand how they were both lost in our new family. The coming of the boys – for both – turned the house upside down. All I wanted: Mimi should quit hitting Davy, quiet down, and stop sassing her father. She should give up trying to trip Nate when he did chores. Shoshie, I wish I had known sooner how to answer your mother's sadness. That's what she means when she swears that as a mother I was no good.

And here's the part what's hard to admit: even as a child, Mimi could be mean; it took an effort, sometimes, to like her. So stubborn. And the things that girl said – such a smart mouth. When Jake spanked, even though I didn't approve, sometimes relief I was feeling. Those slaps on the *tuchis*, they satisfied the itch in my own hand. And they worked – Mimi began to behave better. Or maybe she just got used to your uncles and calmed down. But nothing could stop the things she said – so nasty and pointed. I don't know where she got it – such sureness that only that her way was right. "Mimi, the expert," we called her, and we didn't always say it nicely. It got worse when she grew up.

I know, I watched how she favored Aviva, no matter how we tried to tell her different. Jake even yelled once, begging she should be more fair. But did she listen? No, and not even your father could convince her. *Ai yai yai*, it was hard to see how she made you feel the same hurt what she knew with me. But maybe there was something hidden, a strange gift, in all the tears Mimi shed in her childhood. Strength it gave her, a sense of purpose. You think her spoiling of Aviva demanded the same by you?

Don't roll your eyes. Listen, you never know where the stones what make up the house of your life come from. For Mimi, the chimney rock – it was a present she got from Mae Cherney.

Who she met the same day I did, the afternoon of the Guardians. You remember what happened? Mimi came into the picture after Davy and I piggybacked down the hill.

"Where have you been?" she asked when we panted across the yard to meet her.

"You saw us," Davy said, plopping on the porch and taking a big breath. "Papa showed. We saw you pointing."

She ignored him and bit her lip. "Mama, why weren't you here? You're supposed to be when we get home from school."

She's right, Shlima insisted, perching on the porch railing. *Neglecting your own for a group of foreign ghosts. Be ashamed.*

Better it might have been if Shlima had never nagged me. Her words, a reminder of all I'd learned up there on that hill. Maybe I didn't need to be so afraid of what I didn't know. Maybe it was all right, Mae and I, we should be friends.

She put me in mind of the wrong I'd done to my new neighbor that morning. So I rubbed my angry daughter's head and made her a bargain. "If you get out of those clothes quick, there's a trip I want we should take together. I got a basket of food I forgot to give our new neighbors. You want to come with?"

Running off again? Mamale thundered, appearing above my head in the apple tree. *Haven't you had enough of strangers today?*

Davy rubbed his tired foot against one of my roses. "Mama, I don't want to go."

Mimi leaned against the screen door and made a face at her little brother. "Mama didn't invite you." She rolled her eyes. "You're too young and besides, bringing food is for girls. Haven't you noticed yet that you're a boy?"

Well, she's got your mouth on her, Rheabie, Mamale sniffed, floating down to stand on the ground besides Gitl. *A spitting image of you, so fresh, at the same age.*

"Enough! No one is going anywhere around here without a little niceness,"

I insisted, speaking to both the dead and the living. "Go get changed, Mimi, and no words about it. Davy, find Papa and tell him we'll be gone for a minute and be back just as quick."

Some quick, Shlima spat. *If you get back in less than an hour, I'll faint.*

Mimi skipped through the kitchen doorway as Davy smiled. "I'll tell Papa, but first – a cookie?"

"*Oy*, you and your cookies! Here." I filled the greedy hands of the boy who held my heart. "And one for Nate and for the big man too. Can you carry them all?" I looked at Shlima but continued talking, "If Papa grumbles, tell him supper is an hour away."

So proud, so tall – Mimi walked beside me, holding a basket of fresh bread, last summer's jam and a few quarts of canned tomatoes. Beauty rushed into her face, making a flush and a smile that reached all the way to the curls on the top of her head.

The beauty faded a little when we knocked on the door and an angry Mae opened it. "Who's this?" our new neighbor snapped.

"Friends," I said in a calm voice, "come to visit you." Mae didn't move, so I braved a look at her dark eyes – green like moss what grows on oaks. "True friends, like the kind what you asked for earlier." A trembling in my voice, Shoshie, but still I said the words. "A promise I'll make, you still should want it from me." The green of Mae's eyes deepened. "Please. You'll have us?" I asked, meaning: I'm sorry. An apology I made with every word.

Light: like the sun through trees jumped into Mae's face. Her cheeks, a mess of freckles, looked like stars – on fire with delight.

"Good," I sighed and leaned back against the wall of the house just as your mother stepped forward. Frowning at what she felt in the air between us, Mimi held out the basket. "We welcome you to the neighborhood," she said with just a *bissel* of a question in her voice.

"My pleasure." Mae opened the door and smiled. So bold, she winked at Mimi. "Rheabie, why didn't you tell me you were growing such a gorgeous girl?"

"Who had time with all your questions?" I looked down at my daughter, standing glad like a proud flower. "Did you give me even a second to brag?"

"Well," Mae wiped her hands on her apron. "I am very pleased." She got serious and asked, "Do you ladies have time for a cup of tea?"

Mimi looked up at me, pleading.

"All right," I gave in. "But very quick. A hungry papa we got waiting at home."

"*Oy.*" Mae reached out for Mimi's hand. "I've seen the man eat!" She led the child into her messy kitchen, full of unopened boxes. Then she laughed, and, as if Mimi was twenty years old, said, "Such an appetite, your father. I bet there's trouble when you keep him from his food."

So shiny, Mimi's eyes, when Mae seated her at the table. "Please," she asked, "may I have a glass of milk?" And she sat, with her hands in her lap, while Mae hurried to serve her. Such talk between them, Mae asking questions about Jake, how the pullets were doing, the best place in Petaluma to get groceries. The painting in the corner, did Mimi think it should hang somewhere else? Your mother's shoulders got wider: she loved, I understood suddenly, playing an adult.

This, the gift from Mae: to see the ancient woman what lived inside my daughter. To recognize Mimi's mind, a whole world of opinions, of rights and wrongs. Mae could see that Mimi wanted, more than anything, to be taken seriously. The key to making peace with that girl – like a grown-up we should treat her.

"But she's only seven," I thought as we hurried away much later than I'd wanted. "What's the crime she should stay a child?"

A crime of holding back, of remaining blind to the wide fields of her nature. Mimi needed more, needed bigger, than to be talked to as a little girl. What more, what bigger exactly, I couldn't name, but at that moment I felt it. As I walked, a pounding, loud as a drum, began to play on my ribs.

"So Mimala," I said. She lifted her head, but stayed skipping ahead of me. "Tonight, as soon as we get home, I want you should help cook supper." I took a breath and let it out slowly. "It's time you learn what all women know."

"Really?" Such joy in her voice as she asked, "You'll let me do it, just me, and not Nate and Davy?"

At her pleasure, I couldn't help smiling. But she didn't know yet, the hours of cutting and mixing and watching. "I'm talking soups and bread and chicken. You're big enough now. I want you should know."

Mimi hopped away. "I am very pleased," she called back, sounding the spitting image of Mae. That moment, it was a start, an important beginning. Your mother's genius with pots and parties, it grew from this seed. Planted by a red-haired woman lonely for neighbors who understood a young girl's yearning. Mae showed me what I hadn't yet seen for myself.

"And when you are ready," I continued. "I got a project for us." A thank you to Mae Cherney. "A party we'll make, a dinner with guests – to celebrate the new folks on Chapman Lane."

Mimi took a dizzy breath. "A party, Mama?"

"Something small. Just Mae and Art and maybe the Blumbergs. You and I, together we'll cook the whole thing."

"Oh boy!" Mimi shouted. She hugged me, and turned a cartwheel. Seven again.

And it's still the same, Shoshana, how it happens with your mother. Have you noticed? When she's trying to be most adult, that's when she slips back, a child. The spirits of her hands rise from her side, even if she doesn't want, and into birds they turn. Something comes flying, full of love, out of her eyes.

Ach, you don't believe? I'm telling you, I've seen it. On the telephone it happens regular, seven o'clock Sunday every week. So *nu*, Shoshie, what will you say when Mimi calls tonight to check up on us? Can you speak to the treasure in your mother, what she keeps hidden away? This is important, what I'm asking. I want a true answer. Are you enough of a *mensh*, my *bubchik*, to hear the birds in her hands?

Chapter 8
SPEAKING TO BIRDS

SHOSHANA

I don't feel much like a *mensh* when the phone rings soon after our spaghetti dinner. I get up and carry the plates to the sink while the bell shrills. Grandma Rheabie raises her eyebrows and puffs out her cheeks as I throw a mess of silverware into hot dishwater. "All right, all right," I mutter at her lined and weary face, and then I reach out my arm. "Mom?"

I don't know if I'm going to speak to the prickly woman who raised me or the sad little girl crying in Grandma's stories. As I cradle the receiver into my neck, I only know this: the woman I've always wanted to talk to, the one I've longed for, has never been. Or, at least, she has never been my mother.

I look out the kitchen window to the hills. The voice I have been hoping to hear all these years belongs to either a ghost named Wina, if I choose to believe Grandma's fairy tales, or is just the filmy comfort of a childhood dream. Anyway, she is not the woman who answers me. "Where were you? I was about ready to hang up and call the police."

"What for? Nothing can happen to us here." I begin to scrape the plates, watching the leftover noodles slither into a mound of old greens in the compost bucket. "Maybe we were outside, talking or taking a walk or something."

"Oh sure," my mother snaps. "You had a miracle happen back there? Don't try to kid me. Your grandmother can't be any better on her legs than me."

"So how are you, Mom?" I feel nothing sweet in her silences. No birds swoop over me in the quiet between the long waterfalls of her words: physical therapy, her doctor, the rude nurse, this week of Aviva's pregnancy and how much Mom misses babysitting that darling, my niece Beth. The sound of Mom's voice, her worries and complaints, is so familiar, for a moment I feel as if I am back in Lydon, drinking a cup of tea.

Except Lydon didn't have a sharp-eyed old woman at the kitchen table who frowns as I listen, nod and rinse plates. She shifts in her chair, impatient, and motions for me with an angry arm: Come! Sit down beside me. "Stop," she mouths. "You talk. It's your turn."

I shrug into the chair and fiddle with a glass of lemonade sweating onto the wooden table. The drops bead against the finish as Mom ends a story about plans for Aviva's baby shower. I can picture Viva, stomach straining against the maternity jumper I made for her birthday, laughing at the corny invitations. "Your sister loved them. She's looking forward to the whole thing so much."

"Of course." A wave of longing rises up from my belly. If Aviva and I were together, listening to Mom orchestrating the shower, we'd be rolling our eyes.

Grandma scrawls a note and shoves it under my wet fingers. "Talk," she's written in big loopy letters, scattering my sense of my big sister. "Speak to the birds."

I look up at the eager lines of Grandma's face, the half-moons cupping her mouth, and I am eight again, sitting on the bed next to Viva as Grandma finishes telling us another fairy story. I pleat my pink PJs, hearing the laughter of Baba Yaga when she comes upon the ignorant maiden lost in her forest. I believed every bit of Grandma's magic, acting out the tales with Aviva afterwards. When we argued over just how smart Baba Yaga really was and what exactly she would say, Dad shook his head. "It's only a story, the work of your grandmother's imagination. She means well, but don't take it so seriously. In this world, you've got to be able to know what's real and what's not."

Will I believe Grandma once again and make the effort to speak to something she's promised me still swoops and flies inside my mother? Or will I place my hands flat on the table, my father's doubting daughter, and trust only what I can feel – the touch of the hard wood under my skin?

"So *nu?*" Grandma asks loudly, her eyebrows raised.

"Is that your grandmother coughing?" Mom sighs. "She's not sick, is she? Let me speak to her."

I hesitantly finger a rose fading in the vase on the table. "Grandma's been showing me old pictures of the ranch," I begin, afraid she'll get angry, as usual, at the mention of her past. "There are a lot of cute shots of you."

"*Feh.* Everyone's cute as a baby," Mom says. "Even you girls – and look what happened. That's a joke."

Grandma watches me roll my eyes, and then she winks. She sits up and reaches forward to pat my hand.

"Listen," Mom drops her voice. "You know better than to believe any of her stories. Don't make me have to say out loud, once again for Christ's sake, that your grandmother's a liar. Can't manage her money. Can't take care of herself. Tells stories. You know as well as I do that for years now, she's not been right in the head."

"Who in this family has ever been right in the head?" I think.

The last light floods the window, paling Grandma Rheabie's arms, marking the way the skin sags across her elbow. Her chest rises and falls with a deep sigh. When I was little, sometimes I pretended she was a witch or, at least, my fairy godmother. She was coming to rescue me in a shower of sparkles from the dullness of my life. "But she..."

Mom interrupts. "I didn't want to tell you because I thought you'd worry, but last time I was out, I talked to Doctor Kendall about Alzheimer's. All her property, her business – it's a mess. That fool Kendall said he didn't think so, but there's no test, so what does he know?"

"He's a doctor."

She ignores me. "Whatever she tells you, show a little sense. Don't believe her. You can be nice: just nod your head and listen. The poor senile thing needs to talk – God knows we all do – so just let her go on."

"Mom!" I swallow something close to a shout and feel words waiting at the back of my mouth. If this isn't the mother I've always wanted to talk to, why don't I just tell her the truth? Listen, I imagine saying, I don't care if Grandma isn't the business woman like she used to be. There's plenty of money in her checking account – I've been paying the bills. And what does it matter if she exaggerates when she tells her stories? The point isn't a debate about what's real or what's true. It's simpler than that: she's lonely, and she loves you. Why can't you quit doubting and love her back?

My mother waits for me to speak, but I can't make my mouth shape anything close to what I'm thinking.

"Shoshana?" she breathes. The quiet on the line gets deeper. I clear my throat, try again.

I like Grandma, I want to say. If you knew how much, would you treat me any differently? Would you talk about me in the same mean way you talk about her?

But the words won't come, and so finally I give up and hand the phone to Grandma. I don't even try to hide the tears that blink from my eyes. Grandma glows like a candle, a star, a light shining in the darkness. Then, "Mimala," she shouts, warmth filling our little kitchen. "You remember your first party? I was just beginning to tell Shoshie."

For a moment, I imagine that the room is full of wings.

Chapter 9
THE PARTY

RHEABIE

So here's the story of the party. We began with cooking lessons that night. Every day, a big fuss in the kitchen, as if an egg in our house was near to hatching. The worried hens, my family ghosts, squawked and cackled. Roosters, your grandpop and the boys, crowed over each burnt pan. But we survived, your mother and me, because Mae was *mensh* enough to throw herself into the project. Almost every afternoon, she found an excuse she should hurry over to the ranch.

"Here, try this recipe, Mimi. It's good and simple." She brought ribbons. "Just right for your braids, dolly. Looking nice makes a girl a better cook." Each sad piece of coffee cake our neighbor ate without blinking. Every burnt potato Mae coated in a cream of fine words.

"How do you do it?" I asked once, after sending Mimi up to the egg house for a new half dozen. As soon as our young cook slammed the screen door, Mae put down her plate. Such a sorry cake. She didn't even try to eat anymore.

"To be honest, I don't taste," she laughed. "Instead, each bite, I see the hunger on that determined girl's face."

Your mother: hungry to make bread that rose and borscht worth eating. Hungry to watch the boys gobble a supper, not knowing who made what. And when she was discouraged, Mae could give a lift. "Don't be in such a rush, *bubelah*. You'll get it."

Mimi would sigh and straighten her shoulders. "You think so? Really?"

"I promise," Mae said firmly. "The best cook in the world you're going to be."

Never before had our house known such a woman, as bright and shiny as the kerosene lamp in the evenings. Mae taught the boys the latest union songs or new dance steps from Los Angeles. Such a glow on her face when she leaned across the table, arguing with Jake over world events. And after supper, she could talk to the *kinder* about homework in English instead of Yiddish. Born in the madness of New York City, Mae was, remember? She knew from the sounds I found so foreign in my own *kinder's* words.

What I mean, Shoshana, is that she breathed the same air they did and understood the sentences they made from it. At that time, Jake and I, we still had Russia in our mouths.

Once, she told Davy a story in Yiddish and English. Such a look, big with heart, on her face. I shook my head. "You are a regular piece of patience."

Davy jumped off Mae's lap. "Why, Mama?"

"Because a boy I know asked twice this morning for the exact same story, and someone was kind enough to tell it to him."

"I know," Davy smiled. "And I listened good so now I can tell Malka just what Mae said."

"Good," his storyteller nodded. "It is a boring life for a cow, chewing grass all by her lonesome in the pasture. A story like that is just what she needs."

"See?" I said as he rushed down the porch steps. "You know all the answers, how a mother should be."

I was asking, you understand, what we had not discussed yet, in spite of our "tell-everything-to-each-other" friendship. Yet so far, there'd been no words to explain why Mae, ten years older than me, had no *kinder*. Such an emptiness in a house, it was rare those days. And sometimes, as Art explained history to Mimi and the boys, Mae would blink fast and swallow. A look of sadness took over her face.

The kitchen got quiet now at my question. A *bissel* tears, like mist through trees, fogged Mae's eyes. "I wanted but could not have," she said slowly. Then she sighed. "So – there were other things to do. First the needle workers' union, then nursing and Art's work with the Educational League in Los Angeles. Still, your *kinder* I understand – Mimi especially. She's too much like me."

Always full of surprises, this new friend. "Like you?" I couldn't see what string in my anxious daughter ran to the heart of Mae's bright life.

She leaned back in her chair. "She's in such a hurry to grow up, that one – like she's an old woman already. Do you ever see the *bubbe* that lives in her eyes?"

Shoshana, of course I saw. Since that day when she was dancing, at three, I'd run away from the old lady living inside my daughter. Those tantrums, I thought, it was the old one. The sour, wrinkled woman, she was to blame. "Yes," I admitted, twisting my fingers together. Then: a sign of how far we'd come in friendship. I asked, wanting an honest answer, "What should I do with her? Mimi doesn't want to be young."

You don't have to ask Mae for advice, Shlima wailed from the left-hand corner of the ceiling. *That's what you have family for. Besides, what can a stranger know?*

"I didn't want to be young, either," Mae confessed. "My poor, scared mother. From her I demanded the world – everything in life, years before my time."

Mamale shook her head at me from the rocker. *I don't know why you are spending time with this meshuggeneh. What do you need with another Mimi in your life?*

I ignored her. "You were hard on your mother?" I asked, thinking of Mimi's latest fit, a tantrum ending with two broken plates.

"She didn't trust her strength, so she tried to hold me back." Mae looked out the window toward the gum grove. Then she sat up and leaned toward me. "Rheabie Slominski, you are stronger than you think."

Strong enough for what? Gitl jumped down off the top of the tallest kitchen cabinet.

Mae placed a thin hand gently on the table. "Trust your girl, all the age that was born in her. Let Mimi find her own road."

Road going where? Mamale huffed. *Down the lane, on to Western Avenue, right out of Petaluma? You want Mimi to waltz away from your life?*

"I don't understand." Already my ribs were aching. "What are you telling me to do?"

"It's time," Mae declared with a smile, "overdue, this party business."

Only that? Such a small road, I thought at the time, a little path maybe. Mae saw deeper. Like Mimi, she had an old woman's wisdom in her knowing eyes.

"The girl's ready," she said quietly. "She's worked hard. Don't keep the reward from her anymore."

No! Shlima shook her head. *Not yet.* She whirled through the air. *It'll be a mess, you do this now.*

I ignored that worrywart, my sister, and watched instead the sun tracing the bones of Mae's face. The lines and angles melted when I said, "All right, so we got a party next Friday night."

Only a week, a tizzy of anticipation. And you know how your mother is – there was no living with her, once the day had been set. A fuss she made out of every step of getting ready. Such planning and lists. And worse, a hunger in her for beauty. Not just a few flowers brought in from the garden but napkins folded, plates arranged, and food decorated within an inch of its life.

What's wrong with just eating it? Mamale wanted to know as Mimi played with a salad one night for practice. She frowned as her granddaughter placed cucumbers and tomatoes in a pattern around the rim of the bowl. *A waste of time, all this fussing. Once you make the dressing and toss that salad, who's going to see?*

There's something wrong with that girl, Shlima worried, poking an invisible finger at the nasturtiums Mimi used to decorate slices of applesauce cake. *Where did she learn to be so fancy? Only the rich care about such things.*

Maybe we got an artist here, Gitl offered, standing behind Mimi and leaning over her shoulder. *It matters to her: colors and shapes and making things pretty. When have you seen Mimi having such a good time?*

This is only food, Mamale squawked, floating up to the kitchen ceiling. *She should worry how it tastes.*

It tastes fine, I snapped. *I've made sure. Now quit fussing over the poor girl.*

Wasn't it was brave of me, Shoshana, how I stood up for your mother? A first, I want you should know, defending Mimi from Mamale's harsh tones. But, here's the truth: under my words, just like my ghosts, I was worried. With every day closer to the party, your mother grew an another inch. As she hummed over flowers and table settings, she stretched herself. Pleasure she made from things I could not know. Like that fairy story from when you were little – "The Ugly Duckling" – I saw for the first time, the face of my daughter, the swan.

In the story, it's good for the swan, yes, to grow into her true beauty? But what about the family what loved her? The Slominskis – nothing could change the fact that we were plain, brown ducks. That night, a Wednesday, I bit my lip and thought, "Mae's right. This is a new road Mimi's walking." Here was the surprise. I missed the daughter I knew, small and smart-mouthed; I wanted the tantrum thrower, she should come home.

Have you lost your senses? Gitl moaned. *Look how the boys are smiling.*

It won't be this peaceful the night of the party, Shlima predicted, leaning her back against the plate cupboard. *Trouble's just waiting to walk in and live at this house.*

She already does, Gitl sniffed, *and her name is Shlima, so frightened she sees cobwebs in every corner. Pay no attention, Rheabie. The party will be fine.*

Fine: like the way it dawned that Friday morning. A clear day in June we had, sharp and smelling of heat. "Chicken-killing weather," Jake grumped after a quick breakfast, hurrying off to check the brooder houses. Mimi and I rushed our baking, hoping that the sky would stay cool. But by ten o'clock it was near ninety already. Jake returned, just as we pulled the knishes from the oven, swearing over the loss of ten chicks.

"Smothered!" he growled. "In a corner, piled on top of each other. You'd think they'd have more sense." He ran a hand through his hair and looked up at me. "Tell me what we're doing on a chicken ranch. Raising imbeciles – what kind of business is that?"

"Papa, you want your tea?" Mimi asked, trying to calm him.

"Try this." I set a glass of water on the table to cool his temper. As Jake took a long drink, I said, "I remember how you liked needlework better, the intelligence of top coats. So smart, that wool." Then I cut him a slice of rye and got out the dill pickles. "What brilliant conversations you had together when you sewed."

Jake sighed so loud I knew he was feeling better. "Well, needlework was cleaner." He tugged at his beard. "At least, the wool didn't do its business on my feet."

Your mother and I both bent for a quick look under the table. Please, I whispered, Jake remembered – yes – to take off his shoes when he came in the house. That scamp, your grandfather, wiggled his toes at us and laughed.

"I'll take the boys to Art's pond for a swim later to keep them away from the cooking." He stood up and smiled at us. "Mimala, those knishes smell so good. It must break your heart not to give your papa one."

"My heart is not broken," she insisted, wiping her wet hands on her apron. "There's just enough for everyone to have two. You can't have any missing at a party."

"*Feh* on the party," Jake said quietly. "This is your papa we're talking. Family." He bent down to look right at her. "Be careful, *bubee*, about what's important. This party – it's going to be over tomorrow. It's not your whole life."

I looked at the man, wise in his way, and shook my head: "*Sha*, don't say this." I didn't see the point in making clear the hard fact of what was to come. Somewhere in me, where I didn't want to know, I could feel how much Mimi was changing. More than family, more than her papa, this party – it had already become her life. What she wanted, who she would grow to be, what mattered. Before our very eyes, like in that story, our duck had shed her brown feathers. That night, the swan, so fancy, would flap her wings.

But not until dessert, not until we were full, leaning back in our chairs and feeling sleepy. Such a perfect party; *oy*, was I *shepping naches* from how well Mimi had done. So what did it matter, the potato soup was a little thick and the lettuce in the salad was wilted? On such a hot day, who could expect less? Not us, full and happy. Even your mother, showing that dimple at the side of her mouth, was pleased.

Until Moysche Blumberg asked, "You read that letter in today's *Freiheit*?" He had the nerve to slurp his tea. "Birobidzhan – Zionism in the USSR, the writer calls it. No better than Palestine, he said."

By the time he finished speaking, the room was silent. Such a bombshell, it was as if he'd told us the pope was really a Jew. You know from Birobidzhan, an important piece of Soviet history? No? Ach, what do they teach in school these days?

Birobidzhan – a national homeland for Jews in the new Soviet Union. Someone's bright idea after the revolution – we could overcome years of hatred by giving our people a piece of land. Under the Czar, it was against the law Jews should own and work acres. Our life we could not draw from the Russian earth. And dolly, because we didn't work and suffer beside the Russian people, we got the blame for a bad harvest. You know the rest: riots, *pogroms*, murders. Losing Mamale, Shlima and Gitl to the Ukrainian

Nationalist Army – who wanted their own homeland, no Jews included – what came from not having dirt on our hands.

Well, that was how we figured it then, and all these years later, nothing has shown me different. If two peoples don't plant their hands in the same earth – that's when hatred can begin. The glory of socialism – everyone living from the blood and breath of each other – would stop such misery. A part of the great experiment we were, all the way across the world in Petaluma. Birobidzhan, so we could live what was forbidden our fathers. Birobidzhan, like how Jake kept our family safe by working the land.

"What do you mean?" he roared. Everyone at the table jumped. "That writer has the nerve to compare Birobidzhan to Palestine? A homeland in a socialist society is no English colony. In Birobidzhan no one sits on his ass dreaming about the Messiah and spreading religious poison. Can't he see the difference here?"

The room woke up. Mae leaned forward, her elbows pressed eagerly into the oil-cloth. Art slid his glasses back up to the top of his nose.

And Moysche, one of the hot heads at Jewish Center meetings, stared into the center of the table. "The writer has a point," he insisted. "Why Birobidzhan? The Jewish people don't deserve a piece of land warmer than Siberia? What keeps the government from offering a settlement where it really matters – the Ukraine or Bessarabia – a place what's in the world?"

Out of the corner of my eye, I saw Nate, full of sighs, quietly folding his napkin. Davy kicked at the rungs of his chair. All right, so maybe for them this discussion wasn't so interesting. For me, it was different. "*Mazel tov*," I thought, fiddling with the fancy skirt Mimi insisted I should wear, "finally, we have more to talk about than food."

Fine lines showed between Mae's eyebrows. "You're questioning the Party's commitment to overturning anti-Semitism?" For a moment, the question made Moysche look small.

But the man was always stubborn. Taking a breath, he slapped the table. "No. But can't you see the larger question? Maybe a territorial solution is repeating history, making another Pale of Settlement. We're talking danger here."

Beside me, I felt Mimi begin to stand up. Already she had her eye on the door, ready to slip away. "Sit," I whispered, my hand on her arm. "You still got guests, and your party is lovely. A hostess has to stay and be polite."

Her father wasn't doing so good in the polite department. "What danger?" Jake yelled. "How can Birobidzhan be like the Pale?"

Even Art raised his reasonable voice. "For God's sake, Blumberg, you have a brain. Use it. All this was debated before Birobidzhan was formed."

"Not debated enough," he growled. "I'm telling you, we are open for attack, everyone living in one place, just like before the revolution."

Jake shouted. "Don't be stupid. It's a whole new world, organized by principles. What, you've turned Zionist now? Be ashamed, Blumberg. You think socialism doesn't mean a thing?"

My three ghosts joined the debate, floating just above the kitchen table. *Zionism, feh!* Mamale screeched, *as if the Party would ever be so bourgeois and counter-revolutionary.*

Gitl flung her arms wide. *In Palestine they are still competing for property. Birobidzhan is the opposite of that.*

And Shlima crowed, *What did I tell you? Trouble, trouble, trouble!* Then she pointed her finger at the real drama in the room. *Rheabie, look! The pot is boiling over. Mimi's going to cry.*

And this is the important moment, the very second your mother first showed the reason for her new feathers. She stood up and knocked her chair back, fully a swan. "Stop it!" Mimi screamed. "All your stupid fighting. You're wrecking the party." Then, the bird of my womb hurled her glass into the kitchen wall. It broke, shocking the room into silence. The dinner – in flying pieces now, broken by the force of her arm. And yes, Shoshie, you're right. This angry girl was exactly the child I'd been missing, with her temper and bitter mouth, come home just like I'd wanted. You think I was grateful? "Mimi Slominski." I yanked hard at her elbow, wanting to die from embarrassment. "Be ashamed!"

But shame she didn't know, your mother. "This is a party," she howled. "Don't you know how to act?"

"Shut your mouth this instant," Jake yelled. His tone was dangerous, so different from his roaring over politics. I knew what was coming. In a second, he'd be ready to use his spanking hand.

"Apologize!" I demanded, trying to head off the fight. Moysche's mouth was still open, and poor Luba had begun to cry. "Apologize," I demanded again of Mimi. "Look what you've done."

But your mother wailed, "I don't have to apologize to anybody." She cried, the old *bubbe* fierce in her voice. "They were wrong. They should apologize to me."

Here is where your mother left us, taking a road to a world of her own making. In her defiance, Mimi had the courage to look each person at the table right in the eye. And we all looked down – ashamed, unable to stay with that angry girl and keep her company. None of us knew what she needed or wanted, what this new road meant. Everyone failed her – her mother, father, brothers, guests and ghosts. Everyone except Mae Cherney. As I counted red checks in the oil-cloth covering the table, I heard a firm voice say, "Mimala, come here."

And then footsteps across the glass, until Mimi reached Mae's side of the table. Our neighbor swung the unhappy girl up into her lap. "So you want an apology," she said calmly. "Why? Do you think this kind of party is not the place for the furious things we say?"

Art straightened and looked at Mae with a light in his face, and then he nodded. "A party **is** the place," he said in his quiet voice. "You need to understand, child, there's purpose in what we're doing. From talk like this, we build a better world. For you, so you can grow up to live in it: a place of justice." He leaned over to tap Mimi's arm, then looked to Nate and Davy. "There can be no better kind of conversation. To discuss, to struggle with ideas – it makes a life something. This is the biggest thing I know."

Moysche cleared his throat to speak. "He's right, *kinder*. Ideas – they make a man feel like a person." He tapped a finger on the table. "And when a man feels that, he has courage. So *nu,* then what happens? Courage, ideas, talk – a revolution he can bring to the world."

"But it wasn't like that, what you were doing," Mimi objected. She put her mouth back on the argument. "You weren't listening to each other. You just yelled."

"True," Mae said, "so now we come to the truth of it." She smoothed Mimi's hair down with her freckled fingers. "I need to understand, dolly. What's wrong if we shout?"

I held my breath, as if whatever Mimi said would make sense out of her new feathers. This lovely daughter, who had she become?

"It's not polite," your mother said.

Polite? Mamale asked. *What, she wants us to talk world events and be quiet? Who could do it?*

Even Gitl was puzzled. *It's polite to discuss what's important as if it doesn't mean a thing?*

Mimi leaned into Mae's chest. Then the heart of it came out of her. "And it scares me," the poor girl cried.

Scared by a little noise? Shlima wondered. *But Jake yells. She's used to it. And our Mimi's not bad in that department herself. Now she's a fraidy-cat? Rheabie, check her temperature and see. Maybe she's just sick.*

But no such luck, the excuse of a fever. *Listen to what she says.* Gitl shook her head. *Mimi wants we should act different with company. Something she learned in school, maybe. She thinks quiet, it's nice.*

My sister was right. The new swan in Mimi needed a still pond to swim in – something calm, with lots of high bushes. Like your house in Ithaca – all that garden, so much green. You know what I mean: very pretty, but boring. And the talk there – the life taken out of any discussion with your mother's rule: no one should raise a voice.

Don't look at me like that. It's true, what I'm saying. All right, so all these years later, maybe I should be able to accept how your mother and me, our tastes are different. You'd think I'd be used to it by now.

I'll tell you one thing. That night of the party, even though her fear made no sense to me, I admired the *chutzpah* in my daughter. So brave, her request that the world should be polite. I marveled but knew, sure as I could feel the table under my fingertips, that poor Mimi wouldn't find what she wanted in our house.

She was leaving me, and the very thought made my bones hurt. Still, even though I was aching, in my chest I felt something else. Somehow that night, your mother, she took a broken glass and gave me the pieces. In her hands she held them like it was some kind of gift.

Yes, ashamed I was, embarrassed too, how my child behaved so badly in front of company. I thought that was the reason what made me cry as I watched Mimi rock slowly, back and forth, in Mae's arms. But as she quieted, I realized I didn't care, even though I should, about tantrums and broken glasses. I only cared that Mae smiled at me, warm and happy, over Mimi's head. And so, I spread my hands wide on the oil-cloth and tried to find my own *chutzpah*. What in the world did I need different?

The question was so strong that even Mamale heard it, floating up near the ceiling. *What?* she screeched, clutching her elbows and glaring down at me. *Nothing needs to change here. The nerve!*

Shlima scowled from where she had come to rest on top of the icebox. *I told you this party would be a disaster! Oy, Rheabie, what have you begun?*

They were smart, my ghosts, because that night I started a story that it's taken me all these years to finish. Here's the worst part. For reasons I can't tell yet, we're not even close to the end. And a little voice has told me we have to hurry. Everything might depend on you, *bubee* – what you've done with your own wings, dolly. And I'm tired now so I'm asking: please, Shoshie. Do you trust me enough finally to open your mouth and tell one of your "once upon a times"?

Chapter 10
FAIRY TALES

SHOSHANA

Once upon a time, a young woman had her world turned upside down when she came south to nurse her sick grandmother. She heard so many wild stories that her head walked on the ground and her feet swung free in the air.

Once upon a time, the woman's grandmother sat on a creaky porch in the mornings and talked about magic. She said she was telling family stories, but each time she mentioned a familiar name, she waved her wand, and they became someone else.

Once upon a time, on a Tuesday in late September 1980, this confused girl finished the lunch dishes and tiptoed past the bedroom of her napping grandma. In the room where her uncles had grown up, the girl stared at family pictures, framed in wood and arranged neatly in chronological order across an entire wall.

"Cut the storytelling," I say out loud, raising my hand to stroke the frame of my parents' wedding picture. "It's time to quit it." I close my eyes. "No matter what Grandma says, the problem isn't about trusting her. It's whether or not I want to live in the middle of a fairy tale."

It's a relief to breathe the air of this room, cooled by the leaves of an old apple tree. The desk and plain chair are as neat and calm as the pictures on the wall. It's so simple that I lean against the door frame, trying to pull the peace into my lungs as if it could douse the heat in my body. When my grandmother tells her stories, everything I know about my family gets confused and hot.

For instance, she's barely mentioned Uncle Nate, and when she does, she makes him out to be so stern and quiet. Where is the laughing uncle who always joked his way through a visit to Ithaca, hardly touching his plate at dinner because he talked so much?

Or Davy, withdrawn and silent at family gatherings, drinking beer after beer in the blue easy chair he moved to face the corner. Before he arrived, Mom always warned me to ignore any odd behavior. "It was those two years in the Nazi prisoner of war camp," she whispered, sounding like Grandma Rheabie all of a sudden. "I wouldn't wish them on my worst enemies. What he suffered over there, I hope you never know." I can't believe that the man who shrugged his shoulders and wouldn't answer when I asked, "Do you want more chicken or potato salad?" is the dreamer in Grandma's tales.

And then, of course, there's Mom, who I can't even begin to recognize in my grandmother's stories. That passionate little girl, on fire about entertaining, is a million miles away from the woman who complained if Dad invited a client or someone from the firm home for dinner – "Oh Abe, not again." I don't understand why throwing a glass at a wall when she was seven makes her into some kind of hero. To me, it only means that, even when she was little, my mother was a brat.

So, after lunch I come here, to this little room where Grandpa Jake hung the family history on the wall in neat squares, framed in some kind of order. Here where the graduation and wedding photos, the collage of proud parents and grinning children, make a quilt of who we might be. Today, I trace the reflection of apple leaves on the glass caging our family's New Year's "portrait." The four of us, posed on the couch in Ithaca when I was sixteen, makes the sweat bead beneath my ear.

Dad is smiling, though he had let out a rare "goddamn" at Aviva and me a moment before for sniping at each other and squirming while he set up the camera. Viva laughs, her dark head thrown back a little, not knowing she's about to receive my very best pinch. And Mom smiles, smothering the fury that will erupt as soon as the shutter clicks because when she nagged me about keeping my legs crossed, I whispered, "All right, already. Just shut up."

"Don't you talk to your mother like that," Dad growled when we got up off the couch. "I won't have it in this family."

"Why not? Because we're all so happy and normal?" I asked, slamming the door to my room.

From the time I was small, I knew that these kinds of pictures recorded only the surface, the shiny paper wrapped around an important moment. I was smart enough to realize that the truth was covered with tissue, hidden inside a box. But do I really want to learn what was folded up under my smart-ass remark to my father? If Grandma were telling this story, she'd find something mythic and wonderful about it, part of a fairy tale, running beneath my words.

It comes down to this: I don't know if I'm brave enough to live in a world that is hot and sticky with hidden meanings.

"Of course you're brave enough," I hear Grandma say, cocking her head to the right, the way she did for this forty-fifth wedding anniversary picture. During the party, my uncles danced close with their wives while my cousins snickered. Grandpa had to stop his speech about his years with Grandma because he was crying so hard. "To a coward, about all this I wouldn't tell even a whisper," Grandma says from the photo. "But you don't know from scared. Shoshie, you're brave."

"What you say about everyone doesn't make sense," I protest, "compared to what I remember. I miss the truth from when I was growing up."

"Well," Grandma shrugs, lifting a shoulder of the blue silk dress she wears in the photo, "do you hear anyone asking you should give up what you know?"

In the silence that follows, I hear her snore in the next room, and I am disappointed that our conversation has all been in my imagination. These are the rantings of a woman who can no longer tell what's what.

But even my disappointment is surprising because who is it, anyway, who is hearing voices? Maybe I have been too long in the company of an old woman who talks to the dead. I clench my fists and force the breath out between my teeth. If I didn't think it would wake Grandma up, I'd start shouting who I am, just to remember: Shoshana Cohen, waitress at the Kitchen Kupboard, Josie's employee, Mark's girlfriend, Lillian's neighbor. "You don't have the ability," I whisper, "to put together what she says with what you know."

"Why not?" asks a voice I have heard in a dream from some bright place in my childhood. The air in the room shimmers as an ancient woman melts through the walls and says, "Someone has to teach you to spin straw into gold."

Once upon a time I saw a ghost, a Guardian from an ancient California Indian nation, standing in my Uncle Davy's bedroom. At first I wasn't sure if I was staring at Davy's memory or falling into a dream. Then the ghost said in a voice that rumbled like gravel, "You are bothering yourself with unimportant questions." She laughed, spreading the fingers of both hands on her strong thighs. "What matters is not who but what you believe."

I believe in Wina, the Guardian with the blue tattoos on her chin, who came to talk to me today while my grandmother was sleeping.

I believe that I must hear the rest of my grandmother's tales.

Looking at the photographs in this room, I know that what kind of sense I make from it all is no one else's business. In the same way that Grandma saw a glass that shattered in this kitchen a long time ago, it is up to me to turn the pieces into a gift.

I am not good at fairy tales, but once upon a time, Grandma, the world turned over while you were napping. It didn't look the same when you woke up.

Chapter 11
MIXING WITH GHOSTS

RHEABIE

Shoshana, don't you have something important you want to tell me? Listen, from me you don't have to hide: Wina was here with you. You think that Guardian doesn't have a smell I know after all these years? It woke me up from a dream, and I called out to her. Shame on the both of you, talking so loud you didn't hear.

I was dreaming about Jake, so happy I was to touch his face. But as I bent for a little smooch, the dream ended. Just like that, he was gone.

But then I smelled wood; something leafy and cool told me Wina was here. Wina! Who I haven't seen in a month of Sundays. Wina! Such a knowing in her eyes, she turns me young.

So *nu*, and where was she? With you – in Davy's room. Such a pleasure. The two of you laughing like you'd known each other a thousand years.

But because you didn't hear when I called, I had to fuss all by myself with the walker. So long it took to get up and out of bed. For what? By the time I banged myself down the hall, Wina was gone. A little selfish, Shoshie, you should keep such company all to yourself, maybe. What, you didn't think I might enjoy a look at my favorite Guardian's face?

Well, of course, I'm in a bad mood. I'm seventy-eight years old, and my bones are giving out on me. I missed Wina, and I got a dead husband who won't visit my bed – not to mention trying something more interesting in it – in a dream. And who knows if I have enough time to get done what needs doing before I keel over? The first step: I need you should sit down, *shirrup*, and hear the rest of my story. And if Wina took it on herself to come see you, time is not something we have anymore.

So let's stop with the being nice already and get down to business. I hate all that "Oh, poor Grandma" stuff your mother taught you was polite. Mimi learned it good, trying to run from my temper when she was a girl.

Yes, my temper, the summer after Mimi's first party. Compared to my moods during that time, your mother, the tantrum queen, was nothing. When your mother talks about "the nightmare" of her childhood, that's part of what she means.

And why? Because Mae and I, we weren't speaking. Worse yet, her mother had fallen from a stroke in New York, and so Mae was gone. Even if I'd wanted to make up the fight we'd had after the party, there was no one at her house I could apologize. And our quarrel, I'm sorry to say, it was my fault. When Mae tried to talk about Mimi's tantrum, I shouted down the truth in her words.

"So what makes you so afraid of Mimala's yelling?" she asked one afternoon a few days after the party. Mae took a sip of iced tea and leaned back against the trunk of the apple tree. "The look on your face when she broke the glass – I thought you'd break too."

"I wasn't afraid," I protested, but I was lying. "My hand itched to give that girl a good smack."

Mae's eyebrows went up, lifting her face into a question. "I thought you didn't believe in spanking." Then she looked hard at me. "Not afraid? Are you sure?"

I couldn't admit it. "What? You think I don't know my own mind?" I straightened the napkin on my lap. "Besides, what kind of mother is afraid of her own daughter?"

Mae snorted. "Mine was, and I knew it. Mean as a factory boss I could be, threatening to get my own way. *Oy,* I used her with my temper, and now I'm sorry." Her eyes darkened. She looked up at me again. "I don't want Mimi, much as I love her, should do the same to you."

My ghosts hurried out from the house. *Stop right now. There's no more use in this conversation,* Shlima shouted.

This time, Gitl urged, floating to my side like a pullet feather, *you don't need to listen to what Mae says.*

Daughter, my mother commanded, rising up from the grass at my feet, a black shadow in a dark dress, *You have never been afraid of Mimi, and you do not feel that way now.*

"Listen," Mae insisted. "You give in to that girl, trying to avoid a tantrum. You'll give Mimi anything she wants to keep the peace."

"Not true!" I banged my glass down on the dirt. "How was I giving in at the party? You're saying I had something to do with why she threw that glass?"

"Mimi thought you were ignoring her, thinking about Birobidzhan. For the first time all night, she wasn't the focus. You were thinking about what you wanted to say."

Mae was right. "So what's wrong I should have an opinion?"

"Nothing by me," my friend said, on the verge of losing her patience. "We're talking Mimi here, what she wants and gets from you. And how scared you are when she acts wild. She knows that and uses it to get her way."

Phui! Shlima sputtered. *The woman doesn't even have kinder.*

Mae touched my leg. "Rheabie, believe me, I'm not criticizing."

"Then why are you saying this?" I didn't like how much my voice shook.

"Because in this friendship, we have promised to tell the truth." Mae took a breath and pushed on. "You don't stand up to Mimi, and she needs you to." Her eyes got soft, like Jake's in a moment of tenderness. Then her voice dropped. "You don't stand up because you're afraid."

Gitl wrung her hands. *No. Mae has too little experience and too much imagination. Don't believe her?*

Mimi's fine, Mamale insisted. *Between the two of you, nothing needs to change.*

Shoshie, why do you think my ghosts were so sure Mae had the story wrong? Why did it matter what she said, I shouldn't believe? Maybe if I'd stopped a minute and asked them, the worst wouldn't have happened. Instead, my pride guided my tongue.

"It's none of your business, Mae Cherney, what goes on between me and my daughter." My hands shook, but I hid them in my lap. "Do you hear me? Mimi is not your concern."

"All right." Mae pressed her lips tight together and put her glass back on the tray. "Then I am concerned because I have a friend who is a coward. She can't live up to what we agreed."

Coward? Mamale hissed. She shook a stubby finger in my face. *Didn't I tell you not to trust this one?*

Looking at Mae across the picnic cloth, I realized I hadn't trusted her. Think of it! In all these months of friendship, not a word had I mentioned about my ghosts. The biggest part of my life, and my best comrade didn't have an inkling. Just like Jake, she had no idea who I really was.

And why would you want to tell her? Mamale asked, her face startled. *Besides, Mae's American-born, so what can she know from ghosts? A graveyard haunting she'll never see her whole life.* Then my mother leaned forward to look at me with pity. *Rheabie, give up wanting your life should be normal – this trust business, friends who tell everything. For you, it's not meant.*

It was not meant, at least, that I'd keep to what Mae and I had promised in friendship. All our hours together, and I'd been holding back. Such disgust I felt, smelling the stink of my failure. "Then maybe this friendship, it's not one we should be keeping," I declared in shame beneath the apple tree that June afternoon. I was angry: at myself, at my ghosts, at all my secrets. How could Mae stand to spend even one more minute with a liar like me?

Mae flushed red as a bantam's comb as she rose up beside me. "You are a disappointment, Rheabie Slominski." Her arms crossed her chest. "Someday, maybe you'll find the courage to leave your life – so small and cramped, made from fear."

"Wait!" I called as the words we'd spoken hit the bottom of my belly. *Oy,* such an ache there. "Mae, I didn't mean..."

"Listen to yourself," she shouted, hurrying past the barn.

Mazel tov. Shlima congratulated me as I began to clean up our picnic. *For being so hard on our Mimi, boy, did she have it coming. I'm proud, sister. You told her off, but good.*

I couldn't know from good with my chest feeling so heavy. At that moment, the whole world it seemed had shattered.

Have more pride! Mamale insisted, and she was smiling even. *What kind of mother can listen to such insults about herself and her daughter? I didn't raise you to be a fool.*

But by evening, what Mae had said didn't seem so insulting, only mistaken. I was the one with the foot in her mouth.

No, Gitl soothed, *you're too upset to think clearly. Maybe you were a bit hasty at the end, but that's because something bigger was at stake. Don't go over there,* she advised as I folded the day's laundry. *Mae needs time to realize that as a mother, you are the expert.* She popped up between the sheet I was creasing and pointed. *Look at Mimi, such nice cards she's playing – with Nate even. This time, it never even crossed her mind to cheat.*

My sister was right – by some miracle that night, our house was peaceful. There'd been no squabbles at dinner, no making fun even when Davy spilled his milk. So maybe the Slominskis were all right, and about us Mae had made a bad analysis. Would it help things, I asked myself, to walk over and tell her she was wrong?

Still, I could apologize for my temper and all the things I'd kept from her.

No! Mamale yelped. *You'll explain nothing! Listen,* she calmed down enough to try and pat my shoulder as I walked past her into the boys' room, *What do you want with Mae and her cockamamie kind of friendship, anyway? Your life was fine before she came.*

It wasn't, I argued, slapping a stack of underwear into its drawer.

Poor Rheabie, you're tired, Shlima commented from the hallway ceiling. Kind she sounded, almost. *Look at the time. It's so late. Go over tomorrow. Tonight you need a rest.*

A mistake – because early the next morning came a telegram with news of Mae's mother. Without a word between us, her bag was packed, and she was gone.

It's your fault, I screamed at my ghosts. *What a fool I was to listen!*

And as the days passed, my whole body ached from how much I missed Mae Cherney. How could I have guessed she'd become the bread and butter in my life? A little nosh, what made the whole day taste better. I walked the ranch in a hunger for a rye I couldn't have.

And so I became a knife, trying to slice away at my loneliness. So sharp

I got with Jake and the *kinder* – well, truth to tell, Shoshie, I turned mean. About cleaning the eggs or dusting or feeding Malka. Making their beds, tracking mud in – nothing they did was right. Jake shrugged, surprising me by never trying to fight. How he kept that temper of his in check, I don't know. The *kinder* slunk away, shaking their heads, looking sad or frightened. Still I kvetched, hoping that Mamale, Shlima or Gitl would butt in to say, *shirrup, hold your tongue, can't you be a little nicer?* But no, they kept quiet, knowing I was begging to fight with them.

After a month, I'd gone so far past what I thought of myself, I didn't know the woman I saw in the mirror. Nothing about that stranger made sense until one day – when I was crying for no good reason in the barn.

I was just wiping up after milking Malka when I heard the side door open softly. "Jake?" I called, "is that you?"

"No, me," Art said, moving out from the shadows. Then he saw my tears. "What's wrong? Oh, my poor dear." And, before I knew it, he had his arm around my waist and had pulled me to him. In two seconds, we'd begun a kiss. Juicy and long, and no pulling away either. Such touching: a shock, a surprise, a thrill.

Rheabie! Mamale screamed. *What are you doing?*

I didn't know, standing beside him and catching my breath.

Stop it right now, Shlima yelled.

"Such a pleasure," our neighbor, the history scholar, smiled. He ran a hand down my hip and over my backside, what made me weak between the legs. "So what do we have here?" he asked.

Trouble. Gitl shook a sorry head at me.

We had a man who, ever since Mae left, had become famous for both his egg production and bedroom antics. We had a woman so sad and angry, she didn't know who she was. But I began to remember, even with my heart going too fast and my lips warm from his pressing. I stepped away, much to my ghosts' relief. "It's not right, you should get fresh with me."

Art sniffed and pushed his glasses back up on his nose. "What's fresh if you enjoyed it?"

You didn't enjoy, Mamale insisted.

But that wasn't true, and she knew it because of the link between her spirit and my body. Whatever happened in my bones, she felt. *Oy gevalt*, my poor mother moaned. *Never have you been so bad.*

Art didn't think so. "Look, we're two emancipated adults here, freethinkers." To give him credit, he didn't push. But he said my name with everything he wanted to do in it. "Rheabie, my lovely Rheabie. We're not bound by bourgeois convention. You decide."

This was Art's cleverness: to hit me in the chest with politics. Such a touch and tease from that man, right where I believed. In our movement, like the hippies in the sixties, we talked free love. But no one lived it, not really. Most stayed married – without the piece of paper – and slept in one familiar bed. For women, doing anything different was risky. Who wanted to end up alone with all the work of a ranch and *kinder* to feed?

But at that moment, just like Art's other ladies, I was giving the idea some serious consideration. What would it feel like, I wondered, a *shtup* different from Jake's?

Nothing you need to know, Mamale flapped in the air above us.

Please, Gitl begged from the barn rafters, *don't do this thing.*

Have you ever felt, Shoshie, this kind of moment? A time so slow you notice even the bits of dust floating in the air. In front of me, Art: slight but strong, a vein in his neck moving. A bulge where I shouldn't look in his navy pants. Pants which, I saw, had dragged in the mud, making the cuffs dirty. A little bit of manure smeared on his shoe.

Plus: there was his blue corduroy cap, brim dirty from a grease stain. A couple of toast crumbs never got brushed away that morning from his cheek.

Well yes, it's true, I'm not the cleanest of women, but I couldn't get close to that kind of pigsty. In the split second it took to decide, all I could see was Art's shoe. You'd think after all those years on the ranch, I wouldn't let a little manure keep me from something I wanted. Ah, but what I wanted, I realized, was not Art, but Mae.

Mae? Mamale asked. *But why? She's a nudnik.*

Shlima put in her two cents. *Under her spell you are. There's nothing you need from a redhead like her.*

Don't argue! Gitl shouted. *What's the matter with you? At least she's staying out of Art's arms.*

That was the moment I came back to the woman I'd been before Mimi's party. More than anything in the world I wanted Mae here, so I could ask: how do you put up with Art, a man with such sloppy personal habits? What kind of peace have you made with his freethinking ways? And how long will you be in New York, tending to your mother? Most important: Mae Cherney, will you forget what I said and be friends with me again when you come back?

"So *nu*," her husband coughed. "Aren't you going to answer my question?"

"Yes!" I said loudly. "I'm proud to be a comrade of Mae Cherney." Straight in the eye I looked that man. "Don't you try nothing like that on me again."

Art blushed, and suddenly I felt bigger. Tall enough to stare him down while he backed out of the barn. Then I washed that man off my mouth.

Ach, good riddance. And stepped back into the woman I had been. First, dinner: a good meal tonight and I let Mimi cook, for the first time since the party. Patient I stayed, even when she took a good fifteen minutes to decide what kind of chicken to make. Then dessert, and the boys got to help with the chocolate cake – spreading icing. I pretended not to see how much went into their mouths.

"So what's the big occasion?" Jake wanted to know as we sat down that evening.

"An apology for the last month." I announced. "I am sorry for acting like a bear."

"We had a bear in the house?" Jake pretended to growl and winked at the *kinder*.

"A wild animal I was." I shook my head. "But not anymore."

"Good!" Jake clapped his hands, giving me the first real smile I had seen from him since Mae left. Such a big mess he could make with his own temper, but the minute I started in, he got scared and disappeared. But now, things were finally back to normal. Jake patted his stomach. "Look at all this! *Nu*, let's eat."

And so by the family, the matter was closed, done, finished. Jake and I made our final peace in the sheets that night. "Putting Art in his place," I thought, pulling your grandpa to me. I kissed him and such a feeling, like it was the first time. His mouth, his body – a hunger, what rose up between us. We twisted together, same as our early, wild days. But it was better, Shoshie – now, that our hands had years of knowing each other.

"Rheabie, I've missed you," Jake whispered, stroking my face afterwards. "My *shayne maydele*, where have you been?"

I couldn't tell him; I only cried, and your grandpa held me. Inside the comfort of those arms, I decided about Art he didn't need to know. "And neither does Mae," I thought as soon as Jake started snoring. "Tomorrow I'll write and get us back to being friends.

But Mamale had a different view of the whole business. *You've got canning to do*, she reminded me in the morning. *Besides, to Mae there's nothing you need to say.*

What are you talking? I asked her, sorting the bushel of early tomatoes. *From our fight, I have to make right.*

I don't want you should make up to her, Mamale declared from on top of the kitchen table. *I know she saved you from Art yesterday, but think. You and Jake are all right. Finally, you remembered how to be a wife to him. What do you need from Mae? It's not a good idea.*

Are you out of your mind? I asked, looking at the red fruit I was cutting. *Mae's my friend.*

Some friend! Criticizing how you raise Mimi. Mamale shuddered. *And now you want to tell her about us? Such wild ideas she puts in your head.*

I didn't say anything, just bit my lip and held tight to what happened in the barn yesterday. I remembered last night – how it was with Jake and me.

Rheabie, Mamale said again, stamping her foot on the table near the knife I was using. *I'm your mother. I'm doing this to help you. I forbid you should see Mae when she comes home.*

I was careful, Shoshie. I took a minute to check on the boiling water in the big pot, counting to ten to hold on to my temper. One long breath I sucked in before saying, *No.*

Mamale swooped over to darken the air just above the stove. Whenever we argued, she always floated somewhere above me, so I would have to look up. *I did not come out of my grave,* she hissed, *that you should disobey me. The last twelve years I could be sleeping peacefully in Terlitza. But instead I'm here, in a house what stinks of chickens. Oy, what I've done out of love for you.*

The canning tongs slipped out of my hand into the hot water. *Love, shmove,* I snapped at my poor mother. *You came to run my life, and such a misery you've made it.*

Well, someone has to be in charge! she shrieked. *What little sense you ever had, you've given over to that Mae Cherney. Too ignorant and stupid you are to live on your own.*

Then from this minute, living on my own I'll start learning, I yelled back. *Get out of here! I want you gone.* The house got quiet; even the birds stopped singing. After my words, for a long minute, there was no other sound.

Mamale's eyes got big, and then she started crying. *To think I raised a daughter with such meanness. Oy, my poor breaking heart, what have I done?*

Usually, one look at her tears and the argument was over. Down on my knees I'd get, to beg forgiveness, so we could make nice. But not that day, not about Mae Cherney. Stubborn and hard I felt, like a stone.

Don't you talk to our mother like that, Shlima said, putting an arm across Mamale's shaking shoulders. *Where's your respect?*

The rock in me looked at both of them. *Gone. It won't come back until she stops telling me how to live.*

But you're her daughter! That's what a mother is for. Gitl shook her head. *Oy, Rheabie, you've forgotten yourself.*

No! I declared, placing six quarts of tomatoes in the boiling pot. *Finally I remembered.*

Mamale floated above me, shaking a finger in my face. *Better we should go back to Terlitza than live with an ingrate like you.*

All right, so the shame came finally, making my face red. After a long minute, I opened my mouth to make the apology Mamale deserved. But no matter how hard I tried, my tongue wouldn't work. In me, I swear, there wasn't a single word. We stood looking at each other for a long while as the pot on the stove boiled. Finally, I shrugged at the next group of tomatoes waiting for me at the table. *So go already*, I said. *Leave me and mine alone.*

I began cutting as they left, a huff of wind what sliced through the kitchen. Six more quart jars I filled, ready for the big pot. Then I looked at the clock – the first batch was done – time for lifting, wiping, and lining the jars up on the table. So hot it was in that kitchen. I kept working, but with a rock living in my heart. Finally, fifteen quarts – the end of the tomatoes. *Mazel tov*, at last, my stubbornness was done.

Oy, such a mouth, I scolded myself, taking off my apron. *To your own mother look how you talked.* I stepped out on the porch, hoping I should see her. Nothing. No one. Not even the *kinder*. But wait. Was that Mamale? I heard a cry. Yes, Mamale going at it, with Shlima and Gitl helping. Up at the barn, crying, I guessed. I sighed and then made myself go.

To apologize. To ask she should forgive me. To make right, so guilt would not know my name.

Ach, but they weren't in the barn, my spirits. Every corner of it I searched and not a whiff. *Mamale*, I begged, *tell me where you are.*

Standing outside the barn, I listened. She didn't answer. *Please.* A sound, so faint maybe it was my imagination, came from far away. *Is that you?* I thought I heard it again. There, yes – in the gum grove. That's where they were.

But not crying anymore, not all by themselves and lonesome. As soon as I stepped into the trees, I could see that the Guardians, all eight of them, had come. Standing in a group, and worse, watching my mother. Can you imagine? Multiply Wina by seven, all that leaf and wind and magic, and you'll know what I mean. There was the priest, the Irish girl and a man what looked long and slinky. A young soldier in an army uniform, a boy of Wina's tribe. Then a dark-haired woman, what looked to me Italian or Mexican. The last, a scruffy man with a big beard, graying, in old-fashioned clothes.

I trembled, for me, for my sisters, and especially for my poor, terrified Mama. The look on her face, I still see in my dreams. I began to run, slipping on leaves and cracked branches. Thirty feet I had to cover maybe, but in two seconds I was there by her side.

Mamale? She ignored me and kept her eyes on the Irish girl, the one what'd made Davy a piggyback. *Mama, please*, I begged. *Are you all right?*

What do you care? she hissed and turned back to stare at the Guardians. *Well*, she asked them, *what do we need to do?*

Shlima came closer to me and whispered, *The old one, she just told us that we're not supposed to be here. They don't know how yet, but they want to help us go home.*

What? I was so shocked, I almost fell over. Gitl hurried to me. *They can send you back to Terlitza?* I asked her, barely able to believe.

She shook her head. *It's not that easy, dolly. We are a special case, it seems* — she smiled, just as she used to when I was little — *because we came with you.*

Mamale did not try to put such a good face on it. *This mishegoss is all your fault. What you did, evidently, in the graveyard, was break a few ghost laws.*

With our help, Gitl added quickly, stepping closer beside me. She threw Mamale a look. *We're all to blame.*

So bad I felt, making such a problem for my family. But, I thought, glancing over at Gitl and straightening my shoulders, at fifteen, how was I to know anything from spirits? Even now, it was news to me they had laws.

I leaned forward and stared at the eight Guardians, ghosts so big they could help my family get all the way across the ocean to Terlitza. Their faces — watching us carefully — filled with something what felt like love. Love, which took all what was sad and small in me and stretched it bigger. Love, which filled my bones and made them feel like stars. Full of quiet, like when you look up on a winter night and the sky is bright and winking. All that space, a place of wonder. *Who are you?* I asked.

The Irish girl laughed. *Aye, you are a forward lass.* She shook her head at me, still smiling, then answered, *We are a knowledge, part of what you learn when you die.*

But... I began, glancing at Mamale's hard face, the frown on Shlima's.

The Guardian nodded. *Poor dears, they did not stay long enough in the graveyard. Can ya not see that's what's making them so sad?*

I'm not sad, Mamale said, stamping her foot. *I am spit-making angry.* Then she turned the full force of her glare on me. *Who wouldn't be, twelve years suffering where she doesn't belong and now,* she took a hot breath, *now I am no longer wanted? What kind of afterlife is that?*

Wina looked at my mother like she was her dearest friend and started laughing. If Mamale would have permitted it, I think she would have given her a hug. Instead, Wina chuckled and then said in a slow and leafy voice, *I can see that the living will be a part of this. Since they helped you come, they must help send you home.*

Not they, Mamale corrected, putting all the scorn she had in her voice. *Only Rheabie. This whole business, it's her fault.*

But, of course, I said, getting brave enough to look at my mother's face, all the lines and longing. Twelve years beside me as a ghost, and I never really saw her sadness. Such a selfish girl I'd been, thinking only of me. *Forgive me,* I begged. Still, she wouldn't look at me. *So nu,* I tried again, *who else could help you home?*

The priest Guardian spoke up for the first time. *One isn't enough. It will be too much for her.* He looked over at his group. *Don't you think they should each make a choice?*

But what do you mean, too much? Gitl asked. As if I was six again, I could feel how much she wanted to take my hand.

The Irish girl shook her head. *We don't know enough, dearie, except that to do this will be hard on everyone. We are righting a balance, don't you see? Putting you back in your place, shifting things – that's not easy to do.*

So how can you ask so much of Rheabie? Gitl spoke sharply. *I don't want she should be hurt.*

The slinky Guardian, with something like a wild cat about him, smiled at Gitl. Like a riddle, he spoke, but I have always remembered his cloudy words. *Each great task has a cost,* he told her. *Let your sister hold on to it. Only then will she discover if it also contains a gift.*

What cost, what gift? Mamale sneered, and I knew that I was not forgiven. No matter how many apologies she heard, letting go of an argument was not something our mother did. Unless she could have the last word, something sharp and sour. Unless she'd proved enough that we were wrong, and she was right.

So I straightened again, ready for a piece of nastiness. Mamale made herself even taller and lifted her chin. *Let's get down to business here. Isn't the first step in this "great task" choosing the living helpers?*

The priest Guardian nodded.

Well, I have my choice already. She spoke to Wina, not looking at her family. *Rheabie can do what she wants for Shlima. I don't need her. Mae Cherney – the one driving us away – she'll be the one who helps.*

I gasped. A choice made out of spite, spoken in meanness. Mamale had taken seriously this cost business and meant, of course, to cause Mae harm. But as she spoke, I saw the cat Guardian's eyes go wide, and he smiled, as if he'd been given an unexpected present. The man had the *chutzpah* to look over at me and wink.

And then I understood Mamale's big mistake. Do you, Shoshie? With her own mean mouth, she'd gone and made Mae part of the story. For anything to happen, I had to tell her about my ghosts.

I grinned, feeling light and giddy. So happy I was, I thought about twirling around. Who cared, I might slip and land on my fanny on the slippery leaves of the gum grove? Mamale made it so I didn't have to worry about this business by myself; someone else would be in it with me. For the first time since the *pogrom*, another living person would know.

And the point is, Shoshie: you don't need to face Wina alone either, my dearest granddaughter. Mixing with ghosts – believe me, dolly, it can be strange. Things from you they want; a price they ask for their company. I'm telling you, nothing is at is seems. So if you want, I'll come with you when next you see them. I'm not too steady on my feet and the walker gets in the way, but to be in this with you would give me a thrill. But *nu*, we have to get started soon because, truth to tell, I can feel my clock ticking. We're talking seventy-eight years already. I'm honestly not sure how much time I got left.

Chapter 12
MOVING FORWARD

SHOSHANA

I have time, time to trace patterns in the gray hospital linoleum while I wait for Grandma at physical therapy. Time to make up a list of questions to ask her doctor while she's being made to stretch and bend.

I leave a message for Grandma with the physical therapy receptionist, then hurry across the parking lot to Dr. Kendall's office. "Can he spare a few minutes?" I beg his nurse.

"You're lucky," the gray-bearded man says as he steps around her partition. "We just had a cancellation. Well, so how's my favorite old lady doing today?" He winks at me. "Now don't go and tell your grandma the 'old lady' part. She'll have my hide."

Dr. Kendall's mouth stretches too far when he smiles; his teeth are enormous. He's too hearty, too laughing, as if nothing is wrong. I make myself ask the question: "How soon is my grandmother going to die?"

His eyebrows shoot up, disappearing into gray clumps of hair that are carefully combed to the side in an attempt to cover his bald spot. "Who says she's dying?" he asks.

"She does," I insist but then realize that isn't strictly accurate. "Or at least she says she's worried about it."

Dr. Kendall has the nerve to laugh. "Your grandmother was worried that she wouldn't live until your next visit either, and look what happened."

"Yeah," I frown, picturing her wiping her red face with one of the scratchy white towels at physical therapy. I feel words begin to ball in my throat but say them anyway. "She had to break her hip to get me to come."

Dr. Kendall shakes his head. "Don't fret. Your grandmother doesn't know how to do anything else but worry. She told me once that it's in her DNA." He folds his hands neatly on the green blotter that covers his desk. "Listen, except for the hip and her high blood pressure, everything is in good working order. You're making sure she's still taking those pills for the pressure, aren't you? Good. Her heart, her liver – the latest tests are negative. She's a strong old bird."

Of course she's strong, but the man doesn't understand what I'm asking. I sit up straight in his maroon leather chair to try again.

Dr. Kendall doesn't let me interrupt. "Okay, yes, statistically speaking, a broken hip is often the beginning of other problems." His eyes cloud for a moment. "Your grandfather fit that pattern to a 't.' But I haven't seen anything in Mrs. Slominski to cause concern, and I'm not the kind of guy to keep bad news to myself. If you want to worry, focus on what could happen because she flushed her blood pressure meds down the toilet. For years, we're talking. Then she'd come waltzing in here and tell me she was fine. As a result, we're going to have to keep an eye out for heart attacks, kidney failures or stroke. You know what to look for? Here," he reaches to give me a pamphlet. "This will tell you the symptoms. Bring her in – fast – if you see anything at all."

I frown, and he clears his throat. "Young lady, I'm not one of those doctors who believes in 'protecting' patients. Bad news is made to be shared."

Then share this, doc – and I hate how my voice shakes as I say it: "But she told me the other day that she's having trouble breathing. Sometimes at night it feels like a rock is on her chest. She isn't sure how much time she has left."

"Well," Dr. Kendall leans back in his chair and rubs his eyes, finally taking me seriously. "She actually said that?"

I nod. "I don't like it," he rumbles. The stethoscope on his chest rises and falls as he sighs. "I love your grandmother, and I've been in this business long enough to know that she may feel something in her body that we haven't detected yet."

I grimace. That's not much comfort. Then he lifts his eyes to look at me, a pale blue glance. "I told you – there's no protection here. I can't do my best unless I tell you what may be the truth." He shifts in his chair, then begins a small smile. "But if you want, I'll order more tests, focusing on her lungs and the areas I told you about. I know your grandmother will fight them. Are you willing to work on that stubborn woman and get her to come in?"

I nod, feeling my breath become lighter, glad there's something to do.

"Good." Dr. Kendall stands and shakes my hand. "I can tell you're as tough as she is, missy; it's grand to have an ally." His eyes shift and darken. "I'm glad it matters so much to you."

Of course it matters. The hot air of the afternoon billows around me as soon as I open his office door. How could that doctor, so blue-eyed and laughing, think it didn't? I take quick, short steps across the steaming parking lot. Everything matters now that Wina has come to visit and Grandma needs me.

No. I stop, staring into the windshield of some hippie VW bug, cracked and dirty. Feathers hang from the rear view mirror, a mess of rocks and shells on the dash.

No, Grandma doesn't need me. I need her. Like I needed the twin lakes I used to walk to near Lydon, my boots kicking up leaves on the wet trails as I stared into gray water. I feel that coolness now, a wave that washes down the heat of the hospital asphalt. I close my fist as if I have just bent down to pick up a treasure, some worn, brown rock.

I need Grandma: to tell stories, to demand answers to nosy questions. I need her to believe in the magic that lives in her house. Who else would be matter-of-fact when Wina came, wanting to hear exactly what happened? Who else is certain that I had something important to say to a Guardian?

I lean back to look up at the hard-edged sky, as bald as the back of Dr. Kendall's head, without a cloud in it. Admit the truth, Shoshana. Since you left Lydon and the Kupboard, you have become as peculiar and strange as your grandmother. Mark and Josie wouldn't know what to do with you, because even though you don't show it, you believe in her ghosts. They'd shake their heads and run the other way. So would your mom and your poor rational father is turning entire somersaults in his grave. You don't want to lose the one person who understands this odd change in yourself. You want Grandma to live another thousand years for you – not for her.

So what's wrong with that? I think as the driver of the bug honks at me, a woman with long hair like sheaves of wheat. "Hey!" she yells. I have been blocking her way.

I scoot over to the sidewalk and wonder if, for the first time, I am willing to move forward into all that's hidden and mysterious in my grandmother. Or maybe I am shifting into reverse as I rediscover the wonder of the woman who told me such lovely, outlandish stories when I was a child.

"You always were a sucker for her fairy tales," Mom reminds me on the phone later. "Am I going to have to spend my entire life telling you not to believe her? Haven't you grown up enough yet not to be told?"

"So I'm grown." I pick a sprig of dill from the herbs I have planted in a row of little pots in the kitchen window and try to keep my tone gentle. "But what's the crime in Grandma teaching me a little family history? Better I should stay ignorant and not know?"

"I didn't say that," my mother snaps. "But you can't trust her version. Why don't you ask me?"

Because you are always so angry about the past, I think. Because you can't see anything good about this place that I am coming to love.

Mom gathers her breath into a windy sigh. "If I'd thought you'd enjoy this visit so much, I wouldn't have asked you to go."

For the first time, I feel pity for the woman held prisoner by her hip. I picture her sitting on the flowered couch in her living room in Ithaca. The air conditioner is probably on the fritz again, since she's complaining about being sticky and warm. But besides that, there's a note in her voice. For the first time, I give the familiar sound a name. "You're just jealous of Grandma, Mom."

My outraged mother shrieks, "I'm no such thing." And I giggle. I can't help it. It makes me laugh – how hard she has to pretend.

"What's gotten into you anyway, Shoshana?" she asks. "I expected you'd be back home by now. Grandma's well enough to live on her own. If I can handle it, so can she."

I bend into the crisper drawer for lettuce and cucumbers, our dinner salad. "You've told me a hundred times how Grandma can't take care of herself. You think she's too mixed up all the time."

But Mom's words have opened a possibility that I've pushed away for weeks. For a moment I imagine being back home in Lydon, fixing my own small supper. Mark would still be at the bar, and I'd be rehearsing my "it's been great, but it's over" speech. I'd stop my cooking to listen for the wind and feel the comfort of Rasputin purring between my legs.

I shake away the vision. "I saw Dr. Kendall today and he said Grandma's progress is taking a little longer than usual. He wants to do more tests to make sure nothing's wrong." I straighten and place the vegetables in a neat line on the kitchen counter. "It's nothing to worry, he said. But remember – unlike you, my dear mother, Grandma's old."

"Who are you calling old?" she asks, thumping her walker carefully into the kitchen. "What tests?" Grandma slaps it down on the floor and stops, glaring. "I don't need any tests. I did better than those young boys, the long hairs from the motorcycle accident, at therapy today."

"Now you've gotten me in trouble," I tell my mother. Winking at Grandma, I pantomime the wings of birds with my arms, holding the receiver under my chin. Grandma stares for a moment, raises one curious eyebrow, and then grins.

"Well, I'm glad you're in trouble," Mom huffs. "You're not listening to me anyway. But you should think about it. After those tests, if the results are good, it's time you went home."

To what? I wonder as I sit on the porch watching the sky grow dark after dinner. Dating some other silent logger? Serving meat loaf and luncheon specials at the cafe? The Kitchen Kupboard seems so far away. I'm in no hurry to get back to drinking too much coffee with Lillian while she bitches about her ex in my small house in those dark woods. Or maybe I'd be moving, packing stuff in boxes on my way to some other logging town. This place is dry and ugly and brown, but Wina and the rest of the Guardians speak for it. And so does Grandma, spinning her long stories about the past to tell me how to live. I face the sliver of moon rising above the lights of Petaluma, the one causing the O'Dell's dog to howl, and realize that I'm the one who has begun flying. The wings are mine. Please, I ask the night sky, don't let Grandma die now that I know I've finally come home.

Chapter 13
NOT OUR KIND

RHEABIE

So what's home? The place you live with all your *chotchkes*? Or family, the folks what knew you since before you were born? Maybe home is a sick old woman you got to take care of. A duty, because you're a good girl who does right by her family. But tell me the truth, Shoshie. Are you tired of nursing me? Your mother called while you were in the garden. It's time you went home, she says. So selfish I am, keeping you. A regular mess I'm making of your life.

No? You're sure? Ach, I'm so glad to hear it! If I could, I'd get up and dance. But I don't need to break my other hip and keep you here forever. Though I'd love that, dolly, if you should ever be so inclined.

But for now, yes, it's a good idea, we celebrate instead with a story. I've been dying to tell you what in my life came next. You remember, the summer of 1929, with Mae east with her mother and my ghosts driving me crazy. That meeting with the Guardians in the gum grove, and how they said that Mamale, Shlima and Gilt needed to be sent home. But then, in the middle of arguing about it – surprise of all surprises! – your Uncle Mas walked into the midst of us. Only eight years old he was then, but it was clear that boy could see – Wina, Shlima and Gitl – everyone. And worse, he acted like he understood our every word.

Picture it: the minute after Mamale took Mae as her living helper. The smile on the cat Guardian's face broke apart when Mas popped out from behind a tree. To Gitl he went and said something in what was maybe English. Or some other foreign language. But anyway, Gitl understood him. So startled she looked at his words. *It's my turn to pick a helper this boy says,* she translated, *and he says it should be him.*

Wina laughed, but everyone else looked ready to fall over. Mamale was so pale, I thought if she wasn't dead already, she might faint. But Wina ignored our shock and floated over to Mas. Up she lifted him in her ghostly arms and asked, *What do we have here? What kind of little acorn are you?*

He nestled against her for a moment. "A boy acorn," he giggled, sounding just like Davy. A little older, maybe, a little thinner, with shiny black hair and what to me then were such strange eyes. Wina smiled at him and asked in a voice as gentle as any Jewish *bubbe*, *Well, boy acorn, why are you here?*

"Some ghosts were crying," Mas said in his foreign language as Wina put him down. Gitl again translated. "I came to help."

It's not our fault, Shlima defended, throwing a sour look at the rest of us.

If she wasn't a spirit already, Gitl's look would've finished the life of my worrywart sister. *Stop with the "fault" business!* she hissed at Shlima. *Hasn't there been enough of that today?* Then she sat in the leaves next to Mas and lifted a branch from where it was stuck on his shoulder. *Don't mind her,* she reassured him. *Shlima didn't mean what she said.* And surprise, surprise. On Gitl's face, such a feeling, full of longing. In her eyes, an ache for what she could never have.

Understand, Shoshie, Gitl had died too young, unmarried, never having the pleasure of raising her own family. Her intended, Mottel Golub, and the four *kinder* they'd dreamed of – two boys, two girls – had been snatched away in 1915 by the war. But now that dream was back in her cheeks, making her mouth soft. Such a look, it never crossed her face for Mimi, Nate or even Davy. I felt a pang. What did this child have that my own did not?

Such a brave boychik you are, she said to Mas, her whole body tender. *You heard us and came?*

Mas grinned. Then he spoke, so serious, just like he does today. Gitl made sure we understood his words. "Will you pick me?" he asked. "I'll help you get home."

My sister looked at Wina, her eyes full of worry. The she turned back to the boy. *Bubee, it could be dangerous.* She shook her head. *You're so little, and there's not much about this mishegoss that I understand.*

I didn't understand either, any of it, and especially all this talking. How come Gitl could make sense out of Mas's words when he was speaking English or Japanese and from it she didn't know a word? And Mas, he might've been smart, but what Oriental boy knew from Yiddish? With my own ears, that's what I heard Gitl speak. But any fool could see that they understood each other, comrades already. After a minute, Gitl even made bold enough to give Mas's cheek a little kiss.

Shlima squawked as if the world was ending while Mamale started swooning. Finally, she sagged, just like one of Mimi's sock-dolls, giving into some kind of a faint. In the fuss that followed, I thought: Wait a minute. She's dead; Mamale wouldn't be so mean to pretend to faint, would she? Just to get Gitl back by her side?

Because that's what happened, with a run and yelp from my sister. The Guardians followed, all eight of them, making such a tight circle around Mamale I couldn't see. But better she got – and fast. In a minute she was strong and standing. Some kind of thank you she nodded, and then the Guardians said goodbye.

They would come back when they knew more, they said, and we should think on things, but not to worry. What had happened today had given them some ideas. *And by the way,* the cat Guardian smiled over at me, *the living hear the words of ghosts in their own language and vice versa.* The Irish girl winked as she rubbed the top of Mas's head. *Lassie, you're the only one who can't understand what the boy is saying. If you want to talk to the lad here, it's the English you've got to learn.*

And no, they weren't going to make him forget the whole business, like they had with Davy. Wina shook her head, *This one, he's a different boy. What he knows, we might need.*

And then *so long, see you,* and in a blink of an eye, the gum grove was empty. All what was left: a pale Mamale, a worried Shlima, my tender Gitl, and then that skinny Mas and me.

Shlima started in, *Oy vey, such a pickle we got here.* Her nose she wrinkled, like Mas was a rotten cabbage. *What are we going to do?*

Gitl clapped her hands together. *What else? Take this boy home and give him a cookie. You'll make a basket, Rheabie, for his busy mother on moving day.*

For Mas, I realized finally, must belong to our new neighbors, about whom the whole street had been talking. The Shapiro's chicken ranch had failed a few months back after a pox epidemic; the bank finally sold it. But who bought it and when they'd join the rest of us on Chapman Lane, no one knew. It must have been today, and I hadn't noticed, so busy with my canning and fighting with Mamale. Since Jake had taken the kinder to the town, he wasn't there to see the Tanaka's truck as it rumbled up the lane.

And after the cookies, Gitl glared hard, so no one would say anything different, *we're going next door to meet our new neighbors. We will welcome them like we do everyone else to Chapman Lane. But you haven't told us your name,* she reminded Mas gently.

"I'm Masaya Tanaka," he answered, his small voice filling up the clearing. "At school, they call me Mas."

Messiah? Shlima screeched, *as in the Coming One, the deliverer of the Jews and all that backward nonsense?* Then she placed a hand over her mouth. *No disrespect intended,* she added, quick and sharp.

Gitl laughed, the loudest I'd heard from her since coming to this country. When she could catch her breath again, she wheezed, *It's going to be some joke if the deliverer of our people should be an Oriental. I can't wait, the day the Zionists should find out. But you,* and she actually leaned forward to worry Mas's hair, *I think you are only a little boy. Lost maybe. Tired and your family must be worrying. So nu, what are we waiting for? This child needs he should go home.*

Never before had I seen the bossy side of my sister. I'm ashamed to say I didn't like it, this new brightness what shone from her eyes. A light for this skinny boy who talked a mile a minute all the way up his long driveway. Mamale and Shlima sulked behind while Gitl translated his every word.

And it was bad enough, the jealousy, but then there was also this Japanese business. Asian foreigners, we're talking: strange ways and odd food. I'd only passed Japantown in San Francisco once, but *oy*, the smells there! Dried fish, odd vegetables, garbage. People pushing and shouting. Never had I seen anything so *farfufket*. Now, a whole family like this we would have living on our road? *Oy vey*, was I afraid!

Understand, Shoshie, we'd studied; we knew the history, the economics, the wrongs of such unprogressive thinking. From childhood on, the stirring words of Marx and that good Jewish boy, Trotsky, rang in my ears. I had been raised to see the working class, the whole world over, as my brothers and sisters. To equality for labor I'd given my life for years.

But equality in Terlitza was a matter of Jews and Gentiles. Even in New York, organizing for the needle trades, I worked a few times with gabby Italians and here and there a freckled Irish girl. No Blacks. No Orientals. No Mexicans. Except for a different kind of hair or nose, everybody looked the same.

But now here was Mas, with his golden skin, thin eyes, and hair as shiny as a black bird. So different he smelled – a mixture of ginger and soy sauce with a little incense thrown in. Of course, I couldn't know the delicious bits what made up his smell yet, but *farshtinkener* is what I called it. He's not our kind, I kept telling myself. A little boy, an eight-year-old, and still, I let myself be afraid.

Be ashamed! Gitl scolded when Mas ran to the house ahead of us. She took a good look at her mother and two sisters, hanging back from following after – we were not even being polite. *This is just another ranch family, getting robbed by the bank for the mortgage. Working chickens, the stink and feathers, just like us. Where are your egalitarian principles? Don't tell me*, my sister looked ready to raise her voice, *you're going to abandon them now.*

And who are you? Mamale asked, putting her hands on her hips, *suddenly so high and mighty? What did that strange boy do, put a spell on you with his eyes?* She ignored Gitl's angry hiss and pointed *Look!* at the Tanaka yard, a mess of boxes, crates and suitcases. No adults anywhere – just the legs and shouts of a thousand *kinder* who were playing chase near the barn. *Such a pack of hooligans!* Mamale sniffed. *Tell me, angry daughter, did you think your principles would look like this?*

But surprise! Some of Gitl's principles looked more than a little familiar. Mimi, Davy and even steady Nate were a part of the hooligan crowd.

Davy broke away from the pack and ran toward me. "Mama," he shouted, holding the hand of a panting girl. "Listen to Emi. She can neigh like a horse."

They threw back their heads to whinny and began laughing. *Vey!* Shlima got dramatic and struck her chest. *We can't have this. It's worse than I thought.*

I hate to admit it, Shoshie, but for the first time in twelve years, I agreed with my middle sister. The *kinder* mixing with these foreigners – who had germs maybe or bad habits – it wasn't a good idea.

And look at that! Mamale pointed to Nate chasing a bigger boy around the rain barrel. She gasped *Gevalt!* as Nate lunged, almost falling, trying to tag the boy's back.

"Ken is really fast," Davy said.

"Where's your sister?" I asked, trying to hold my boy tight beside me.

"She's hiding from Nate by the truck," he grinned, and I saw a familiar brown head bent behind the hood next to a black one. "Over there, next to Sumiko," he explained.

Rheabie, this has gone too far, Shlima wailed. *You'd better do something.*

Gitl shook her head, the soft look back in her face. *What's to do? It's too late, already done.*

And she was right, even if I was too ignorant back then to want it. The very air, it held the shape of our tie to the Tanakas what was to come. And how did I know this? Because the wind stopped, just at that very moment. Everything was frozen: Mimi looking around a tire; Ken beginning a small step. Only Mas moved, turning around to look up at me. He spoke, but I couldn't understand him. Gitl translated. "Don't be afraid," he said. "Everything will be all right."

And then – the world began to move again, dizzy and rushing. Mimi danced, Ken walked and Jake, another surprise, shouted from the kitchen door. "Rheabie, good! You found us." Before I knew it, Mas was introducing me to his father. "Hello," Matsu said in English, and then he bowed.

Bowed! As if I was a cross at the church, something to worship. Such an embarrassment! I blushed, redder than my own borsht, and waved my hand in his face.

All right, yes, this is what we call today a clash of cultures. He teases me about it now, but back then, how could I know from what in Japan was polite? Mamale poked a ghostly hand in my back, *Straighten up and look proud*, and I felt my face get cold like a statue. Matsu swears I was the quietest woman he'd ever seen.

But I wasn't worrying about quiet; I was too afraid from realizing that Mamale and Shlima stood right beside me. Think about it! Maybe this whole race, the Japanese, they had eyes for ghosts.

Calm down, Gitl shook her head at me. *No one but Mas sees us. The only one with your talents*, she said as Matsu turned and stepped through her body, *is that sweet boy.*

Who was pulling me inside at that moment to meet his mother? I tripped over myself, so afraid I was to go through that door. And then, I couldn't remember how to put my hand out and say "How do you do?" in English – like Ethel Rabbinowitz, my hardworking night school teacher of English in New York, had taught me. Instead, I took one look at the woman and stared.

Back then, Kiyo Tanaka was some kind of beauty. Such hair. Such eyes. Maybe you can't tell from how wrinkled she looks now, but *oy*, that woman had a smile! One small grin and the world turned lovely. Even the little kitchen, full of boxes, got warm.

But nothing could warm me that day, so nervous and tongue-tied. Normally, I'm a woman full of questions, yes? But about the baby she carried, I couldn't even ask. And you know who it was, that kicking girl what was pushing out her mother's big belly? Yes, your Aunt Mari! Davy's sweet wife I met before she was even born.

I'm ashamed to say, though, at first glance I thought: *Not another one? Don't they have kinder enough, already?* I stayed silent so long that Jake broke my rudeness with his business English. "So happy to have met you. It's time for us to leave."

"Mama, why aren't you pleased?" Mimi asked me on the way home. "When we first saw you near the barn, you looked almost afraid."

"Not afraid," I corrected, "only tired."

Mimi nodded, pretending to believe my lie. "But isn't it funny? They're all the right ages except Mas." Then she put her finger on it. Your mother the hawk, her with the vision. She looked right at me and said, "He's the only problem. Who's going to be his friend?"

"Maybe you all will," Jake insisted, catching up with us. Finally, he'd torn himself away from a last bit of talk about chickens with Matsu. A yellow apple he threw, a parting gift from the Tanakas, up into the air. In his smooth catch, I couldn't tell how much Jake liked our new neighbors. He'd never let them see it, of course, but was he also worrying over how they were not our kind? "So how important is it," he asked Nate, "a whole grade's difference between you? I don't want you should ignore Mas like I ignored your father. Hard it might be on him, if you should leave him out."

Mimi shook her head. "No, Mama found Mas first like I found Sumi." My heart got cold as she shook her head. "Mama, Mas belongs to you."

And she was right, Shoshie, never mind how much I fought against the whole business. What do I need with a friend like that, a young boy and so foreign? Could he talk world events or help put up apples? No. And when he did try to help, like the next day at lunch, leaving a game of tag to set our table, it just didn't seem right. "Why didn't Mas stay and play with you?" I *kvetched* later to your mother.

She shrugged. "He doesn't like games. Mas is a different kind of boy."

Do you see, Shoshie, what was bothering me? Your mother did. The next morning, as I snapped and snarled my way through breakfast, she said, "Mama, you look different. Like you don't belong here anymore."

Maybe she only meant the skirt I'd put on to make myself feel better. A town dress – foolish to wear around the ranch – something Mae might like. But Mimi's right, I thought, as she skipped into the yard to meet Sumi at their new playhouse. I'm not at home anymore in this life.

Why? Because it was plain that everyone in my family was making nice with our new neighbors. The only one hanging back – it was me. Especially with that ghost-seer Mas. And that morning I finally admitted why: I hated that it was the boy and not Mae what had eyes for spirits.

Mae, a friend in politics, a companion in chores, the only person in the world I wanted. That day my missing her, it was so strong, I leaned back against the kitchen table and closed my eyes. And I swear I saw her, Shoshie, standing alone on a corner in New York, sad from burying her mother. We hadn't even heard the news from Art yet, but by her smudged face and the ugly black dress, I knew. Short-sleeved and plain, it made her neck and arms so white and freckled. The way she looked down at a key in her hand – her mother's apartment, maybe – I knew she was just about to walk up four flights of stairs to tidy the remains of a life. Three thousand miles I reached across the country to give her arm a squeeze, to send a little strength maybe. I heard myself say softly, just like Mas when I went to his house, "Don't be afraid. It will be all right."

Dearest Mae, I wrote, my handwriting shaky, because I didn't know if she should want to hear from me, *I am so sorry to learn the sad news about your mother. For you, I write from the bottom of my aching heart. Please, forgive me, our fight before you left, my stubbornness and temper. If it is not too late, I promise to be the kind of friend you want, telling everything I've held back, when you come home.*

And wouldn't you know it? Mas slipped into the kitchen just as I signed the letter: *Love, your comrade Rheabie.* He looked at the Yiddish curiously and said something in that proper English of his.

"What?" I slammed my hand down on the table. "I don't understand you." And then all my sadness and spite, it came to my tongue. "What are you sneaking in for, coming where you're not wanted? What's the matter with you? I'm a grown-up. Go on – out of here. *Gey avek.*"

Gitl swooped in through the east wall. *Sha! Shirrup!* she shouted, spinning like a whirlwind in the center of the room. When she grew still enough to stand, she threw her arms to comfort. *You and your loud words. He can't understand, remember?* She drew the scared boy to her chest. *From all that yelling Yiddish of yours, he doesn't know.*

Then you tell him to leave me alone, I croaked, ashamed but still angry. *Make sure he understands that he's too young. We're not friends.*

He can't leave you alone, Gitl stared at me over the top of Mas's head. *I'm making him my choice, right now, this very minute. The two of you have to get along to send me home. Don't you see?*

I didn't see anything except that my sister had just tied me up with someone too strange and different to even think about getting next to. A child, a foreigner, who somehow thought that me and my business was something he could understand.

You keep worrying, my sister said, *about the boy and how he's so different. Look in the mirror, Rheabela, and be honest. You don't want him because you and Mas are so much the same.*

We're not, I insisted, while tears hurried to my eyes.

Take a look, Gitl said sternly. *He reminds me so much of you when you were little. Open your eyes. What do you see?*

I saw a lonely child who didn't want to play games with the others. Knowing and sad, he was, with eyes what saw too much. I saw a boy, skinny shoulders and thin hips, making a life in a strange country. Up to his ears in family, he seemed always alone. Even the worried way he watched my face was familiar. "Mrs. Slominski," he said softly, "please don't send me away."

"Why not?" I asked as Gitl translated.

"You're the only one I know who can also see ghosts." Then the boy stepped forward and put a hand on my arm, in exactly the same place I had imagined touching Mae that morning. "Please," he said, dark eyes begging. "No one else sees what I see."

Only eight years old he was then, Shoshie, but going on eighty. A whole lifetime, full of too many tears, he carried in those young bones. I could feel it, an ache what rose up from him and spread into the air of my kitchen. So familiar, like smoke from a *pogromed* building, or a goodbye forced too soon. You know what I mean, that kind of quiet with too much in it? Like how your house felt, after your father's funeral or the way Davy's eyes looked when he came home from the war.

Mas's ache sank into my body like the heat of the sun coming in through the dusty kitchen windows. That light, bit by bit, it worked its way up my arms and across my chest. And burned away everything I'd been holding tight from the summer. My meanness. The fight with Mae, that friendship lost maybe. This fear of foreigners. What kind of life I'd have when my spirits went home. I saw all my worries, what had already happened or what might come, right between my fingers. I opened my hand and looked at it. What was actually there? Only air. No fight to relive, call back, make different.

No promise about what might be. In my hand – just the clock ticking away that very minute. In front of me, the sad face of a little boy.

Who I saw, finally, and Gitl had been right – there was nothing foreign anymore between us. Mas's loneliness – I knew from it like the thumping of my own heart.

"Well, you're not alone now," I said in a stumbling voice, talking to him for the first time like a comrade.

He smiled, and Gitl spoke his words, "No, and I won't be ever again." Then he leaned his head to the side, just like a pullet. "You want to know a secret?" Mas asked, smiling. "The Guardians told me – this is home."

Home, Shoshie: not a place or people you want, but truth – that someone should hear it. A sharing, even if it comes from a person what you don't expect. For Mas and me, our home was built from this ghost business. I don't know why we could see them, but it doesn't matter. What counts is what we did with such a sight. And you, heart of my heart, now you've got a home too. You talked to Wina. You're one of us. So *nu,* what are you going to do about it? What does it mean?

Chapter 14
CLIMBING THE HILL

SHOSHANA

It means that when I hang up the phone after Mom's Sunday call, no longer angry with her for interfering in my life, I stand in the late afternoon sun that floods the western windows of the kitchen. Dust floats in the wide washes of light, bouncing up and down on waves created by the revolving fan. I try to follow just one mote on its journey, swept up above the pots cluttering the dish drainer, then swallowed into one of the cracks in the tile counter top. I think, "What dust is falling on me?" and smile at the answer I make, spoken in Grandma's voice: "Ach, the dust of peace."

Peace in the dill, oregano and basil plants close to outgrowing their green plastic containers on the window sill; peace in the spice rack, bottles tilted slightly to the left above the stove. As I move to straighten them, I feel the heat of the afternoon infusing me with the scent of dried eucalyptus and thirsty tomatoes. Peace: as if I am the sun tea, brewing on the porch railing, growing minty and dark. Peace: as if I am a crow, the black shadow swooping low to circle the apple tree, croaking happily over the fruit.

"Maybe I should get up there with some cheesecloth to protect the rest of the apples," I suggest to Grandma. "If he's going to taste them all, we won't have any for ourselves."

She smiles, the lines in her cheeks crinkling like bleached paper. "You like my apple sauce that much? *Oy* dolly, let the old bastard alone. The tree doesn't mind. And we're rich enough to share."

We're rich in silence, rich in sweat, rich in our solitude. Lydon feels so faraway, and it's a relief. What matters is what's right here: Grandma, the sunlight, and that greedy crow winging his way over the garden. He reminds me of the dinner I have yet to cook.

"I'm going to pick zucchini," I announce, bending to get the vegetable basket.

But the phone slices through the sleepy air of the kitchen. "Who's bothering us now?" Grandma demands, but her face lights when I tell her it's Mas, calling from early the next morning in Japan. "How are you, Shoshana?" he asks.

I don't know why the hairs on my arms lift at his voice, and I feel cold as I hand the phone to Rheabie. I find myself trying not to listen to what she says to him and frowning instead at the load of breakfast dishes waiting to be put away. What kind of mess have I allowed in this kitchen? Plates from lunch litter the sink, crusted with potato salad, because I was in a hurry and didn't take the time to rinse them. Lemon halves, left over from making lemonade, are cupped into each other in a leaning stack. They should be cleared away and hidden from view in the compost bucket. All the counters should be wiped down, clean and spare. If he could see it, what would Uncle Mas think?

"He wants you," Grandma interrupts my critical inventory. I take the receiver, feeling the remains of her sweat on the cold plastic. Even though Uncle Mas has been in my life since the beginning and is someone sweet and wise in Grandma's stories, I do not really know him.

"Thank you for taking such good care of Rheabie," Uncle Mas says over the bad connection. "I can tell from her voice that she's enjoying you and doing very well." Then he pauses, and I can hear the silence all the way to Asia. "Have you hiked up the hill recently?" His voice is suddenly loud and strong, as if he is calling from just next door. I peer out the glass to the house where no one in his family has lived for more than thirty years. "There's something at the big rock," he says, "that I believe you need to see."

"I see too much," I want to say, meaning Grandma flushed and waiting to talk to him again, thumping the kitchen floor impatiently with her walker. Meaning Wina, who I expect to appear as a dark shadow in the doorway at any minute, looking in with a smiling face like she always does in Grandma's tales. Or maybe I mean the younger Mas, thin-shouldered and scared, in ragged shorts and a striped tee shirt, burdened by magic in Grandma's stories.

Not the elegant, confident man in European suits or dark slacks and expensive sweaters whose strange eyes notice each tense moment at family parties. Not the one who watches me from across the room, but who never condescends to say a single word, content, instead, to wave an eloquent hand. "You can trust me," that stranger urges from Tokyo, as if he's read my thoughts. "Don't wait to walk," he laughs for no reason, as I have heard him laugh a thousand times before. "Shoshana, believe me. I promise it will do you good."

"Good for what?" I've wondered in the few days since, refusing to follow his advice, to leave Grandma all alone for an afternoon and hike up there. Why should I? How can that weird Mas Tanaka, aloof and traveling through his ancestral homeland on business, know what's best for me just because Grandma told him about Wina and now he knows that, like him, I too can see ghosts?

Still, I examine my hands as I carry the mail up the long driveway at the end of a dusty morning, wondering if my fingers have gone soft like his since I've stopped waitressing. Later, pushing an empty cart through the grocery store parking lot, I stop and stare at my reflection in the big, plate-glass windows, watching the shadows in my eyes. Is there anything in them that resembles Uncle Mas?

Ever since his phone call, I keep searching for what we have in common. I can't help wondering: how did Grandma, Uncle Mas and I get this ability to see?

I need to know, as I stroll across the parking lot of the grocery store, what exactly it is that links us. Feeling the sweat trickle down the bridge of my nose as I place a week's worth of celery and milk, chicken and ice cream in the trunk of the car, I burn at the thought of being part of this odd group. When I slam the trunk closed, I finally allow myself to ask the question I've been ignoring. Before he called I felt so good. What happened? How come all of a sudden, I feel caught – trapped?

I feel set off and marked with chalk, like my tires the very moment I decide, with an impulsive swerve to the right, to park under one of the big oaks in front of the library. The meter maid smiles at me as she brushes the rubber with her long stick. "An hour," she calls from her cart. Her grin feels just like Grandma's fingers and Uncle Mas's words: made of steel, a chain around my wrists.

And why doesn't she mark the VW bug that's tried to hug the shade, creating its own parking spot between two official ones in front of me? As I pass it on my way into the air-conditioned building, I recognize the car from the hospital parking lot – all those shells and feathers cluttering the dash. I shake my head. Maybe there's some sort of parking ghost watching over that brown-haired hippie girl.

But no one watches over me. This afternoon I am deserted as I try to find books about spirits and hauntings. I curse Wina and the rest of the Guardians in Grandma's voice: "What, you're too secret for the library? Why don't you come through the walls and help me here?"

Not even the librarian can assist me. The only thing I have to show for my seventy-minute venture is a yellow slip from the meter maid, a ten-dollar charge, because there were plenty of books about ghosts, but they didn't say anything about the people the spirits visited or about how they were chosen and why.

"So *nu*, what took you so long?" Grandma asks when I arrive home, my cutoffs clinging to my thighs, my mood hot and grumpy. "Where were you?"

"At the library."

She raises one of her bushy eyebrows and folds her hands, waiting for more.

"Looking for books." I slam a bag of groceries, the one with the milk in it, on the kitchen counter. "On ghosts."

"What does the Petaluma library know from ghosts?" Grandma Rheabie shifts sideways in her chair so that the fan can reach the front of her blouse. "Shoshie, what are you doing? You think it will help, chewing over the 'why' of this whole business? A waste of time, dolly." After she slurps the glass of iced tea I place in front of her, she pats my arm. "In political arguments your grandpa used to yell, 'Why never answers the question.' So stop already, eat something and tell me what the question really means."

"I don't know what it means," I want to scream as I unpack the groceries, feeling like a swallowed sneeze, all tickle and frustrated explosion. I shove the soupy ice cream into the freezer and sniff at the chicken: is it still good? Why, in that God-awful heat, did I waste my time at the library?

"So, I have been wondering," Grandma says, ignoring my silence as I hurry the unspoiled fryer into the refrigerator. "Why are you mad at Mas? What did that poor boy say the other night to get your dander up?"

"Nothing," I lie, banging the celery into the crisper, throwing the Monterey Jack to the back of the middle shelf.

"Shoshanala," Grandma scolds, "after all this time, you want to pretend I can't see who you are?"

I slam the door to the fridge shut. "What do you know?" I shout. The sound feels good. And then it comes, like a cough rushing up my throat: "So you told him that I talked with Wina, so what? That doesn't give Uncle Mas a reason to boss me around."

"Humph." Grandma leans back in her chair and watches my face carefully. A concerned look crosses her face, and I hate what's coming: a smile and then a question. "So wolf-girl, it is true? We are bossing you?" she asks.

I feel fourteen again, folding my arms across my chest and leaning sullenly against the kitchen cabinets. "From your bossing," I say, "even my mother could learn."

Grandma tries hard not to laugh, biting her lip, but her effort doesn't make me feel any better. "Uncle Mas told me to go climb the hill," I protest, sounding like a pouting kid. "There is something," I try to imitate his cold voice, "you should see at the rock."

Grandma ignores my sarcasm. "Then there is," she nods, as if there is nothing more to say about it. She laces her hands together on the table. "Mas has a vision beyond me."

"What vision? He doesn't even know who I am!" My voice rises again, louder than the whir of the fan. "I don't take orders, especially from someone who never gave me a second's thought the whole time I was growing up. He has no right to tell me what to do."

Grandma sits up straighter in her chair, her cheeks flushed. "You couldn't be more wrong." She leans on her walker, knuckles tight and white. "Be ashamed,

Shoshie. You, a girl who grew up in a family with no eyes. Never once did they see the bottom of your heart. But we did – and from the very first."

Grandma shakes a finger at me. "Mas and me, all these years we've been waiting. Watching. Until now. Until you could see for yourself."

"See what?" I wail, pressing my palm against the kitchen tile as if its coolness could quiet me. It doesn't. "I don't see anything."

"Yes, you do," Grandma insists. "But like your mother, you are trying to blind yourself with fear. Feh!" She spits. "It doesn't work as a cure."

Grandma Rheabie looks past me to the herbs on the windowsill or out to the garden; maybe she sees all the way to Uncle Mas's old house. Then she glances back again, meets my confusion with a shake of her head. "You haven't let the world teach you anything, Shoshie. It's time you should learn to live with people – ones with eyes, like me or Mas. People what like you for who you are."

"No!" And then I'm out the door, out into the afternoon, out under the warm sky in the heat and wind and brownness. Down the driveway, across a field and up a packed dirt trail that hurries past clumps of dried grasses and slick slopes until it reaches Uncle Mas's rock. "Damn it," I shout to the entire world once I realize where I am going. "What am I doing this for?"

I don't have an answer the entire time it takes me to make my way up there. I'm moving too fast, and it's too steep to do anything but breathe. I can't imagine why I'm putting myself through this, but I keep walking. I swallow the afternoon heat in gulps, watching my feet to avoid seeing whatever might be ahead, waiting up there.

As I near the hulk of gray stone, the trail flattens for a moment, and I stop to rest, turning back to face the heat waves shimmering above the valley. I look down on Grandma's white house, the checkerboard of lawns on Chapman Lane and the string of roads leading east to Petaluma. "*Feh* to you too," I snort at the impossible old woman who's probably searching the window for some sign of me. I can picture how she's holding her hand to shade her eyes, sighing and wishing that I'd come to love, as she does, this small and dusty town.

"For what?" I ask. I turn north, imagining my dark house, damp with late September mist in the Lydon woods. But all I see is a pile of Mark's empty beer cans by the living room couch and wool socks hanging on the wooden clothes rack. I close my eyes and smell bleach from where I have taken a toothbrush to the shower grout, trying to beat back the mold. Today, there is no comfort in the thought of the cabin with its one-burner stove. Even Rasputin, curled up and purring by the fire, twists away when I imagine patting him with a lonesome hand.

"All right," I say out loud, "so no memories." I take a long, slow breath and slowly turn around toward the rock.

Toward Wina maybe, sitting silent and still, waiting to make another show of her wild magic. Or Mamale, Shlima or Gitl, long dresses stiff in the breeze, arms folded, ready to share some secret about Rheabie. Surely, that's why Uncle Mas sent me here: for something important, for magic, for Grandma.

Not for the dirty bare feet I see when I open my eyes, the figure with long hairy legs under a flowered skirt and a skimpy tan top, her arms wrapped around a German shepherd wearing a faded blue bandanna. "Hi," the hippie girl of the messy car says to me with a smile. The parking space stealer, the collector of shells and feathers, holds out a canteen. "Thirsty? My name is Heather. I had a feeling I'd bump into you again."

Chapter 15
TAKING A HARD LOOK

RHEABIE

Ai, yai yai, do we have a problem! Yes, *tsuris*, some serious trouble. It came to me, *bubee*, this afternoon while up on the hill you were. So good, you went. You walked. You spent time with that hippie Heather. Did she tell you – Luba Blumberg's niece she is? And a nice girl too – the kind what could be a real friend. But Heather, she's not the trouble I'm talking. We got something bigger – right here in the house.

Fear! Keeping us small. Keeping us separated.

What fear? Me, I'll tell you plain and simple, I'm scared of dying. My body, it's been telling me that time, I don't have too much left. And *oy*, how I want more: to see the end of the story we're making between us, to witness with my own eyes who you'll someday become. And that's your fear, Shoshie: turning away from living by the vision what's been given you. Wina wasn't kidding around when she put her hands on you when you were eight.

So while you were off with Heather, I realized finally – what *nebechs*, the two of us! And old woman and a beautiful young girl, scared of what might be. Or worse, frightened by what hasn't yet happened. But the truth is – about the future, what do you or I know?

We're not like Mas, who's made a friend from time – knowing her business. Backwards and forwards with her your uncle can go. Ask him to tell you about it sometime. But here's the point, dolly. By him and his gift, I got taught I should turn an eye on what's scary. Well, him and Mae, the two of them together – my good teachers, who showed me how to make like a rock with fear and turn it over. Maybe if I tell you what happened, Mas and Mae, they can teach us again.

We start with Mae, come back to Petaluma from burying her mother. You remember how I'd been waiting for her? Aching to tell, I was, everything about my ghosts. And then, of course, there was this business of Mamale choosing her to help with the big return to Terlitza. A million things, Mae and I had to discuss.

But in the six weeks we'd been apart, New York, it had sucked all the marrow from the bones of my poor comrade. Such a skinny woman Art met in San Francisco, stepping down from the Pullman with shaky feet. She looked bad, he told me later: washed out, sad and tired. "I tried to pretend everything was all right. Honestly, Rheabie, such a big welcome I yelled, and I held up the flowers. 'Your comrade Rheabie,' I told her, 'wanted I should give you these.'"

"For what?" Mae answered, and then Art's eyes filled with tears. Telling this story at my kitchen table, he could barely continue. "My own wife folded her arms and stared like I was a stranger. Such a terrible sniff she made – like I was a rotten piece of cheese."

Art never mentioned how Mae pointed at his polished shoes and ran a hand over his clean jacket – this I learned from the horse's mouth a while later. "So dressed up," she whispered. "What woman made you neat?" Then she pulled her coat tighter around her thin body. "Ach, don't bother to tell me who you've been fooling with. I can guess, but I'm too tired to care."

Too tired to talk the two-hour ride home. Too tired for the chicken soup I brought over that evening. All my excitement, the drum rat-tatting in my chest, stopped the minute I saw her. Such a hard line, her jaw. And no, she'd never gotten my letter. From the apology I tried to make for our long-ago fight, she didn't want to hear.

"It doesn't matter anymore," Mae said. In her bathrobe, at the screen door she was standing. Past my disappointed face she looked – up to the foggy hills.

"I'm glad you're back," I said, wanting she should notice me. Stop pretending, I wanted to say, that I'm not here.

Mae finally faced me. "Oh, I'm sure you're glad." Then she shook her head and let the screen door close.

"No!" I wanted to yell. Where had it gone, I wondered, all the warmth what had once lived between us? All right, so I expected she should be sad, poor thing, but why so wrapped up, like in a thick, wool blanket? What did it mean, she was still so far away?

Such foolishness, Shlima scolded as I cried my way home. *A brass band for a welcome you thought your dear friend Mae, she'd have?*

Mamale joined us, her ghostly hand patting my shoulder. *It's all right, bubee. Maybe you made it all up, this friendship with a wonderful comrade.* She shook her head. *Too much imagination you always had.*

Some comfort, my family, always knowing how to make me feel better. Still, in spite of their harsh words, I stopped sniffing and wiped my eyes. "I don't know who she is now," I declared out loud to the ground, placing my feet on the truth I was feeling. "So distant, so cold. Like she was still in New York."

Maybe she is, Gitl offered, floating in the air above me. Like a bird she looked in the twilight, all swoosh and feathers. *Rheabie, be patient*. Before she joined the wind, she called, *that woman needs you should give her time.*

I did. Two long days later, Art finally drove over with her for a visit. Five whole minutes it took, he should get her to leave the truck. At last, Mae stood next to me. "He made me come," she sniffed. "I hate this fussing. You should all just leave me alone."

I took her arm. "Come inside," I begged. "Sit down."

Mae didn't want tea; she didn't want applesauce cake; she was hoping not to be bothered with the *kinder*. Good thing they were all three playing at the Tanakas that afternoon. So the two of us sat at the table – words thick and heavy in the air between us. Well, my words anyway. That Mae, she didn't seem to have any. She just slumped in her chair, looking outside.

No words, at least, until Mas came with a cup of flour his mother had borrowed. So quietly he put it on the table. Then that boy, he looked at us with glad eyes.

"You didn't have to do this. Mimi could've brought it later," I said slowly in English. Yes, English! As soon as I stopped being afraid of Mas, I'd made it a point to speak that hard language. For our conversations, I didn't want my spirits should have to translate. Would you have trusted what Shlima said?

And it came easy, the English, just like Ethel Rabbinowitz, the night-school teacher, had promised. So many years of hearing the words – I knew more than I thought.

But Mae wasn't noticing my words. Too busy she was staring at Mas – looking the boy up and down. And that brave child, he stared back, until Mae's hands started to shake. Quick, she put them in her lap.

"Who's this?" she asked, speaking for the first time.

"One of our new neighbors," I began.

Mas interrupted. "I'm Mas Tanaka. I've waited so long to meet you, Mrs. Katz."

Mae shuddered, as if Mas's words were ants, crawling over her body. "No!" she choked, and then she stood up. Mae was in such a hurry, she bumped into the table, trying to leave it. "I need to go home."

"Wait!" I called, but she hurried out, knocking Mas hard in the shoulder. Almost deliberate you could think it, the way she turned.

"Come back!" I pleaded as the screen door slammed.

Let the fool go, Gitl urged, rising up from the floor. She rubbed Mas's sore shoulder. *Now, don't pay the missus any mind*, she comforted him. *She's upset, she's sad. Hurting you she didn't mean.*

"Yes, she did," he said, watching Mae walk home. He blinked, and then, like any little boy, began to cry. "Why doesn't Mrs. Katz like me?"

I brushed at my own tears. "I don't know."

That woman, she should be hung, Shlima declared, flying in fast circles just below the ceiling. *The nerve, to push our Mas that way.*

Our Mas? I looked up at my sister suspiciously. So, what had happened, he was suddenly more than Gitl's chosen child? Like a member of the entire family, as if Mimi or Davy had been insulted. *Mazel tov*, I wanted to say to Mas, *you've won her over*. And then, *oy vey, you poor boy*.

"I'm all right," Mas said, watching Shlima whirl. All her Yiddish curses made him smile. "I just want to know why."

Why, shmai! What's to understand in such rudeness? Mamale huffed from the corner. Back and forth she rocked in one of the chairs. *I don't know, Rheabie, how such temper you can stand in a friend.*

This is the same comrade you've chosen should help you go back to Terlitza, I reminded her.

You think I don't know that? Mamale glared at me. *Her I chose, yes, but not from being friends.*

From meanness, I declared, saying her reason out loud for the first time. It was the truth, but like a knife, those words, they cut the room.

Gitl shook her head and knelt next to Mas on the floor. *There's too much fighting in this house today, boychik. What do you say, we go play outside?*

Mas looked at Mamale and me, both of us with red faces. Ashamed we were for not holding our tongues. He tilted his head to the side, "You don't have to worry about me."

"Good," I said, "because I'm worried about Mae. I'm going over there." I looked at my mother, by way of making an apology. "However it happened, we are all wrapped in this together." She kept frowning. "Listen, it's too late now. What's done is done."

But you know Mamale – always she had to have the last word. *Rheabie, this is not a good idea*, she protested, although her voice was softer. *Stop and think. Do you really know who you are going to see?*

Like always, she'd put her finger on it, my mother. *No, and that's the point*, I answered even though my heart started a worried beating. *In this we have to be together, a union shop. How will I know about Mae if I don't ask?*

Sour her kitchen smelled when I let myself in without knocking. Bad milk or ammonia maybe. "Hello. Anybody here?" I called.

I stood still and sniffed. What was that odor? Then I realized: what we had here wasn't any kitchen smell. A stink like from the Terlitza *pogrom*, a little gun smoke, some screams, sharp and bitter. My nose remembered – a sharpness, like bad cheese. The small of fear.

I heard a noise upstairs, and moved toward it. "What are you doing here?" Mae Cherney yelled from above, leaning over the stair railing. Her hair: mussed now, tangled at the edges. Her eyes: big and icy, a coldness like I had never seen. A wild woman we're talking, who made my knees knock together. I swear to you, Shoshie, the look of her scared me. And then she started yelling. "You got no business here, Slominski. Go home!"

What would you have done? Left, like the madwoman asked, and gone about your business? My first choice. I took a step back, away from her anger, meaning to leave. But then, the light from the window on the landing caught her cheek, and I thought I saw a tear there. Tiny. Sharp. A piece of wet silver. It cut the muscle of my heart.

And so, for the first time in my life, I decided not to run from what scared me. With a quick breath, I put my foot on the first riser. "Go away," Mae yelled, but I kept on. Afraid, my heart shaking. But bit by bit, I climbed those steep stairs.

"*Gey avek!*" she screamed. "In this house, you don't belong."

"I do," I said, surprised at the strength what lived in my voice, "because, whether you like it or not, I am your friend."

"Well, I don't want you!" Down on the floor Mae sat, twisting her arms between the stair railings. Pressing her head into the wood, I heard a low murmur, "Some friend you are – rolling in Art's bed."

"What?" Surprised, I sat down too. "I didn't do a thing."

But I could see she didn't believe me. As I steadied myself, Gitl whispered from inside the wall behind me, *Tell the truth, Rheabie. You got nothing to lose here, so don't be afraid.*

"Listen, the man asked, but I wouldn't have him." I spoke slowly. "You think I'd lie with a comrade what can't keep himself clean?"

Mae lifted her head and stared at me, in her eyes a question.

Go on, Gitl said, her face flickering in the wainscoting. *Tell all of what happened that day.*

"Muddy pants," I explained, "and chicken manure on his shoes. Really, Mae. Don't you think I have better sense?"

"Art always washes first," she excused him. "And he can be so convincing. The man can talk."

"Then *feh* on his talking!" I threw up my hands and looked right into her eyes. "Okay, yes, for a moment, I admit I considered. Flattered, maybe, he should think of me. But he didn't really have much to offer. And that little, it wasn't worth hurting you."

A quick smile, a swallowed laugh and then poor Mae started crying. Ach, how the sound stabbed at me! A thousand curses I threw at Art as I hurried up the rest of stairs.

"I don't know who I am anymore," she whispered finally, "now that my mother is gone. Even the usual things, like Art's funny business, don't make any sense."

"Yes," I nodded, settling my back against a wall. "The world is a different place."

"Harder somehow or maybe meaner. Even though I didn't like her much, this hurts," she patted the top of her chest, "so it's hard to breathe."

"I remember." Closing my eyes, I could feel the jolt of the cart that carried me out of Terlitza. The long trip to America I had begun. For months, my ribs were so tight around my chest, never could I find my breath. Colors, conversations, the shapes of buildings, all seemed strange. Once, seeing a face in a shop-glass window, I felt pity for that sad girl what looked at me. It took a full minute to realize – that reflection, it was me. Worse – when I understood finally, I didn't cry but instead started laughing. Out of my mind with sadness, that's how I was. "Whatever you do, how you react, it's a surprise, yes?" I asked Mae that afternoon. "You never know what'll bother you."

"Yes!" She smiled at me. "Thank you. You are the first who actually understands." The way Mae lifted her hands – touching the loss what we now had in common – reminded me of Mas, our talks about ghosts and spirits. The shy light in her eyes, the eager smile – it was the same. "So," I asked after a while, "about that boy you ran down in my kitchen this afternoon?"

"What about him?" Mae's face got dark. She turned her head away.

"Why did you leave like that? What happened, *bubee*? What made you so afraid?"

"I don't know." There was quiet, and then: "I just don't like him."

Like you, Shoshie, the way you describe your feelings for your uncle. It makes sense to you – yes? – what poor Mae felt? Ach, but not to me, so I asked again, in a worried voice, "Because Mas is an oriental?"

"Of course not! What kind of fool do you take me for?"

"Then what?" I pressed my palms together, needing to know for Mamale and all the Guardian business we had to do together.

Oy, but Mae was no better than you, Shoshie, at explaining why Mas scared her. She frowned, worried her lip and then said simply, "Those eyes. He sees too much."

Of course, this is exactly true, but her words puzzled me. How could Mae know? I gathered my nerve and asked, "Well *nu*, so what did he see?"

Mae blushed. "Not see exactly," she stammered. "Well, maybe. Or something worse. Crazy." She bent her head and spoke in a breathy whisper. "He made me feel like my mother was in the room."

"And was she?"

"What kind of question is that?" All of sudden Mae's face closed shut, like a door slamming. In a huffy voice she said, "My mother is dead and buried in New York."

But that same sourness filled the air, the smell of Terlitza thick in the hallway. The fear, it was so sticky I spoke fast, afraid it would gum up my words. And Shoshie, I swear, I wasn't thinking about anything except the *pogrom* and how I had to run from the army to keep living. But the way Mae's chin shook and how her hands twisted together, made me say right out, "Your mother buried? Aren't you lucky? Mine has been following me – twelve long years since the day she died."

Rheabie! Mamale shrieked, bursting up through the painted floorboards like a rocket. She hung in the air over my head, screaming, *Why did you have to say such a thing!*

Big mouth! Shlima flapped, taking form from the lace curtains that blew at the landing window. In a dress as black as a vulture, she hurried up to the ceiling. *Foolish girl. Shameless sister. All the stars and the moon should fall on your empty head.*

What have you done? Gitl asked quietly, perching uneasily on a step a little below us. *Rheabie, use your brain a little. This is not good.*

You know it had to come out, and I told the truth, I defended. *Just like Gitl told me.*

Oy vey! Mamale pressed both hands into her chest and rocked back and forth with her eyes closed. *Oy-oy-oy! That kind of truth she didn't mean.*

Such a loud laugh broke up her wail. Mae sat up, looking about her with wild eyes. "This is your mother?" she asked and pointed at Mamale. Mae took a big breath. "Rheabie Slominski, on your life, tell me the truth. I'm not crazy? It's not just you and me in this hall?"

"It's not," I said, too shocked to try lying.

So now she can see us? Shlima yelled, pulling her hair in astonishment. *Ai yai yai, this is it. The world has just come to an end.*

"Well, it will," Mae said out loud in her nurse's voice, "if you don't calm down. You're going to give yourself a coronary." Then her eyes went wide, and she had the nerve to giggle. "But what do you care? You're already dead!"

Go ahead, Shoshie, laugh. That's exactly what my dear comrade was doing. For the first time since she came back, I heard the sound of the old Mae. "Rheabela, I'm so relieved. I'm not out of my mind. Either that, or we're both crazy. With such a *mishegoss*, what are we going to do?"

"Enjoy every minute," I said, placing my hand on Mae's knee and introducing Shlima and Gitl. "These two like Mas because he's polite when he talks to them. I'm glad to have someone else here as fresh as me."

"Mas?" Mae got still, looking frightened again. "What do you mean?"

I grabbed her hand. "Listen, this is not anything I understand, but for years I've been alone in this business. Then, Mas's family came, and from the first day he could see them. You get back, and suddenly you've got eyes too."

And a mouth, Shlima scolded, folding her arms across her chest, *that doesn't know from respect.*

Mae ignored her. "I heard Mas talk to my mother in your kitchen." She gave a shudder. "Without saying anything out loud, he told her it was all right, that it was time she should go home." Mae sighed. "And she did, just like that. Without a goodbye, even. Now she's gone."

"Your mother?" I sat back again, needing the wall to hold me up. "You mean, she was there, at my house, and I didn't even see her?" I took a long breath, then looked at my friend, *"Vey,* I'm so sorry. I wish we could have met."

"No, you don't." Mae shook her head. "It was hard for her to say a good word about anything."

Mamale butted in, shrugging her shoulders. *Looking at Rheabie's kitchen, the state it was in, what good was there to say?*

"Wait a minute." I looked up at my mother, swaying in the air above us. "You saw her and kept quiet about it? For shame, you didn't say a word!"

Mamale rolled her eyes. *Don't get yourself so excited. She was hardly there, a shadow. No face, no form, barely a whisper. Who it was, until this very moment I wasn't sure.*

"She was there strong enough for me to hear her." Mae shrugged. "Each mile west, what I could see of her faded – but that voice, talking on the train every minute! Just like in life, she drove me wild with her poor mouth."

Be ashamed! Shlima scolded from a bedroom doorway. She almost shook a finger at Mae. *What kind of girl talks so bad about her mother?*

Can you see how it was, Shoshie? Already, without realizing it, Shlima had accepted Mae, treating her to insults like one of the family. I looked at my friend and thought: It wasn't enough you had to lose your mother. Next, you get this for a family? Oy, you poor thing.

The poor thing raised her eyebrows, about to smart-mouth my sister, but Gitl distracted her. *Mrs. Katz,* she said gently, *I'm so sorry for your loss.*

I'm more sorry – Shlima strutted past us, as full of herself as a bantam rooster – *for what loss you have in the way of a husband.*

Mae got to her feet in a hurry. "That's enough from you. Art's my business, and I'm not willing to hear what you have to say. You understand?" Breathing hard, her face red, she looked at Shlima with narrowed eyes.

I pride myself on being frank, my sister stated, drawing back a little.

"That kind of frank," Mae said firmly, "is not welcome in this house."

I swallowed a smile, watching Shlima hurry to make an apology. So many things, I thought gladly, from this new family member I'll learn.

That afternoon – it was the beginning of our true friendship, the moment Mae and I started to see what lived at the bottom of each other's hearts. For me, she was always a surprise, like a box wrapped in shiny paper. Each time I opened it, there was another, smaller one, decorated with ribbons, waiting inside.

Like you, Shoshie, hidden and full of unknown powers. Your gifts they're folded, tied up with string. It's time now, you should begin the unwrapping.

Look in this mirror, my dear granddaughter. When the fear fades, what do you see?

I see Mas, a little shadow, standing just behind your right shoulder. Yes, there. Do you have the courage to take a look at what you know of him? Some kind of *tsuris,* he seems to be for you, a rock, what lies in your path. So *nu*? Turn the stone over! Gather up your courage and take a hard look.

Chapter 16
SEARCHING FOR UNCLE MAS

SHOSHANA

I try to find the Uncle Mas that Grandma sees behind me as I stare in the mirror that evening. The only things I discover are the familiar lines between my eyebrows, my chapped bottom lip, and a pimple forming by the side of my nose. No matter how much courage I summon, Uncle Mas is not sitting like a gnome on my shoulder, crooking a finger and calling my name.

I study the family pictures in Uncle Davy's old room, peering at a younger and grinning Uncle Mas. In those snaps, I can see what Mae meant about his eyes seeing too much. They are dark like ponds, thick with underwater life. In one picture, he stands apart from the rest of the family, his arms folded across his chest, watching the others. I wonder, for just a moment, if the blur below his eyebrows could be tears or just a jiggle of the camera when Grandpa calls out, "Everybody ready? Okay, smile. Say cheese."

The Uncle Mas I know never seemed to hurt when he sat apart before Thanksgiving dinners, alone on the piano bench eating peanuts, not joining Uncle Nate and Dad in the den as they watched a football game and drank beer.

"So it's a crime he didn't like sports?" Grandma argues in my mind. "And as for this 'never hurting' business, what do you really know?"

I know that each time before Uncle Mas came for the holiday, Mom would pull Aviva and me aside and whisper, "Keep clear. Watch out for that man. His Rob is okay, but with Mas himself you have to be careful. That's all I'm going to say."

I thought it was because he was gay or worse, a psychotherapist, one of those California types leading workshops full of tears at Esalen. The frown on Mom's face, her helpless shrug when Uncle Mas laughed, made me worry that perhaps he knew too many secrets, had listened in the high-back chair in his fancy San Francisco office once too often to the intimate things people said. Wasn't that why he watched the family so carefully during dinner, observing our behavior? "As *meshuggener* as his clients," Mom would mutter after having too much wine, when she saw him look up suddenly and smile even when no one had said anything, much less told a joke.

At least, no one we could hear. Who knows how many ghosts came to those November family reunions, making funny remarks about the food? And why is it that every spirit in this family acts like some kind of Jack Benny or Groucho Marx? Maybe the only thing wrong with Uncle Mas was that, unlike Grandma, he couldn't listen with a straight face.

Would I have laughed too, if I'd had the vision then and could hear the smart remarks? Would I have paid attention to the living, like a good girl, or ignored them, leaning back in my chair as Uncle Mas always did, chewing my food slowly while waiting for the best joke?

"So impolite, Shoshana," Dad would've said afterwards with disappointed eyes, "for you to be wrapped up like that in your own dream world."

"You were acting as crazy as your uncle Mas," Mom would've fumed. "I don't know how Rob puts up with him. But I won't. One cuckoo bird in the family is enough."

But there is more than one now, Mama, I want to say to her. I stop digging a load of compost into the old pea bed, preparing it for fava beans. I lean on the shovel, too short and small for this job, and look up to the slopes of brown hills to the west. Maybe this is the rock Grandma keeps telling me that I have to turn over. I lean to pull a shriveled pea plant out of the dirt. I don't want my mother to hate me the way she hates Uncle Mas.

"It's not hate," Grandma explains, making me stop the work to sit on the porch and drink a glass of water. "The soils wants to rest now. You should too. Listen, your mother's too smart for hate. We're talking fear."

Fear of what? I wonder. Fear of the way Uncle Mas stares directly at people when they talk, searching out the truth in their words? Or how he responds to anything left out or camouflaged, answering what wasn't said? Or sometimes not answering at all, letting the conversation dwindle into silence, so that what is meant echoes from each corner of the room. Mom, a woman who buries the truth, piling paragraphs on top of what she really means, must hate that about him. Well, I think, tipping the last of the ice water down my throat, this is one way I am finally my mother's daughter. Uncle Mas's ways scare me too.

Grandma shrugs her shoulders. "You are so like him. It's always been a worry – kept her up nights – that one day Mas would steal from her your love."

"She doesn't want my love," I retort, quick and bitter as Shlima. But that tone doesn't come from a ghost or anyone else in Grandma's stories. That blade in my voice, the hard edge of disappointment, is an exact replica of Mom.

"Of course she wants." Grandma watches me with sympathetic eyes, then hardens her voice. "But she doesn't know from magic, and so she's shut out. Poor *bubee*, she can't see the Guardians. It's not given to Mimi that this she should understand. But Mas now, he's a different story. Naturally, this makes your mother afraid."

"Of what?" Unlike Grandma, I have never known Mom to be truly scared of anything, not widowhood, not hip surgery, not growing old. My mother angers instead, ranting at doctors, her daughters and everyone she doesn't understand. Well, but maybe after all these weeks I'm finally learning a little of Grandma's wisdom. For the first time, looking out over the tumbled garden, I wonder if there's something else in Mom's rage.

But then I shrug my shoulders. Does it matter? Did any of the handymen she yelled at for not cleaning up enough or the waitresses she berated for slow service care if she was frightened? So what if all that anger was really a different emotion and aimed at someone else?

"Why should Mom be afraid of Uncle Mas?" I ask, ready to argue. Or better yet, to get up out of my chair and return to the garden, forgetting about the soft underside of my mother's tongue. But I'm never allowed that kind of escape at Grandma's house, and I have to admit that after all this time, maybe I don't really want it. Perhaps the wanting to hurry away is just a habit, like my mother's frowns.

"You need to understand, a mother wants to protect a daughter," Grandma explains, patting my arm with her arthritic fingers. "But poor Mimi can't protect from what she doesn't know. You should feel for her, dolly. Mas is the one what can help bring you into your own, and this, she's always known. Don't you see? You need him, not her. Your uncle's been a thorn in her side, or a big knife maybe she's pricked herself with, all these years."

"She didn't have to," I begin, seeing the scared face that sneered at him each Thanksgiving. So many sour words and prim thank-you letters she wrote to acknowledge his generous holiday gifts.

"No," Grandma nods. "So unnecessary. Think about it, *bubee*. Will you suddenly stop loving her when, finally and at long last, you become friends with Mas?"

"Of course not!" I sit back in my chair, unsure if what's idiotic is that I am thirty years old and have just admitted out loud to loving my mother, or if it's ridiculous that my feeling for her, as curved and deep as the Mississippi River, could just vanish, dry up and blow away.

Rheabie turns to me with tears in her eyes. "*Oy*, you sound so much like your father. For a moment, I could have bet my life he was here."

I look around the yard, hoping to catch sight of his ghost, a thin man with dark wisps of hair, arms folded into a brown tweed jacket. But there's no one squatting to inspect the flowers in the garden for earwigs or white fly. There's just the ache I always feel for him which flares and then, like a match lit into the wind, sputters and dies.

"A good man," Grandma nods. "A *mensh* if there ever was one. And you know, Mas was one of his favorites, although he took care to hide it from your mother. The phone calls they had when she was at meetings! And letters sent to his office. So blind, that Mimi. In front of her face all these years, and there's so much about your uncle and this family she's never known."

"Really?" I don't know why, but I'm suddenly fighting a desire to laugh, as if I have slipped off a dress that never fit and am standing naked. My arms feel open to the breeze on Grandma's porch. "Daddy liked Uncle Mas?" The air moves across my skin, the wind lifting my bangs and tangling them. I feel as nude as my father, who swam in the buff when no one was home. He made Aviva and me promise not to tell Mom if we returned early from downtown on Saturdays and caught him running into the house with a wet towel. Like him, maybe I can make something with Uncle Mas that she doesn't need to see.

I get up and kiss Grandma on the top of her head. "Enough with this resting, already," I declare, trying to sound as much like her as possible. "The garden is calling. It's time I should get back to work."

"Glad you can hear it talk," she chuckles as I return to the short shovel and the wheelbarrow full of compost, damp and crawling with earthworms. For the next hour I thrust and flex, turning the soil and then taking off my gloves to smooth it with my fingers, enjoying the feel of the dirt on my hands. There is never a rock to interrupt my motions, no heavy stone to lift or jagged edge to catch on my skin. Each time I stand to begin digging again, I'm surprised by how well the handle nestles into my palm now. I turn to wave at Grandma or glance over at Uncle Mas's old house or up at the hills sheltering the Guardians. "Uncle Mas and I will be friends," I declare to garden." Surprised and happy, I begin to sing.

Chapter 17
OFFERINGS

RHEABIE

So *mazel tov*, you've decided to be friends with Mas. Throwing down my good shovel in the peas, rushing in to make the big announcement. But dolly, a week ago you said it. Isn't it time you should do something? Five days he's back from Japan already. When are you going to call that boy up?

I want you should have friends here, someone besides me to talk to. Lonely I don't want you should be. And Mas is a start, yes, but he's a relative. Maybe someone else more your age you need.

So *nu*, what about Heather? The hippie. The one you talked to. A sense of humor, that girl, and such a good heart – like you wouldn't believe. She takes care of Luba – every weekend, her shopping and cleaning. When Luba starts yelling – about making the bed right or how Heather should've gotten ground beef – it's on sale – that girl just laughs. You think I'm a pain sometimes, dolly? *Oy*, from pain only Heather can tell.

And have you noticed? Every night she runs by here, huffing and puffing. Turning her head at our house, she's looking for you. Listen, Luba tells me: the last five years Heather has run all over Petaluma with her jogging. Never once have I seen her on Chapman Lane. But the minute you meet – hah, she can't help herself. So, is it too much to ask maybe you could be out in the yard when she runs by with a little friendly waving? Why not invite her in for a cup of tea?

All right, yes, your grandma is being a *nudzh*, but I only want you should be happy. As long as you're here, a good life you should have.

So call Heather up. You need her phone number? Don't look at me like that. It just so happens Luba gave it to me the other day.

All right, not just so happens, but did you ever think maybe your grandma is also lonely? You're good company, dolly, but it's sad, just us in the house. Years ago, I couldn't think without falling over another person. Now, so much silence. I don't know what to do.

So all right, yes, I'm asking. For the both of us. A little company. Dinner or maybe breakfast. What? You don't want to call? Then okay. I will.

This I learned a long time ago – an idea needs hands behind it. It's not enough, to think, to want. Work it takes to make it real.

This I didn't understand until about my ghosts I told Mae Cherney. She's the one what taught me how to make ideas take shape. And I'm happy to tell the story, if you think it might help you call Mas or Heather. Ach, I see that smile. You, such a schemer. You just want to listen so you don't have to pick up the phone.

All right, already. I give up. Who can fight you? After all this time, wheedling tales from me, this you know how to do. So, we're back to that summer of 1929. A hot August. I'd told Mae about Mamale. She'd talked with Shlima and Gitl. The world had changed, right?

Wrong. I thought as soon as Mae knew the truth, our friendship would come back, everything warm between us. When she found out Mas could see spirits too, they'd be friends. Ach, but that was just my idea. I didn't know how to do nothing with it. I sat back and waited. Nothing changed.

Mae came over every once in a while, ready to run if that *shlemeil* Art had the nerve to so much as smile at me. Over her shoulder she looked, in case poor Mas should come around. But Mas didn't, because that smart boy, he noticed whenever the Katz's came visiting. After a cup of tea, when I pulled Mae into the garden so she could take home a cucumber, sometimes I'd see Mas, hiding behind the water trough in Malka's pasture. And such sadness in his face. It twisted any pleasure I got from either of them, how he watched Mae with such scared eyes.

So what are we going to do about Mas and Mae? I asked Mamale one August evening. Feathers of high clouds covered the sky, but it was still summer: not a spitting chance of rain. I was in the garden, picking tomatoes for another day of canning. I looked up at my mother. *I didn't hear your answer. So nu, what should we do?*

What we? she wanted to know from the melon patch. *You were the one stupid enough to tell Mae who we are.*

I scowled at a rotting tomato. *So who picked her to help with the journey back to Terlitza? You think she's such a miracle worker, Mae could do it without seeing you first?*

But we don't know, yet, if anything is going to happen. Or how. Are you that anxious to get rid of us? Mamale shook her head at me, and floated over to settle in the corn patch. *Quit jumping ahead so fast. Even as a little girl, you never took time to plan.*

It's true. You don't plan enough, Shlima added, appearing from the center of a string bean teepee in a brown dress and red apron. She frowned. *If you did, you would have looked ahead and had an idea already for this kind of trouble. But, is it really trouble? What do Mas and Mae need to like each other for, anyway?* she asked, squatting beside a group of marigolds. Such bright colors, those flowers, next to her drabness – even with the stink. My sister wrinkled her nose, *They're both meshugge enough to like you, so if they don't trust each other, why do you care?*

Trust – it's the one thing we need here, I answered. *Nothing can happen if those two don't get along.* I wiped the sweat from my face. I wanted Wina and the Guardians to just show up and fix everything already. Couldn't they tell us what to do, and then between Mae and Mas make it all right?

Then I blushed. Maybe I didn't understand yet the Guardians' magic, but I knew from laziness when I heard it. Mamale was right. The plan was the Guardians' part, but the only one could fix Mas and Mae was me.

But first things first – the canning. Begun the next morning as soon as I could get the *kinder* out of the house. A hot day it was, and I had a three bushels waiting. A rush it would be to get the job done by noon. And why noon? Because after that – so much sun in the windows, it would boil me. You know how it feels, Shoshie – hot enough to fry an egg on the glass. So I hurried. Putting the water up. Cutting the tomatoes. Fast I tried to be, stuffing the jars with fruit. And when Davy interrupted – "Mama, I'm bored" – I'm sorry to say I yelled at him. Such a sad and startled look on his face. "Oh, dolly," I apologized, setting the first group of jars to cool on the table, "Here, have a cookie." As he ate, I thought quick – what kind of plan would get him out of my hair?

Ah! I sighed with relief just as he finished! "Will you be a good boy and help your busy mama? Get the mail."

Everyday we had the *Frieheit,* a socialist paper, sent out from New York, and it weighed a bundle, all that Yiddish. Then, for Jake, the *Petaluma Argus Courier,* in English, for the local news. Letters, bills – a lot for a six-year-old to carry. Tired he was by the time he stomped back into the house.

"Thank you, *bubee,*" I said, handing him another raisin cookie.

"You won't thank me." Davy's voice shook. "Look." He pointed to the Freiheit, a headline of screaming Yiddish: **Riots in Palestine, Arabs Make Pogrom Against Jews.** This he could barely read, let alone understand. But that boy knew the shadow of death when he saw it. "Something bad happened," he said slowly, his eyes filling. "Mama, I didn't want to bring it to you."

Something bad, which made me catch my breath, changing the air what moved in and out of my body. Terlitza I saw all over again: glass from broken windows, feather pillows torn.

"See?" Davy said, folding his arms over his chest. "Do you hurt?"

"Of course I do." I put my arms around my dearest child and rocked him. In the quiet I whispered, "But from what happens in the world, all the hurts and sorrows, your family you can't protect."

He shifted in my lap, big eyes turning around to face me. So much fear in his look – I bent forward to meet him with all what I had in strength. "You think not knowing makes troubles go away?" I asked my boy. "Listen, lovey, I can promise, this is not how the *meshuggeneh* world works. Much as we want, never can we hide from what hurts." Davy blinked and bit his lip. "Yes," I urged, "this is a rule we have to use for living. A *mensh* does not turn away from whatever terrible thing has happened. You understand?"

Slowly he nodded. "So," I set Davy down from my lap, "now I have to find your papa." I sighed, looking at the bushel of tomatoes still waiting I should cut and can, juice from where I'd been quartering the next batch dripping from the cutting board. Oy, such a mess, but wasn't this bad news more important? Yes, of course, yes. I tussled Davy's hair, then gave him a love pat on the tuchis. "Can you help me, my big boy, by playing quietly until I get back?"

Davy looked down at the paper and ran his fingers over the dark headlines. Then, a quick nod, and he ran off to his room.

Jake, in a pair of muddy overalls, smiled at me when I stood, heart in my mouth, in the door of the egg shed. He didn't stop his work, sand-papering an egg clean, until he took a good look at my face. "What's wrong?" he asked, and suddenly I wasn't Davy's mama anymore, a woman what could make a lesson from killing. Facing Jake, trying to tell about the *pogrom*, I felt young, small as my son. And was no better at speaking, I'm telling you, caught by the memories that terrible news brought me. Finally, I gave up and just threw the paper under your grandpa's nose.

And waited, while Jake squinted over the bloody details. When he got to the end, he shook his head, and then placed both hands on the egg table to announce his thoughts. "Zionist fools! They turn their backs on the Soviet Republic and look what happens." Jake stared at me. "Some kind of joke, no? They get Arabs instead of Cossacks, but it's the same religious poison. Better for them, they should have stayed at home."

"Yes?" I took a step back and leaned against the shed wall, hoping he should be joking. But no such luck. I knew, from how my stomach closed like a fist, that your grandpa meant every word what he said. "A good hundred have died already," I argued, instead of staying quiet like usual. "This slaughter means nothing to you?"

"And why should it?" Jake folded his arms over his ribs. "Those Zionists shouldn't be there. A nationalistic movement, without an inkling of class struggle. Dreams of a holy land – from such ignorance, what do you expect?"

This argument – old and worn-out – cost us many cold nights together in New York. A space it made in the middle of our bed. Your grandpa disagreed so strongly with the Zionists – he threw up his hands, said they weren't his people. For me, *meshuggeneh* politics and all, they were still and always my fellow Jews. I would yell, so loud the neighbors thumped on the walls for me to be quiet, "You think the Ukrainian Nationalist Army cared about politics when they were busy murdering all of Terlitza? Zionists, socialists, communists. When they fired their guns, all they wanted was another dead Jew."

We agreed to put the fight behind us once Mimala was born, because now we had made family. What that really meant, Shoshie – I kept quiet each time Jake pounded a table and told the world all what he thought. And he was not alone at that time; hundreds of Party members shared his cold opinion. I swallowed my own ideas and, instead I'm ashamed to say, let the father of my child talk. Until that August day, when shocked I was to feel hot words in my mouth, wanting I should speak them. I bit my lip – maybe I could hold the argument back? But the way he stood, smug smile, hand in his overall pocket, made me wonder: hold back for what?

"What did I expect? Not this," I yelled, waving the paper at him, "all the killing and burning and orphaned *kinder*." Suddenly, I smelled burnt wood come all the way from Palestine. My foot – it began tracing a puddle where soup and blood had stained a floor.

"Rheabie, wake up!" Jake brought me back to Petaluma with a slam of his hand against the wood table. "Enough with the past, already. Do you have to dive in and swim in it?" He leaned towards me. "So I want to know – how many more years do we got to live the Terlitza *pogrom*?"

I gasped, but that *nudnik* of your grandfather continued his lecture. "All right, yes, it was a horror: losing your mother and the rest of the family. But each time there's a world event, like this little business in Palestine, do you have to start remembering again?"

"You, Mr. Had An Easy Life, what kind of *chutzpah* gives you anything to say about it," I snarled. "From me and my remembering you don't know!"

Grandpa had been safe in America for years when the slaughter in Terlitza happened. When we met – surprised to see a familiar face at a garment workers' rally in New York – the *pogrom* was just a piece of bad news I told him about his first home. He wasn't the one who heard the shouts and bullets. That time in the graveyard – this he didn't know. So how could the worst day in my life be more than just a story to him? Twelve long years, the ranch, three kinder since that terrible time. And that day, I swear, I'd have given it all up for the ignorance what I saw in his eyes.

But *vey*, hadn't I just told Davy it was no good to hide from hurting? The truth, I owed Jake, even if it killed me to say. "What happened then, I still see it, "I got out, between wails and then the sobs that took me. "I live those memories every day."

"*Ai* Rheabela," Jake choked, and then your grandpa pulled me to him, crushed tight against his overalls. Into my ear he whispered, "Sha. Just put it behind you. It's all right. Decide you won't think about it anymore."

"I can't," I cried, wishing I was made different.

"Yes," he argued, wrapping me with his certainty. "You're strong, my Rheabela. Yes, you can."

He was wrong, it turned out, but who was I to doubt the faith of your grandpop? I wanted, at least, he should hold me until the crying stopped.

Maybe you're wondering, where were Mamale and my sisters at that moment, when I could barely breathe from remembering how I lost them? A good question, Shoshie. Strange it was, but always, when the memories of the *pogrom* took me, their ghosts went away. Fled, like the winds of that terrible day were chasing them. Ran off, to hide from what was.

And even if she'd been in the egg shed, I wouldn't have seen Mamale because the rags at my feet, they looked like the dirty cloths I'd had to use to wash her murdered body. No matter what mean thing Shlima might have said about the mess in the kitchen, in my ears all I could hear was her last scream. And so I felt more than alone when I finally mopped up enough to say goodbye to Jake after his comforting. Davy was gone from his room, playing with Mimi and Sumi. The cleaning what waited for me in the kitchen I couldn't bring myself to do.

I headed for the big hill instead, thinking a little breeze, the open fields, might make my lungs work easier. Maybe I could get my breath back being outside. I got Mas instead, waiting for me at the end of Malka's pasture. "I heard you crying," he said softly and took my hand. "It was in the air."

We headed for the trail what led to Davy's rock. Imagine my surprise! Up ahead, Mae – waiting for us where it began to get steep.

"Your mother told me I should come," she shrugged. "You need me. Is that true?"

I nodded, teary again but too tired to say anything. I tried but no words came, so I turned back to the path. Up up we went – the three of us, without stopping. No smiles, no looking at views, no chatting. Like puppets we hurried, pulled by a string.

Pulled by Wina – who else? – sitting on the rock, waiting. When we finally got to her, she nodded her quiet hello. *Your family asked me to come see you*, she said slowly. Then she took a minute to look each and every one of us in the face.

Such tenderness as she peered at Mae, a smile and warmth I'd never seen in her. Pride and a squaring of her shoulders when Wina stared at Mas. But when my turn came, the tattoos on her chin crinkled and her eyebrows bent together. She frowned and then, I swear – by a magic, she drew me up outside of myself into her eyes.

Into a place what I didn't know, where the sky was dark, the air was scorching. A place where I stood, young again and scared past breathing, in the middle of a fire. I was in Palestine maybe, a smoky village where houses burned in the night and children were screaming. Then it changed. *Ai*, my nightmare of nightmares! I was back in Terlitza, hiding in the forest with Uncle Yosl, while neighbors beat at their chests, watching their houses burn.

Maizle Demnakoff, Berel Kenofsky and Tsessie Riefberg. The Lithuanian, Dvosie Elyenkrieg, clutching her sister Ruchel by the back of the neck. And the cousins Bralov – Mindel, Chaya and Munish – uselessly praying. To my right pretty Genya Chernich left her hiding place. "Mama!" she screamed, running back to the burning buildings. A soldier on a horse dropped his torch. Then he raised a gun.

"No," I shouted, wanting to stop Genya, pull her back into the bushes. But I couldn't speak, and my legs weren't working. I had to stand, ashes falling on my shoulders, as that soldier, a thousand curses on his head, shot her with a laugh.

And then Wina blinked and the world came back, a hot afternoon in August in Petaluma. Mas put his hand in mine. "Where was that fire?" he asked, as I stood confused, oat grass tickling my knees.

"Yes, what did it mean, all that burning?" Mae echoed, coming up close beside me. "Are you all right, Rheabie?" She rubbed my back.

I ignored Mae, watching Wina and waiting, she should give me some kind of explanation. Only silence she made, and then, the nerve! She faded away into the rock. I heard her voice like a wind from the trees. *My village burnt once*, she said softly. *We built another. That's the choice you face now.*

"But Terlitza's gone," I argued, leaning forward and trying to see her. Wina didn't answer. "Well, and build with what?" I asked, hoping she would come back.

She just told you, Gitl said, floating down in front of us like a bird, her skirt nestling into the grasses.

Use the brains you were born with, Rheabie, Shlima called, screeching like a jay from a nearby oak.

But I didn't have any brains – just tired legs and a heart gone cold from memories. At that moment, all I felt was spent and dry and old. So I sat down on the dirt and pressed my hands into it, warm and dusty. I looked below to the house where Jake and the canning waited for me to come home. And then, Shoshie, in my fingers I swear I felt some kind of answer. Up from the ground it came, right from the earth. I grabbed a *smidgen* of it between my hands, and pressed. Tightly. Taking a breath, I asked Mae, "The *Freiheit*. Have you seen today's?"

She shook her head no, so I told the news about Palestine. More than that, I made myself spit out the memories what came too. Shlima and Gitl melted in front of me. Finally, I told someone besides Jake the story of the Terlitza *pogrom*.

Two someones, actually. I want you should understand, Shoshana, I wouldn't have said a word to Mas except for the magic of the Guardians. What did a boy that young need to know from such a terrible tale? But Wina hadn't closed his eyes when she put me back into Terlitza. Better, I thought, he should at least understand what she made him see.

Mas nodded as I told how Mamale sent me off to take some chicken soup to sick Uncle Yosl. A little smile he gave at how I slammed the lid on the pot and made a smart-mouth. "It's too late. Too dark. I don't want to go!"

"Enough!" Mamale roared. "There's no one to cook for him. He's lonely."

Gitl wrapped a shawl around me. "Visit awhile. Make sure he eats."

Mas twitched, like he knew the bad news what was coming. Surprised he didn't look when I told how we first smelled smoke. Just a fire, Uncle Yosl thought, on the other side of the village. "Maybe our house," I worried, wanting to make sure everything was all right. Then a popping sound we heard, and Uncle Yosl grabbed me. "Come. Now." Before I knew it, in the woods we were.

And from there I watched – the soldiers, their guns, torches and shouting. Laughter. Curses. And then screams.

"Mamale!" I sobbed after Genya was shot by the soldier.

"*Sha!*" Uncle Yosl put a hand over my mouth. "She's a smart woman. She'll be all right."

But smart Mamale wasn't. She tried to fight the soldiers. The next morning I found her – a knife in her bloody hand. Shlima and Gitl too. The three of them – brave, foolish and full of bullets. "Why didn't you hide?" I screamed over their bodies. "How could you leave me, this kind of alone?"

Mas listened like he could see me, crying on the floor of our burnt kitchen. *Oy*, and the smell! Fear and blood and bodies. Mae took Mas's hand, squeezing it tight, while I finished my tale: the graveyard, the burial, Mamale, Gitl and Shlima coming with me. Leaving Terlitza with them under my skin.

And finally, when I was done, out we stared at the valley. So thick, the quiet between us, not even my biggest cleaver could cut it. Ach, but here's the magic – it didn't hurt, that silence. Something else happened, dolly. Just the opposite of hurting, in fact.

I watched and saw bits of my words get chopped up, broken into little pieces. And then the wind – it picked them up like pine needles or chicken feathers. All that hurt from the worst day of my life – like dust it blew through the air.

And then everything looked different: the scrub oak behind us with the short branches burned by lightning. Or the blackbirds in the meadow, so noisy, what flew in a certain order as they looked over the grasses for food.

Most important, Mas and Mae seemed changed as they sat beside me. A *bissel* light outlined their heads.

In it, I saw the lines at the side of Mae's mouth, like pullet scratches in dirt, thin and crosshatched. For the first time, I noticed the funny shape of Mas's eyebrows, that part at the top what makes like a salute, standing straight up in the air. These two friends, I felt them slide between my bones, making a home there. I got bigger, not from ghosts this time, but from feeling who they were in me.

Mae tried to clear her throat – and surprise – she had tears in it. Imagine – from my story, her eyes got wet. And her cheeks – red, as if her face was burning. In her look such understanding, it moved my tired heart. Even Mas, still holding Mae's hand, noticed the change in her. Slowly, finger by finger, he uncurled the tight ball of her fist.

"There," he said softly when he was done.

Mae shook her head. "Who are you? What kind of boy?" she asked, looking at her palm, flat and open now. In her eyes, a little wonder, a little fear.

For the first time all afternoon, your uncle smiled. "I am Mas Tanaka," he announced proudly. "Now we've met properly. Mrs. Katz, how do you do?"

"I don't know," she replied, wiping a tear from her nose. Then Mae leaned forward to look at me. "So *nu*, Rheabie? What about you?"

All I knew was that by the time we walked back down the hill that day, between Mae and Mas was everything I wanted: her hand rubbing his shiny hair while she teased him into a race, "Who can get to the oak first?"; his hand in hers after he beat her, as they rested waiting for me. And such a welcome in their faces as I trudged toward them. At that moment, I felt as full of air as the sky above our heads. A thought came to me then, even though I knew my ghosts would sniff at it. This thought, Shoshie – with this walk, Mas, Mae and I had made a picnic, eating what happened in Terlitza like it was bread.

I could imagine how Mamale would scoff, *What, you think you baked some kind of rye from our horrible story?*

Or Shlima, *What are you calling a picnic? You had nothing to chew but sad.*

But I shrugged at their voices, because in my bones I could feel the strength of my thinking. Holding me up, it was, helping my legs to walk. *Look*, I wanted to shout at Mamale and Shlima, *Come close and look at our faces* – the shiny eyes and cheeks with color in them. *It's been a picnic, yes, with the best food in it. And not a crumb is left, we're so full from our meal.*

And that was what Wina meant about the choice I was facing. You see, Shoshie, how it was up to me to make a joining between Mas and Mae? By offering up what hurt most in my heart, letting them see my poor, *pogromed*

Terlitza. The rags and ashes I had to give them, all what had burned.

And from that – the start of friendship between them. The three of us, at last, ready to send my ghosts back.

Do you understand, Shoshanala, what your *nudzhing* grandma has been trying to say here? You too have to make something from your thoughts. So start already – sharing what lives in your bones with the people around you. Mas, for instance. Maybe Heather. There's magic, I promise, if you can find your courage and be the one to speak first.

Chapter 18
REACHING OUT

SHOSHANA

The first time I try to call Uncle Mas, my hand shakes the minute I pick up the phone. "This is ridiculous!" I tell myself, taking a breath as I look over the kitchen, the leftover beef stew hulking on the counter, cooling on top of a hot pad in Grandma's biggest stainless pot. I figure that by the time I've finished talking with Uncle Mas, some kind of friendly chat with jokes and comfortable pauses, the stew will be cold enough to put in the refrigerator, steam condensed on the underside of the lid. All I need to do is stop the trembling in my hands and dial.

I get as far as the area code and put the phone back down. "Shoshie?" Grandma calls from the living room where she has settled on the couch with her Tolstoy, frowning over the small print in the battered blue book she's had since she was a girl. "Are you all right?"

"Tea?" I ask, promising I'll try Uncle Mas again as soon as I make her a cup. I set out a plate of cookies and the bowl of sugar cubes on the coffee table so that she can read and drink in comfort. But leaning over is hard with her hip, so I stay beside her to lift the plate when she needs it, to hold the mug when her hand gets tired. Any excuse not to call Uncle Mas. The silly mystery I'm reading doesn't interest me, and so I sneak looks at her in the light, watching the twitch in her cheek as she turns a page, the way the lines in her neck get swallowed by the shadow from the collar of her shirt.

"What?" she wants to know, looking sideways suddenly and catching me in my stare. "I got crumbs on my lip? I'm drooling? Maybe some kind of fairy came by with a magic wand and made me beautiful all of a sudden?"

"You don't need a fairy for that, Grandma," I say, placing my own mug on the table. "You're already beautiful."

"Such a tongue you got on you," she sighs, but I know from the smile she is holding back at the edges of her mouth that she's pleased. "Like your grandfather. With him I always worried – when he flattered, what did he want?"

It surprises me that what I want, more than anything, is for her to know that it's true: she's lovely, with her cheeks crinkled like paper and the hair whisping away from her braid, feathering near the brown eyes I can fall into sometimes, swimming in their warmth when she tells her stories. Something in the way that she sits this evening, back straight to avoid more pain and her shoulders rounded, carrying the ache of her healing hip, hits me in the chest. I want to rub my breastbone, soothe the spot that hurts from looking at her, so old now, so beautiful, so frail.

"I'm not flattering. I'm telling the truth," I declare, shocked at the firmness of my voice, at the way my hands clench in my lap. When she shakes her head and her eyes fill with tears, I'm frightened by my desire to please her, to say words that will hold her longer in this house, reading beside me in the evenings or looking out the kitchen window as I work in the garden, stumping her way to the porch with her walker when she decides I need a break. Everything I do here has her name on it, and that is why, after a moment, I pat her hand and get up from the couch and force myself to the telephone.

"Can you come up this weekend for a visit?" I ask Uncle Mas, willing my voice to steadiness, my hands strong and still.

"Rob will be away, but I'm available. To visit with whom?" he wonders, letting the silence wrap around his words, listening for what I haven't had the courage to say.

"Both of us," I stammer, trying to mean it. Rheabie cranes her neck at the strain in my voice, a concerned face squinting past the lamplight. I don't want to see the worry that has settled into the folds of her chin, so I turn my back and lower my voice. "Listen, she needs you," I tell him.

"Of course." He laughs, a light sound that flutters across the wires like a bird. Then there is silence, and I can almost hear the question he won't ask: "But do you?"

I can see my frown, warped like a circus mirror, reflected in the side of the stew pot. For a moment, I almost feel bold enough to answer his silent question. But the truth – "I don't know yet" – doesn't seem big enough to say.

I don't know anything the few days before his visit as I clean furiously, tooth-brushing the shower grout, reorganizing the broom closet, transplanting the geraniums on the porch into new clay pots. "You'd think the Czar was coming," Grandma mutters, shaking her head as I wipe down the inside of the kitchen cupboards. "We're not talking any royalty here, only Mas. Don't worry. He's seen everything. That boy fed you squash and beets when you were a baby and then laughed when you threw them up on his shoulder. Believe me – you, he knows."

She purses her lips at the cracker boxes, the cereal, the bags of sugar and flour on the kitchen floor, waiting to be put back on clean shelves. "Shoshie, stop a minute and answer a question. You've turned the house into a madness. For why?"

I put my rag down and sit cross-legged next to the three packages of spaghetti I bought at the store yesterday, more than we can eat in a month, even with our guest. The look in Grandma's eyes, warm and curious, forces my words. "I want Uncle Mas to know I am taking good care of you."

She slaps a hand on each knee, and throws back her head to laugh. "Dolly, this he'll know with his whole heart." She reaches into the air as if to stroke my cheek. "You don't think it shows, all the love here? Look!" Grandma gestures to the room, the herbs blooming on the windowsill, the collection of saucepans, copper bottoms shiny, now hanging in easy reach of the stove. "A whole different house we got," she insists, "since you came."

For a moment I can feel how it's changed, the air full of light, billowing from the open windows into the corners of the kitchen, held by the baseboards in some kind of embrace. Grandma nods. "See? Not so empty anymore. For that, I have you to thank."

Her words make me jump all of a sudden, my jeans too tight, my turtleneck stretched and lumpy in the neck. Itchy and nervous, as if Mom is standing behind me in a skirt and hose, tapping one of her leather pumps impatiently, sighing loudly and crossing her arms over her black cashmere sweater. "Look what you've done now," she says, shaking her head. "Grandma's getting dependent on you. What's going to happen when you leave?"

"I won't," I declare to the frowning figure I have conjured up, the sleek woman in wool, who raises her penciled eyebrows at my words. I hate the smug way she presses her lips together, making a stop sign across her face, a red line of politeness designed to hold back an "Oh, really?" or some other comment of doubt. "If Grandma has the good sense to need me," I retort, "that's her business."

"Good sense to need?" she echoes. "She'll only be disappointed. I needed you after your father died, and even though I begged, you stayed selfish. Packed yourself up for college without even a whisper and drove all across the country to get away."

I begin to ready all the responses I have ever made to this argument: "Daddy wanted me to go to Berkeley. I was only following his dream." But the curve of her hand clutching the single strand of pearls my father gave her for their twenty-fifth wedding anniversary stops me. Finally, I understand. The fall of 1968, Daddy's plans didn't matter anymore, because like me, Daddy was gone.

And I can't tell her the truth, that it was her weeping that drove me away, how she cursed him all that summer for his heart attack, sobs and swear words that I could hear at 2:00 a.m., even with the radio playing and a pillow pulled over my head. It was her pale face in the morning, a balled Kleenex in her hand, silently reproaching me for not getting up in the night and crying with her, that made me go.

I flip my hand to brush the memory aside, knocking over a half-opened package of Grandma's favorite crackers. Startled, I look over the chaos I have made of this kitchen, settling finally on the small smile on Grandma's face that blinks at me like a lighthouse beam on a foggy night. How long have I been daydreaming this old and painful fight with Mom?

Grandma laughs, "So *nu?* Look what happens when I give you a compliment. Disappearing into yourself so far, I thought you'd gotten lost." She shakes her head, teasing, "Well, you won't catch me at that again."

I shrug and place the box of Ak Maks back on the shelf, embarrassed to realize that I have my own Shlima and Mamale, appearing at the oddest moments to criticize my work. I consider telling Grandma, whose hands now grip her walker as she prepares to stand, how similar I am to the young Rheabie of her stories. But I don't have to. She knows, of course, just as she knows who I really clean for, hoping that Mas will give a good report of me to his mother or sister and that the message will somehow get passed on to Ithaca.

"All right, so scrub yourself to death," Grandma jokes, thumping her way across the linoleum. "I give up trying to stop you. I'm going outside so I can talk to that smart Heather when she runs by."

I surprise myself by lurching up after her and brushing crumbs from my jeans. "Good idea," I nod. "I'll come too."

Heather is the one who ends up organizing the kitchen, putting it back in order while I cook dinner. She's efficient, quickly returning boxes to the cupboard, baking supplies and flour on one shelf, jars of beans and rice on another. "Done!" she calls, slapping her hands on her sweats to make dust prints just as the timer rings for the spaghetti. She laughs when we collide at the sink, a tangle of hands trying to wash up and pour the hot water off the pasta at the same time. Rheabie rolls her eyes at us from her place at the kitchen table, chuckling as she sets out silverware and napkins, ordering Heather to "step on it, already!" and bring the glasses and plates. Throughout the meal, Grandma interrupts our conversation with wild puns, making us groan and giggle at her bad jokes, while Heather's dog Barnaby thumps his tail at our squeals. And at the end of the evening, when I invite Heather back again, I can tell that it takes every bit of restraint for Grandma not to crow, "Didn't I tell you? So why did you wait so long?"

Instead, she leans against my shoulder while we watch Barnaby lope beside Heather down the lane and sighs into the October darkness. "Tired, Gram?" I ask. "I didn't mean to keep you up."

"From such a evening, there was no keeping," she reassures. "Those kinds of laughs I wouldn't have missed for the world."

"It was so easy," I admit to the half-moon and spattering of stars, remembering how comfortably we sat around the table, the satisfied quiet that rose up as we finished our last cups of tea.

Grandma snorts. "You expected anything different? Listen, I've known Heather since before she was born – that bean sprout is practically family. And besides, it was you, the one what made it easy. You don't know the light what shines, sometimes, from your bright face."

I don't know anything, it seems, about having company and why, suddenly, I am starting to enjoy it: Luba with Heather two days later for a gossipy afternoon tea, Uncle Mas arriving after dinner that evening with his expensive leather overnight bag and warm smile. He looks different to me, sprawled on the couch next to Grandma, talking about his trip to Japan, laughing while he watches her reactions to his adventures. His arms, in a hand-made shaker sweater, seem longer, and he's thicker in the chest than I remember. And when he kicks off his shoes and turns to wink at me after teasing Grandma about her bossy ways, I understand that Uncle Mas has come home to the only person in my family who truly sees him. Somehow I'm expected to have that vision too.

And it's not hard. Or at least it's not hard to talk with Uncle Mas in the garden while Grandma naps Saturday afternoon, discussing the plot of fava beans I have yet to plant and the rest of the tilling and weeding needed to get ready for winter. I squat, my knees caked with dirt, looking up at him from the soil I turned over last week, smiling at how smoothly the dirt still runs through my hand. He nods at the gesture, as if I have just answered an important question or told him something he needs to know. "What?" I ask, standing up quickly, turning to stare into his knowing face.

"Look!" He points to the crest of the brown hills waiting for the first rain, and I see clouds or maybe shadows there that seem to gather together, become thick or solid. I blink. Maybe it's only the wind or a wisp of fog wandering east from the ocean. Or could it be something else: the gnarled shape of Wina and the grassy Irish girl, the wintry priest and smiling cat Guardian? Yes. I can barely breathe, watching their faraway figures move in the wind, and I hope, with everything that I have in me, that they will let the breeze carry them down the slope to join us here.

"We all think you are just what Rheabie needs," Uncle Mas says, speaking as if the entire valley and the magic ones who guard it are listening. He smiles at my excitement. "Do you hear me? She chose well when she chose you."

I prickle just like I always do when he gives me orders. "I was the one who chose to come," I insist, letting my annoyance turn my attention away from the spirits on the hill and focusing on the tomatoes. I pull off a few dead leaves, twist a wandering branch of one through its wire cage – a useless act. There won't be enough sun in the next few weeks to ripen the fruit, and I should just pull the plant up and compost it. "All right," I admit to the frown on Uncle Mas's face, "I didn't come strictly for Grandma. Mom asked me, and I wanted, finally, to do one small thing that might please her."

I am surprised to hear him laugh, a loud peal that rushes past the snow peas and hurries toward the house. The sound will wake Grandma, I know, because she won't want to miss a second of our fun. Maybe it'll bring the Guardians. But I don't understand the joke or why Uncle Mas pats my shoulder and then gives my arm a gentle squeeze.

"Your mother is always a mystery," he says, pushing his wire rim glasses back up his nose. "Someday she'll be glad that you see the love in what she does."

I give a snort of disbelief and a shrug that makes Uncle Mas laugh again. I can no longer see the Guardians on the hilltop and hope that they are making their way down to us. My uncle gets bold and hugs my shoulders. "Ai, such a gift you are, Shoshie," he says, trying to imitate Grandma. His voice and accent are so off that I can't help myself, and I begin to giggle.

"After all these years, you can't do better than that?" I am bold enough to tease him. "*Oy* Mas," and I become Shlima, rocking back and forth in one of her dramatic moments or better yet, Mamale, beating on her chest and tugging at her hair: "What are we going to do with such a *goy?*"

For a moment we touch shoulders as we laugh, and then he motions with his hand, clean, rounded nails and slim fingers, for me to lead him out of the garden. The Guardians have not arrived, but I feel their presence anyway, large and shimmering. As he latches the gate behind me, my elegant uncle grows serious and his eyes darken. "I want to tell you one thing, favorite niece." The words sound clipped suddenly, solemn, weighty and Japanese. "Don't doubt what you know."

He waits a moment, then leans forward to peer at me, and I feel like a character in a fairy tale, a lost girl surrounded by magic, listening to the wise old man of the forest. Or maybe I'm just one of his clients, confused and weepy from my own phantoms, holding my breath at the end of our session, hoping for a final word, some direction or advice, before the hour is up and we have to say goodbye.

"You've gained power here," Uncle Mas states, slipping his hands into the pockets in his corduroy jacket. A blackbird calls from a field, and I look up quickly, hoping it's the Irish girl, but I am disappointed. Uncle Mas waits until I have turned back to him. "Shoshana, it's time," he says firmly. "Trust who you've become."

"What the hell does that mean?" I want to ask, feeling an edge enter my voice, a tinge of doubt and insult, a mirror of my mother. I take a breath to swallow the words, and then I see her, small and sharp, leaning into the rickety garden fence, her bony shoulders hunched. There is nothing Guardian-like about the way Mom's brown scarf catches the breeze or how her tortoise-shell sunglasses, round moons of darkness, reflect the edges of the afternoon light.

"Is that my mom over there?" I whisper, hoping that my question will drive her away and bring Wina instead: sweet, calm and smiling. Maybe what I see is only a shadow falling from the apple tree or a shape made by the pile of tools, rake, shovel and hoe, that I set against the fence this morning. Maybe this ghost of Mom is just a confused memory come alive again, a forgotten moment from the past, a picture I've called up out of my overactive imagination.

The old man of the forest, the famous therapist, pats my cheek. Although he isn't bold enough to do it, I tense my face, expecting a pinch. "Trust," Uncle Mas says, smiling. Then he lifts his arm and waves to Grandma, up from her nap already, her hand shading her eyes as she watches us from the porch.

Part II
Secrets Waiting for An Ear

November 1980 - March 1981

Chapter 19
DREAMING AGAIN

Rheabie wrenches up in bed on a stormy November evening. "No!" she tries to shout, feeling her lungs being squeezed. She shudders, hurrying to draw the night back into her body. Her mouth gulps at the darkness. "Air. I need air."

"So why waste any, talking?" she thinks, pressing a hand into her sternum. Ai, it hurts. The ribs. The dry skin covering them. Such an ache. Rheabie rubs, trying to slow her heartbeat, lesson the hurried patter that races inside her chest. Fear from the same old dream. The pressing, something weighing down on her. A sour smell, like death, rising from her hands. Isn't it time the nightmare should stop already? All right, so she's suffocating. A dozen times now. So boring, the same story every night. Couldn't we try something different, get a little creative? Better yet, the dream, it should get tired of trying to kill her. Just go away.

Not until the danger's gone, Wina murmurs, the words rising like smoke from a dark corner of the bedroom.

The leafy voice startles Rheabie. *You again? Since when have my dreams become Guardian business?* The hand on her chest trembles, so she hides it in her lap. *Things are a little slow maybe? There's nothing else needs you should do but watch me sleep?*

There's danger, Wina repeats.

Rheabie hates how her favorite Guardian refuses to come forward, won't step from the shadows into the orange circle of her night-light. *What? My other hip, it's going to break maybe?* she taunts, hoping to coax Wina out of her corner. But *oy,* as sharp as Mimi – her words. Mamale would scold: *The nerve, talking to a Guardian like that. Didn't I teach you better? Show respect!* But respect isn't what's making Rheabie's heart feel unsteady. She waits for the flutter to stop.

A flurry of rain tattoos the roof, drops battering Rheabie's window. She feels how the sturdy fava beans, stalks tangled together in her garden, have been forced low by the wind. But Rheabie knows they're holding. "Such good work," she thinks, "what my planting girl, my Shoshie did." If only she'd asked her to strengthen the supports under the apple tree. It twists in the storm, branches keening. *Vey iz mir* – the little roots, maybe, are beginning to give way. Rheabie listens, expecting the old tree to topple. A small branch breaks instead, scraping the side of the house as it falls.

The danger, Wina reminds. Rheabie's heart starts pounding again. She doesn't want to hear what she knows the Guardian will say next. *It's bigger than us. We need your help.*

"This," Rheabie thinks, "the *real* nightmare." Not the dream itself, but the broken conversations afterwards. Pieces of glass. Wina – her words, such a mystery. A *mishegoss* what says nothing. After all these years, it would kill her maybe to explain what she means?

What kind of danger? What needs doing? Rheabie asks. The rain has lightened for the moment, making a soft shush against the roof. Rheabie listens, imagining the sound like a blanket, wrapped around her cold shoulders. Any minute now, Wina will tuck her in with the truth. But the rain continues, clanking down the rain gutters, dripping steadily from the eaves. Wina hides in her corner, not saying a word. And the danger – whatever it is – runs cold fingers down Rheabie's arm.

Vey, she moans, knowing the touch is as real as the flannel nightgown covering her body.

Of course, real, she hears Mamale chiding. *Since when did Wina ever lie?*

Rheabie looks for the scowling face of her mother in the murky darkness. She can't see where she's floating in the room. But the voice continues. *Think already. Something terrible we're talking. Not your hip. Not that easy. Something what lies much closer to your heart.*

Rheabie feels the breath leave her body. She begins to gasp for air.

From our own, Gitl whispers, *a member of the family.*

It's your fault, Shlima cries, circling above her. *You. You're the one.*

Rheabie wakes again, her lungs hurting. She makes herself sit up and reach for her robe. "A dream," she tells herself. "Wina, Mamale." The tick of the clock, so loud in the room's silence, tells her that they were never here. "What? So now I get a dream inside a dream?" She carefully gets out of bed and shuffles in her slippers to the window. She can see the fava seedlings, young plants hungry for water, waiting for the first big rain of the season. The apple tree stands with every branch intact, traced by the moon.

All right, what she needs is a mug of tea, maybe. If she's up, a game of hearts with Shoshie.

Then Rheabie remembers, and her mouth fills with the metallic taste of failure. "Shoshanala," she cries, curling her hands around the small pieces of the night. She tries to hold on to what she knows, placing her trust in Wina's long ago kiss on Shoshie's head, her choice, the old promise. But then she sees the hard eyes of her granddaughter. *So nu?* The truth – no matter what kind of face she tries to put on it – Shoshana's gone.

For the first time since Shoshana was little, Rheabie feels frightened about the coming year. Everything she planned, all what she was sure would happen, has cracked apart.

Chapter 20
TRYING TO HIDE

Nov 5, 1980

Grandma, It's raining hard. I made a fire as soon as I got home from work, and the house feels like mine, for the first time since I got here. I thought coming home would help me understand things, but so far it hasn't. I'm still lost. This place doesn't fit, but then no place does.

Shoshana crumples the letter, the third she's started in the last hour, and stares out the window at the clouds misting through the fir trees in Lillian's yard. It's only her sixth day back in Lydon, the second after a full stint at the Kitchen Kupboard, and maybe she'll get used to the breakfast shift again, maybe all the meat-loaf platters at lunch won't seem so heavy on her arm as soon as Jack and Ed and the rest of the regulars get over having her back to tease. It's harder to keep quiet, like usual, to not ask questions as they jabber on, laughing at old jokes or getting hushed as they remember a baby's death or a tree felling gone wrong. Even from the kitchen, cutting two slices of Josie's best cherry pie, the stories pull at Shoshana, and she wants to lean her hip against the counter when she serves them up and ask, "So what happened? Did the doc get here in time and O'Malley make it? Did the Reese's have another kid?" Rheabie has spoiled her, filled her head with the breathy whisper of old tales, and the thought, along with a flare and sputter from the wood stove, makes her bend again to the creamy paper on the table to begin another letter.

Grandma, it's raining and I just got home from work.

Shoshana doesn't let herself write what she most wants to say: "I'm sorry." Sorry for getting scared, for running out and putting the nice but bland Mrs. Nielsen in charge. I couldn't do it anymore, Grandma. And I took care of everything, cleaned out even the garage, and got Heather to finish planting the rest of the fava beans. No, I can't explain any better than this. I just had all I could take. I'm sorry, Grandma. I'm so sorry.

Mimi's not sorry; she's damned angry. Who would have thought that after all these years, all her effort to keep things safe and calm, the voices would come back again? "Shut up," she wants to scream at the rumbling tones in her head, the conversations that are not memories or dreams even, though they have the nerve to wake her up in the middle of the night. Three a.m. precisely for the last week. How is a woman supposed to sleep? Especially now, with a hip to heal and Aviva needing help with Hannah – such a darling baby, but fussy, not like Beth had been as a newborn. Especially since her own mother, endlessly talky and stupid at seventy-eight, seems to be making much better progress in physical therapy than she.

"I won't listen!" Mimi vows out loud, just as she used to do when she was eight, but the voices don't fade. They get louder, the leafy one asking her to come home again and walk up the hill – as if she could, with her hip. And then some girl, windy and Irish, begs, "Surely now, it's time you returned."

"Fat chance." Mimi winces as she stretches to turn on the night stand lamp and then the clock radio beside it, filling her room with Chopin. 3:14 a.m. She is stronger now than she was when she was little, no longer as confused by the sticky touch of the night. Hadn't she learned long ago how to block the voices, to pull out the long fence post that she always imagined ran straight up from between her legs to her neck and beat at them?

So why had they come back? She doesn't know if she can find that old post again, worn away by too many years of taking care of the kids and Abe, of facing life on her own after he died. Maybe she used it so much that now it's splintered, rotting in the ground like the one that Mas picked up after school once and presented to her as if it was a sword. Such a weird kid he was, and even stranger now. Still, he helped her, and in the end she'd won all those battles. She can win again, damn it. She's not crazy. Never was. Never will be.

"Do you know what time it is?" Mas asks. There's a sigh, a rustle, the waiting that Mimi dreads whenever she speaks with him. "Are you all right?" he growls.

"The voices are back again." Silence. She hears him breathe and then can't help it. Why wait? She rushes to explain. "The voices, your voices, my voices. The ones you can't see. The ones you gave me the fence post for. You remember? You took them away once, the voices. Why did you bring them back?"

"I didn't." And then Mas is hushed again, listening in that way she can't stand, trying to sort through what she isn't saying. Well, let him. Let him stare at the clock like she is, 4:07 a.m. her time, only 1:07 on the West Coast. Let him be scared and worried and try to figure it all out.

"This is about Shoshana, isn't it?" she says slowly. The mashed potatoes that Mimi had for dinner turn over in her stomach. "You got to her when she was at Mom's, made her hear the voices too."

The way he doesn't answer tells Mimi that she is right. God damn it! "You sneaky son of a bitch! How dare you ruin her life?"

She hears both sounds from him then, the cool tone as he speaks aloud, the rich warmth of his invisible voice. It's so soothing, she has to shake his words off her shoulders. "She doesn't know it yet, but Shoshie's strong, stronger than you or I."

> 11/12/80
> Grandma, I miss you so much, and I don't understand what I'm
> doing here in Lydon.

Rheabie put both hands on Shoshana's cheeks at the very last, when the truck was loaded up, Mrs. Nielsen had moved in, and it was time to say goodbye. "One thing is all I'm asking," she begged, something near to fear in her brown eyes. "You should go and hurry up about this business. A million years we don't have here. Soon. I want you should come back soon."

Soon, Shoshana thinks, she will tell her grandmother about the odd hollow in her chest that has refused to go away ever since she pulled the truck out into Chapman Lane and headed for 101, the first of the highways that took her north. Soon, it will stop pressing so hard on her ribs, and she will be able to breathe again, will no longer feel the urge to call every day to make sure Rheabie is all right. Maybe then, she will be able to mention the Guardian she saw yesterday on her favorite path through the woods, an old ragged logger in a black hat, red wool shirt and worn boots who seemed more like a tree than a human. He wouldn't talk, just raised his hand as if he knew who she was, and then melted back into the darkness of the leaves. She knows Rheabie would say, "What, you think your vision will just go away, now that you are back in Washington?" and she doesn't want to admit that yes, that is exactly what she wants. She's tired from squinting her eyes to see if a shadow is only a shadow or maybe something more. Too many hidden meanings, too much to sort through, and it's taken so much out of her. Shoshana stops writing. I just need a rest, she thinks. I'll finish the letter later. Soon, when I'm not so afraid.

Back before Mas took the voices away from Mimi, she wasn't scared; she was proud when Miss Williams looked up from her desk after Mimi had finished cleaning the chalkboard after school and asked her about the lovely picture she had drawn at recess that morning.

"No, that's not my grandma. She's dead," she'd said, trying to understand why her teacher suddenly seemed so puzzled. "That's a pretend lady who talks to me before I fall asleep. She makes sure I have good dreams." Mimi didn't say that the lady, whose name was Ema, kept the voices away. Everybody at her house pretended, Davy with his magic rocks and Nate with his pirate adventures. Mama had the invisible voices, Mimi's dead grandma and aunts, who kept her company all day long. They were loud and funny sometimes, but no one else ever laughed at the things they said. Were she and Mama the only ones who could hear them? Maybe, but she didn't tell Mama, so that she could listen to their talk about the ranch. Grown-up talk. All the secrets and worries. And sometimes when Mama got mad at her, Grandma and Aunt Shlima and Gitl took Mimi's side and told Mama she was wrong. It was just at night, when everything was sad and dark and Mimi couldn't get away by playing in the barn or picking a fight with Davy at the table, that they scared her. That's when Ema came into the room through the window or out of the wallpaper and held Mimi on her soft chest. She sang lullabies or told funny stories, and it was easy then for Mimi to close her eyes and sleep. She didn't have to worry anymore about why her mother was shouting at unhappy relatives that Mama thought only she could hear.

"So you just made her up, honey?" Miss Williams asked, and Mimi nodded yes, afraid that she had done something wrong. She stared at the sweet pearl buttons, prettier than anything she could ever have, on her teacher's blue dress. "Imaginary friends are good," Miss Williams said, leaning back into her big chair, "but they are best for little children. We have to let go of them if we want to grow up. Do you understand?"

Mimi straightened and looked into her teacher's face. Here was someone else talking to her like a grown-up, just the way Mama's friend Mae Cherney did. But Ema was bad? She couldn't have her anymore?

"You're a big girl now," Miss Williams smiled, "and it's time you learned that an imagination is fine in small doses. I want my most promising student, with a good future in front of her, to know what's what in the world."

November 15

Shoshanala, Enough already with feeling sorry. You don't say it when you call, but I can hear it in your voice. Just do your business and keep your eyes open. And why aren't you calling your mother? You got her in the habit of kvetching at you every Sunday night. Now, she has no one else to nag but me and Max, who she woke up in the middle of the night the other day. Do us both a big favor and talk a little. What does the world look like to you up there in Washington? You tell me the news, but it's time we both paid attention to what in the world we really see.

Love, Grandma

Shoshana sees her mother, a trim woman in a brown plaid skirt and wool jacket, leaning into the fence in Rheabie's garden. She is tapping her foot against the edge of the shovel, scowling at the mud drying in the crack where the handle is attached. She tells Shoshana that she should take better care of her grandmother's tools, and what is she doing fooling around in the dirt with winter coming on? Mimi folds her arms across her chest. "So Grandma wants these beans planted, so what? They aren't going to grow in all the rain, and you know it. It's just another one of those traps of hers to keep you here, so you can't go home. *Gey avek.* Get back to Lydon. You were only supposed to take care of Grandma for a little while – not move in. You don't belong here. You never did."

Shoshana sits up in her chair by the fire and wishes she was waking from a dream. This vision is not some disturbing piece of sleep, but the nightmare of memory, come back from the afternoon when she saw all of the Guardians for the first time. Just as she and Uncle Mas were getting close, her mother appeared, a living ghost, surrounded by the filmy shimmer of Guardian power. Her mother, in her best going-out-for-brunch-in-Ithaca autumn clothes and makeup, scarf, sunglasses and gloves, took one look at Wina and the Irish girl, and began to scream, "What are you doing to me?"

"Mom?" Shoshana holds the phone tightly in her hand and looks out the misty window. "Are you all right?"

"Of course I'm all right." She imagines her mother straightening up on the pink flowered couch and reaching for the remote to turn the sound down on her Sunday night news show. The announcer's voice stops suddenly. "You don't need to check up on me."

"Maybe I'm the one who needs a check." The words surprise Shoshana. It wasn't what she'd planned to say. "It's Sunday, and I missed hearing from you." Mimi snorts, and the undignified sound coming from her proper mother makes Shoshana smile. She knows that Mimi is surprised and blushing now and has no idea what to say.

"It's kind of strange being back," Shoshana offers hesitantly. When was the last time she told her mother anything that mattered? She runs her finger along the rim of her coffee mug. "I think I got used to being important. You know, taking care of Grandma and the house and everything."

"Of course," her mother answers slowly. "Why not?" The lack of sharpness in her tone makes Shoshana wonder if she misunderstood. Where's the put-down of Rheabie or of her daughter making a living as a waitress, not using that expensive college degree? "So you liked it there?" her mother asks, as if she wants to know, as if whatever happened to Shoshana in Petaluma is important.

Shoshana looks around at the cabin whose walls feel too close this damp afternoon and tries to tell the truth lightly, turn it into a joke. "Call me crazy, but yes, I did."

"You're not crazy," her mother shouts, loud enough to hurt Shoshana's ear. "Do you hear me? You have never been. And you never will."

When Mimi left Miss Williams that day, Mas was the only one left in the schoolyard. The other kids had already gone home. "Don't get mad," he said, falling in step beside her through the field that led to Chapman Lane. "I told them to go."

Mimi didn't know why everyone always obeyed him, even though he was the oddball of the school, the kid they liked to make fun of: dreamy and strange, too apart from the world. Miss Williams told them not to be mean, but Mas was so easy to tease because he never answered back, just looked at them in a way that sometimes made Mimi afraid.

"What do you want?" she snapped, wishing more than anything that she could be alone. She had to think about what Miss Williams said and come up with a plan about Ema and the voices. She knew, even with tears pressing at her eyelids, that she couldn't pretend anymore. She was too grown-up, a big girl. But what would happen when she heard the sad voices tonight?

"Here," Mas said, pulling out an old rotten fence post from the field. He bowed in front of her with it.

"What's that for?" Mimi asked.

"Magic. A sword," and he stopped, looking at her in the scary way that always made her stomach turn over, "for fighting voices."

"You hear them too?" Mimi shuddered: why had she asked such a question? She held on tighter to her books, and her legs trembled. Crying almost, she told Mas the truth for once. "I don't want to be like you."

Mas's voice got gentler than she'd ever heard it. "Don't be afraid." He placed the board carefully in the grass at her feet. "Use this for whatever you want."

After he'd left her, Mimi picked up the post and swung it through the air. "I won't hear you anymore," she told the voices, feeling the grain of the wood pressing into her hand. She was grown up now and didn't need Ema anymore, didn't need to listen to anything in the night. "I just won't hear."

"You're not listening." Mas sat himself on top of the dishwasher in Rheabie's kitchen and smiled patiently. "Shoshana, you have to stop being so afraid and hear me. Your mother is all right. That wasn't all of her out there."

"Then who the hell was that?" Shoshana cried, angry at her uncle, furious with the Guardians, raging at the whole crazy business she had fallen into.

"Grandma, you explain it to me." She turned to the old woman, hunched in her favorite kitchen chair, who hadn't said a thing throughout this whole conversation. Explain what brought the spirit of her living daughter all the way out to Petaluma on a Saturday, her hip healed as if she'd never had surgery. Explain what happened in the garden to make her scream. Shoshana knew perfectly well that her mother was with Aviva in the hospital at that very moment, cooing over Hannah, her newest grandchild. Viva was tired, leaning back against the pillows and trying to nurse. Shoshana knew, because she had just called to congratulate them. She was so worried about her mother that she couldn't feel delighted, as she had been four years ago when Beth was born. And Mimi knew it, because when Shoshie talked to her mom, there was surprise in her voice. "What's the matter? Why do you sound like that? Is Grandma all right?" The sharp way she'd answered Shoshana's breathy question, "What about you? Are you okay?" didn't reassure her.

Rheabie shrugged her shoulders, her hands held high as if she knew nothing, and Shoshana wanted to shake her. What was going on? She always had something to say.

"Listen," Mas tried again, leaning forward and pressing the long fingers of his hands together, "Sometimes living spirits can visit like that. It's not unusual. A part just splits off and goes about seeing to other business. You've probably swooped off to Lydon once or twice while you've been down here without knowing it, looking in on Rasputin or maybe even the cafe."

Shoshana wanted to smash his reasonable, calm face. "You don't get it. Did you hear what Mom said when she was screaming? I was the one who did it, turned my mother into a ghost. I called her up and then scared her to death."

"How do you know she meant you?" Rheabie spoke finally. "Yelling at me she probably was, maybe Mas, or even, nerve of nerves, at the Guardians. All that conniption out there – none of us took even a minute to ask. And then she was gone. Maybe Mimi just missed us or was curious. Maybe her own dear daughter she longed to see."

"Yeah, right." Shoshana shook her head. "My mother has turned into a living ghost, maybe, but a personality transplant she hasn't had."

Mas chuckled. "I don't claim to understand what happened exactly, except that yes, Shoshie, you have some kind of vision – a power to see, maybe." His dark eyes widened. "And it's come to you in a rush, and it's scary. It's more than we thought you'd have, and I'm as surprised as you, but that's not what's important." He jumped off the dishwasher and looked straight into Shoshana's face. "This sight – so what are you going to do about it?"

"Nothing that will hurt my mother!" Shoshana shouted. If there was a glass nearby, she would have picked it up and thrown it. The thought stopped her for a moment. All right, so maybe something in her was as scared, as full of fire as the bratty Mimi when she was a child.

Mas, a waterfall of cool water, stared down her anger. "Your mother's not anywhere close to hurt. She made her choices about all of this a long time ago." He sighed, looking weary and puzzled for the first time. "And why it's been given to you to uncover, I don't know. But none of us can do anything when we're frightened. Stop."

Stop being a coward.
Stop blaming yourself.
Stop trying to hide.

Shoshana uncrumples the letter she'd picked up this afternoon from her narrow slot in the Lydon post office. When she first saw it behind the glass, she'd hoped it was another note from Grandma or Heather maybe, not that aloof, mystery man, the lousy therapist who didn't know the first thing about how to comfort anyone – her uncle. He'd only written four lines, typed on thick white paper: no greeting, no signature.

Ignorance is not bliss. That's the only thing I understand enough right now to tell you. Your job is to hear - from everyone. The first step is to listen. All the secrets are waiting for an ear.

Chapter 21
ASKING QUESTIONS

Nov 22, 1980
Dear Uncle Davy and Aunt Mari,
While I was taking care of Grandma, she told me lots of
stories about the ranch. But Im interested in hearing
some other points of view. Would you mind telling me what
it was like to grow up there?

Davy takes a swallow of whiskey and draws. The charcoal makes a dark smudge across the paper, a smear like a fist coming down. With his palm, Davy spreads the gray, exploding it in a high arc – just like the pain he felt when the clenched hand reached the side of his head, and he screamed. The night was slick and wet. He heard sounds, cries and shouts, and smelled fire. The stars were burning. The night tried to save itself and dove into black water, taking him with it. He was a drowning man.

Still is. No one understands. They think it's because of what happened in the war, and maybe they're right. Davy doesn't know. Mostly, he stays beneath the water. He only feels like he's on the surface when he teaches, finding his feet under him in room 212 at King Junior High or when he asks some scared and confused kid to talk to him after class. But then, just as the world actually starts to seem hard and solid again, something happens: a shadow under a tree in the front yard looks too dark; he smells smoke or gets a letter. That's when the tide comes in, thick and dark and shaking, and he goes under. Goes deep to where the fist still hits.

My mom doesn't have a good word to say about Petaluma,
so I don't really know. I thought you could tell me
- if its not too much trouble.

Mari packs her overnight bag: a nightgown, underwear, *One Day at a Time*, the Al-Anon book she reads from each morning. Socks. Makeup. She leans back against the dresser and thinks. Should she bother to bring her own gardening gloves? Mom's are so small and thin. She won't be able to tackle the blackberries on the side of their house without good leather. Well, that can wait for next time.

She goes downstairs, listening for the chime of the clock in the living room. She only has half an hour before Davy gets back from Saturday soccer practice and there is his dinner to fix yet, the plate of chicken and rice she knows he won't eat. It's hard to make herself walk through the dining room into the kitchen. The air is so dull there, heavy from Davy's art work last night, and the curtains are still closed. But he's never liked her to disturb anything once he's started drawing. She stops and corrects herself. No – once he's started drinking again.

And so, she will leave for the night, and he can do what he wants without her. After all these years, she has given up begging him to stop. And she doesn't even nag him to go to meetings. He'll just use it as another excuse for a bottle. Like he's using this letter from Shoshana. If it hadn't come yesterday, he would have found something else after three dry years. This time, she won't try to figure out the reasons that made him start again. She only hopes he will keep to his usual routine: drink himself silly on Friday and Saturday, stay sober for work during the week. Then start again after he's finished his grading next Friday night.

Well, maybe not next Friday. Despite her years with Al-Anon, Mari still hopes that this binge will be a short one. She should know better, but maybe, just maybe, something will happen and this time will truly be the last. One day, maybe he won't need to drink anymore. Enough of the poison festering inside him will have made its way out, and so he will turn his attention away from it, finally, and fight the disease. The original wound will have drained, and he can begin to heal.

Mari knows that something tore at him long before he came home from the war and she came back from the internment camp. They used to pass each other walking alone at night on Chapman Lane, restless footsteps in the dust. The first time he turned to pace beside her, she was startled to see barbed wire in his eyes. And when he sighed as they turned back toward home, she knew she'd found the only person in Petaluma who could understood how she still felt caged, how she heard the Colorado prairie wind at night, sneaking in under their door in the barracks. And how the Amache guards in the tower still watched her – every hour of every day.

He carried the memory of his own guards in the POW camp, she knew, and the beatings there, a fire on a dark night. She could taste the flames on his skin the first time she warmed herself against his chest. And when she slipped her hands beneath his sweater and traced the outline of his ribs, she was not afraid of burning. All heat and wood, they rolled together in the grass behind his father's barn. The night blazed and Mari dove, unafraid and flying, into the fiery pain. She came out clean, the remains of camp charred into ash.

She'd always thought that her love could do the same for him, that he'd find peace in their grassy bed, and later, their marriage and strong children. But looking around the dining room now, a mess of drawings and empty bottles, Mari understands that his pain has always been too big for her to hold. And maybe he never really burned hers away either. What if it just went into hiding while she got caught up in caring for him? As she leaves the house for the night, slipping the key into her jacket pocket, she wonders: Can you really do anything with that kind of pain once it's there?

> Grandma's given me the big picture, but what about
> the small things? Chores or games? I guess I'm asking: what
> kind of life did you actually have there?

Davy Slominski is a little boy again, and the barn is burning. He is nine or ten maybe and has been working at candling eggs ever since school got out. It's the Depression, 1932 or '33, and Mama is still over at Mae's, Nate is off with Ken, and Mimi is reading in the house, leaving him alone with the chores. Alone with Papa, the stern man who sneers when he calls him "Mama's boy" and has never really liked him much. Papa, the scary guy feeding Malka on the other side of the egg shed wall. Papa is extra mad tonight because the Brucksteins left today. The bank took back their ranch and the whole family, including Davy's best friend Jerry, have gone to stay with their aunt in San Francisco. "Bread lines!" Papa shouts, throwing another bale of hay into Malka's stall. "Forced to take handouts. A whole family ruined – by stinking greed."

Mr. David Slominski, history and sometimes art teacher, understands the forces that made his father's face red that day, the fear that caused his loud voice to tremble. But all young Davy can hear is Jake's anger, and he cringes as he holds another egg close to the candle to make sure there isn't a baby growing inside. There are so many eggs yet to do, and the boy is tired. The light is going. When his father clumps outside to feed the pullets, Davy places the candle in its holder and goes to see if he can find some help. He knows he shouldn't leave the egg shed with the candle burning, but he isn't sure he can find the matches to relight it if he blows it out, and the kerosene lamp is empty. He's not allowed to refill it by himself. Where's Mama? Why doesn't Nate come home? Maybe Mimi will be nice for a change and finish the candling with him.

As Davy walks down the hill, he sniffs. Something isn't right. He turns back to the barn and sees smoke in the egg shed. He screams. Papa is throwing a bucket of water on the fire. It's small and bright. Davy runs to Malka, gets her blanket and stamps on the flames. His feet burn. Eggs crack and break. Papa throws more water. Throws it on Davy. "Get out of the way, damn it!"

He's wet and crying as the fire dies.

"Look what you did!" Papa yells. "How many times have I told you..." He takes a step closer and Davy backs up. "You never listen. We could've lost everything."

"I'll clean it up," Davy pleads. He kneels on the floor, picking up eggshells, trying to fold the blanket. All he can see of his father's fist is an arc of motion, a dizzy whir, and then it hits. Explodes, like the mortars will around him years later in Germany. Stings, like the Nazi bullet that lodged in his leg and led to his capture. And then there is a burst, red and gray and throbbing, like he felt over and over again at the hands of prison camp guards. This first time, Jake hits him on the left side of his head, just above the ear. Later on, he will bruise his back or legs, any place that Mama won't see.

"I'm sorry, Papa. I'm so sorry."

```
Dear Niece,
Your uncle and I were pleased to get
your letter. I have many fond memories of the
chicken-ranch days, but it feels as if someone
else lived them. Can you understand how that time
in my life was like a fairyland? The war
changed everything. Until you wrote, I thought
what happened at the Amache internment camp was
far away too, like our old place on Chapman Lane,
but I wonder now if that is true.
```

When Mari returns home on Sunday morning, she feels as if she is walking into the barracks. She half expects to see Mama's doilies on the crate they used for a table and to hear the murmurs of other families behind their walls. A tightness fills her chest, as if she has just had her first cigarette behind the school building with the other wild kids and hopes that the perfume she sprayed on her shoulders won't allow Mama to tell.

"Davy?" She puts her bag down in the hallway and listens. He is not snoring away his drunk upstairs. After the clock in the living room chimes, she hears him finally – a little sound like falling paper in the dining room, then his sockless feet moving across the floor. When she gets there, he is bent over, settling a drawing that has slipped from its perch on a chair. It is one of twelve that he has left for her to see – like an exhibit at a museum. A first.

"Look," he says in a trembling voice. "Start here." She squints, moving slowly from piece to piece. Each sheet of paper contains shapes, more recognizable than usual: a wall, fingers, barbed wire. The face of a man. Mari feels as if she is being pulled into the images as they pile one on top of the other and come clear. The barn, egg crates, a candle. Smoke. Fire. A scream.

Maybe it is the sound coming from her own mouth, as she understands the story he's trying to tell her. Maybe it's Davy's wail as he starts to cry.

"I'm sorry. I'm so sorry."

She feels him breaking apart in her arms as they slump against the dining room wall, feels herself shatter like old glass. Later, when the sobbing stops, she rubs his arm, then her own, trying to find her shape.

"Honey?" Davy shifts to sit up. "I'm in trouble."

Mari draws a breath. These are the very words she has been waiting to hear for years, but she doesn't feel relieved as she stares into his face, washed clean by all the crying. When he attempts a smile, she feels no satisfaction or joy. What she feels is still, like the center of a pool of water swirling down the bathtub drain. Quiet, like the silent place inside the roaring of Colorado winds. She is sitting on a hill, by herself, staring into the moonlight. She is seventeen again, just back from camp, and trying to find her place in the world. Then, she clamped down tight on the confusion rising inside her, muffled the shrieks and screams. Now she looks down at her hands – veiny and tired, nothing young about them anymore – and finds the strength to tell the truth. "I'm in trouble too."

Shoshana,
These drawings are the best I can
do right now to answer your questions. If you
don't understand, Aunt Mari is willing to tell you
what they mean. I write this 6 days, thirteen hours
and 4 minutes sober, but who's counting? I'd ask you
to wish me luck, if I thought it would make any
difference. For the first time, I'm doing every bit
of this on my own.
Uncle Davy

Chapter 22
ACCOUNTING

Nate puts the phone back in its cradle and stares out his study window, watching the first snow blur the pines in his backyard in Virginia. Jeez-o-petes, but he'd like to hide behind a swirl like that instead of having to sit at the head of the Thanksgiving dinner table, fill wine glasses, and act like nothing is wrong. He's got two hours before the rest of the company comes – can he shake off this mood, cold as those damn Montana winds that used to eat at his bones each January in Yellowstone? What about the way his hands are shaking, the urge he feels to punch the wall, cursing his father at the top of his lungs?

No. Nate crosses his arms over his chest and holds tight. There are baby grandkids in the house. Carol and his daughters-in-law are working their tails off, fussing with the bird and other fixings in the kitchen. He has no call to scare them, just because his brother called up to wish him a happy turkey day and ask if their dad beat the shit out of him too – back on the ranch when things got bad.

Nate shakes his head. What a young fool he'd been to face Dad down in secret, to stand at the back of the barn, straight and quiet, and just take what Jake dished out with the back of his hand. During the beatings, Nate tried to act like those Japanese warriors that Ken Tanaka was always jabbering about: protecting the weak, using the mind to stay strong. He even made plans when he could see Dad was getting riled. Step one: make up some excuse to send Mom and Davy off the place. Step two: kick over the milk bucket or screw up the chores some other way to make his father mad. And when Dad roared and began to use his fists, he'd think, "At least, I'm saving everyone else from this."

What a joke. Turns out, he hadn't saved Davy from anything: not Jake's bruises or, later, the Nazi's beatings – even if he enlisted first, hoping to convince Davy not to go. And hell! He didn't even know until today that he should've saved Davy from booze too. Such a damn fine brother he's been all these years.

Nate takes a swipe at his tears. Well, at least he's made sure he's done better at being a father and husband. His kids aren't afraid to come home. And they make noise when they visit, instead of hunkering down into sullen silences. Listen! Nate leans back in his chair and grabs at the sounds in the house. Upstairs: Ashley, Dawn and Sammy are sprawled on Grandma and Grandpa's bed, playing Candyland. Down here: Charlie, that lunky newlywed, stops Suze on her way to set the dining room table and gives her a loud smack. Luke and Tom are cheering a Lions' touchdown from the couch in the family room. They laugh and act like brats – not the responsible fathers they are now – when their mom hushes them, "Keep it down, you guys! The baby's asleep."

Nate gets up from his chair. He needs an Alka-Seltzer – the usual ironies are turning his stomach over. The best ranger the Park Service ever saw is a bureaucrat now, locked up creating budgets and lobbying big shots for funds from a fancy office in the Capital. And the family that he's made, the folks who make the lousy job worthwhile – for them, he has his father to thank.

December 10, 1980
Dear Uncle Nate,

Uncle Davy told me he talked to you, and so I'm writing to ask tough questions.

Did Grandpa ever hit you too?
How much did Grandma and Mom know?
Did Grandpa ever hit them?
If you don't think it's being too nosy, what effect did those times have on the rest of your life?

Please be blunt. I need to know what happened. That's the only way I can understand.

Love,
Shoshie

Dec 15
Shoshie,

1. Yes, Grandpa hit me.
2. No one else ever knew about any of it, until now.
3. As far as I know, Grandpa never touched Grandma or your mother. I don't think he could have lived with himself if he did.
4. Enclosed is a financial report about what those years cost me. I can't say that it really adds up.
5. Understanding isn't all it's cracked up to be. There are some things it might be better not to get.

Itemized Financial Report
For Nathan Slominski
Budget Analysis of the Chicken Ranch Years, 1929-1945

Accounts	Income	Expenses	Balance	Net Worth
Ken T	Shared outdoors; first one to tell me to become a ranger with Forest Service	WWII- took care of his ranch while his family was locked up	Even	Unshakable friendship; got a career
Davy	Told magic stories	Tried to protect from Dad; enlisted first; cut college short	He got hit anyway; his 2 years in the POW camp; GI bill paid for rest of college	A brother who calls now; helped me understand Luke, who's just like him
Mimi	Taught me how girls work	Lots of fighting and nagging; always told me what to do	Learned how to stand my ground quietly	Drives me crazy but still matters
Mom	Loved me no matter what from the get-go	Tried to protect her from Dad by sending to Mrs. Cherney	He never hit her; she taught me how to love	Immeasurable. Got Carol and marriage; saw what to do and what not to do.
Dad	Adopted, fed and clothed Davy and me	Hit me.	Learned obligation and duty; showed me how not to be	Watched him change later; gave me a chance to forgive

Nate puts his tidy chart back down on the desk and imagines the laugh Carol would get out of it – and then, how she'd lean forward out of her chair and give him holy hell. "What does it mean, cowboy, that you've reduced it all to debits and credits?" He'd be in for one of her wifely lectures: "Is income and expense what it's really about?"

No. But the columns put the whole thing in some sort of order. They give him something to put his hand on that makes sense. The net worth, for instance: isn't that a clear way to say what he's gained in the long run? Even when the balance was negative, it's obvious how he got what Luke, his smartest boy, calls a "backwards gift."

"Well," he hears Carol ask, "why can't you just tell Shoshana straight out, instead of turning the family history into a business transaction? Honey," he can feel just where she'd run a finger down his stiff jaw-line, "what are you afraid to say?"

And because Nate is alone in his study, he can imagine giving her an honest answer. "I hate how much I owe him," he stutters. "I can't stand it that I never told him after he changed."

"I know it's over and done with," Jake declares, pulling Nate into the hallway during the big forty-fifth wedding anniversary party. He wipes his eyes, "But such a fool I was back then. Stupid and afraid. I shouldn't have done what I did."

"It's okay, Pop," Nate says, even though it isn't. He shifts a little so he doesn't have to feel his father's hand on his arm.

Jake closes his eyes as if the move hurts him. "Such a good boy you were – you deserved better. Believe me, from the bottom of my heart, this I know."

"It's all right." The air in the hallway, so warm and thick, brings Nate close to fainting. He takes a big breath. "Enough already. The subject is closed."

As he walks away, he is sorry he doesn't have the balls to turn around and say "*Mazel tov.* I've waited so long to hear that." Or the courage to pull them both outside and tell his dad the truth: how Nate kept a close watch when his boys were in their teens and held his temper. He's proud that during all those upside-down years, he never raised a hand. "You were my example, and I made sure I didn't do anything like you. I tried as hard as I could not to be your son."

But I still am, Nate thinks now, crumpling up his nice chart and the letter to Shoshana. The rock in his ribs, which he hasn't felt since his father's funeral, has come back again. It's all mixed up: his father's fists on his back when he was a boy and the way those same hands felt when Papa was dying. His yells in the barn and the series of loud gasps he made at the very last. There are all the times that Nate put off going home and how he sat at the far end of the couch when he got there, refusing to look at Papa. There is the night he climbed up into the hospital bed and gently held his dad when the delirium made Jake wild. Why was he shouting about Birobidzhan, the Party and Russia? Who made him cry out, "I'm sorry, so sorry" so many times?

Nate shakes his head. Some things are just never settled, so why should he have to put words to them? He's always tried to be a good uncle, but "No!" he declares out loud to his niece. If he could, he'd send Shoshana a Yellowstone "No Trespassing" sign. "Listen," he'd write her in a short note. "This is private. You don't need to know."

Chapter 23
SOLITAIRE

It's not fair, Mimi thinks, up again in the middle of the night and playing solitaire, that Davy should have mentioned anything about Papa to Shoshana. All right, so her nosy daughter asked, but still... Mimi's hip aches as she shuffles the deck in her tidy kitchen and begins to deal. Seven of hearts. Ten of spades. Shoshie adored her wild horse of a grandpop and the piggyback rides he gave her when she was little. She'd squeal each time he'd shout, "Who's my best girl? and throw her up in the air. Tonight on the phone, Shoshie sounded cold, as if she were wrapped in ice. For the first time since she returned to Lydon, between them Mimi felt the full three thousand miles.

And what timing on Davy's part – now that Papa's gone and unable to defend himself. Even if it's true – and it might not be, since her brother is also a drunk – where can they find Papa to ask? He's floating out in the Pacific, resting in a crab shell. Maybe he's a piece of bone swallowed by some fish. "Monuments he didn't want. No grave stones, no cemeteries," Mama yelled when they were arguing about the funeral. "He begged to be burned and scattered. Why can't you give your father a little peace?"

"He has peace," Mimi remembers interrupting her mother, "all he wants – for the rest of eternity." Abe jerked her arm, trying to stop her mouth, but she was too full of her own misery to pay attention. Tired beyond knowing from that long final night in the hospital, she wanted just one thing: not to let Rheabie win. "A grave is for us – to remember him. To show the great grandchildren." At the look in her mother's eyes, so stark and teary, Mimi lowered her voice. "It's so we – everyone left behind – have somewhere to go."

She never thought she'd need a grave to visit so she could ask her father some hard questions. "Daddy, honestly, those times when Davy – or Nate even – came in crying from the barn, had you just been yelling like usual? Or was it because of something worse?"

A black seven, a red six. Mimi sighs and moves them to another pile, revealing the ace of diamonds. She concentrates. More than anything, in the 3:00 a.m. darkness, she doesn't want to cry.

And why hasn't Davy talked about the hard times back then and how everyone was running scared because it was the Depression? Their family was never sure if they could make ends meet. The price of eggs wasn't high enough to even pay for feeding the damn chickens. And all hell broke loose when the mortgage was due. Abe gave his life to the firm so that Shoshie and Aviva would never know from those kinds of worries. About the things that made Papa crazy back then, how can Shoshana possibly understand?

And what about Mama's part in it all, Mimi thinks, allowing herself to get a little angry. She's sure that Davy never thought to mention that. Poor Papa. If Mama wasn't wailing to him about money, then she was off poking her head into the neighbor's business. She kept herself busy helping to deliver Mari or nurse Mas. And then there was that famous uproar about the Brucksteins. Mama begged to take them in when they lost their ranch. "As if we could have managed to feed three more people, for God's sake," Mimi thinks, beginning to feel a bit better. She sips her tea. "Mama never put our family first."

"Look at this!" Mimi remembers Jake shouting when she got home from school one afternoon. He pointed up the hill – the chickens were thirsty. He shook his finger at the cold stove – supper wasn't on. As Mimi set her books on the kitchen table, Papa fumed. "Hours she's been gone, off to who knows where, as if it doesn't matter. What kind of mother leaves her *kinder* to starve? And have you seen the garden? Every plant means more on the table. How could she let it get so full of weeds?" Yes, Papa could make the whole house shake, the way he stomped his big feet across it. And the dishes rattled in the cupboard when he yelled. But after he got it off his chest, he could smile – at least at Mimi, busy chopping a pile of beets and carrots. As she put the potatoes up, he patted her on the shoulder. "My *shayne maydele*! Without you, I don't know what I'd do."

Mimi lays the nine of clubs on the ten of diamonds, the red queen on the jack of spades. She's won her game, but somehow, tonight's solitaire isn't giving her any satisfaction. It's only kept her from feeling a brush of cold air on her skin. And distracted her from looking closely at the room's shadows. She doesn't like the ones that pool near her feet on the floor. They're familiar, too long and bony. Mimi gets up fast and stumbles, as if a pair of slippers has tripped up her feet.

But there's nothing there: no hush puppies worn in the toe, no cold pipe in the ashtray. No matches, a dirty coffee cup, or scrawled note. She holds tight to the lip of tile around the sink as if the press of her fingers will stop the crying. Loneliness takes her with its usual grip. "Where are you?" she wails at Abe. "How could you leave me? Everything's so upside down now. What am I going to do?"

"What do you mean, Mom?" Shoshana asks. Her daughter has gotten even more distant in this phone call, low-voiced and calm. "I'm not sure I understand."

Mimi takes a breath and tries to imagine Abe sitting beside her. It's one of their family conferences, when they plunked the girls down on the living-room couch and had a talk to clear the air. "Things were more complicated than the way Uncle Davy has explained them." Mimi tries to find the tone that Abe used – reasoned and unemotional – which always made the girls listen. But the tears are pressing so close, she can't hear anything in herself that sounds warm. "You need to know that Grandpa was upset in those days because of the Depression and Grandma. In what happened to Davy, both played a part."

Mimi leans forward in her favorite armchair and holds the phone tighter. Despite all her plans, she's having trouble remembering what she wants to say. "Grandma," she begins again, and the very name makes her dig her feet into the living room carpet. If Mimi can just hang on tight to what she knows here, she won't feel so lost. "Your grandmother was gone all the time, fooling with the neighbors. You wouldn't believe how much, especially, she played around with Mae." Mimi didn't think talking to Shoshana would be this hard, with all sorts of odd feelings come back to haunt her. She almost feels as if she's stuck in the Petaluma kitchen on a deserted afternoon. Her voice sharpens. "And while she was having so much fun, who do you think was left to pick up the pieces? I did all her chores, and poor Grandpa was so tired, he couldn't see to spit."

But it isn't her pain that makes her sit up so suddenly. Before her, as if he's pacing the porch once again, she sees her father's worried frown. "You have to understand – Grandpa thought he'd lost Grandma. Even though she still slept at home, Mom was never there. And it was always Mae this and Mae that – as if she was the one who was most important." Mimi knows she sounds bitter, but she can't help herself. "About her own family, Grandma didn't give a damn."

Mimi hears Shoshana stir, as if she's about to say something. If she could, she'd reach through the phone to stroke her daughter's face. At least, she made sure Shoshie never had to feel so left out, so alone and uncared for. She made it a point to put her children and husband at the center of her life. "The worse times were when Mae had the nerve to come over. Poor Grandpa – so hurt and mad. Did they even notice – not those two, so wrapped up in each other? It was like we weren't there."

"Mom," Shoshana interrupts, and the tone of her voice is tender. Mimi feels as if Shoshie has slung a grateful arm around her neck. "Are you telling me that Mae and Grandma were lovers?" Then her voice gets hard. "And that's supposed to make beating Davy okay?"

"Of course not!" Mimi yells. "How could you think such a thing?"

How could she not? Mimi snivels, hours later. Even her arm feels shaky as she throws another Kleenex into the basket beside the bed. And that's nothing compared to the way her legs wobble when she tries to swing them to the floor to go to the bathroom. God, I've been stupid. Every muscle in her body feels severed. She's been cut loose, unhinged.

For the first time since Abe died, Mimi is glad that he's not sharing the bed with her. She wouldn't want anyone to know how the very thought of her mother and Mae makes her want to throw up. And all the tears, for pete's sake, which she just can't stop coming. She's a boat without moorings, drowning in her own sea.

And it doesn't seem to matter that she's always been good with Mas, accepting his partners and acting the liberal. All those tolerance speeches that she's given her uptight friends at the synagogue don't mean a thing. It's different somehow, this business of Mae and her mother.

And then she's angry all over again at the thought of their lying and sneaking. Under the very noses of the whole family – god, the two of them were bold. Thinking of Papa starts another round of crying. All right, so he had a temper and was maybe a hard man to live with, but he was good and trusting. Who knew he could be so blind?

Except – and the thought makes her grab her walker and wrench her hip – she never knew her father to be blind about anything. Oh my God. Mimi makes a hurried clump to the bathroom. What if Papa knew?

"Of course he knew," Rheabie says, sounding proud of it. "Your father and I, we never lied."

Mimi wants to block her mother's voice because suddenly she feels as if she is being crushed into tiny pieces. She's an old milk bottle, broken hard under someone's foot. Or the wineglass, shattered at the end of the wedding ceremony under the *chuppah*. After all the celebrating, she'll be wrapped up in a napkin and just thrown away.

"Mimala," her mother sounds close, warm and concerned enough to be in the room with her. "Understanding I don't expect, but I want you should know: between us, it was a matter of principle. When we married, a vow we made – each other, we did not own." She pauses, as if she is leaning forward to touch Mimi's hair or hand her another Kleenex. "A hard promise it was to keep sometimes. I'm telling you, each time he had a little adventure, I thought I'd die."

"Stop!" Mimi demands, ragged and edgy. "It's not fair, Mother. You're twisting things around to make this be about Papa. That's just like you to try and get off the hook."

Rheabie is quiet, listening as Mimi sniffles. The two of them are as far apart as they've ever been. And all the years that Mimi has tried to tame her tongue, to be nice when her mother's so aggravating – where has that gotten her? The peace that Abe tried to make between them is completely gone.

"You betrayed Papa and the rest of us." Mimi has nothing to lose now by being honest. "What you did with Mae was wrong. I'm ashamed that you could do such a terrible thing to your family. Who the hell did you think you were? It's not fair."

"Fair, *shmair.*" Mimi sees Papa for a moment in his leather chair, the one she and Abe got for him after they were married. She remembers how he interrupted a complaint she was making (about Abe? his job? their apartment?) and looked at her from the corner of the living room on Chapman Lane. "Such a pretty wife you are, all grown up to be the spitting image of your mother." She cringed – until he leaned his head toward Abe, standing outside under the apple tree talking to Davy. "And look at that good man you picked. May you have a happy life."

Then he took her hand and craned his neck to make sure that Mama was still busy washing dishes in the kitchen. "Shh – a secret. Just between you and me." He sighed, "I had to learn the hard way, dolly, it pays to watch your temper. More important, you should watch what you want." Papa smiled, pressing down hard on her fingers. There was so much sweetness in his eyes, it made Mimi want to cry. But she listened instead, as he nodded at her. "You need to learn, honey, that fairness in life – it's just not part of the business." He winked. "Don't wear yourself out, chasing something that can't be."

Then Papa nodded at Abe again. "Fairness doesn't keep the bed warm. You hear me? Fairness won't give you the years with him you want. Only love, *bubelah* – that's what we're talking. In the end, it comes down to how far you can stretch. So take an old man's advice and live from the promises you made each other. It might not be easy, but that's all you've got."

What Mimi's got is a raging desire to burn down the ranch. Just wipe that hellhole off the face of the earth. So what if her father grew understanding by the time he was old and tried to pass on a little bit of wisdom? She can't listen to him, not now. Not after what her mother did with Mae. It's so embarrassing. If she could just move Rheabie into a convalescent home and sell the place to someone else. They'd tear that ratty little house to pieces and build something lovely. Something spanking new. And then, the whole Slominski clan could forget what happened and start over. They wouldn't have the past hanging around their necks.

Or weighing down their stomach, settling like a rock in the belly. Mimi sighs, rubbing the place that aches. "Oh, damn," she thinks. She'll never be able to get rid of the ranch as long as her mother is alive. But afterwards… Rheabie's gotten so frail this fall. Mimi can hear it in her voice. It won't be long now.

Maybe she shouldn't have spoken so harshly to her. Mimi takes a sip of her coffee. Honestly, who does her mother have left? A few crazy friends like Luba Blumberg? The closest relative, a worthless son like Davy, a drunk? Even Shoshie's gone, come to her senses finally. "Face it," she thinks. Rheabie needs her. Both Abe and her father would want Mimi to apologize and make peace.

"But she betrayed all of us," she can't help arguing.

"So *nu?*" she hears her father say. "A betrayal it wasn't, what I did to Davy and Nate with my hands? Always, afterwards, I was sorry. Take it from me, Mimala. Sorry – it's hard to live with, unless you say it out."

Mimi makes her shaking fingers dial the number in Petaluma. "For you, Papa. Because you'd want it, Abe." She takes a breath, hearing the phone ring. Then her mother's panting hello. "Mom? I'm calling to say I'm sorry. I apologize."

Mimi closes her eyes and tries to picture how Abe would sit when they were having an argument. When the sharp words were over, he'd pull his chair in close so their knees would touch. She holds tight to the memory of his hand stroking her arm. "How you and Papa lived," she tells Rheabie, "is really none of my business. That's between him and you."

But the sense of Abe fades, and the space across the kitchen table feels endless. Mimi hates how her voice shakes when she asks, "Did you love Papa? That's all I want to know."

There's a pause. The quiet at the other end of the line is like a rock, one of those gray ones in San Francisco Bay. And then, a burst of noise: the sound of her mother crying. Mimi hasn't heard tears like that since her father died. "Yes, I loved. Of course, yes."

"Then how could you?" Mimi flattens her hand against the table and knows that if Abe were here, he'd motion for her to be quiet. She looks around the kitchen, so tidy without his mess, and is certain that if he were still living, she could talk it over with him and wouldn't have to ask.

"Mimala," her mother answers with a voice full of catches. "Him I loved – like you loved Abe." She pauses, sighs, "But the truth – a difficult man, your papa. An equally difficult woman – me. We survived by living from what we believed."

Mimi closes her eyes and strokes the place mat already set out for tomorrow's breakfast. "You asked so much of each other." She straightens the matching napkin. "I couldn't do that."

"No," her mother laughs now, "we were out of our minds." And then she pauses, and Mimi imagines her looking out the kitchen window. Is she turning her head to see Mae's old house? "Well" – and Rheabie is back again – "You and Abe, you were a little more traditional." Her voice is warm. "Of what grew between you, I've always been proud."

"You have?" Mimi wishes, more than anything, that Abe were sitting right here to hear this. What she wouldn't give at this very moment just to see his face.

"Besides," her mother continues, "it was a hard thing what your father and I tried – this business of freedom. So much *tsuris*. Truth to tell, I'm too tired now to want to live it again."

"Do you miss him?" Mimi asks, looking to where she keeps Abe's favorite mug – as if he might come back and use it sometime. Twelve years later and her basement is still full of his clothes.

"*Oy*, dolly," her mother sighs. "That father of yours – he's a hole in my chest. Even right now, ready to kill him for this secret business with Davy, I miss him. Oy, I hate him. But I miss him, yes. Every day."

"Me too," Mimi wails, six again and fully fifty-nine, but wanting her mother's comfort. She is surprised and grateful when she gets it, for the first time in years.

Mimi wakes from a dream of cranes tearing down her mother's house in Petaluma to sleet on her window. She hears a familiar Irish voice whisper to her, "We're here. Get up." And she thinks she's still in a dream when she sees eight people standing in her bedroom. They look so strange: big and wavy, dressed in old fashioned clothes. There's a priest, a pioneer girl in a calico skirt and a young soldier. A lean man, a young boy, a Mexican woman, and a forty-niner. Standing in front is a very old woman with a wrinkled face. Mimi gasps when she realizes the old hag has bare breasts. "Get out of here!" she shouts, scared and lurching to reach for her bathrobe. She holds the cloth tight: these are the voices, but she's seeing them for the first time. So she must be slipping, becoming more and more crazy. Like a scared little girl, she wants to call for Ema but instead makes herself sound her age. "What do you want? Why do you keep bothering me?"

And then Abe is in the doorway, coming towards her in his red sweater with the leather patches. He's crying, tears falling down his stubbled cheeks. She begins to sob, reaching up and pulling him to the bed beside her. It's been so long, she doesn't care who else is in the room and might see. She kisses his beard, the veins in his neck, his Adam's apple. She locks her fingers through his bony hands. And then she is falling down into the years of comfort between them. Over and over she tries to turn in his arms. And is held still once more, as if the last twelve years have never happened. As if he will never again have to let her go.

Chapter 24
TIME TRAVEL

UNCLE MAS

February 22, 1981

My dear niece,

The truth is that I time travel, and I can't control it. I know that your grandmother has mentioned this *"tsuris"* of mine to you in the past, but perhaps now, after months of Rheabie's tales and hearing family secrets, it might make more sense. It's a part of myself that I'm tired of keeping from you. The way you've pursued the truth in your family this winter and gone to the heart of the secrets shows both strength and wisdom. It's time for you to understand the forces that have shaped your Uncle Mas.

Time, or *Jikan* in Japanese, is a living thing, a beast or a being. To me, she is a lady, *Jikan Fujin,* a mythical creature with a thousand eyes. Or at least that's the way I saw her when we first met. You could say that she took me captive then, and I have belonged to her ever since.

But I don't think that's the real beginning of this story. It starts, I'm afraid, at my birth. Or before that, whenever it was that I was given my calling. I came into this world with a gift, a vocation: I hear. I hear the voice of the wind and the cries of all creatures in nature. I hear the whispers of ancestors who tell me tales. Most important, I can hear hidden thoughts, the rude or selfish or embarrassing things that people are too afraid to express. That's what makes me a good therapist. I pay attention to what isn't said.

That ability also drives people away, but I simply can't do anything about it. Did you know that I came out of my dear *Okasan's* womb with big ears? That's a joke, dear niece, but it's also true, if you look at the family pictures. I'm the elephant, always standing a little apart. In my favorite shot, which rests on my desk right now, Kenji has his arm over my shoulder. Like always, he's trying to pull me in. "Get your feet on the ground, be practical," he urges. My brother doesn't understand that the hard realities I deal with are the ones that he can't see.

But he's right. I'm not good at the small things that other people seem to find so important. Ken says that's why I hardly seem to be there. Am I just as absent to you, dear Shoshie, as I seem to the rest of the family? Maybe once you hear what happened between *Jikan Fujin* and me, you will understand.

I am writing to tell you another story for your collection, this one about a young boy who thought that he, alone, could rescue three lost and lonely ghosts. You'll have to forgive him. He was only ten and dreamed of being a hero. But I'm afraid that he ran into trouble and almost drowned. Or, if you prefer, he flew too close to the sun, and his wings melted. We can use any of my favorite mythological metaphors here, but the main point is that I learned the hard way that I didn't have as much power as I thought.

I wanted to find a way to send Mamale, Shlima and dearest Gitl back to Terlitza. I was certain I had it in me to be the gallant boy who'd lead them home. I wanted to prove my skills, to do something real with my mysterious ability to hear things. I wanted to create an adventure from all the secrets that I heard.

The deepest truth, I suppose, is that I was lonely. No other kids wanted to play with me, even my brothers and sisters. I was a little too strange, too odd a creature to fit into their games. And compared to what I heard in the wind or trees, I confess that their play bored me. I was more engaged when I had the stimulation of grown-ups like Rheabie and Mae. But when the stock market crashed, they suddenly had no time for me. They were busy trying to hold on to their ranches and just survive.

So I immersed myself in the troubles of Mamale, Shlima and Gitl. Those strange women loved me. I felt important listening to all their complaints. That would have been fine, except that I couldn't control my desire to do something about it. Every month or so, I'd come up with a plan to get them home. But each one I presented to the Guardians was gently rejected. Wina always tried to smile at me when she said, *No, little oak. This won't work.*

Once, after I was particularly disappointed and began to cry, she took me on her lap and held me. *Little one,* she said, *you are a special boy, and the spirits have given you great powers, but you need to move slowly. This is a time of learning, of finding patience. Be very careful. You must understand how to listen before you can act.*

I know now that even though I heard how much Gitl missed Terlitza and how much often Shlima wailed at night, crying over its shabby houses, I wasn't listening hard enough. I didn't hear beneath the surface to the meaning below. Of course Rheabie's spirits weren't asking me to rescue them. They realized, though I didn't, that I was only a little boy. All they wanted was for me to hold their suffering. They needed me to cup their stories in my palm and simply place them between the muscles of my heart.

I didn't understand, and so I made grand plans that always managed to place me in the middle of things – the big hero. I filled my days with the most delightful dreams. And all this served a legitimate psychological purpose – helping me to compensate for my outcast status in life. I couldn't know that, of course, and to be truthful, I think I took the pun of my name a little too seriously. It makes me laugh now, but really, what boy wouldn't want to be a

Messiah to Gitl, Shlima and Mamale if he had a chance?

One rainy afternoon, when I was sure that I'd come up with a solution to the Terlitza problem, I put on a clean shirt and hiked up to the rock, pushing against a strong wind. Bowing respectfully, I begged the Guardians to come and listen to me once again. The only one kind enough to oblige was Padre Guitierrez, who'd been a father at the San Francisco Solano de Sonoma Mission. After death, he'd become a spirit of storms.

Child, he said, *This is not weather for the living.* I remember how he put a hand on the cross that hung from his rope belt. *I beg you to go home.*

But I was a little samurai, in love with his own bravery. I refused.

Padre Guitierrez, always courteous, listened as I puffed up my plan with big words and lengthy explanations. The rain had soaked through to my underwear by the time he reluctantly shook his head. *I will take this to the others, but it doesn't seem very different from your last one. There was that fatal flaw, you remember. It could not be done.*

But I've fixed that, I insisted, still trying to feel like a warrior. He bowed to me when I finally began to cough. By seven o'clock that night, I'd come down with a bad fever. *Okasan* sat beside my bed and put cool cloths on my head as I got lost.

I was drowning in a sweaty dream, a part of *Jikan Fujin's* waters. The fever led me to a wild river, wet and hot and humid, and there I was captured by a medusa with a thousand eyes. *Jikan Fujin* seemed as real as the Guardians when I found myself swimming toward her in that fevered darkness. Nothing about her frightened me as I dove at her legs, still as rocks. Instead, she gave me a cool place to rest and something to hold on to. I caught my breath in the circle of her arms.

When I regained my strength, she lifted me out of the river and showed me a road through dark trees and stars shining above them – it was Terlitza! Dry and calm now, I walked between the houses and heard families talk over the evening meal. A girl ran out into the snow; it could have been Rheabie or one of the girlhood friends she sometimes spoke of. I thought my chest would burst. Imagine! Masaya the Messiah had found the place. Then Gitl came, with an eager face and rushing heart, to walk beside me. I heard Shlima cry behind us, *Oh wait. Wait for me.*

"I've done it," I thought, beginning to run toward the bonfire in the middle of the village. It looked just the way I felt – red and tall and proud. I heard the fire call me, and full of my accomplishment, I didn't think about the danger. I stepped forward to enter the heart of the flames. The heat and the light swarmed over my body, beginning to eat me. An ancient woman, older than Wina, beckoned to me from the center of the fire.

"Stop!" someone yelled. A roar, a buzz, a swarm of bees darted all round me. "You're safe now," *Jikan Fujin* said as she protected me from the stings.

Five days later, she released me, and I came out of the fever. I opened my eyes to see *Okasan* bending over me with trembling hands. Mae stood behind her in a smudged shirt, holding a mustard plaster. I didn't understand why there were tears in her eyes.

"Welcome back," she said in a trembling voice, and it was only then that I realized that I'd come close to dying. Maybe the fire, the bees and even *Jikan Fujin* had been real.

We couldn't let you get hurt like that, boychik, Gitl cried, hovering in the air near my shoulder. I turned toward her sweet spirit, and all I wanted to do was curse. Why were the Terlitza spirits back here in Petaluma? Hadn't I led them home, just as I promised? Why didn't they have the sense to stay? I could see a worried Mamale spinning above my dresser. Shlima frowned at me from the ceiling, *What, you think we'd accept your sacrifice just to get back to our old town?* She came closer, and I could swear she was crying. *The nerve, Mr. Fancy Messiah. Just who do you think we are?*

"Trapped ghosts," I remember saying rudely, and then I closed my eyes and sleep took me. But instead of resting, recovering from my illness, I dreamed of failure. Over and over, the dreams were the same. I was looking for my pocketknife or *Otosan's* gold watch and I couldn't find it. I had to walk a street whose name I never knew. Walls popped up in front of me, and then there were fences. Wherever I turned, the way was barred.

Okasan fed me broth when I woke the next morning. Rheabie came for a visit and put her soft hands on my throbbing head. "There, there," she comforted the small child nestled into a tangle of blankets. But I didn't want to be a sick boy. I should have been the triumphant hero. Those ghosts cheated me. I was ashamed.

Gitl tried to explain. *If we'd stayed in Terlitza, you would have died, no ifs or ands about it. The Guardians have learned that someone dying is the only way for us to go home. They had wondered about it for a long time, but what you did proved it to them.* She stroked my damp forehead. *Dolly, we decided it costs too much. Content we are to stay here.*

There must be another way. Don't give up, I argued. *Let me try to save you.*

There will be no saving, dolly. No sacrifice. Gitl placed her ghostly hand on mine. *Sha! You have nothing to say about it anymore. We have made our choice.*

It was a blow to realize that the choices weren't mine, that the spirits wouldn't let me help them. I had to learn how to use my powers in other ways. But I didn't know how, until the tentacle of *Jikan Fujin* pulled me down beneath her waters again. She became my teacher, and in return, I'm now her companion for life. Anytime she wants, I am plucked from the present and sail with her to a thousand different places. We visit what has happened and what will be.

Can you imagine how hard it is to have a practice, write books and find love with those kinds of constant interruptions? Believe me, I've had to work hard for everything "real" in my life. I put my foot down, and now *Jikan Fujin* will not pull me away when I'm with a client. But any other time, she can crook her finger and call. My mind drifts, and suddenly I've joined her for another adventure. When I get "lost" in thought, I'm usually traveling with her. Bless Rob, for putting up with his detached partner all these years and the home he's made despite my "absences." When I return from one of my journeys, that good man always wants to know what I've seen.

The past and future are all the same, Shoshie, when viewed from the banks of *Jikan Fujin's* river. The only constants are the truths that are never said. That's why when I became an adult, I promised to listen to all the wounded stories, but as a monk, not a warrior. I've finally found a good way to use my big ears. It's my gift to bring the speaker to say what he or she already knows: the truth too strong or scary for hearing. *Jikan Fujin* taught me that I don't need to change anything. I hear, but refuse to fix.

However, dear Shoshie, the years have taught me that listening makes its own kind of magic. That's the secret I was too young to know back then. So I write to ask you this question, favorite niece: what has happened now that you know the hidden truths in your family? What kind of magic will you make from the tales?

Chapter 25
MAKING CHOICES

Nate shuts off the hockey game – Montreal was unbeatable tonight – and shakes his head at the way his slippers shuffle on the family room floor. He's walking like an old man already, well on his way to the *alter kocker* he'll become. "You'll be the best old fart there is," Carol would tease, if she could see him. But she's upstairs, reading and waiting for him to get his A.K. ass up to bed.

The shadow of his hand on the wall as he reaches for the light switch startles him. Nate looks again. Damn, but his mitt looks like Dad's. He turns both palms up, as if he's making a scoop to throw kale seed into a bucket, and stares at his fingers. All that swelling around the knuckles is just like his father's. And their fingertips could be the same, the way the skin is red and cracked. Nate doesn't have the farmers' salve that Dad used when he disked the kale field in February. All the mud chapped Jake's hands, and then the fine chaff from the chicken feed made them sting.

Nate shakes his head. He's got it easier than his pop – if he remembers to use the stuff the dermatologist gave him. With his soft job, inside a damn office and swearing at numbers, those cracks will disappear in a week. But if he uses the medication, he'll lose another memory of the ranch and details like how to seed the kale might not come back to him. Nate doesn't know why, especially after all his talks with Davy, it should matter so much these days.

"Guilt," Carol says when he mentions it, "because it's still bugging you – how you never answered Shoshana's letter. Keeping secrets, just like your dad did. Are you putting the memories in the bank to leave to her?"

Of course not, Nate thinks, slowly climbing the stairs. His hunger for little pieces of the past, the good things – the sight of wild mustard in a grassy field or their smell after a cloud burst – is part of something else. He pauses on the landing and looks out into his neighbor's icy yard. For years, he's puffed himself up with how far he's come from the Petaluma and how little he misses it. But now, when some bus belches exhaust, Nate actually longs for the clean stink of the chickens. The noise of the Beltway at rush hour reminds him of the unholy racket the gum grove made in a storm.

Nate tugs at his sweatshirt, bulging over his belly a little more than he would like. All right, so he has to face facts: Petaluma was never as far away as he wanted to think. Tears nip at his eyes when he admits what he's known ever since Davy told him about the beatings at Thanksgiving: cursing Dad, doing everything possible to avoid his bad example, was just like loving him. Ass-backwards maybe, but even when he was too dadblamed full of pride to see it, Nate kept his father very close.

```
March 2, 1981
Dear Shoshana,
The most important thing about my growing up on the
ranch was all the scrapping with your grandpa.
He beat the crap out of me sometimes, but our fighting
taught me how to be a man. Or how not to be - because I
spent every waking moment trying not to be like him.
Hell, I probably ran from him even in my dreams. But
I didn't understand until now how that wasn't really
running. Jake Slominski was always there, determining
my life.
And that goes for Uncle Davy too - we've spent hours
on the phone yakking about it. We both agree, it never
helps to turn your back. So, here comes the lecture.
Honey, keep whatever is bothering you right where you
can see it. Make sure it stays in front of your face.
```

Shoshana stares at a blurred photo of her grandfather. He's dancing with Aviva at his forty-fifth anniversary party, laughing as he awkwardly does the twist. The small wooden frame looks odd propped up against a mossy log in the forest clearing outside Lydon. Shoshana doesn't know why it's so important that the picture needs to be facing north.

Or how come one of Uncle Davy's drawings, wrapped in plastic to keep it dry, must sit catty-corner from Grandpa. She clears fir needles from a rock, setting the picture carefully on the lichened stone. This sketch is the most explicit of all the ones he's sent her. She can smell the smoke and hear the shouting in the barn, as Grandpa's fist is about to hit.

She wipes her eyes and positions Uncle Mas's letter and the one she got yesterday from Uncle Nate around the circle. She adds a 50's snapshot of the entire Tanaka clan and one of her dad from that same time, playing golf. Grandma lounges next to a pine in the line drawing that Shoshie doodled while Rheabie napped in October. She places Aviva's Hannuka card, the one with the picture of she and Bob looking down at Beth holding baby Hannah. The goofy grin on Beth's face makes Shoshie smile. The formal portrait of Mimi in a red silk dress rests on a broken stump near them. Beneath it, Shoshie lays her latest phone bill to represent all the surprising talks they've been having. She hesitates, then sets a single black feather, from the collection in Heather's car, to the east.

There is only one more thing to add – the faded picture that Rheabie sent up over a month ago. "This one – only a few I have left – is precious. You'll be a good girl, yes, and give it back?" And even though she didn't ask,

Shoshana can hear the question that still hovers above Grandma's notepaper. "So *nu*, aren't you going to tell me what you need this for?"

She didn't know then, but now Shoshana slips the print from its envelope. Placing it gently on a small branch, she says in her best Rheabie voice, "The whole family it's not, if we don't have Mae."

So now what? Shoshie opens the plastic tarp she's brought with her and sits in the middle of the circle. For a minute, she feels foolish and is afraid someone will stumble on this spot in the woods. Well, but what would that stranger see? A woman in a blue jacket and wellies, hoping that she has correctly guessed the weather. A strange collection of objects around her that, if she's wrong, are going to get wet. Anyone approaching would hear the Russian folk song that Shoshie sings now, even though she's not sure why she's doing it. She imagines someone shrugging a shoulder, muttering "crazy hippie," then backing off, leaving her alone beneath the big trees.

Alone to let the stories come, to hear the unsaid things from the photographs and letters. Alone, to see what might rise up from what they have to say. She opens her hands, as if politely asking them to speak. Then Shoshana stops singing and tries to hold still as a whirl of pictures slams into her chest.

She feels Mae's skin under her surprised hand, a first kiss that is terrifying. In the grip of a red heat, she raises her palm to slap Davy, then Nate. And chops onions for borscht or practices a dance for the Obon festival. She wanders in a time-fever through the grassy hills. Inoculates chickens, picks orange poppies, runs from the sound of a man sobbing. Flinging herself beneath the apple tree, she becomes Shlima wailing, *Now, we'll never, ever, get home.*"

Shoshana is crying, holding her hands tight around the kernel of her own question. This, she understands finally, is what she's come out here to ask. "But where do I fit here?" Her voice is as raw as the wind when she shouts, "Where is my place?"

Mimi lifts the file folder from the center of her desktop and shuffles into the kitchen. It's 3:00 a.m. again, and what else is new? The voices have gotten her up. "So, tonight maybe you'll indulge in a cup of tea?" she asks her two visitors, a lean catlike man and the pioneer girl. "How about a game of double solitaire?" It's a silly request; she knows they'll laugh and refuse. What Mimi wants most, of course, the voices no longer seem willing to give her. All eight Guardians have never come again, bringing with them that wonderful moment with Abe.

Her guests settle into the chairs at the kitchen table and watch as Mimi opens a file folder, turning over the pictures of the apartment buildings she's collected. Each time she looks at them in the presence of the voices, Mimi feels as if she's come home. Not to where she's going to live herself, of course – this house is fine, thank you. But the apartments are some place even better – a monument she wants to build to Abe. If he had lived, this was the kind of spot they'd planned on for retirement. They'd saved for years so that all his hard work would culminate in something they could touch.

A place for nice people. Mimi imagines running her hands over the well-tended lawns or walking across the hard surface of the tennis courts. She can smell the chlorine from the Olympic-size pool. And then there will be the flower beds, filled with all the plants that Abe loved to grow in their garden. Pink roses will line the walkways, yellow pansies at their feet.

It'll be beautiful, Mimi thinks, a testament to who Abe was and all he gave her. She sniffles for a moment, flipping through the yellow sheets in the file, rereading all her notes. "But none of that now," she says out loud to the ghosts as if they were the ones crying. After twelve years, Mimi's done with mourning; this is for him, finally. She wants to give Abe something lovely, but sound and practical. Something that will make the family a little money, to give them ease. Davy and Mari, for instance, who are barely getting by on his teacher's salary. Mimi wants them to have something more, to fix up their run-down Berkeley house. And Nate – she says to hell with his job – retire early and build that cabin you dream about outside of Yellowstone. No more budgets – just fishing and long tramps with Carol. She wants him to read his cowboy books by the fire and to keep fit by chopping wood.

Everyone will benefit, if Mother will consent to give up some of the land she's bought with the money Abe left her. All right, so Mom is an ecology nut and might not like the idea of building on Chapman Lane, but she owes Abe, Mimi thinks, almost as much as I do. He made her old age comfortable. Papa wasn't a planner – he didn't leave her enough to sneeze. Abe came to the rescue. Working for her, for all of them, wore down his heart. Surely Mom will see reason. And after all the talking they've done in the past few months, Mimi is hungry to try a project with her mother. She smiles, imagining the two of them designing the complex together – a lot of talk, a little arguing, like the way it used to be around the dinner table – as they work to turn Chapman Lane into some place great. For Abe, for love, for the family. Mimi sips her tea and nods at the ghostly pioneer girl who watches her from the kitchen's shadows. They'll be doing it as a mother and daughter come together again, making peace.

Dear Shoshana,
    At first, I didn't want you to know any of the bad stuff about your grandpa. I thought you might be hurt by the truth. But if the Park Service has taught me anything, it's that a body always has a choice about what to do with

information. Keeping secrets - that's when the options disappear.

So little darlin, I want to remind you to keep choosing how you live, and what you take from this family. Now you know the things we've never wanted to talk about.

It's yours, free and clear.

Choose.

Uncle Nate

Shoshana chooses to look at the Guardian who has come to her in the woods as she's been crying. She wipes her eyes and stares into the bearded logger's face. Behind him is an older Indian man with a fishing spear and a young girl carrying a woodpecker basket. There's a boy in a World War II Navy uniform and an army nurse. They step quietly into her circle, careful not to disturb the pictures and letters. She hurries to stand up and face them, feeling almost afraid.

But the logger's smile, a warm burst, calms her. The young girl sets down her basket and cups her hands.

Here. She throws something to Shoshana, who automatically reaches out to catch it. She gasps as she sees it's Rheabie, there between her palms.

Or an image of her, like a photograph, as she stands and looks out the kitchen window. Shoshie is holding the whole house now, feeling it settle into her hands. Her fingers become the hills, a thatch of new grass and mustard flowers. Her legs take root in the gum grove and feel the weight of Davy's rock. A centipede scurrying between stalks of fava beans brushes across her chest. A gopher burrows between her ribs.

Your place? the logger asks — or maybe she's mouthing her own question. The only thing she can be certain of is that finally, it's begun to drizzle. Shoshie knows she has to hurry. There isn't much time left. Her voice flutters in her throat. "I have to go home."

Mimi smoothes the airline ticket that will take her West next month to surprise her mother on her birthday. She imagines the shouts, the hugs, the excitement that will fill the house. And Nate and Carol are thinking of joining her. "We'll turn it into a mini-reunion," Mimi keeps saying when she calls her brothers. She goes over their plans with whatever ghost shows up to keep her company at three in the morning. It's funny, but Padre Guitierrez, the polite priest, has become her favorite. Each time she shows him the blue-prints she's drawn up of the apartment building, he nods so seriously. She doesn't know why, but the look on his face always makes her laugh.

Shoshana speeds down the highway, singing one of Grandma's Russian melodies. Even though Rasputin yowls in his cage beside her, she only grins. "Soon," she promises him as the names of towns become familiar. "Just a little bit more, baby," she says, and sings the foreign words again. It's a song about coming home to stay but not feeling sure how that will make things different. It's about the need to hurry, to hurl down Highway 101 like a lightning strike, aiming for the difficult and the unknown. "So, I'll have a place at last," she thinks, as she shifts into second for the last hill before Petaluma, "but what does that mean?" She rolls down her window when the town's lights fill the valley. Cold air whirls through the cab of the truck, waking her up. She peers at the spread of homes, the shadows of the dark hills behind them. "It's so big," Shoshana thinks, comparing it to Lydon, "not like I remembered." Rasputin growls. Shoshie shakes her head, trying to feel the certainty that sent her south again, eager to live inside the magic with Grandma. "The Guardians told me to come," she reassures herself, holding that damp afternoon in the woods up like a beacon. The gray light that shone through the trees that day comes back clearly. So does the feel of holding Grandma and all of Chapman Lane between her fingers. But then it began to rain. "And I said it," Shoshie remembers. "I'm the one who decided." She puts her blinker on for Grandma's exit. "Holy shit. I hope this isn't a mistake."

Rheabie sits in the evening darkness, trying to push away the nightmare. Such *chutzpah* – coming over her any time now, not even waiting she should be asleep. Indecent – the way her breath gets short, and on her ribs she feels a rock, something hard, pressing. "*Gey avek!* Go away!" she shouts, while her heart races. It surges, the accelerator stuck, like Jake's old Ford.

And then there's the dread: a smell like the Terlitza *pogrom*, rising from her belly. A sour taste, something bitter at the edge of it, fills her mouth. She feels a finger tracing her spine, marking her arm with an icy touch. "So hello, Danger," she says, not needing Wina to name the feeling anymore. Rheabie greets the companion who's seen her through this hard winter. "With friends like you, an enemy I don't need."

You're your own enemy, Rheabie hears Shlima cry, *too stupid and blind to see what's in front of you.*

It's true. Rheabie leans forward, trying to find the hard lines of her sister's ghost in the dusky kitchen. The shadows hold nothing, just an empty sweep of wind.

It's time you should remember.

The small light over the stove, outlining the big pot of borsht she's made for Shoshie, shakes and wavers. Rheabie closes her eyes, trying to steady herself. *What, remember? Jake hitting the boys and how I didn't see it? All the suffering what lived in this house I didn't know?* Her fists clench. *Davy's drinking, maybe? The mean things Mimi said about me and Mae?* Rheabie sighs, or maybe the room does. *Remembering – it's all I do. Thinking over what happened, it doesn't make right.*

That's not the danger, Wina calls in a breathy whisper.

I know from Danger! Rheabie shouts. *By me, he's made a friend.*

You don't know anything, Shlima argues.

Yes, Rheabie agrees. She doesn't know what she's supposed to do with what happened between Jake and her boys, the dirty secret of her family. She doesn't know what Wina wants from her each night, hiding in a corner near her bed. Last fall, it seemed simple – Rheabie should tell Shoshie the real story of the ranch and the future would take of itself. But Shoshie left and discovered parts of the story Rheabie never knew. So now what happens? Rheabie's sight has gone blurry. The future – so fuzzy now. *Mamale, help me,* she calls to the empty room. *Oy,* so much she can't see.

Rheabie stands at the kitchen doorway and peers out into the darkness. The truth curls around her, so tight and grasping she can barely breathe. She's afraid – afraid that Mimi's been right all these years – maybe she's just plain crazy. Maybe all what she called magic – her spirits and the Guardians – never happened like she thought. There's nothing to tell Shoshie, no story to inherit. All her plans – they're not promised, not something Wina can make come to be. All Rheabie knows for sure is that the April night is cold, smothering the seeds in her garden. It wraps its fingers around them, withering the new sprouts. The touch reaches north, ruffling the hair of a young girl singing somewhere down the highway. Rheabie sighs. She knows, finally, that Shoshie can't fix any of this. *Vey iz mir,* her coming – it's only going to make things worse.

Part III
COMING TO TERMS

MARCH – SEPTEMBER 1981

Chapter 26
AN UNCERTAIN WELCOME

SHOSHANA

Why did I wait so long to move here, I wonder, as I place four bowls in the cupboard next to Grandma's set. My blue glass plates and her handmade stoneware make what anyone would call a match. They balance, like the small grater I unwrap and set beside her tall worn one on the second shelf in the utility cupboard. My medium-sized frying pan nestles in the pullout drawer beneath the oven, right between her big skillet and the small one we use for scrambled eggs.

"I fit!" I want to shout to Grandma across a mess of unpacked boxes and crumpled newspaper. The pleasure of seeing my things next to hers shakes the upper muscles in my arms. Or maybe it's the sight of our two favorite mugs on the counter, steam from the cups twining into the morning air. "Look," I start to point, but the puffy cast to Grandma's face makes me hesitate. Something's wrong in the way she sits quietly at the kitchen table, not talking and rubbing her plump hands.

I look at her closely. There's been something wrong since the moment I arrived the day before yesterday, receiving only a reserved hug and a bowl of soup while we made awkward conversation. I thought it was just the late hour and her tiredness, all the work of cooking and getting ready for me. But I have to admit I was disappointed. What happened to Grandma's usual buoyant and talky welcome? Maybe it would be back this morning, I thought yesterday as soon as I woke. But she spent the morning reading her Chekhov in the living room. She ignored me for most of the afternoon. I decided last night that if I hurried and unpacked, things might get back to normal. Surely she has stories to tell, important things I need to hear. But the tension in her face, a sharpening of the lines around her mouth, makes me doubtful.

"Are you sure my moving in is all right?" I ask, getting down off the stepladder. It's a silly question at this late date, because where would I go if Grandma didn't want me? The way I high-tailed it out of Lydon, just up and quitting on Josie and the landlord with no notice, I can't go back. But I guess I don't have to live here, if she really doesn't like it – no matter what I saw in the circle of Lydon Guardians. If I had to, I could find a place of my own.

I sit down at the table. "Grandma, tell me the truth." She looks up, frowning. "Having me here. Is it really okay?"

"Sure," she shrugs, and it makes me wonder if I've asked the right question.

"My own wolf girl, here to stay – exactly what I wanted all these years." Then she shakes her head, "But it feels a little funny, such a big wish I get all of a sudden. You're such a *macher* now. You think this small house, the two of us can hold?"

"It's still your house," I reassure her, but I don't think I've understood what she's really saying. Ever since that day in the woods when I decided to come, I've felt sure of things. All right, so I got a little cold feet when I got off the freeway, but that evaporated. Now I'm just confused.

"Not just my house anymore, dolly. Can't you see?"

What I see is a scared old woman, biting her bottom lip, her eyes full of questions. And the skin beneath them looks dark and a little flabby. Where is the storyteller the Indian girl tossed to me, the wise woman I held between my hands?

"You grew up into yourself over the winter," Grandma says now, worrying her index finger, "a woman to be proud of." She manages a smile, looking straight at me for the first time this morning. "Holding back you're not, anymore."

I'm so pleased that I cup my hand to her cheek. "So don't you hold back either," I insist and then try to imitate her. "I don't want you should make yourself small on account of me."

The words are a surprise, and so are the tears that fill Grandma's eyes after she hears them. "I thought having you here would take care of all the unfinished business, but maybe it doesn't," she sniffs as I hand her a Kleenex. "I hate it – getting so old I'm not sure about anything anymore." She makes a helpless movement with her shoulders. "Maybe I've just been *meshugge* all these years, like Mimi thinks – the Guardians a piece of my mind, made up. Crazy as Mas's patients. A sickness, maybe. Nothing magic in them at all."

The kitchen falls into a hush, as if the bowl of fruit next to the refrigerator and all the glasses in the cupboard are listening. "But Uncle Mas and I saw the Guardians too. How can you explain that?" I ask gently. I move my chair closer to her and rub her arm.

"You're *meshuggeneh* too, maybe," Grandma argues. She shakes my hand off. "They say it runs in families. Genetics. That's what I read."

"Grammy." I look at her sternly. "This is not about genetics and mental illness." It hurts, the way she only half-listens, shredding the tissue in her lap. "What, you think you gave the vision of Wina to me – as if she's catching? Maybe instead of being crazy, I have a Guardian flu?"

She doesn't laugh. I try again. "I haven't told you yet what happened when I saw the Lydon Guardians. That's why I'm here, because of the big meeting we had out in the woods. And I know they're real, but what's happened that you've turned doubtful?" My voice catches when I ask, "What did Mrs. Neilson do to you while I was gone?"

"Mrs. Neilson, *phui*," she says, pushing her chair back impatiently. "That nice woman couldn't affect a soul. This is not about her, but I don't know what exactly. Too tired and scared to think I am anymore."

"Scared of what?" I ask. She doesn't answer. "Tell me," I beg in my softest voice.

Grandma turns away and looks out the window. I twist to try to see what she's gazing at beyond the glass. Then she sighs and turns back, her voice trembling. There's an edge, almost like my mother's, in her sharp words. "So how come, now that you've come to your senses and are here finally, the Guardians have left me?" Her cheeks are red. "The minute you came, they disappeared. Wina and Molly, the Irish one – every night with me this winter – and now nothing. If the Guardians are so real, how come you can't tell they're missing? Even the air in this house, it's different. Waiting for them, I am. Lost. Like in a nightmare. And they're just gone."

The kitchen fills with a dampness that has nothing to do with the March weather. The cold fingers of a shadow reach for my leg. And a breeze, which seems to have come south from Siberia or maybe Terlitza, hurries through the cracks in the windowsill. Grandma pulls her sweater close and shivers. "See?"

I do, and so I stand up and open every single cupboard. "Look!" – at the stacks of different plates, the two types of glasses, the bigger row of spices. I yank each drawer wide, revealing the piles of utensils and dish towels neatly lined up inside. "And this too," I promise, as I empty what's left of my boxes out on the floor. "It all belongs here," I declare, standing in the middle of the mess as she shakes her head, "like you and me together." I make my way over to Grandma's chair and crouch at her feet. "Who cares if the Guardians are gone? We'll either find them again or go on without them." I take her hand. "Don't you get it? Whatever happens next, you are not alone."

Chapter 27
CONFUSIONS

RHEABIE

But I am alone, *bubee,* no matter from what kind of sweetness you want to tell me different. This *farshtinkener* road I'm walking now, you can't come. And I wouldn't want you should. So foggy and dark the air, even though I'm sorry to say, I know where I'm going. The final destination I'm not afraid, but it's the getting there what gives me chills.

Of course I'm dying. Where are your eyes? You can't tell from looking? I thought you were a girl once what knew from smarts. No, we're not talking a disease or something for Dr. Kendall. My problem? Too much living. It's just time.

How do I know? The *chutzpah,* such a question! What's the matter? You don't trust your grandma anymore? I know because when I wake up in the morning, I feel it. Some kind of cold touch, a danger, what lives in my bones. And it has the nerve to talk: "Listen up, a big change is coming." I pull the covers over my shoulders. Still it whispers, "Enjoy what's left. There's nothing you have to do anymore."

After your grandpop died, I thought I'd be glad to hear that kind of news – I could rest, already. Be done with staying busy. Free to live easy at last. But instead, my hands close up – holding tight to the sheets. Even watching you, with tears in your eyes right now, Shoshie, can't make my fingers stretch. I'm like Mae, that day on the hill when I told about the Terlitza *pogrom.* You're Mas, trying to open up my fist.

Ach! I don't understand why I'm living my whole life over again – circling back around when it's time I should grow knowing. But worse! I keep trading places with people in the old stories, becoming someone else. Some days I get out of bed, scared as Shlima about what might happen. Other times, in a fury like Jake I am, raging about the price of eggs. I should know better than to act like him after all these years! *Oy,* how it galls me. The things I hated most in them, I've become.

And I get confused – the way their eyes look out of mine at the kitchen. *Get in here and make my tea!* Jake demands. *Trouble. We got trouble coming,* Shlima predicts. *Such a mess it'll be when Mimi comes.*

Don't look so shocked. Of course she's coming. For my birthday. A big party. A surprise. What? She didn't tell you the plans? How come I know? Because from me, when could your mother ever keep a secret? In her voice

I heard it, what she doesn't say. But don't worry. I'll pretend when the time comes – a shock, a faint – she'll get her pleasure.

But about Mimi I wasn't talking, right? Wrong? Now I'm lost again. Can't tell what's what. Getting so confused in the mornings. You here. Putting your stuff everywhere. Nothing can be found. I get lost.

And then I cry because Mae's gone, a long time now, but my hands still hurt from missing. Mamale, Shlima, Gitl, Jake – pretend different I try, but they're gone too. All what I've got left is a voice in my bones saying, "Hurry up. Your life's almost over." I'm not ready yet, I tell it, but then I don't know. Everything's upside down; the world's going backwards. Did I tell you that Mas, he called last night? This morning? Two days ago, already? *Oy*, nothing makes sense.

I don't like how you're looking at me. Stop. Quit staring. Such a big *macher*, suddenly you're in charge of my life? Just because I wanted you here doesn't mean you should boss me. Don't put your books on my shelf. You take those pictures down.

I'm wise to you, Shoshie, you and your bad business. You're not going to take over here and then kick me out. Wanting my place at the Ecology Center. Or maybe my money. An easy life – living off what I've earned. You can't fool me, you and your tears. Phui! I'm on to you.

Am I all right? In the pink of health – except for you and for dying. My ankles? Of course they're thick. Years I've lived with these fat feet. You haven't noticed maybe because you're too full of yourself – putting your things all over. Such a mess you've made, pushing me away.

Don't look at me like that. The rain's coming. Can't you hear it? Thunder we got. It's going to roar. Get the chairs inside. A picnic I left out in the garden. Stop staring. I need you should get the plates. A danger, I'm talking. They're getting wet in the rain.

Shoshie, what are you doing? Get that coat away from me. Stop it, already, you with your hands. The car? I don't want the car. I want you should clean up the garden. It's raining. Mae's in the barn.

Do you see her? Mae. Shiny, shiny like tin foil. Over there. My Maisie, bright like sun on snow. She's coming. She's going to take me. Let me go. I have to get up to the barn.

Stop shoving. I can't breathe. Such a weight on my chest. I want Mae, her with the hands.

Stop the car. This minute. Turn around, I said. I need we should go back. To the danger. To Mae. The rest of the family. The barn, Shoshie. I want my Maisie. Poor Maisie. So much rain.

Chapter 28
HOSPITAL MOMENTS

SHOSHANA

"Kidney failure," Dr. Kendall says, looking at me over his glasses in the hospital hallway. "Her potassium level is really high. We're going to try to control it with a diuretic to see if she can let go of all those fluids – that's what the puffiness is from. But if she hasn't improved by tomorrow, we'll have to try dialysis." He motions toward Grandma's room. "You did good – bringing her in before anything too terrible happened. Guess you read those pamphlets I gave you and were smart enough to notice the swelling in her ankles. Listen, she'll be okay."

"But what about not breathing?" I ask.

He shakes his head. "A panic attack, nothing more. I guess she was really scared."

I feel my hands for the first time that morning, still twisting the handles of Grandma's navy-blue purse in my fingers. The bag, full of lipstick and Kleenex and cough drops, bangs against my knee. Her brown wallet has one ten, two fives and three singles in it. "Count what's there and hold on tight," Grandma begged as the nurse was wheeling her away for tests. "Don't let the pullet buyer steal anything from me."

"She's so mixed-up and angry," I say. "Confused about where she is and furious with who's around her."

"Uremic poisoning," Dr. Kendall gives it a name. "The kidneys aren't filtering as they should, so all the toxins are in her bloodstream. That'll take a while to go away." He looks at me closely. "Guess she scared you too, huh champ?" Dr. Kendall pats my shoulder. "Don't worry. The worst is over. She'll stop her yelling, and now that we know what's causing it, we can get it under control."

Nothing feels controlled. The voice on the hospital intercom is wild and fuzzy. The lines in the mottled linoleum wiggle around my feet. I try to stand more firmly on what feels like a moving floor as he explains the dialysis. "If the Lasix doesn't work and she has to go that route, it will be three times a week," the doctor nods, "and no missing, because her life will depend on it. If you need, we have a service that can ferry her back and forth."

I don't know what I need right now except for Grandma to come back to herself, to know where she is and who she's talking to. I want the rock she keeps telling me is pressing on her chest to go away. All that is just a panic attack? Nothing Doctor Kendall is saying makes any sense to me.

"But why?" I ask finally, peering down the hallway into an approaching gaggle of people. "What caused this to happen now?"

He looks concerned. "That damn high blood pressure," he explains, "along with her angina. I bet she quit taking her pills the minute you left. Of course, what we're seeing now is years of neglect, all that lying she did about her medication. The long-term hypertension led to the angina. She didn't mention it to me until a few months ago."

I know I look blank, and he translates the medical words. "Angina is a heart condition, sort of like a cramp or charley horse. The heart doesn't get enough blood, so the muscle seizes up. We tried to control it with medication, which she probably didn't take either. It's a sign that the heart is beginning to fail."

I clutch her bag against my belly. Doctor Kendall sighs. "God love her, your grandma never took her hypertension seriously. It has three choices of where to show up: the beans," he points to his kidneys, "the heart or the head. Lucky for you, we're not talking a stroke here. But the bottom line, toots, is that she's just too old, and that's the real problem. Her parts are wearing down."

"And she knows," I want to tell him. "She hears that voice in her bones talking." Instead, my eyes fill with tears, and I can't say a word.

"The Lasix may be the ticket." The doctor pats me again. "We're probably not talking years here, but she has time."

That's what Uncle Mas says too when I call him, sobbing, gulping my words from the pay phone in the hospital lobby. Grandma is settled in her room, finally asleep. I stroked her white hair, then made myself run downstairs to the phones, leaving her to the nurses. *Please,* I asked the Guardians, *make sure she'll still be here when I get back.*

"She's got time," my uncle reassures me, his voice cutting through my stutters. "Shoshie, listen to me. This isn't it."

"You're sure?" I run my hand over the rumpled edge of Grandma's little phone book. There are so many names written in pencil here on the "T" page.

The first Tanaka listed turns his voice into something close to a smile. "You forget," Uncle Mas jokes, "we have inside information. From *Jikan Fujin.*" Then he sounds serious again. "Have you seen Mamale, Shlima or Gitl flying around her?"

"I've never met them," I sputter. "Only through her stories. I have no idea what they look like."

Uncle Mas laughs. "If they were there, you'd know. Such steamrollers, those three. They know how to make a noise. Besides, they'd want to meet.

Would make it a point. And I promise you – until they come, don't worry. Rheabie's not going to leave you yet."

I close my eyes, holding tight to each word.

Uncle Mas listens to me breathe. "I don't have any clients tomorrow. Rob and I will drive up as soon as I'm done tonight. You can expect us between nine and ten."

"The *Jikan* person won't pull you away?" I ask in a small voice. I feel six years old, holding my daddy's hand as I walk down a San Francisco hill to some fancy party. The sidewalk is so steep and I'm so scared that I grab at him, slipping and almost falling in my patent leather shoes.

"Make sure *Jikan Fujin* doesn't pull at you," Uncle Mas says, chuckling. "And eat something. You'll need some kind of sustenance to get through the day."

I put down the receiver and hurry back to Grandma's room in case something bad has happened. I begin to believe Uncle Mas when I find that she's asleep, curled away from the noisy hallway with her face to the wall. I can only see her back with the three moles lined up like Orion's belt just below her shoulder. I leave the door open just a crack and tiptoe toward her. "Are you cold, Grammy?" I whisper, pulling the blankets up.

"No," she startles me by answering. "Not even for you can I make this right." She shifts away from my hand, pulling at the edge of the sheet with an angry gesture. "What kind of animal would do such things to his own *kinder*? An ape, hitting his chest in the jungle. But those big males, they don't hurt the babies. Even they know better than you."

"Grandma." I move to the foot of the bed to make sure that she can see me. Very gently, I reach under the covers and begin to rub her cold feet. She shakes her head, "Jake? Where are you going?" She lifts up slightly to look around the room, empty of ghosts and nurses. "Such a coward. I got plenty more to say. Of course, you'd leave."

I press into the arch of her right foot with my palm. "Maybe he'll be back. He's probably waiting for you to get better."

She frowns. "Not that stinker. Too sad, he is. Hiding, all those years, his hitting. Now he's sorry. He got caught." Grandma sighs as I concentrate on working each toe in her foot, then pressing the tender skin between them. She leans back, closes her eyes. "What am I going to do, Maisie? Davy, poor Davy. And big brave Nate."

"I'm Shoshana," I want to remind her, but for the first time today Grandma is smiling. I can't take away whatever pleasure she finds in this nasty room.

Then she returns to herself and struggles to sit up, frowning at the blood pressure machine clicking beside her. "Shoshie?" she asks, pointing to the red numbers which change every minute or two.

"Your kidneys are sick, Grandma," I explain, sitting next to her bed. "They went on strike and refused to work."

"For a better contract?" she smiles, and I know that for the moment she is with me. "What, more wages they needed? More time off?"

I take her hand. "They're giving you pills to make it better. If that doesn't work, they'll try dialysis."

"No dialysis!" she insists. "They stick you with a needle. Did I tell you Moysche had it? Married he was, to the machine. Poor Luba, tied like a cow to his comings and goings. She just followed, pulling at the rope. My work I've got. Ecology Center. Sierra Club. Dialysis I can't do!"

"We'll see what the doctor says." I try to calm her down. Grandma ignores me.

"I need to go the bathroom," she declares, clutching my wrist with strong fingers. "Now."

"Good," I tell her, even when she doesn't quite make it to the toilet. "That's my fault," I assure her, as she stares at the urine dripping down her leg. I kneel at her feet, wiping the floor with a towel, trying to explain that I took too long unhooking the blood pressure cuff. "The nurses wanted to give you a catheter, but you said no. Do you remember?"

She ignores me as she sits on the toilet. "*Oy*, so much I'm going. What's all this?"

"Just what Dr. Kendall wants," I say, helping her back to the bed. "You need to get it out of you."

"I have to go again," she cries after ten minutes and we try the bedpan this time. I'm clumsy, pinching her skin as I jam it under her legs. "Sorry, Grandma," I apologize over and over.

She wipes herself angrily. "What do you got to be sorry for? You're not the one making the stink."

By the time I've cleaned everything up, flushed and rinsed and wiped, she has closed her eyes and is dozing. As I tiptoe past her to the door to ask a nurse where I should put the dirty towels, she grabs at me. "Mimi," she begs in a trembling voice. "Don't leave."

My hands are full of urine-soaked cloth. "I'll be right back, Grandma."

"No," she protests. "You always leave."

So I don't, letting the nurses discover our mess when they come to give her more medication. We spend the afternoon in a rhythm: bedpan, clean up, sleep. Sometimes she knows where she is and that I am with her. Others, *Jikan Fujin* has snatched her up, and I become my mother or uncles, Aunt Kiyo or Mae. Then, just before dinner, she snorts awake and is back with me. She looks around her little cubicle. "I hate this place," she declares.

"It's not great," I agree. "A little lacking in the aesthetics."

"My mind is going," Grandma folds her arms. "Too confused I am here." She sits up. "Let's go. You take me home."

"The second they let me," I promise, lifting the plastic cover off of her dinner tray. A sad piece of meat loaf and a ball of mashed potatoes sit next to some overcooked string beans. Grandma takes one look. "What *dreck. Gey,* already. Let's get out of here. Out of my mind it's making me."

I shift in my chair. "Doctor Kendall said they'll need a couple of days to get your kidneys back in business." I explain again about the dialysis.

"I don't care," she interrupts, glaring at me. "I want I should go home."

"I can't do it," I reply to each of her requests, which get louder and louder. "Not yet. Only when you're ready. Grandma, please," I beg when the Yiddish curses begin.

"I thought you loved me," she shouts.

I begin to cry. "Not enough to kill you – which is what going home would mean." We are quiet after my words, smelling the meat loaf and listening to the sounds of the hospital parking lot. After a door slams and a car starts, I grab a Kleenex and find the courage to ask, "Is that what you really want – to die now?"

Rheabie's body goes still, and I know I shouldn't have asked that question. I'm talking as if she's the woman I expected to meet when I returned to Chapman Lane. I wipe my eyes. I miss my nudging grandma, the storyteller and comrade in magic. "I need you to come back to yourself and the house. I want much more time together." She looks puzzled. "Don't ask me to break the doctor's orders," I continue. "Things are bad enough. Do you want to rush this whole thing?"

"I don't want any of it, Mae," she declares, looking more afraid than I have ever seen her. "So tight my chest. Hard to breathe."

I push aside her dinner plate and climb into her bed. Grandma Rheabie's mouth is a surprised circle, an "o" as I insist that she scoot over so I can lie down on top of the covers. She trembles as I gather her up, careful not to tangle the line from the blood pressure cuff. "I need you, Grandma," I whisper over the top of her head as she settles against me.

When she falls asleep, I feel the weight of her body pressing into my hips and pulling at my shoulders. Is this the kind of stretching, I wonder, that I've traveled all this way to do? It's not fair, I want to shout at the hospital ceiling. There's so much I need to learn from her. I can't do this on my own.

Yes, you can, I hear a leafy voice say, and I turn to see Wina glimmering in the corner. She puts a finger to her lips, *Hush,* and smiles at Grandma with a shady love.

Where have you been? I want to ask. *Why did you desert her? She's been wanting you so badly, so why are you showing up now when she's asleep?*

But my questions and the noise of the hospital, the garbled voices from the nurses' station and the beeping machines, retreat while I watch her. Wina's calm and knowing look drives them away. I let myself rest in the breeze she creates that swirls leaves through the closed window. The creaking branches lift me out of the building and bring me to the eucalyptus grove at the ranch. We are lying on a blanket beneath the trees, watching the evening shadows. Though I can't see them, I know all eight of the Guardians are there.

Make her well, I ask, tears pricking at me again, and I hold Grandma tighter.

Try another question, Molly requests in her Irish lilt.

Help us make good use of the time we have left, I beg, turning from the trees to watch her blood pressure machine flash another set of numbers. This is the lowest they've been all day.

"There you go," Molly soothes or maybe it's the older nurse, Marge, who's just pushed the door open, a paper cup with two green pills in her hand. "We have more meds, and it's time to check vitals," she says cheerily as I wake Grandma. "Did we have a nice nap?" Marge asks while I slide slowly off the bed.

"Now you're set," she declares a few minutes later, after writing down temperature and blood pressure. "You're just fine, but you need to rest now. Doctor Kendall will be in shortly to check on you." She pats the chart. "Now just take it easy, Mrs. Slominski. You've had a big day."

Grandma purses her lips, as if she's actually understood Marge and the words are making sense. "What does she think," Grandma asks, the minute the door closes, "I'm going to get up and dance?" I smile at how clear her eyes have become; the Lasix must be working. Grandma shakes her head. "Such a phony baloney, that girl. A bedside manner she hasn't got."

"So you're a connoisseur now?" I tease. "After all your experiences, you know what's what?"

I'm relieved to get a smile, instead of anger. "Years ago, I learned about it," Grandma says proudly, sounding more and more like her old self. She picks at her cold meat loaf. "From a professional I learned." She wrinkles her nose at the beans. "Did I ever tell you Mae was a nurse?"

"You haven't told me half enough, and I'm waiting." I feel the eucalyptus grove, the quiet that the Guardians gave us. I put a little of its peace into my next words. "Grandma, I'm counting on your kidneys getting better, so I can hear all the stories. I won't let you go until you've told me every single bit."

Grandma watches my face, then squeezes my anxious fingers. "I like who you've become, Mimala," she states. "A good girl grown better. And I never thought it possible, but more patience than me, you've got."

"Grandma," I begin, but I don't have words, only tears to show her. A rush of wings whirls around my head. Guardians, I think. Maybe Padre Guitierrez and his breezes. Then I realize: no, it's Mom. Even though I haven't called her yet, she's here with us in the room.

"What's going on?" Dr. Kendall asks, throwing the door open.

"Such an interrupter." Grandma raises her fork, a canned peach in its prongs. "So tell me, Mr. Pill Pusher. Is this the best your place can do by dessert?"

Chapter 29
Days of Mae

RHEABIE

I want you should understand Mae, Shoshie. Such a nurse she was, with hands what could cool a fever. A voice demanding you should get well. So calm, that time Mas tried to send my ghosts back. Him and his pneumonia, such a scare. Dr. Smith told Kiyo and Matsu – died, he would have, if she hadn't been there.

Mae, so long ago, teaching me from sickness. Not like these nurses, so bright and cheerful. "Are we hungry yet? How are we feeling this morning?" What's the matter, they don't know from the word "you"? All the poking, the pills. So many interruptions. And did you hear? Dialysis today, they wanted me to do.

I told them – no. Such words Doctor Kendall and I had about it. Threw me into a wheelchair, he did. Took me off.

To the needles. In a cold room. All alone. No Mae. No Mamale. Just nurses. Voices too sharp and loud.

Where were you? Why didn't you stop it? Such a lazy girl. Sleeping in while I'm sick. I'm telling you, I needed Mimi should make a big stink for me. A fight. Loud and yelling. Why hasn't she come?

And where's Mae, her with the hands what could make me feel better? What she could do – I'm telling you, I never felt anything the like. I know, I know. I haven't told you yet, how it was between us. So hard, so sick now, so *farpotshket*. But oy Shoshie, did we make some kind of heat!

What started out innocent, that touching – just comrades being together. The love, we didn't mean it should grow. But it did – born from a hard winter. Such a feeling, it was a ghost come back from all what died between Jake and me.

Your grandpa always claimed it was the Depression what drove the wedge between us. Nineteen thirty-one it started, the pinch of the crash. In the twenties, egg prices always rose and fell. Ranching, it's not an easy way to make a living. But that year – down to eighteen cents a dozen – life was a squeeze. Jake growled the entire winter, always yelling. So worried about money, your grandpa couldn't sleep.

To the barn, he went. Tossing and turning the mortgage. A blanket in an empty stall – this he used when, finally, he could shut his eyes. Each time I asked he should come back to our bed, he growled. "Not now! Can't you see I'm busy?" All the fire gone between us. In my chest – like how I felt this winter – such an ache.

Enough already, Mamale said. *This is what happens in marriage. A man, he's hungry at first. Then – and you never know when – he's done.*

But I'm not done, I told her, making our lonely bed in the morning. *This kind of farfufket marriage, it's not right by me.*

Don't fret. Gitl patted my shoulder. *Jake's just worried. The price of eggs picks up, and he'll be back.*

So all right, worried, Jake was – but the man I saw in the morning looked the spitting image of his father. The Terlitza rabbi. Such a holy *shmuck,* that hypocrite, him with a heavy hand on his sons. Jake told me stories about his growing up: beatings, black and blue, a whirlwind of shouting. He wanted I should understand why he ran away so young and never went back.

Like my poor Davy and Nate, suffering from their father, who suffered from his father too. A whole line of boys we got, Shoshie, bruised from hitting. Who knows how far it goes back? Phui – I spit on all those men – who could have done different. Each one – like his father – he didn't have to become. On them all I throw a thousand curses. And then – this secret business – Jake made it ten times worse. Unfair? You think I'm being unfair? *Oy,* Shoshie. Look in your Uncle Davy's eyes and tell me I'm wrong.

Ach, but I've gotten confused again. So much I hurt. From the story. From the dialysis. So many pain pills. My nightmare. Who knows what's what anymore? But trying to follow Mae, I am, a string through the gum grove. One bright thread, from her house to mine. But so tangled, every time I think of Jake and what happened between us. I can't separate it out. So mixed up.

Ai, yai yai. It presses on me, how I don't want to see my part.

Me, the wife, what ran from home, over to Mae's house. Any kind of excuse to be with her – I was gone. Sewing a birthday dress for Mimi, maybe. Ordering seeds for the garden. The Yiddish chorus, she got me to join. And like always, our ranches kept working together. Cleaning the brooder houses, inoculating the pullets. Such a good comrade, she made even the stink fun. I laughed, making jokes. Jake worked beside us, angry. Art watched closely, pushing his glasses up on his nose.

I didn't want to know what made me fluttery each time I saw her. Birds, I'm talking, a rush of air in the chest. Even the warnings Mamale gave, *What are you doing, Rheabie? Why are you blushing?* I ignored. Too much worry. Such a grab I made for that warm feeling, me with my empty hands.

Foolish! Silly! I should've listened to my mother. Even Gitl tried to tell me: *Watch out for Jake.* But I didn't look, and missed the first time he raised his hand to Davy. Ach, it's killing me now. I was there but didn't see.

The fire in the egg shed, you remember? In March. Late in the afternoon. At Mae's I was, helping her make the garden. Dizzy from how she looked, spading the beds. So strong. So beautiful. What I wouldn't give to be the shovel in her hands. Getting dark, it was, but still we kept working. To separate we couldn't bear.

Then, I sniffed. Smoke! I looked – a dark smudge. From our barn it was coming. Such a scream I gave. And then ran.

But by the time I got there, no flames. Only hissing. The barn – full of smoke and yells.

Davy drew it right – a mess, the lines of Grandpa's anger. Even from outside, his screams I could hear. Red-faced Jake was, his overalls wet, holding an empty bucket. At your uncle he roared and wouldn't stop. And where was Davy? Hiding under the candling table. Was he burnt? Had the fire hurt him? So dark and cloudy that room. "Fool! Idiot!" Jake yelled.

Down to the ground I went, to hold my Davy. In my arms I took him, so sobbing and wet. Jake cursed. "You should burn like the barn. You should suffer like the egg shed. Hours I sacrifice for you, and this is what I get?" Then his face turned white, and he threw the bucket at us. "Get up. Out of there!"

Never before had I seen your grandpa this angry. Something sharp and mean took over his face. Past the spanking temper Jake had gone, the yelling we'd grown used to. Bad enough that was, but this, dolly, it was something new. Slowly, he raised his hand, looking right at me. "Your fault. If you'd been home this afternoon." His eyes, Shoshie. "Every day you leave us. For Mae. That god damned Mae." His arm moved. I knew I was going to be hit.

But nothing happened. Because Mae came. Throwing her weight on your grandpa's arm, holding him back from punching. There was steel, what couldn't bend, in her voice. "That's enough."

"Get out of here!" Jake screamed, trying to shake her off. "This is my house."

"Stop." She held tight. Not afraid. Not flinching.

"Where do you get off?" Jake sputtered. "You don't have nothing to say about this."

"But I do," I said, calm all of a sudden. Such courage I felt, holding Davy to me. I faced Jake. "Enough is enough."

Big I was. Protected. Because Mae was there. We were safe. So out I crawled from under the table, pulling Davy with me. "Let me look at you, *bubee*. Are you all right?"

Then I noticed a mark, and I turned toward Jake. "You with your big mouth, all that yelling. Look how he hurt his ear, trying to get away from you!" *Oy*, so stupid of me! So blind. I thought – poor Davy, banging into the table. His cheek – red from pressing into the ground. Not bruised from what I know now – Jake's fist, the first hitting. Right before my eyes it was, and I didn't see. "What kind of father are you," I yelled at Jake, "making such fear in your own *kinder*? Ready you were to hit the both of us. Be ashamed!"

"He set this place on fire," your grandpa roared again, "leaving his candle. Stupid. Careless. How many times have I told him? Never, never leave it alone."

Davy shook from fear, and I stroked his head, trying to calm him. Mae stood quietly, watching me with proud eyes. Jake yelled on, but him I didn't pay attention. Instead, I looked at her. So warm, her face. So comforting. The only place, that minute, I wanted to be.

"*Sha!*" I stopped Jake finally. The barn got quiet. I looked one last time at Mae, then drew a breath. "If you ever lay a hand on any of us," I vowed to your grandpa, "this family is over. Just one touch – I take the *kinder* and leave. We won't come back – not once, not ever. Gone we are, you do any such thing."

But *ai*, the damage was done. Poor Davy had already had his smacking. All my brave words, they were too late. But here's worse. Because of what I said, Davy never opened up his mouth to tell me. Poor boy. If he did, our family it would break up. Such a fool, I was. A bad mother. Full of herself and her love.

Of course I fussed over Davy's hurt. Rushed him back to the house, so he should feel better. I cuddled and fed my boy, then put his upset bones to bed. But all the while, thinking about Mae. What would happen when next we should be alone to talk the business over? I trembled, looking forward to having her to myself.

And not another word Jake said about what happened. How could he admit the hitting when he knew how eager I was to pack? Ach, I felt proud that day: for once, I'd stood up to the man's temper. Nothing more would happen, because I was watching out. But can't you see, dolly, how I helped with the lying? Who could tell the truth now, with me ready to pull the family apart?

"Make sure you don't start using your hands like your father," I spat at Jake when I left the barn that day. Maybe he'd stay out there tonight. Happy I'd feel, for once, to be in our bed alone.

With thoughts of Mae, a bright and fluttery feeling. With shock and shivers from when I walked her home later and *oy*, she leaned over to give me a kiss.

Where? On the path, at night, when no one could see us.

What time? Late, I don't know. After the *kinder* were in bed.

And my spirits? Right there they were, feeling like usual everything what happened in my body. Maybe they squawked, I don't know. Hung from the sky I was, looking down on the two of us and watching. I was both in my skin and outside at the very same time.

And then I broke away, like a shy girl, and ran for home, too moved to say anything. A hand I kept pressed against the glow what burned in my chest.

The next morning, I saw the *kinder* off to school, then collected eggs like usual. Only short words between Jake and me, before he left for town. And we went on like that, as people do, because how could we live any different? Between Mae and me the loving grew, short breaths snatched from the rest of our busy lives. For six years, I had her, to love like that, on one hand, a great brightness. On the other, there was Jake, his sullen moods and yells. *Farpotshket,* like I said, and no separating. His hitting the boys and the kissing, all mixed up.

I miss my Maisie, her what turned my whole world over. All these years without her and still, I'm never used to it. So alone I feel.

So now, it's just you and me, Shoshie, the two of us. Together.

Who's coming later to visit me, you said? Mas? Good. Maybe he'll tell me one of his stories.

He and Rob are staying at the house, yes? So *nu*, why aren't they here yet? Ach yes, right you said so. They're coming later. Shoshie, you don't need to get so impatient with me.

Such a little boy Mas is. Only eight. Smart beyond his age.

Yes, I'm tired. Yes, confused. I can't remember. Did I tell you? Dialysis like Moyshe they made me do. This morning? Last night? I'm not sure when it happened. The needle, it hurt. Look, the bandages. Too tight they wrapped it. A good nurse I wish I had, like Mae.

Her with the voice, so calm and cheerful. So much love she has, in those eyes. Mae, where is she? Now I need her. Go get her, Shoshie. Up at the barn. I want Mae, she should bring me home and make me better. Out of here, I need. There's a danger. You'll get Maisie, please?

Chapter 30
VISITING HOURS

SHOSHANA

On the way home from the hospital, Uncle Mas makes a surprise left turn onto a side street from Western Avenue. "Where are you going?" I ask, not recognizing the name. I don't want to be taking any detour. Can't he see how I'm tired from a long day of listening to Grandma wander? After her story about the fire in the barn this morning, *Jikan Fujin* came and got her, and she stopped making much sense.

"It'll get better," Dr. Kendall promised when he visited. "Be patient. Let that dialysis do its work." He patted my tense shoulder. "At least you got a story out of her today. Be proud."

But I'm not proud. I'm hungry. And cranky. I long for quiet and the gourmet meal that Rob has spent the day cooking for us at home. Why is Uncle Mas pulling off like this, parking under a group of twisted sycamore trees? They line what seems to be a hidden little park, perched on a grassy slope above these cracked sidewalks.

"Come on." He walks quickly up a series of stone steps.

"Wait a minute!" I follow him, trying hard not to show my impatience. When I get to his side, I realize that we're not standing in any park. It's an old cemetery, full of plastic flowers and leaning headstones. What are we doing here?

Uncle Mas strides down a path and then stops in front of a neglected grave. He crouches, bending to pull weeds. "Rheabie never let it get this raggedy before," he says, clearing a spot at the base of the headstone. "Poor thing," he mutters. "It must have been too much for her to come."

The weeds are tall, so it takes me a moment to make out the name on the headstone. *Mae Cherney Katz.* "Oh, no!" I draw a surprised breath at the dates. *1892-1937.* "Back then? But I always thought…"

And then I'm not certain how I have explained Mae's absence to myself. All this time of listening to stories about her and where have I been imagining that she is? Dead perhaps, but in the last twenty years, like Grandpa. Or somewhere far away, like New York or Philadelphia, because maybe she and Rheabie had one of their big fights. I ignored all the clues – the fact that Rheabie doesn't have any modern pictures of her. Or how when Mom reminisces about Thanksgiving dinners before we moved to Ithaca, meals that were peopled with friends from Petaluma, she never mentions Mae's name.

I sit hard on the ground. But Art was there, I realize now – smoking cigars and hurting the fingers of all the kids with his tight handshakes. Even though it was impolite, Viva and I tried to run away whenever he came near. Mom said we should feel sorry for him because his wife died, but he pinched too hard when he squeezed our cheeks. Art – grown old and wrinkled behind thick bifocals, still holding tight to flesh. I smile at the thought of him, the free-thinking womanizer, who in his old age, reduced little girls to giggles. We meowed behind his back, playing with his last name, then ran away when he turned around. But how could I have not realized that Mr. Katz, the Cat man, was the same Art who belonged with Mae?

Uncle Mas sighs. "I had to come by and see if any part of her was still here. Rheabie needs more than I can give her right now. Something's going on that I don't understand. That nightmare she keeps talking. The panic attacks and danger. I thought maybe if Mae…"

Then Uncle Mas shakes his head, tugging on a periwinkle plant. "You'd think I'd have learned after all these years. Always wanting to rescue the Slominski women. Give them the impossible. I was just being silly. Of course Mae's gone."

How? I want to shout. What happened? And then I'm struck by the edge in Uncle Mas's voice and how his face has grown cloudy. If I close my eyes, I know that I'll see him, a little boy standing in the rain pitching his latest plan to the Guardians. He's still trying to make up for his failure to send Shlima, Gitl and Mamale home.

Tears crowd into my throat. The aloof Uncle Mas I've always known has melted into the vulnerable boy of Grandma's stories. For the first time, I feel all of who he is. And I like him – this crazy psychologist who reads thoughts and rambles through time. "Listen, if you'd saved those Slominski women, I'd be in big trouble."

The graveyard goes suddenly quiet, bird cries and rustling trees melting into silence. Uncle Mas lifts his head, waiting for me to continue.

"You wouldn't be here," I explain, feeling as if even the air is listening. The Guardians seem very near. But I don't know what they want of us or why my words matter. I push past the sense of them to get to the truth. "I couldn't deal with Grandma and all that's happening right now on my own."

"Yes, you could," Uncle Mas disagrees, but the shadows have faded from his face. I hear a redwing blackbird call. "Shoshie, you're much stronger than you think."

"No. You don't get it." If the Guardians were here, they've now retreated. I feel a breath of wind on my face. "I'm trying to tell you that I'm glad you're around."

"I know." Uncle Mas smiles. "I'm telling you something important too."

I look at Mae's tombstone, the carved words that catch the last of the day's light. *She fought to build a better world.* "So, are you going to tell me how Mae died?"

Uncle Mas shakes his head. "That's for Rheabie to do. All her life she's been wanting you to know. I won't take that pleasure from her. Wait until she gets home. Once she gets started, she won't be able to stop."

Grandma is so much better two days later, after her second dialysis, that I have hopes of Doctor Kendall releasing her. Rob, Uncle Mas and I wait for his midday visit on a windy Sunday afternoon. "Too brisk for golf," Rob declares. "He'll be here soon." Today's nurse, Colleen, smiles at the mild joke as she squeezes past us to check Grandma's vitals. She never scolds, like Bobbie did yesterday, about how much we've crowded the room. Maybe the ease is because of Rob, who we've coaxed into staying with us instead of going back to the house to cook. Maybe it's his homemade chocolate chip cookies, which he offers to anyone who walks through the door.

Grandma beams at his attention, his corny jokes, the quiet way he rubs cream into her arm after Colleen gives her an injection. A big man with steady hands, he makes our little bit of the hospital feel safe. And he keeps Grandma in the present, instead of worrying about the times with Mae. "Robbie, look at what Mimi sent." Grandma points to the big bouquet that sits on the tray table beside her. "Maybe you want you should see the card what she wrote?"

For the fourth time that day, he opens the little envelope that came with the flowers. "Get well soon, Mom," he reads out loud slowly. "I'm so lucky to have a mother like you."

Rheabie's cheeks flush. "From Mimi we're talking here. The one I couldn't do right by." She smiles, playing with the ID band that hangs loosely around her wrist. "Such a surprise, that girl. Read it again."

But Rob doesn't get a chance, because the door to the room swings open. We turn, hoping for Dr. Kendall but see Uncle Davy's tense face instead.

This is the first time he's seen Grandma since November, I realize, since he quit drinking and told about the beatings. He wouldn't visit, I remember her writing, "He just can't – well anyway, not yet." His hunched shoulder and stiff jaw show me just how much it's cost him to come back today to Petaluma. Clean sober, with nothing to muddle the memories. Clear-eyed, trying to loosen his mouth enough to smile at the eager woman in the bed.

Grandma grabs at his arm holding a few narcissus from Aunt Mari's garden. "Davala, *oy* mine Davy. I'm so sorry." She squints up into his face and bursts into tears. "I should have done more," she cries, "I should have known about Papa." Davy flinches and tries to back away, but Grandma holds him tight.

"Why didn't you tell me? *Oy*, what you had to go through all alone," she wails, "your stinking father. If he was here, I'd kill that man this minute for all what he did to you."

"It's all right, Mom," Davy gulps. "Stop."

And then I'm out of the room, pulling at Rob and Uncle Mas, to give Grandma and Uncle Davy some privacy. I can hear them both crying as I shut the door.

Rob wipes his own tears away. "That's what's really poisoning her," he says, "not the damn kidney."

Uncle Mas nods, his smile warming the cold hospital walls. Slowly, with a sweetness I have never seen in him, he leans a shoulder into his partner's. Rob's bald head drops, and he whispers something I can't hear.

I feel surrounded by private moments, alone and shut out of the feelings around me. The hospital smells – Lysol and ammonia – swirl around my head. I turn toward the windows, wanting the sun or some real air to heat me. Instead, I see Guardian Molly waiting beside a hesitant figure down the hall.

It's Aunt Mari, looking as awkward as I feel, etched in the light of the main doorway. I walk quickly toward her, my chest still heavy from Grandma's sobs. "Oh, I'm so glad you came."

For a moment, Aunt Mari's face becomes a Sierra granite canyon. Her eyes look like stones, with dark hollows carved beneath them, sculpted from the press of glaciers. Then I blink, and she returns to the ordinary woman I have always known, dressed in black stretch pants and a gray turtleneck sweater. The stillness I sensed behind her smile fades when I give her a hug.

"Was it you who finally coaxed Uncle Davy into coming up here?" I ask, standing close to her side and sounding like my mom, a little light-hearted and breezy. Then I give up on the Mimi talk. "Grandma's really needed him, maybe as much as he needs her."

Aunt Mari steps back and takes a long moment to look at me. "He couldn't come until he was ready," she says. And then she smiles, linking her elbow with mine. The aunt I always described to Aviva as soft, like a piece of marshmallow or cotton candy, suddenly takes me in hand, walking us firmly up the hall.

I feel confused by her strength, as if the world has suddenly gone blurry. If Aunt Mari has changed so much, then nothing I see might be real. No familiar shapes, no edges. I'm surrounded by water, watching the people I know melt into an amber liquid. Everything I thought I could depend on in them slides away from me and grows sticky, becoming something else.

Maybe it's your eyes that have gone sharp, Guardian Molly offers, popping out of the wall to walk next to me, *seeing the truth now.*

I don't know what I'm seeing, I tell her, watching her blue calico skirt swish against the linoleum floor.

Aunt Mari presses my arm, and I see her in the red plaid skirt she wears as a young girl one windy April afternoon in Colorado. She's kicking at rocks behind the high school barracks at the Amache internment camp, only fourteen and angry and alone. Aunt Mari hunches down, wraps her arms around her blowy clothes and is surprised to feel tears coming. The strong sobs pushing their way into her chest shock her. After all, she is more than two years gone from Petaluma and should be used to how the family is scattered, Mas, Sumi, and Emi having won permission from the authorities to attend school back east and Ken serving in the 442nd. What's the hurt in being alone in the small barracks room with a stoic Mom and Dad? Who tell her to be *gaman-suru*: persevering, patient and hard working? *Shikata ga nai*: it can't be helped. We just have to go on.

But Mari cries for her favorite rose hollyhocks, the ones she begged Mother to let her plant, which might be starting now outside her old room near the yellow plum tree. She cries for the poppies, the ones she told her secrets to, that have just finished flaming the hills behind Chapman Lane. And mostly for Yuki, her black cat, who is the proud mother of another litter of kittens. In her latest letter, Mrs. Slominski wrote that she is keeping one for Mari this time and giving it her name.

"I didn't know you could see things," my aunt says, bringing me out of her past and into a crowded hospital hallway. She smiles gently. "You're getting more and more like Mas."

"Which is a compliment, of course," he says softly, greeting his sister.

She tries to laugh at the kiss he places on her cheek. "You know I never meant it to be anything else."

Uncle Davy opens the door and gestures us back into Grandma's room, his face strained. Aunt Mari takes one quick look and then squeezes past me to hold his hand. They stand together at the foot of Grandma's bed, making a double shadow on the blanket. Rheabie is a ball of misery against her pillows, pale and small.

I hurry to her side, wanting to straighten the sheets, to get her a Kleenex.

"*Sha!*" she orders, waving me off. "There is a something what needs I should say."

The room stills, like the air did yesterday at Mae's grave, as if the Guardians have come with their storms and hilly wisdom. I look around, expecting Wina or Padre Guitierrez, but they're not here. Even Molly, who was watching us all in the hallway just a minute ago, is gone. There is only Grandma, rooted like a twisted oak to her bed, holding us quiet with her eyes.

"I want you should know that I spit on Jake's memory for what he did to Davy and Nate." She twists, struggling to sit up straighter. "The truth – me, it was he wanted to slap."

I start to protest, but Grandma folds her arms and scowls in my direction. "Every single punch," she says, "it had my name on it – and Mae Cherney's. Our private business Jake took out on who couldn't fight back." Now she turns toward Uncle Davy. "Shamed I am that I didn't know. So blind, so stupid. What kind of mother was I? This is where the blame lies."

Rob shakes his head, but she ignores him and lifts up off the pillows. She leans toward the slouched figure at the foot of her bed. "Davy, you hear me? Nothing was your fault."

"But we're not talking fault and blame," he says after a long moment, pulling at her blanket with weary fingers. His voice begins to waver. "All we need is the truth. That's what this is about."

I wait for him to explain more, but Uncle Davy stays quiet. The silence grows deeper in the crowded room. Then I realize that he's right. This is not about what happened with Grandpa and Mae in the past. The truth is right now – the way the light comes through the window and shows the veins in Grandma's arms, the bruises from the IV turning yellow. The truth lies in the quiet that changes tone, becoming peaceful and cool, the silence rising from where Uncle Mas sits in a chair. And Aunt Mari, remembering the blue camp skirt that her mother made over and embroidered with small yellow flowers, showing *gamen*. Each stitch made beauty out of *shikata ga nai*: it can't be helped.

"Grammy," I call softly, but I'm really speaking to all of us. I feel linked to each person in the room, held in the strands of a spider web, full of tears like dew. "Uncle Davy and Aunt Mari came. Uncle Mas and Rob are here. For you."

My family is watching me now, the room hushed and warm, waiting. I try to put every leaf and flower I have ever touched at Chapman Lane in my voice. "What happened back then, what Grandpa did, it shouldn't have been. It was terrible. But," and I stumble, not sure exactly how to say it, "in spite of him – or maybe because of him – something else happened." I watch the tears begin to fill Grandma's eyes again. "Look at us here," I beg her. "How come there's so much love?"

Chapter 31
THE PAIN OF LOVE

RHEABIE

I don't know from love right now, Shoshie. That's the bitter truth. *Oy,* such a sour taste what lives in my mouth. And not from the medication. Or that *dreck* they call food in this hospital. The thick head what I carry on my shoulders, it's from me and Jake.

No, don't worry. I remember – yesterday we had a little surgery. A shunt. To make right for the permanent dialysis, yes? Some big shot, a surgeon, he took a piece from my leg and sewed it in my arm. So it won't hurt so much, the dialysis. So they can do me three times a week for years. But *bubee,* that's not the problem. This pain, it's what can't be fixed.

It's killing me – Jake. What he did to Nate and Davy. Such a secret what lived in our family. How did it happen? I keep asking. To stop it – what different should I have done?

I curse Jake at night, hoping to call him back, so we can have words about it. So loud I yell, the nurses come. Last night – or the night before, after Davy visited – that nice Angie came running. "Are you hurting, Mrs. Slominski?" she asked.

"Yes," I told her. Crying I was, "but not from pain. From a *shmuck* what wronged me and my family." I didn't have the nerve to tell – my own husband, him what was the *shmuck.*

Angie sat with me, that nice girl, until I should stop crying. Good with a Kleenex, she was. Almost like you. Then I saw, when she thought I wasn't looking. A little squirt of something in my apple juice she put, so I could sleep.

This morning – I woke and could think again. Ai, Shoshie, such a pleasure. The first time in days, my brain it's returned to me. And no nightmare last night, the same one what's been bothering me. No pressing and twisting, what Dr. Kendall is fool enough to call a "panic attack." As if it's not real, all my worries. As if the past, it's not holding me down with a hard hand.

Today, I can see Jake and me, how between us things got tangled. Like bad yarn – so twisted, so many knots. And I've been wanting it should be all his fault. Or if not him – then me. Searching I've been. Trying to feel better by pointing a finger. Like Davy said, I should be smarter than just making blame.

So young I've been acting, silly and foolish. A nineteen-year-old, what doesn't know from squat. Full of ideals, mad at promises gone wrong – like the girl I was when Jake and I married. You think life might've taught me a little more by now.

Ach, but back then. From what I didn't know, you could fill a roadster. A model T, like the one Jake and I used to come west such a long time ago. We left a few days after our wedding. A January in New York it was. Foolish to travel then.

But the snow had stopped. So we made a big party. After everyone left, your grandpa took me outside. "The stars, Rheabie. Look."

His hand I held, watching the sky closely. Then I said once again what I promised in private before. "Marriage is not a leash, Jake. Maybe other women might make you a pleasure."

Jake laughed. "No one like you."

"I won't object," I declared. "We are free human beings."

Your grandpa lifted me in his arms. "For me the vice and versa."

"But no lying about it," I promised, "not now, not ever. In our life – even the little things – we are big enough to know from each other the whole truth."

Dolly, I remember exactly how Jake looked when he answered. His dark eyes shining. Wet, from a tear maybe, or a piece of his pride. "This is a marriage of principle," he shouted. I thought even the sky was glad for us. "Rheabie Melnick." Like a bear, he hugged. "By you I will live the truth."

There were no "ifs" or "ands," Shoshie, no talk of exceptions. He didn't say, "But if love comes to you by a woman, all promises are off." Do you think it was my mistake, not seeing how much being with Mae made different? The hitting – maybe it wouldn't have been if she'd been a man.

A week after the fire in the barn, I told him – when things between Mae and I looked serious. Before we snuck off to lay down together, I needed he should know.

This is different from what you promised, Mamale squawked from her chair in the corner of the kitchen. *What's your hurry? Nothing's happened yet.*

But it will, I retorted, suddenly breathless. The very idea, it made me have to sit down quick. Oy, such a tingling there was in my stomach. And my ghosts, they knew. That kind of hunger, they could read in my body. Such a long time it'd been since Jake and I, we lay together. Who knows? Maybe they were a little curious and hungry themselves.

Wait 'til the damage is done, Shlima advised, floating near the ceiling. *Don't give yourself extra problems. What the man doesn't know won't hurt.*

You think when he finds out afterwards, that's going to make it any better? I glared at Shlima from my place at the kitchen table. *He'll be mad I lied.*

He'll be mad, no matter what. Gitl spoke softly and stared at me from the top of the kitchen cabinet. *Rheabela, are you sure?*

Telling Jake she didn't mean, my sweet, scared sister. An old-fashioned and prudish girl – she still hoped this business between Mae and I would just go away.

I'm sure, I told her, hanging on to the only piece I felt certain. A rope it was, this feeling for Mae, something hard and strong.

Something wrong, Mamale corrected my thought, *and you should let go right this minute. From this rope, the whole family is going to hurt.*

She was right, my mother, but I was too full of love to listen. Besides, I wanted a chance I should live up to my freethinking ideals. Since we were married, Jake had one adventure – a woman in San Francisco from his old union. Hard it'd been on me, but we stuck to our beliefs. He told me – no lying – and things turned out all right. My turn now, I thought, taking off my apron. Asleep the *kinder* were already, so I went off to find Jake in the barn.

"I have something to say," I announced. "I want you should listen."

"So say," he shrugged, sitting up in the stall where he slept. "Then *gey and gezunterey.* Leave me alone."

A big breath I took at the man's coldness. Then I tried to remember the warmth what lived in Mae's eyes. "I want you should know between Mae and me there is a something."

"What kind of something?" Jake spat.

"Like how it was between you and that Hirsch woman." I bit my lip, surprised at the sharpness in my words. I hadn't cared about her back then. I knew between your grandpa and me, our love was strong. Ach, but this winter, when he wouldn't come near me, I'd hidden the thought until now – maybe it was her he wanted again, not me. "You've been thinking about Sonia, maybe, full of missing?"

Jake ignored my question. "Phui," he spat, turning away. His stiff shoulder, it stabbed me just like all those nights when I begged we should touch a little. That's all what I had to look at when he rolled away in bed instead. Time for the truth now.

"I'm missing what we had," I tried to explain. "Your coldness is killing me."

Jake shifted. "It's not my fault," he muttered. "Don't blame this on me."

Yes, I realized suddenly. Mae wasn't something what rose from the *farfufket* state of our marriage. What I felt for her was separate, all its own. A warmth, Shoshie, such as I had never known, even in the best times with Jake. A feeling in myself I never knew enough to name.

And she knew me – who I was – in ways poor Jake didn't. Mamale, Shlima and Gitl she saw. No secrets. No spirits in hiding. The full truth in me she could talk and laugh with, touch with the palm of her hand.

"Not your fault," I agreed with Jake. "But I have to do this."

"No." Jake began to rise and shake his head. "You can't." His eyes went hard, close to the way he looked when he yelled at Davy. Then he raised his fist.

Watch out, Rheabie, Mamale screamed.

Get out here, Shlima yelled. *Run!*

"You can't stop me," I said, sure for once. "No matter how much hitting."

"You're sure?" he asked, stepping close.

I spoke quickly. "Don't you even think about it. One touch and I'll leave."

Don't! Gitl sounded shocked. *You'll hurt him.*

What do you think he wants to do to me right now? I asked her. Shoshie, I swear, there was something bad in his eyes.

Still, I looked Jake right in the face. "I'll take the *kinder* and then you'll have no one to help you. If you hit me, you'll lose the ranch."

"No," he gasped, the look dying.

"Then let me be."

And he did, your grandpa, but I know it cost him. Cost your uncles too, what I didn't know then. So blind, so happy, I thought our life was fine – even with this *tsuris*. The rare moments Mae held me, worth the trouble it seemed. Worth the fights with Jake – him turning away, not speaking. Worth the sad looks from Art, his head shaking. Once, he cornered me in the egg shed. "My Rheabela. Why her and not me?"

My Rheabela? Mamale huffed. *Since when did you ever belong to him?*

Shlima floated nearby, looking Art over. *So skinny. Not like Mae at all. What makes him think he's such a prize?*

I didn't answer. To Art I simply shrugged. What was there to say?

Once, after a year, the four of us talked. The men's idea – in the spirit of honesty, of comradeship and principle, we should speak freely what needed said. But that night, at our kitchen table, Art turned quiet. Out the window Jake stared at the barn.

"So *nu*?" Mae asked. "A big meeting you wanted. Now you have nothing to say?"

Art slapped both hands down on the table. "I say enough. Jake and I are fools for putting up with you. The whole world should know the shame of what you've done."

"What?" Mae threw down her napkin. "What kind of shame are you talking, Mr. Free-thinker? Haven't we been over this a thousand times?"

"A crime against nature," he sputtered. "We deserve better. Most important, the family, the *kinder* – they should have more."

"The family?" Jake's voice was almost a shout.

"Sha! You'll wake them." I motioned toward the bedrooms, Mimi, Davy and Nate sleeping just down the hall.

Jake growled at Art in a whisper. "We're all ruined in a minute you should open your big mouth. The talk gets out – think of the *kinder*. Tortured at school. Think of us, laughed out of the county. Use your brain, Art." Jake took a breath. "We'd lose the ranches if anyone should know. "Ach, the truth, Slominski. All you care about are chickens." Art folded his hands together. "What kind of man are you to just sit by?"

"A man of principle." Mae defended Jake for the first time in months. "Besides, Comrade Casanova, what big wound has all this brought you? How many new women? I'm counting. Three? No, you got a welcome in four new beds."

"A grieved man's got a right." He reached for his tea.

Mae handed him the usual – two sugar cubes. "So has a woman. Don't try and tell me any different, Art Katz."

Silence stretched the walls of the kitchen. *Oy*, how I shuddered waiting for it to break. What broke was Jake's pride. "All right! Enough! No more discussion. I say now and forever, we make an agreement. Keep it secret. The subject is closed."

"You're a fool," Art hissed. "Shamed I am to see such weakness in a comrade."

"*Shmuck*," Mae spat at her husband. A string of words, worse than I can tell you, came out of her mouth.

I raised you for this? Mamale asked, rising from the floorboards. She hovered in the air near me and had the nerve to wink at Mae. I'm ashamed to say, Shoshie, she looked ready to laugh.

What's so funny? I asked her.

Shlima answered with a smile. *So much talk, this fighting.* She grinned at the men. *For what? You and Mae. It's not going away.*

Yes, I nodded, smoothing down the edges of my napkin. We were a fact, like the pullets in the brooder houses, like the price of feed. A part of the ranch, no matter what the men said. And this meeting, I thought, maybe it's something they need to feel better. A little roar to save their pride. Because, it was clear to me finally – this mess, it had something good for everyone. Art could wander like he always wanted. The difference – Mae didn't hold him back anymore. And Jake, he could worry over the ranch all he liked. I didn't stop him. All night long he could work, without me nagging him to bed.

What mattered most – I looked down the hallway – the *kinder*. From our love, they shouldn't be pulled apart. Mae and I never thought, like people do today, to rearrange, to move somewhere else, to live different. For the *kinders'* sake, and maybe for our own too, we tried to keep it all the same.

And what did Mae and I get for it? Lost time, what we could never get back again, hours robbed from being together. So many whispers, hurried talks and broken visits. Our rare private times, we'd look at the clock and make ourselves pack up and pull away because, we said, keeping the family strong was most important. *Oy*, some strong we're talking. All we were keeping was a lie.

I'd get back, and one boy or the other was in his room, eyes red from crying. "What is it? What happened?" Nate'd shrug and not say, refusing to look at me. Davy had words. "Go away!" he'd yell. "Leave me alone." And when Jake came in for supper, he rolled his eyes. "That fool son of yours. We had a business in the barn."

Such a *nudnik* I was, not asking more questions. Not listening hard enough to hear what they hadn't said. When I saw Davy after his bath – bruises on his leg – why did I believe his whisper, "Don't worry, Mama. I just fell down"? *Oy*, how it haunts me, Shoshie, like that dream I told you. Every little piece, I keep turning over: that thump in the barn, a boy crying. Why didn't I walk in?

I hate Jake for all what he did, and I hate for how I should have done different. I curse and spit at the two of us, but *vey*, with such an ache. Because all my yelling, what good is it? The tears, they can't take away poor Davy and Nate's scars. Nothing, not one little bit, can ever make my good boys better. And Jake's gone. Even if he were here, what's to say?

It's over, he'd argue, so long ago, so why make such a fuss about it? Why bother with regrets?

But I do regret – so many things what we did badly. You call what we had any kind of marriage? Our own ideals we failed.

Okay, okay, so yes, Shoshie, you're right. All those years, I admit, there was more than failure to them. So complicated, so tangled, I can't take it all apart. Love? Of course, love. Jake would always tell me. Up and down he'd swear – even then, I was the root of his life.

A root – and he is that for me, but maybe it's the tree itself what's gone rotten. I keep asking myself – the forty-five years with him, the six with Mae: so much pain, the cries and beatings. A thousand memories of sweetness too. Was it all a mistake?

Chapter 32
HARD RECKONINGS

SHOSHANA

"Grandma's doubting everything," I tell Uncle Mas that night on the phone. The house feels full of shadows, a little skewed or off-kilter, and definitely cold. I wipe down the counters as I talk, even though they don't need cleaning. Tomorrow, if Dr. Kendall sees fit, she's coming home. "It was hard this afternoon," I tell my uncle. "She couldn't stop crying. She keeps asking me if her whole life with Grandpa was a mistake."

Uncle Mas listens and, for the first time that I can remember, his silence is a comfort. I let my own words drift back to me, listening hard to what I've said. "That's not a question anyone can answer for her" – I shake my head at the herbs on the window sill – "and I think I might be angry that she's asked it. I was kind of short with her a couple of times, and I don't want to be."

"Well, Rob will be relieved." Uncle Mas surprises me by laughing. "He was beginning to doubt if you were even human. Saint Shoshana he's christened you – guardian of old ladies, bedpans and fava beans."

I smile at my new name, feeling the comfort of being teased. I never thought I'd be able to joke with Uncle Mas. "Isn't it confusing," I ask him, "life with a good Catholic, and then the whole Jewish side to the family? Doesn't the Buddhist in you get a little *famisht* sometimes?"

He laughs again, but I realize that I've asked a question that I need answered: how to balance all the identities – granddaughter, caretaker, and Guardian seer – that I've taken on. Uncle Mas hears my thoughts. "Shoshie, it's all right," he reassures, "to be impatient with Rheabie. She doesn't need you to always understand." His voice gets slower, and I can hear his deep feeling for my grandmother. "What you don't know might help her to get close to the pain."

"She seems pretty damn close already," I want to snap, surprised at how quick I am to defend her. But I try to stop the thought, wondering what Uncle Mas is seeing as he looks north from San Francisco toward Chapman Lane.

"It's Rheabie's time," he tries to explain, "to look at her failures. She's put it off for a long time. And there's something else. But *Jikan Fujin* hasn't shown me, and I'm not sure. But the failures, yes. It's a reckoning time."

"She hasn't failed!" I insist, remembering the look on Uncle Davy's face when he first entered her hospital room. It was love, not failure, that brought him back to Petaluma, the place of his worst memories and pain.

Uncle Mas's voice firms, becomes professional. "The best thing you can do for Rheabie right now is to just listen to her stories." Then the psychologist softens at bit. "I know it's hard, but the biggest danger is cutting off the process."

"But..." I interrupt.

"Saint Shoshana," he admonishes. "Don't try to fix anything. That's my role, remember?" I close my eyes and see a young boy on a rainy hillside. A bonfire in the distance calls his name. "Yes," Uncle Mas says, as if he's seen my vision. "The circles here go deep." He takes a long breath and then whispers. "We're repeating something old, getting a chance to work it another way. You can't control this. Just let Rheabie talk and react from your gut."

I shiver, feeling the walls of the kitchen close beside me. An odd stillness floats in the air. Then I remember the other reason I called. "Wina and Molly are at the hospital every day," I report, "but never where Grandma can see them. Why won't the Guardians sit with her anymore?"

After my words, the line goes quiet. "Uncle Mas?" I feel clumsy and uncertain, as if maybe I've said the wrong thing.

"Good for you," he says, and I feel like I just got an A on a hard test.

"Yeah, but..."

"We'll see you on the weekend," he declares and hangs up.

So I guess I put my finger on one more piece of the puzzle. But what does it mean? I ask the kitchen, looking it over one more time to make sure that it's ready for Grandma. Everything she loves is clean and in its place. The soup pans hang above the stove, their copper bottoms shiny. The pots of basil and oregano lean against the window glass, thick with new shoots. She'll be glad to be back, I comfort myself, flicking off the light, and maybe that will help her make sense of things. Being home, I tell the tired hardwood of the hallway, will ease her worries and make things good again.

"Good for what?" Grandma asks late the next afternoon, propped in her own bed once more, looking small against the pillows. "Going ahead, as if nothing happened? Pretending that whatever Jake and I did, mistake or not, was all right?" She stares at me, frowning, and sets down her glass of ginger ale. "We are talking here, a whole *mishegoss,* a terrible, sorry business. You want I should just cry a little, snap my fingers and then make nicey-nice?"

"Of course not," I argue, insistent and cold, way too much like my mother. I look past Grandma out the window to the apple tree, hoping it will take Mom out of my voice. But I have to wonder: Is this what Uncle Mas meant about fixing last night? Am I really asking her to just get over this, to hurry up and move on? The buds on the tree are near to flowering, the first small promises of Grandma's August applesauce. But, I realize – and the shock feels like a January ocean wave breaking across my chest – I don't think that she'll be here to make it this year.

I sit on her bed and smooth down her blanket. "Grandma," I whisper, my voice full of tears. "I'm afraid you're going to die."

"So what else is new?" she asks, shrugging. "I already told you."

"But soon, way too soon," I choke, "and I don't want you to." She pats my hand, and that only makes me cry harder. I wish I was little again and could crawl up into her arms. I'd beg for her stories, for whatever wild answers she would make to my most pressing questions: Why did Ginger the dog have to die and where did she go? How come Jamie, Nick and the rest of the guys won't let me play ball on their team? And who are the Guardians, really? What does it mean that we see them? Grandma, I want to ask, I moved down here to be with you and the magic, but how do I live with it and make some kind of daily life?

But I understand now: she can't answer that, anymore than I can tell her if her marriage was a mistake. *Vey iz mir*, I think, trying to sound as much like her as possible, about this we both need to find our way alone. The thought frightens me, and I lift one of her worn hands and rub it against my cheek, feeling uncertain. I'm not sure that I understand a single thing anymore.

Except for the feel of her fingers against my skin, the press of her arthritic knuckles. And the one fact about her pain that I know, and she does not. "The Guardians were with you the whole time in the hospital," I tell her, hoping to ease her loneliness – or my own. "Wina and Molly haven't deserted you, but they never appeared where you could see." Grandma stares, watching me closely. "Do you know why they don't want you to talk to them?" I ask. "Why do they want you to go through this on your own?"

Grandma flushes and the color stays high across her cheekbones. She looks out the window, then lifts up to meet my gaze, her eyes filling with tears. "You're a very smart girl."

But she won't say anything more and I bite my lip, holding back a thousand questions. I've won the booby prize again, but I still don't know why or how smart I've been. "Please don't be like Uncle Mas," I beg finally. "This is important. Tell me what it's about."

She leans back, looking embarrassed, but also determined. "*Oy* dolly," she says. "Sometimes your grandma is a fool." Then she sighs. "Maybe it's me what's been keeping the Guardians away with all my weeping and wailing. From fear. Those panic attacks. For months, ever since Davy told me, I got the guilt. I wanted to die from shame."

I press her hand, and she glares at me. "The trying to make me feel better – from you and Rob, from Nate and Davy, all that love and protection – that's what's wrong."

Grandma pauses and folds her arms, covering the IV bruises. "My own part in things I didn't want I should feel. So I made lots of noise, kept myself confused with nightmares. Such a fool I was, running the Guardians off. *Vey iz mir*, after all these years, you'd think I'd know better. What a *tsuris* I made all from wanting not to know."

"But know what exactly?" I ask, sensing that Grandma had left something out of the story. Or maybe it's just her guilt, rising up like dust to cloud her words again.

"Forty-three years," she mutters, watching the wind move the branches of the apple tree. Then she looks at me, pain etching the slopes of her face, shadowing her cheeks to a grayness I have never seen before. "I still don't want to know how much I lost the day Mae died."

Chapter 33
STORIES OF GLASS AND STONE

RHEABIE

Such a loss, *bubee* – Mae's going. A window breaking. Like the cold frame Jake built for my tomatoes. Smashed – letting the March air in. The Slominskis and Katz's – both families cold and shattered. In splinters, the balance between us. A million pieces – all what anchored me to the world.

Or what kept me from it, maybe. That cold frame – a little shelter. Making blooms too soon, before the right season. Helping what shouldn't have grown.

Ai, dolly – so long I've waited to tell you. What I learned from watching Mae die, I want you should know. To make easier, maybe, the hard time what's coming. My own death – even you, who doesn't want, can smell it now. I thought Mae's story – it might help with the tears, the changes. I wanted you should be prepared.

But now, truth to tell, I don't know. Looking back, from that whole business maybe nothing I learned. I thought – such a bad time, but getting through, it made me better. Some better. Only a teaspoon, maybe. The real truth – I didn't change. It's all a lie, those nice lessons, what I wanted I should tell you. Whatever I thought – it's broken apart.

I got glass in my hands right now, dolly. Hidden, like Davy and Nate's old bruises. From a long time ago already, but can you see how it makes for scars? I know. You want I should tell you anyway. But it's hard to talk, dolly, what with this pebble I got in my mouth.

A little stone, like the lump in Mae's breast the very first time I felt it. So small it was, that rock. Just a bump under my hand. "What's this?" I asked on the hill one fall day – one of our hurried, private moments. "Feel. It's not right."

"A woman change," she said after rubbing the place with her fingers. Mae had the *chutzpah* to smile – touching her own death. "Very common, we get older," she explained in her nurse's voice. "Things harden, get bumpy. Nothing to make a fuss."

I should've trusted the feeling in my stomach – like lightening, a zigzag. Such a heat, what rose up there. But Mae smiled, and I thought the fire came from something different. "*Bubee.*" She pulled me down next her. "Don't worry." And I believed.

Like I believed when I got home. "That Davy," Jake said, "Such a smart mouth." Your grandpa, he leaned his shoulder into Malka's flank, busy with his milking. "So I want you should know, I yelled a little." That man, he looked over his shoulder at me. "When's Davy going to learn to behave? Like an five-year-old, acting up every time you're gone."

"Who's acting?" I should've asked – your grandpa, the only one upset at my going? The one taking out his feelings on the boys? Or my favorite son, hiding in his room afterwards? "I'm just reading, Mama," he told me when I asked what happened. "I'm fine."

"Try not to make Papa angry," I begged, brushing the hair back over his forehead.

"It doesn't matter," he sighed, opening his book again. "He gets mad no matter what I do."

True, I know now, but at the time, I couldn't see it. So much staring me in the face those confused years. I turned away. And wonder: what would have happened, if the truth I'd coaxed from Davy? Would it make a difference, if sooner to the doctor I'd gotten Mae about her breast?

A whole winter of sharp words and then quiet. So many fights we had the next spring, me *nudzhing* her to see Doctor Smith. "What's so hard about a little visit?" I'd beg each time we sneaked off alone. "If the lump's such a big nothing, why don't you want to go?"

"Enough already!" Mae turned away, then sat up on our blanket. Up on the hill we were again, our favorite place – the shade of Davy's rock. "That doctor – he has plenty of sick folks he needs should see."

"But he likes you." The sun, such a fire it made on her hair that day. "He won't mind a visit."

Mae frowned, then began pulling on her clothes. "I don't need to pay good money – what we don't have – to visit."

"For me," I begged. "Please, Maisie. Just to make sure."

"What? You think I don't know anything?" she growled, buttoning her dungarees. "I'm a nurse. Leave me alone."

Such a huff she walked home – no good-byes, no last kisses. Nowhere near my house she came for a few days. A long absence – even Jake noticed. He grinned after lunch one day. "Trouble in paradise?"

"Don't look like you enjoy it," I snarled, picking a few early cucumbers. He grinned, then called the *kinder*. "Let's take the afternoon off. To the river. A swim! "Such a big production he made out of that picnic. At the last minute, he leaned out the truck. "Sure you don't want to come?"

I shook my head, bent over the bushel basket. "Look how many I got already. These pickles can't wait."

"Liar!" he cackled, gunning the engine. Mimi – looking grown-up already, dressed for boys – smiled beside him. "You're too miserable, but suit yourself,

Missus Lonesome,"Jake called. "Enjoy."

But you think I made for the kitchen the minute they left? Not on your life, Shoshie. I waited, watching – my heart in my mouth – 'til the truck, it turned the corner. Then that basket of cukes stayed right where it was. I ran to Mae.

Hanging laundry she was – one of Art's shirts blowing. Behind her, a field of kale, ready for cutting. Such green under that late May sky. A painting: her red hair, the white shirt, the kale field. "Mae Cherney," I should call it. "At Forty-three." Or "Cancer: Not yet Showing." The truth maybe, something simple. "Love."

"Hey," I called, "you with the washing."

She looked up, then frowned. *"Nu?* What do you want?"

"To say I'm sorry!" I ran up, not caring if Art should be looking. "I'm sorry ten times." I held her. "Don't turn away!" Such a string of apologies I whispered in her ear, Mae started laughing. So big, so many, even Mamale blushed.

Have more pride! she urged, perched on the clothesline. *Wanting she should go to the doctor – you're only looking out for her. That's not wrong.*

Shlima agreed, floating like a crow over the kale field. *Worry!* she yelled. *It's a sign of love.*

Gitl stayed quiet while Mae grinned, then ran to tell Art how we were going walking. I hurried back to our place, grabbing the blanket what we hid in the barn. *Pay attention!* Gitl whispered as I fished it out of the egg shed. *Watch closely. Be smart,* she urged as we rushed up the hill.

But listen I didn't, glad for an afternoon with my Mae smiling beside me. Such a wildness what took us that day. The blanket we threw away, in our pleasure rolling right on the grasses. Touching the mustard flowers, the poppies, each other – full of spring. But a watch I kept on my hungry hands. Not once allowing they should come close to her breast.

Until, two months later, the lump got so big even I could see it. Until, she had to stop, panting, when we were only halfway up the hill. Such a cough she had. From that June cold, she kept excusing. Nothing to worry. Just a new syrup she needed, what would make it go away. But finally – in August – Art and I dragged her to Doctor Smith. And the man, he didn't like the sound of the cough. To Mount Zion Hospital in San Francisco he sent us. Doctor Abraham Cohen – a young boy, too full of himself – told us the bad news.

"A very serious cancer," he said, pulling at his beard in the quiet office. "Breast and lungs. Surgery is your best bet."

I heard a crack then, Shoshie. The cold frame breaking. But no, I told myself. Maybe it was only Mamale's scream.

What? She wailed in the air above us. *How can he know? Just out of school. Too quick. He can't be right.*

Gitl put a hand on Mae's shoulder. She looked sorry but didn't say *I told you so.*

"Surgery for what?" Mae asked, shrugging Gitl off. The nurse had come back to her voice, so calm, so scientific. Only a few feet from me she sat, but a million miles away.

Dr. Cohen shook his head. "Maybe you'll have a better chance, if we try to remove it. It's the latest treatment – not common – but can give you more time."

Ai yai yai, Shlima moaned, floating near the room's only window. Her hands she wrung in its small light. *We should've come sooner. Vey iz mir.*

Noise from the street – the trolley, the newsboy shouting headlines. I didn't hear it. Only silence. The sound of Mae's breath.

"What kind of time are you talking?" she asked, her fists balling. Holding tight – the pieces of our life together, maybe. She looked up quick at me, opened her hands. On her knees they went. "*Nu?*" She stared the doctor right in the eye.

So brave, so foolish, my Maisie. Just like her, she should want to know the worst. Time – so she maybe could measure, make right, not die sudden like her mother. Time – so she could say what needed said. Such heart in her, Doctor Cohen, he couldn't face it. At Art he looked instead, sitting quiet in his chair. Then shook his young head. "I can't tell you. These kind of cancers we never know."

See, there's hope, Mamale told me that night. *Oy,* was I crying! Even Jake, he took pity on me. His blanket he brought down from the barn. "You want me to stay?" As company, by my side – in sadness. Feeling sorry your grandpa was. But the whole truth, Shoshie? I'm sorry to say, in his eyes, a little something. Satisfaction, maybe. Happiness. What made a *bissel* light.

Mamale, not good at seeing, turned his words into a sign. *Already we have miracles. You don't know what will happen. Wait and see.*

What miracle? I asked, pulling the pillow over my head. *If Mae dies, Jake gets me back again. Already he's counting the seconds. He's glad.*

Unfair I was – speaking from meanness. Maybe how I'd feel, the Hirsch woman got sick.

Be ashamed! Gitl scolded. *So unfeeling. Have a little trust. Jake's bigger than that.*

I couldn't trust. I couldn't see. But already I heard the glass breaking. *Enough, already!* Shlima shook a finger at me. *What, you know the future? Nothing's happened yet.*

But I knew, from the cramp of sorrow what lived in my belly. From the way the bones showed under Mae's cheeks. Only eight more months we had, and believe me, I counted every minute. Eight months nursing. And this too: eight more months, Jake beating the boys. A sad fact – the hitting stopped the minute we got Mae buried. Davy told me. Never again.

And it's tearing at me now, making a hole in my side what's aching. Whatever gift I thought lived inside this sad story, it's gone away. Me – what's always wanted we should hold what happened with Mae between us. Ai, Shoshie. Now I don't know where, in all the years since then, the truth about her lives. In a place of glass and rocks, maybe, everything broken. The only thing I got left to give you – stones, *oy,* such stones.

Chapter 34
SORTING THE DIRTY LAUNDRY

SHOSHANA

Grandma's right. Her stories are like rocks, all these tales about how Mae's death and Grandpa's hands shaped the family. Even though I want to know what happened, I keep tripping over the rubble, and it's hard to hear. And now, no matter where I go on the ranch, I can't help but see them. Mae, worn to bone, but with a swollen liver making her look six months pregnant. Yakkov Slominski, pulling on his dark beard, worrying about foreclosure. They accompany me to the Recycling Center or when I work in the garden. But as soon as I put down my shovel, finished with spading in the favas, Mae drifts away on the breeze. Jake stays, shouting, "Damn it! What do you know from planting? You've done it all wrong." Yakkov is the shadow dampening the apple tree, making its leaves curl. He's the furious ghost who curses in Yiddish and then scurries away whenever I come into the garage.

"Grandpa!" I call, wanting the man who carried me on his shoulders around the garden when I was little. "Please come back," I whisper to the smooth dancer who told me, during a waltz at his forty-fifth anniversary party, that the only way to live a long time is to follow your heart. "You can do it, like I did," he said, his eyes welling. He hugged me when the music was over. "Shoshanala, I'm counting on you."

Counting on me for what, I want to ask, now that I know his secrets? The answer is easy. Counting on me to love him since Grandma can't.

Or maybe I have that wrong, as she cries and tells me piece after piece about those rough years during the Depression. The argument about the Brucksteins needing a place to stay and how he wouldn't let them. How he got into a fight with Moysche, the two of them throwing punches in the front yard, about the great strike in San Francisco in 1933. And then the yelling about Mae: how he refused to let Grandma go to San Francisco for her surgery. How he wouldn't let Mae stay in Mimi's room afterwards to be nursed. "I won't have her here!" Jake yelled. But he couldn't stop Grandma from spending everyday at Mae's, feeding her soup, changing her bandages. She cries when she talks about how Mae screamed the first time she saw her terrible scars. There are so many tears that I'm beginning to feel as if I'm the one who's drowning. And the truth is, I'm not sure anymore if Grandma's crying for herself, for Mae, or for Grandpa too.

"It's wearing me down," I tell Aunt Mari on the phone one night when she calls to see how we're doing.

She thinks I mean the nursing, the grocery shopping and sitting with Grandma through endless Sierra Club newsletter planning sessions. "It's a lot of work, honey. We're proud. You're doing a good job."

"I'm not complaining," I try to correct her impression, but I don't know how. What comes out surprises me. "Is it hard to listen to all of Uncle Davy's stories right now?"

My marshmallow aunt laughs shyly, and then her voice transforms into that surprising Sierra granite. "We have a lot to say to each other," she rumbles, "things we've never said."

I blush, ashamed for asking such a personal question. Or maybe it's the personal answer that makes me red. I picture them up late at night in their tiny Berkeley house, filling it with tales about Amache and the German prison camp. Uncle Davy is drawing it all, I know, precise charcoals, red and gray, but now the lines are firm and strong. He's sketching more than just what happened in Petaluma. Grandpa's shadow no longer dominates their dining room wall.

But that shadow lives here, an anger and loneliness I can feel under the driveway when I walk it. It pulls at my feet as I return with the mail.

"I need a job," I tell Aviva, calling to coo over the latest drawing that little Beth has sent to her Aunt Shoshie. I anticipate a long conversation about normal things: ragged nights because Hannah still won't sleep for more than four hours at a stretch without nursing, the unholy cost of her diaper service and those unexpected visits from Mom. "My back pay from Josie finally came today, and it's not enough."

"You already have a job," Mom answers instead of Viva. For a moment, I wonder if I've dialed the wrong number by mistake, then realize they're both on the line, speaking from two extensions. This will grant me another letter from Viva – a rant about how Mom never lets her alone when she comes over, not even when she's on the phone.

Mom sighs loudly. "So much *shlepping*, the cooking, and laundry. Grandma couldn't do it without you. You're her Mrs. Nielsen now."

Aviva is silent, but I hear her impatient breathing. It's good to feel how we continue to take each other's side. "But I can't take Grandma's money for that," I argue quietly, not wanting to wake Grandma from her nap. "She hardly has any. And for family, she shouldn't have to pay."

"That's right," Viva backs me up. "We need to help her now. I can send you a little cash."

Mom laughs. "Don't worry. Grandma has plenty and more to spit at. Who knew a good communist would be so sharp at making a buck?"

She's delighted at our surprise: Viva's gasp, my stutter. "Daddy was good enough to leave her something," Mom explains. "All the investments, the property – it's a joke, the way she's made it grow."

There's something more that she's not saying and so I wait, letting the line fill with silence. Mom gets breezy. "We'll talk about it more when I come next week. In the meantime, just remember – she'll pay anything to keep you there. Get a monthly salary out of her that's worth your while."

I don't want to get anything out of Grandma except for her tears to end and the blame and guilt to go away. I hate how she keeps beating on herself, the way she used to hit the braided rugs on the clothesline when I was little. "It's the only way to do it right, dolly. Grandpa fixed it so I shouldn't wear myself out, but the vacuum be damned." She's damning herself now, sure that she's at fault. *Everybody had a part in it,* I declare to Mae's cancerous ghost and the grandpa I knew, conjuring him up from a wavy line near the refrigerator. Grandpa's spirit looks too faded to be really here – not sharp and clear like the Guardians – but I talk to this piece of my imagination as if he's real. *So why can't you explain things to her?* I ask, *or get it over with and fight it out.*

"Rheabie **is** fighting it out," Uncle Mas argues later that day in a phone call after dinner. "You're watching the process." He gets quiet, and I can hear another voice talking vaguely on the line. I'm envious of the lighthearted tones I hear, the chuckles and laughs. "I wonder," Uncle Mas begins, sounding surprisingly hesitant. "Are you having trouble sorting this all through?"

"Of course!" I want to shout. "Who wouldn't?" I sigh, afraid that he's heard my unspoken words. So I tell him the truth. "When Grandma tells stories, I'm seeing everything she says as if it's happening right now. Everywhere I walk, Mae and Jake – who he was back then – is here. Mae's all right, but I can't put Jake together with my grandpa." The tears rise in the back of my throat. "The guy I knew wasn't like that."

"Can he be both?" Uncle Mas asks, the background conversation quiet now. "Maybe it's important for you to keep paying attention to what you see."

"That's your only advice?" I ask, talking more softly now since Grandma has turned off the television.

Uncle Mas snorts. "Well, Rob has some for you, Saint Shoshana. Get out of the house, I'm supposed to tell you. Call up Heather and go out for a beer."

I do, amazed at the pleasure I feel in the smoky bar, the smell of sawdust and cigarettes. The jukebox is playing country music, and the weepy guitar makes me grin. I breathe deep, watching the flick of a match and a woman's gold necklace catching its reflection. She leans forward as some guy in a Greek cap, looking vaguely like my old boyfriend Mark, lights her lipsticked smoke.

For a moment, I wonder if he's with Lillian. Nah. I shake my head. Like me, they've both moved on by now.

Heather laughs at my interest in the couple. "Girl, your eyes are sticking out. Be careful. I think you've been hanging around too much with old people. Not that I don't love Rheabie," she adds, watching me carefully. "But, like Aunt Luba, she can make your ears fall off, the way she likes to talk!"

Later, walking Barnaby on a quiet street, Heather tugs at my arm. "I think I was unfair about our old ladies and their stories." She lifts her head to look at the stars for a minute, then turns. "They want their lives to mean something. And so they have to tell us. 'Learn already,' Aunt Luba always says, 'from what I did.'"

"Maybe by telling they're still learning too," I add, hearing the wind rustle the tall spring grasses.

Heather grins. "So what's Rheabie trying to learn right now? What's she teaching you?"

"More than I ever wanted to know."

I'm learning about Jake Slominski, the force and fire that was my grandpa when he was young. I'm learning about the anger and tenderness Grandma felt as she watched her lover die. So much fury and love on the ranch at that time. But it all feels jumbled and *farpatshket*, as she likes to say.

"I'm going to make sense of it," I vow the next morning, sorting the laundry. I haven't done the wash for a few days, a rebellion against Mom and my Mrs. Nielsen job. And I haven't talked to Grandma about money either, and I don't intend to. I don't want her to think I'm going to steal from her, like she worried when she was sick. Maybe that was just the uremic poisoning, but I don't want to take a chance. It's enough right now to concentrate on the small things. Reducing the huge stack that overflows the hamper is all that I can do.

I throw a heap of bed sheets and dish towels into the laundry-room corner. The linen is worn, a little faded and comforting – like Grandpa was when I was small. I stop for a moment, a wad of clothes in my hands, furious that I can't even do the laundry without seeing him. But here he is, smiling – Grandpa, the magician, pulling surprise quarters out of his pockets. Grandpa the clown, willing to laugh at my worst knock-knock jokes. He gave piggyback rides, tickled my face with his beard, and listened to everything I hated about high school. "Don't give up," he said each time I complained.

That's so different from the fierce father he was to his sons. The man I'm trying to understand was as stiff and rigid as my blue jeans, caked with garden dirt. All right, so this will be young Jake's pile, I decide, making a mound of the muddy pants I've worn all week and my favorite pair of crusted overalls. Damp wool socks. Old sweaters. Two flannel shirts, both an angry red. I want to turn my back on them and bend down to run my hands through the delicates. I long for the soft touch of Mae's memory, Grandma's and my tender clothes.

But no. I'm trying to figure the worst of it, so I kneel in front of the jeans and sweaters, seeing Jake Slominski with his hand raised. His feet are planted in Malka's stall, and he leans back, thick-hipped and muscled, ready to strike someone. *Stop!* I call out, but the furious man who became my grandpa doesn't hear me. His jaw shakes. His left foot arches. Then his arm swings and comes down.

A rush of air, a brush on my face, the sound of sobbing. A small boy in a *yarmulke* and *peyes* stares at me from where Grandpa stood on the pile of clothes. A bruise mottles his cheek, and the right side of his upper lip is swollen. He ducks his head, pulls up his knickers, then wipes his nose with a dirty fist.

I draw in my breath, not wanting to scare him. My ribs start to hurt as I look at his sullen face. An old country boy, throwing rocks and chasing birds on the muddy streets of Terlitza. Skipping *shul,* coming in late for meals, trying to avoid his father's hand. *Come here, bubee,* I whisper, wanting to hold him. My arms ache to rock Grandpa as a child, the beaten boy who grew up into the raging man.

But he shakes his head no and I watch as his form fades slowly in front of me. I feel empty, my body turned in on itself and twisted, when he is finally gone. I don't know whose pain I'm feeling, his or mine, as I hold one of the sweaters against my chest and start crying. I feel old, stretched past what I know, as I rock back and forth on the laundry room floor.

"Shoshie?" Grandma calls. "What are you doing?" Her walker clumps toward me. "Dolly, are you all right?"

"Grandpa loved you," I sob, feeling fierce for the small boy, sharp and protective.

"Of course he did." A rush of color hurries into her face. "This you think I don't know?"

"You taught him to love," I insist, hugging the hand-knitted navy pullover. "He'd grown up mean and you showed him how."

"I didn't show him enough about the boys," she says and taps her walker against the floor. "Better by them, I should have done."

"No," I stand up, angry still. "He did that all by himself. It's not your fault." I point to the clothes. "This is the mean father, over there, all that stuff in the corner. This is how he was – a bigger pile, see? – when I was a girl. He changed, because of you, and who knows? Because of your loving Mae, maybe. Anyway, he made himself different from when he beat the boys. By the end, he wasn't the same."

Grandma stares at the piles of clothes: the dark cold wash, the dark warm, light warm and light delicate. "*Oy,* Shoshie," she shakes her head, "you are something else." But there are tears in her eyes. "So Jake loved, like I did, and after a lot of practice, we got better at it. All right. This is true. But what about the suffering along the way, the ones what got hurt from our learning?" She watches me leaning back against the washer, my hands holding on tight to the metal. "I don't want I should discourage you, dolly," she says softly, "but by my heart, I don't know anymore if love's enough."

Chapter 35
DAYENU

RHEABIE

Love – it's not enough it should make up for the bad things we did, Jake and I, between us. Not enough it should change what happened, make the scars go away. You think, Shoshie, life's a chalkboard and love, a big eraser? You get enough, maybe, the slate comes clean?

No. I want you should understand, Shoshanala, some things are written. No matter how much you want it should be different, love can't take them away. A hard bone to chew, I know – it makes my teeth tired. But believe me, dolly. This is truth.

I was young. I thought different once. Love, I promised Mae, was more than enough. Enough, we should have our hurried meetings together. Enough, in them she should make me live from the root. All what I was and no hiding. No secrets between us. My ghosts, the Guardians – the whole *mishegoss* we shared.

But then her cancer. So all right. We would make good use, the short time given. Not long, those last eight months. *But a whole world, a lifetime,* Mamale promised, *if you should stay smart and pay attention.*

Keep your eyes open, Gitl urged. *So much you have between you. Hold on tight every minute. Don't forget.*

But ai, so much work, Shlima worried, walking home with me one night after a long day's nursing. She patted my tired shoulder. *So much trouble. And – who knows? – maybe Mae, she's going to die on you. All this time with her, you're sure it's right?*

Of course I'm sure, I yelled. *We're talking Mae here.* Up to Davy's rock I looked, the hills what had known our pleasure. *Whatever she wants, she gets.*

"It's worth it, yes?" Mae asked as the weeks flew by and better, she didn't get. Worth the trouble of going downstairs, Art carrying her into the garden. Worth all what special soups what Mimi and I cooked, trying we should get her to eat. Worth it: the clouds making for a good sunset. Enough: a funny get well card from the Yiddish Chorus in the mail. Small things she marveled: the perfect shape of an egg, a bit of wind through the curtains. When Art wasn't home, my hand tracing her scar.

"Make me well again," she pleaded, wanting touches between her coughs, the old fire twisting between us. Later, too sick, content she was with just my hand on her head. Then two weeks before she died, a surprise! A day with smiles, sitting up in bed and eating a little something. Then after, down she pulled me beside her. "I'm hungry," she begged.

"More toast you want, maybe?"

"No," Mae smiled, the world shining from inside her eyes. "You I want. One last time."

I cried, holding the toothpick what was left of her body. So much love in me, Shoshie, it split my ribs apart. Out came a rush, the heat of big feeling. Such a fire, it roared past what I'd felt before. Each touch – between us, more than melting. Her skin, her bones – they burned into me. So large, our warmth, I thought, the world can't hold us. So *zaftig* those flames, we were made over new. But surprise, Shoshie. In the afterwards, no magic. Still her swollen belly. All that love, more than ever felt in my life – but her cancer, it didn't go away.

Disappointed I was, but not Mae. *Oy,* how she smiled. "*Dayenu*," she called out.

"Sha!" I hushed her, embarrassed that in her sickness and our love she should go religious. "What, you're Moses now? Out of Egypt you just led us? *Ai yai yai,* what if the neighbors should hear?"

"I don't care!" She shifted slowly, lifting herself up to look at me. In her eyes, tears. "Remember our first time together?" she asked. "Yes, like Moses, freed from slavery. Happy I would've been – just for that. But look – we got years more. Enough. *Dayenu*." Mae faced me, her green eyes, shining. "Ashamed I'm not to say it. Enough – you loving me backwards and forwards." She began to cough, but held tight to my arm. "*Dayenu*, you're here now."

"Yes," I thought, crying with her. "So what if Mae can't sit up anymore to look out the window? So what for a garden now, she's got my roses in a jar?" Gitl and Mamale were right. What we couldn't have, it didn't matter. Enough, already, how much we did.

My whole life, a tribute to that moment. Living by Mae's memory, to her enoughs, I've tried to be true. Yes, so she died at forty-three, so young and cheated. Yes, our six quick years together – barely a sneeze. It was enough – the peace Jake and I made in the afterwards. And when we had to give up chickens and sell two acres of the ranch to pay taxes? Enough, I told myself. Still the garden. Enough, the two acres we got left. *Dayenu*, Davy came home alive from the war, never mind damaged. *Dayenu*, the job for Nate in Yellowstone and the promotion for your father, the move to Ithaca 3000 miles away. *Kinder* have their own lives. At least once a year, we had those visits. You girls, shiny creatures what made the fire leap up in your grandma's heart. Enough, it was always enough.

But now? Maybe enough – it's a lie, a foolishness. Maybe it was, all those years, only settling for less. Phui on *Dayenu*. I spit on all the ways I tried to make the best of what's not there.

Not what Mae meant, I realize now. Ai, how it cuts me. Her *dayenu* – a cry for something else. Not settling, but breathing big, going further. Living from the fire, making courage in the eyes. Not what I've done – with all my hiding and keeping secrets. So mad I've been at Jake for not telling about his hitting. But look at me.

A woman what couldn't say her own truth: about spirits and Guardians. The magic what I saw in the world from him I hid. So who did Jake think he loved all those years? A girl afraid of her own shadow. A girl what couldn't live up to the bigness of Mae. Her love, what we shared – this I didn't use to make better what came after. Back in my bed I took Jake, but never once did I let my ribs break. Cheated him I did, and also the *kinder*. Their own mother, never did I let them know.

Think about it. After a day arguing with Mamale or talking with the Guardians, on the edge of Davy's bed I sat and told "Bluebeard" or "Rumplestilskin." After tucking him in with kisses, I then went to Mimi's room and said, "Pick. You want 'Sleeping Beauty' or 'Snow White'?" But never once did I think to make up a story from the magic what lived all around me. Molly's hillsides, Wina's leaves, the funny things Shlima said – such good tales I could've made. But too scared I was, not trusting my *kinder* to know from real ghosts and spirits. Afraid they might laugh, maybe – my secret world.

The worst part? Even now, I don't know if I can tell them. Mimi will scream, "Oy, the Alzheimer's. Didn't I tell you?" That Nate, he'll shake his head, "Mom, what kind of foolishness is this?"

Oy, how I want the truth it should live between us, so much it makes an ache. Davy with his brown eyes, clear now finally. My brave Nate, him what knows how to laugh. And your mother, getting warmer every phone call, a peace finally between us. A big project she keeps talking – "Wait 'til you hear, Mama" – something just the two of us, she wants we should do.

Do you understand, Shoshie? Like Mae I'm trying to be – who she became from the dying. Big. Feeling love and going further. Facing pain and making right. Making right by Jake's shadow, him everywhere in the house among us. Making right by my own secrets, all what I didn't say. But how? What do I say when the *kinder* should walk into this kitchen? Who are they going to see waiting for them in two short days? I'll tell you. An old woman, that's who. Standing scared.

Chapter 36
FAMILY REUNION

SHOSHANA

When they get here, my uncles see a shrunken creature who trembles as she watches them through the kitchen window. Grandma leans into the glass, panting like she's beginning a panic attack, and raises a shaking hand. She bites her lip when the car doors slam, and they clump up the porch steps. Uncle Nate muscles his way through the screen door first. "Mom, are you okay?"

Grandma gasps when he gathers her up into one of his big cowboy hugs. "Where's the honey cake?" he chokes, his voice sounding wobbly. Then he clears his throat. "I have to have some before Mimi gets here. You know how she is. I'll never get a bite."

He puts Grandma down gently and looks her over. The warmth and worry in his gaze makes me want to cry. Grandma starts, so Uncle Nate takes up his teasing. "The nerve, Mama. Who told you to lose all that weight and send it to me?" He slaps at his thick waist, then demands his favorite dessert again. She laughs a little, but can't get a word out her mouth, despite his pleas.

"Of course we made you one," I interrupt, worried about the flush on Grandma's cheek, the way she stands, holding tight to the table.

Aunt Mari puts an arm around Grandma's shoulder, steadying her. "Well, for goodness sake. I did too."

"Two cakes?" Uncle Nate chortles, sitting down finally and leaning back in a chair to peer at his mother. He makes a quick dab at his eyes while she's hugging Uncle Davy, making sure that she can't see.

"There now," Aunt Carol beams when we finally settle down to chat around the table. She pulls her chair close and places a palm against Grandma's cheek. "Such a pleasure, Rheabie. I've missed you so much."

Grandma breathes deeply, the panic gone now, and presses Aunt Carol's long fingers. She squeezes, then gives a great sigh. "So, you are hungry? You want lunch? How was the flight?" she asks, sounding more normal. Then she shakes her head, "No. That's not what I want to say."

"What, Mama?" Uncle Davy pats her shoulder.

She turns to look at him. "It's your first time in this house since you told about Papa." Her eyes fill again. "Memories, all the bad memories. Doesn't it hurt?"

"I came for you," Uncle Davy says, "and I'm glad to be here. I don't know how it's going to feel."

"You'll tell me?" Grandma begs, folding her hands together. "I don't want anymore hiding. Whatever you need, it's all right, you should do."

No one hides during lunch, a painful discussion about AA and what it's been like for Uncle Davy since he got sober. Then Aunt Mari shyly tells us about her work with the Japanese American Citizens League. She's hoping to testify in Washington before the Wartime Relocation and Internment of Civilians Commission. "I have a lot to say."

"So how about a rest?" I suggest to Grandma after the meal, noticing how pale her face has gotten. She leans back in her chair and simply looks. Then, after a long pause watched by everyone at the table, she nods her head, "All right."

But when I get Grandma settled in bed, she whispers, "I want Nate. Go get him."

"No," I refuse. "Grammy, you need a nap."

"Who can sleep?" she argues, the lines of her mouth going stubborn. "There are things – private – to him I should talk."

After Nate goes to Grandma's room, I herd the rest of the group outside to the rickety lounge chairs near the garden. "Well," Aunt Carol asks me as we sit down, "how's she doing? Tell the truth now." Her fingers work a blade of grass. "God, she's gotten frail. Is Rheabie really okay?"

I shake my head. "No. It's hard – the dialysis and so many medications. And the panic attacks…" I stumble, but Aunt Carol's eyes, so brown and thoughtful under one of Grandma's big straw hats, coax the truth out of me. "Grandma's had a tough time the last six months. I can't tell you how much I wish I hadn't left."

Uncle Davy leans forward, tugging at the brim of his baseball cap. "It's hard for her to take in what happened," he states quietly. Then he smiles at me, excusing my absence. "I think it was good that she had the time to come to terms with it alone."

She hasn't come close to terms, I almost say, but bite the words back. If Grandma really does all the talking she wants to this weekend, revealing her secrets, they'll be able to see soon enough.

Aunt Mari nods, "I hate watching her suffer like this. Until now, I've never thought of Rheabie as old." She lets her words drift off toward the newly planted bean bed. We sit together for a few quiet minutes, feeling the afternoon breeze. Then Uncle Davy shifts. "How about a walk?" he murmurs to Aunt Mari. She gazes into his face, something rich and old rising up between them.

"Well, how about that?" Aunt Carol whispers to me as they walk down the lane, their shoulders touching. Then she shakes her head. "I don't know why, but it's hard for me to remember that you're only Luke's age. You seem older, somehow. I don't feel like I'm talking to one of my kids."

If I were Mom, I would use her comment as a polite invitation to ask about Luke and the rest of my cousins. Instead, I stare at the comfortable woman who, like me, listened intently to everyone at lunch, but didn't say a thing. "Well," I tell her, trying to remember if she talked much at the family Thanksgiving dinners, "you don't feel very much like an aunt anymore."

She laughs. "I guess I don't know who you've become in the last six years, but I like it." She looks up to the hills, toward Davy's rock, and then asks another question. "How's it been for you, staying here?"

"Okay," I nod, surveying the soil I've worked, the lettuce sets I've planted. I'm surprised at the rush of feeling in my throat. "More than okay. If Grandma will let me, I don't ever want to leave."

I realize that I mean after she dies, and I'm startled. For the first time I'm talking about Grandma's death as if it's sure to come soon. For the past couple of weeks, I've let her fears, all the worries and stories about the past, distract me from the tale that her body is telling. Why do I care what she says to her kids or if she can reconcile with Grandpa? All I really want is for her not to go. "It's because all of you are here," I admit to Aunt Carol, "that I can say what's going on and not feel out of my mind because of it. Of course, she's not doing well. I haven't wanted to admit how much of the last month I've spent feeling afraid."

And trying to fix things – just like Uncle Mas told me not to do – so Grandma will have some kind of peace for whatever time is left her. Filling up my days with her worries, so I don't have to face my own.

Is that why Uncle Mas spent so much time with the Guardians? I'll have to ask when he comes this evening. I picture stealing a quiet moment with him. "I understand now about the fixing. It takes you out of yourself," I'll tell him. "So what were you running from as a boy?" Will Uncle Mas give me an honest answer? It's more than coming to terms with the magic, his long journey to accept his gift. It's bigger than the loneliness that Grandma could see in him.

Then I smile at myself. It's so easy to slip into questioning someone else when I want to avoid my own fears. Aunt Carol has been watching me dance around my last words to her about Grandma's death. Now she turns to look at the garden. It's come along in the last month – now fully planted. So much work, but I never thought that it was just for me. Who else will eat those beans, the tomatoes and the cucumbers? I don't want them if Grandma isn't here to make a fuss over their taste and size.

"When my mother died," Aunt Carol says finally, "I thought the world had a hole ripped in it. Even with Nate and the boys, I felt orphaned – without anything to hold me down." She leans over to pat my hand. "Honey, I envy how you're anchored here. That's not going to happen to you."

"I don't know what's going to happen," I whisper, feeling the fact of Grandma's death moving away from me. A whirlwind, a rush of fear rises up from my belly. "I just hope I don't have to deal with it very soon." I want to be back in the house and checking on her, making sure she's resting. How can Grandma get through this whole weekend, with the big party tomorrow, if she exhausts herself the first day?

Aunt Carol laughs at me, and then picks up the novel she's reading. "Go on now. See how she's doing. Send your uncle out to me if they're done."

But they're not, because I can hear slow murmurs from behind the closed door of Grandma's bedroom. She's crying and talking at the same time, and Uncle Nate sounds as if he's trying to stop her. "It's okay, Mom. That's enough."

I try not to wonder if she's talking about Grandpa or finally telling him about her spirits. Which part of her past will she reveal? And how will Uncle Nate react to it?

When he finally emerges, he wipes his eyes as he stands in the kitchen doorway watching me cut potatoes for dinner. He shakes his head when I put down the knife, "No, don't worry. She's finally asleep."

The awkward way he stands, leaning on his left hip and hugging his own arms, makes me want to hug him. The concern about what happened between them evaporates. I feel eight years old again, in the company of my favorite uncle, holding the red birthday balloon he just gave me carefully against my chest. Then, I was too scared to crush it into me and run to him to say thank you. But I don't have to be afraid now, I think, moving across the floor towards him. Who cares if the balloon breaks?

"You are a surprise, cowgirl," Uncle Nate says, releasing me finally. "Your dad would be proud."

That makes me teary, so we stand side by side in the kitchen without saying anything. I feel Grandpa's wispy spirit, my imagined ghost, grip my feet. I'm embarrassed to admit the feeling that his warm touch gives me: a sense of peace.

Chapter 37
SEARCHING FOR PEACE

RHEABIE

Ai, but there's no peace in this house: too many ghosts, too many slaps and hitting. Can you see it, Jake – all that hurt, what lives in the walls? The mark of a thump. Was that you, what made that dark spot? Listen! A boy's crying. Everywhere, all the sounds what I refused to hear.

Look at Nate, so grown up, laughing. To my eyes, a young boy still, biting his worried lip. Forget the jokes. Forget the man wanting his honey cake. He's fifteen again, the first time making a stand against you. Shouting back, his neck thick like Malka's, hard and tight. "Why are you yelling, Papa? Stop it!" I watched: a fist balled, then forced open. "Stop. We can hear you just fine."

Me, I can't stop hearing – all what came before, the terrible things what happened. Everywhere I look, it's you and me, Jake. Such fools we used to be.

Remember when Nate asked Mimi, she should help with his chores, the time you wouldn't let her? In high school they were then, junior and seniors, eager to play. "I forbid it," you shouted like always. "Responsibility you have to learn."

"No," Nate shook his head. "Why are you being so unfair?"

"Unfair, shmair," you stuttered, ready to burst.

Mamale floated above your head. *Watch out, Rheabie. Jake needs you should all be careful. Who knows what the man might do. Oy, is he mad!*

As mad as Nate, Shlima added, coming up out of the floorboards so she could stand right there, some kind of wispy shadow beside her nephew. You saw her maybe, yes? Was that the reason you backed away? In your snarl, anyway, a smidgen of surprise, something different. Shlima looked proud, patting Nate on the shoulder. *Good for you, boychik,* she crowed, *So strong you've grown.*

Rheabie, say something, Gitl advised from the top of the kitchen cabinets. Was it an echo of her voice, maybe, what made you look up? So surprised I was to see how you frowned. She shook her head. *Before anything worse happens, the family needs you should stop this now.*

Nate wasn't willing to stop. "You don't care about responsibility," he argued. Then he took a breath, my brave boy, and told the truth on you. "Dad, you're just being mean."

Meanness, Jake, what we allowed to live in the house between us. Me with Mae, not caring how you should suffer. Keeping my ghosts secret. You with your hidden slaps. So long ago, you think it should be over and done already, over. But it's not, my Yakkov. This visit with the boys, like a bad penny, it's all come back again.

Here in the house, our Davy with clear eyes finally. A big fight he's making – every single day – he should not take a drink. And he keeps at it, the same like he did candling eggs when he was little. So stubborn, even though it was bedtime. "Let me finish!" Standing up on his tired legs, not willing to quit.

Now Davy laughs like I haven't heard in years, a sound with a little *boychik* in it. Remember that way he had – such a big giggle from his small chest? Such a smart son, him with the laughing. And all those fancy things, our Davala, he liked to say.

"Listen to my special rock, Mama. A story it's telling. Stop cooking. I want you should come outside. There's a dragon in the clouds."

So why didn't I put that the spoon on the stove, stop everything, let myself play with him? Tell me, what was so big and important, out of the kitchen I should shoo that boy? Yes, I had work or Mae to see or Mamale to fuss with? *Be a better mother,* she always told me. She meant a mother what didn't get distracted by the Guardians or a Jewish Center meeting – *ai yai yai,* so much I put in our poor Davy's way.

Tell me, Jake – how can I make right by our boys? This talking I'm doing, it's not working. Just now – Nate, I tried to tell him how it was. "That you're calling neglect? Forget about it." About Shlima and Mamale and Gitl, he just laughed. "You and your stories! When my boys were young, I tried to be like you. But that kind of gift – for making things up – I don't have."

"A story it's not," I argued, but our eldest, him with the reason in his eyes, he didn't believe me. Tell me, Jake. What should I do?

Get up, I know. Try again. Be stubborn like Davy. Out of this room I need to go.

But make myself, I can't. Too scared. Too shaky. Like some nights, that first year after Mae died. Remember how tight you held me? So many tears. So much missing. Why, I want to know, wasn't I brave enough to tell you every single reason what made me sad?

Mamale gone. *Oy,* how I missed her! Not just Mae, but Gitl and Shlima too. Maybe you would've laughed, like Nate, thinking *My wife, such a meshuggeneh.* Maybe no. The truth you might've seen, what lived in my eyes.

You felt the shyness, I know – a bashful woman, your wife, without her spirits. Each time we touched, like a glass at a wedding, I broke apart.

Smashed under a napkin I was – from being so lonely. Missing Mae, you thought. Yes, of course. But missing so much more too. Would you've understood how odd it felt – just you and me and the pleasure? Without my ghosts in my body, some kind of inexperienced girl I became all over again.

So gentle you were, Jake, with your new virgin. Under my hands on your skin, such a difference I could feel, how much you'd changed. From Mae's illness it seemed – is that when it started? Yes? No? Well anyway, until then, your *meshuggeneh* wife, she was just blind.

And like I told Shoshie, maybe at first you were glad, a cancer what came to your rival. But this I didn't say – that gladness, I could feel how it gradually melted away. And yes, in a spitting minute of meanness, to San Francisco you wouldn't let me go for her surgery. No, you yelled, nurse her I couldn't in our house when she came home. But once you visited and saw her pain – the lines on her face, the thick bandages – big enough you were to stop fighting. The day you watched Art hit a hole in their kitchen wall, then start crying – a different man you tried to be.

Swallowing the anger, walking away from any yelling. All those times I came home late from her house – dark already, not a bit of food on the stove. Such a stare you gave, ready to shout, "Where have you been? A man needs his supper!" But then you stopped. I watched, I saw the big swallow you made for your words. And before I knew it, for eggs you'd sent Davy. "Tonight, we eat scrambled." When I got up to fix, into a chair you ordered me. "Nate, pour your mama a cup of coffee. Mimi, cut toast."

Jake's changing, Gitl whispered afterwards, helping with the dishes. *Of him, I'm proud.*

No pride in me those days – in my heart lived too much sadness. Your help – like Mamale breaking ghost rules to mop the kitchen floor or Shlima pinning up laundry – I let go by without a single word. So sorry now, Jake, I couldn't find in myself a "thank you." The last two months before Mae died, such a *mensh* you were! All I ever wanted a man should be.

And it didn't stop, the minute we got her buried. From me to the boys, you turned your eyes. All right, so maybe it was too late by them, but remember how the Forest Service you studied when Nate decided on it? All those articles you mailed, so a hopeful something he should have to read between bombing missions over Italy. And when Davy came home from the war, all night you stayed up with him, the poor boy, he couldn't stand sleeping. So what he couldn't say anything, just stared at the wall? Cards you played or interesting items from the paper you read him. Remember the first smile you got from that boy – reading the letter, from the Tanakas, they were coming home?

He couldn't know, you didn't tell, all your extra work to keep their ranch going. Those years locked up in Colorado, it was you what kept it afloat so they should come home to something. And remember how Davy, he left the house for the first time – but only if you should go with him – the day we went over there to clean? Such a pleasure it was, to make ready for that homecoming. How eager, his fingers, to do that work.

And Davy stayed that night – when the gun you had to get because those stupid hooligans, they were coming. Out on the porch with you he stood, facing down those drunks. "Jap lover!" he told me they yelled, slurring the words over and over. But no fists, like the old days – you it was what kept Davy calm. In Yiddish, making up curses to call down on their ignorance. In English, quoting the constitution, remembering from citizenship class.

Grown tall you were by then, Jake, doing right by me, your sons, and the neighbors. Such courage it took, you should learn to live a different way. I'm sorry I forgot how you much changed – all these months, so taken up with the hurt of Davy's story. No – not forgetting. But like the stubborn woman I am, couldn't feel. Only Nate's old pain. My own. Yours. The whole business. Now the big picture – it's coming clear.

And if you could change, my Yakkov – you think maybe I have it in me to join you? You think I'm big enough so the secrets what's left, their telling I can do? It's my turn, yes, for the hardest work in my life I've been doing. To make peace in this house, now that's my job.

Peace: for Davy, for Nate and for Mimi. What I want should bloom between us. Peace for Shoshie and what's to come.

But *oy*, so scared I am, Jake. Afraid it's not in me. Please. I'm asking, on my knees even. I have need. I want you should find me. Jakey, please. It's your wife what's asking. Come back. I want. I need. You. Your hand.

Chapter 38
MAKING THINGS RIGHT

SHOSHANA

The peace I felt with Uncle Nate fades as soon as Mom arrives, with Uncle Mas and Rob slipping in quietly behind her. She brings a whiff of the evening, dusky light and strong breezes, which push against the house. "Shoshie, what a haircut – you look so different I never would've recognized you. Oh my God, Mom. All sticks and bones. You need to put on a little weight." She greets each brother and sister-in-law with a loud smack and a flurry of criticism. The sting in her words, I realize after looking at her closely, is to keep us from noticing her own scrawny figure and slight limp.

Uncle Mas nods and draws me to him, his arm around my shoulder. He doesn't say anything, just sighs and gives me a little squeeze. Rob sets a tin of chocolate chip cookies down behind Mom on the kitchen table. Making sure that she's not looking, he rolls his eyes.

Mom takes charge of the supper preparations, and makes her own salad dressing instead of Grandma's favorite. She *tsks* over the pot roast I've cooked and then shrugs. "Well, it'll have to do." I move around her carefully, managing not to get impatient, until she sends me to count the plates at the table in case I missed anyone when I set it earlier. "You don't think I can add?" I hiss, fourteen again.

"Don't mind her, dolly," a pale Grandma whispers from the couch in the living room where we've set up the big family table. She interrupts the weepy conversation she's having with Uncle Davy. "Your poor mother is only trying to find her place."

Mom doesn't fit, I understand, as she leads the conversation during the meal: asking Uncle Nate intelligent questions about his work and Uncle Davy about this year's soccer team at his junior high school. But she's too loud, too quick for everyone else to get a word in. "You should retire, Nate," she declares. "That job is no good for you. Davy, when in the world are you going to fix up that house?" The worst moment is when she puts Grandma on the spot. "What did you decide to pay Shoshie for taking care of you?" I slam down my glass of iced tea and get ready to yell.

Uncle Mas stops me. "I know the main celebration is tomorrow, but I want to thank Mimi for this little reunion and birthday party." He bows his head at her. "It was her idea and organization. Without her, we wouldn't be together now."

Without her, I think, we might all be having a good time instead of looking at our plates with red faces. Without her, we might be quietly making a circle around Grandma as she begins this uncertain time – it should take a long while, please – of saying goodbye.

I sit up sharply in my chair. Maybe Mom doesn't know, maybe she can't see all the changes in her mother. Then I hear Aviva's sarcastic voice in my head. *And maybe the Pope is a Jew.*

Of course Mom knows, and she's just as sad and uncomfortable as Uncle Nate and Davy. I can tell by the way she sneaks a look at Grandma that she's hungry for more of her – wanting time. But she's clumsy and awkward about it, just like her reply to Uncle Mas's compliment about bringing us together. It's not in her to say thank you. Only a sharp "So what's wrong with the rest of you, you didn't think of it first?"

Uncle Mas has the nerve to laugh. "Why has it always been so hard for you to accept a pat on the back?"

Mom flushes a surprising red and softens her voice for the first time that evening. She hesitates, then admits, "I don't know."

"I do," Grandma interrupts, getting teary. She takes a breath. "Praise I didn't give Mimi enough, so what kind of practice did she get with compliments?" Grandma pushes her fork around her plate, then looks directly at her daughter. "All of you – I neglected something terrible. I'm sorry, *bubelah.* It's my fault."

"No it isn't," Uncle Davy says gently. He sets his fork down next to his second helping of fudge cake. "All afternoon you've been talking about the past and everything you didn't do right by us. Enough, Mama. I'm not willing to hear anymore."

"She was only taking responsibility," Mom defends, puffing her chest out like one of the ranch's old roosters. "Apologizing – it's about time someone did for all the *mishegoss* that happened around here."

"Wait a doggoned minute," Uncle Nate begins. "It's not all Mama's fault."

Mom won't let him interrupt. "Why are you so quick to shut her up and pretend that everything is okay? What's Mama going to say that you don't want to hear?"

"I've heard it all," Davy insists, his voice gone hard and stubborn. "And the 'I'm sorry's' do no good, anyway. Enough is enough."

"She must've been reading your Big Book, Davy." Mom is mean enough to sneer a little. "Isn't saying 'I'm sorry' one of the twelve steps from AA?"

Everyone takes a breath as if Mom has hit us. Uncle Nate glances quickly at his brother and almost stands up. "So who's going to apologize for Dad?" he shouts with a white face, ready to spit at his sister. "Since you were his favorite, maybe you can explain what he did with his hands."

"Cut it out," I yell at them all, ready to do anything it takes to stop the arguing. "This is Grandma's house," and I look at her weeping face for a minute, then scowl at the three of them. "You can't talk like this here."

Stupid, selfish, I want to say, thinking only of yourselves and not your mother. Can't you take a little care for her and just shut up? Because what must it be doing to Grandma to see Nate clench his fists in his lap and look ready to take a beating? How it must hurt to watch the coldness come back into her daughter's eyes. And then there's Uncle Davy, curling into his seat as if he's actually getting smaller. The laughing man who made jokes all afternoon about his teaching, his kids and even his drinking, is gone. Grandma is crying, of course, pulling at a tuft of hair just behind her ear. She stops working the gray curl to wipe her eyes. "How could you have lied to me?" she asks.

"We're not lying," Mom says, her own voice shaking, but I can't tell if she's trembling from sadness or anger. "This is the first time anyone here has told the truth."

"Whose truth?" I demand to know, thinking of young Jake, the bruised boy I held in the laundry room. And what about Mae? Who speaks for her?

"What hurts," Grandma says again, the word stumbling and broken, "the lies. *Oy,* so many lies."

When she looks past me, I realize that she is not talking to us, but to Grandpa's ghost – a real spirit, strong and fluid, not the wisp I've imagined – who stands beside my chair suddenly at the foot of the long table. He's in worn overalls, a bit of mud caked at both knees. And the Guardians are here too, all eight of them positioned in the room's shadows. They have made a circle around our chairs, shafts of silence with flickering eyes. Uncle Mas nods at me, *Yes,* and then his slight smile deepens. *Trust what you see,* he says in a voice that I hear in my head.

So ashamed I was, Grandpa answers Grandma, *afraid you should leave me. All those years I lied so you should stay.*

Uncle Davy answers his mother, too. "We wanted to protect you, Mama. Maybe it was a mistake."

A mistake, Grandpa says, *a stupidity, a wrong – my hitting. What I did, I could hardly live with myself sometimes.*

Uncle Nate shakes his head. "We knew how much it would hurt if you knew. And I guess it's crazy, but we didn't want the family to fall apart."

"Better it would have been, maybe," Grandma says, "if it had." She is crying again, looking up at Grandpa's ghost. "You I stopped from telling me a dozen times – not wanting I should know, not wanting to hear it. My ear I didn't give you when I should."

I didn't think the truth, it could live between us, Grandpa replies, choking a little. *So far we'd come together, all those miles, I was afraid we'd lose them.* Tears begin to tremble in his voice. *Ai my Rheabela, without you, it was me what didn't think I could live.*

"And just where could we have gone?" Mom asks impatiently, twisting her coffee cup on the tablecloth. She looks up at her two brothers. "It was the Depression, for pete's sake. You think we could have had a better life if we left Papa and starved?"

"It wasn't a good life here," Uncle Davy answers. With the words, his face grows smooth and straightens. It's as if he has come back to some sure thing that he knows. He runs a hand over his fork and looks calmly at his sister. "At least for me."

A lie you turned everything good by not telling, Grandma weeps to Grandpa. *So blind you kept me to my own part.* She stares at him, holding tight to her napkin. *By the time Davy came home from the war, weren't we strong enough already? After everything what happened? Together the truth we should have faced.*

It was me, not brave enough, he replies, crying too. *I couldn't stand it, you should leave me and run away.*

No, Grandma shakes her head, tears marking her cheeks. *How could I run? Like my own hands you were, so much we'd grown together. All those years, what roots lived between us, couldn't be undone. And then there were my lies too – about my spirits, about the Guardians. So shamed I am. Please. I want you should forgive me. Who was I not to trust what you'd become?*

Mom has been frowning and watching Uncle Davy. "I don't care what he did to you – Papa was a good man. He took you in. Gave you a home. Made you family. When you came home from the army, he fell all over himself trying to right by you."

Uncle Nate growls, "Too little too late by then. You," he points at Mom, "could never see who he really was. You only saw what you wanted."

Can you see all of me now? Grandma asks in a whisper. *I want you should know the truth. But I need to know. Is what we had – never mind the lying – enough?*

Mom argues, "Well, who says the ogre that you talk about is the one and only truth?"

Grandpa shakes his head. *Of course, bubee. But something more needs should be done.* He walks quickly to kneel down beside Uncle Davy. He puts a ghostly hand on his and starts to speak. *Your forgiveness I ask – for every single hit and bruise. A fool I was, so stupid and angry.* Grandpa takes a breath. *Mean to my beautiful son, who looked too much like me as a boy.*

Uncle Davy turns to face his siblings, "Well, here's one thing I know is true. I was too screwed up after the war to care what Dad did. And mostly too drunk to notice. But now it matters – a lot. At least he tried."

"See?" Mom says, glowering at Uncle Nate. "You don't have the only angle on the whole business."

Uncle Nate sounds all of twelve again. "Well, Miss Know-It-All, neither do you."

Grandpa gets up and moves to his other son. *So proud I am, how you tried to protect Davy and Mama. Out of my way you kept them, took their punishment for your own. I'm so sorry, my boy, for all what your ignorant father did to you. Will you forgive me this time, now that I ask again?*

"The point is," Uncle Nate begins, but then, as if he can see Grandpa peering at him, he starts to look uncertain. Grandpa pats his cheek. *Such a good son, I have.* "Oh hell," Uncle Nate gives up. "I don't know my point."

Aunt Carol jumps in for the first time. "What matters is how you took what was given and used it." She looks right at Grandma and says, "I can tell you that Jake's mistakes made Nate a better father. How he was with our boys, that's the point."

Grandpa stands up and nods at Grandma. *A woman to be proud of. Like you, heart of my heart – she's got a good mouth. Your mouth it was what kept me here all those years, made me better. About your spirits, you didn't have to tell. So much love without knowing. All the best what I am,* he sways a little, then wipes his eyes, *I got from you.*

Oy Jake, Grandma wails, and she sounds so shaky that I want to get up to hold her.

Don't, Uncle Mas silently cautions. *Let them be.*

Grandpa lifts his hands and presses them against his chest. *Could we have done better? Yes. By each other and the kinder. But you're the lucky one, my Rheabela. What I wouldn't give for the time you still have left.*

"Daddy was a hard man," Mom admits slowly, "full of complications. Mean and kind he was – both. And it may be hard to believe, but I think he was sorry. From the little bits he told me, he regretted what he did."

"Maybe," Uncle Nate surprises her by agreeing. He pauses to looks up at Grandma, then goes on. "I never told anyone, but he apologized to me once – at the anniversary party." He bites his lip. "I couldn't accept it. Man, is that something I regret."

Grandma continues to cry, watching her son and Grandpa's ghost standing just behind him. There's a hunger in his face as Grandpa weeps too.

"Regrets," Uncle Davy declares, his voice somehow both young and tender, "only keep you in the past." He shakes his head. "Some things you can't get back. There's time you can't make up."

He pulls his chair closer to Aunt Mari but continues to talk to his mother. "You think you're sorry for what you did? What about me, the family drunk?

How can I make that up to Mari and the kids – all that I lost? All the time I didn't give them?" Aunt Mari puts a hand on his arm, and he stops to sigh at her. By the time the breath has come and gone, I can see that Uncle Davy's eyes are wet. "Mama, listen to me. I just have right now – the only thing I can give anyone. I don't need your apologies for the past anymore. All I want is enough of you in the present."

Grandma really begins to sob now, and I am crying with her. "Mama," Uncle Davy begs, "just be with me."

Grandpa speaks to her over the tears, a loud voice tumbling down the length of the table. *You got time, my Rheabie, so use it. You want love? You got it. Look at what's here.* And then he fades, and the Guardians fade with him. They leave us – still and shaken – sniffling in the quiet room.

Chapter 39
LISTENING TO THE QUIET

RHEABIE

Too quiet, this house, full of dreaming. Danger, mine enemy, it's you I can feel, how you're here. How come this visit, you with the cold hand on my shoulder? What do you want, waking me like this? Stealing my breath, making my lungs breathe tight. Sitting on my chest, bringing the smell of death. Enough already, you with the nightmares. What's it going to take, you should finally just go away?

It's not enough, tonight's dinner – the heart of the family broken? Jake, down on his knees, begging forgiveness – you want more than that? Listen, we made right – finally – between us. All what happened – the beatings, the arguing and betrayal – that we can put to rest.

That's not the danger.

No? But I thought ... I was sure ... *Oy vey*, Wina. Between you and my friend the enemy, this I don't need – another mystery in my life. Hard enough, this one. All the twists and turning. So many little pieces, so much of my life cracked apart.

So *nu*, why don't you show yourself, already? Stop hiding in the shadows. It would kill you, maybe, to just say straight out what you want? A little hint. A tiny bit of guidance. You should know by now, guessing games I can't do.

No guessing. A matter of thought and consideration. The problem is beyond us, as Guardians. It's your task, a concern for the living. Something has been left undone.

No! What do want from me? So tired I am with all the doing. So late. So close to dying. Use your eyes.

Use yours, Rheabie. Listen. A gift was given you long ago. It's come time that you need to use it. Feel the song that lives in your hands.

So tired. Too tired. I can't feel nothing.

Hush, lassie. Listen. Something big is at stake.

Bigger than Jake, what *tsuris* he brought to the family? Bigger than my part, how in ignorance I helped?

Bigger. It's a danger and hurt to all you hold. Listen. The quiet knows.

Chapter 40
MAKING PLANS

MIMI

The quiet in this house is too loud, damn it. It's such a roar that it pulls me out of a dream in the middle of the night. I'm snatched away from my place at Aviva's kitchen table where I'm holding my new grandbaby. Hannah's blanket feels so real against my skin, for a moment I forget where I am. Nothing can locate me: no shush of cars speeding down the expressway. No groan from the refrigerator. The silence is complete.

Then the wall clock chimes. The quiet shifts around me. Three somber gongs announce that I'm at Mom's house, trapped in Petaluma. And it's real, not a nightmare, this California darkness unbroken by streetlights. I catch my breath, scared at being back in this solitary place again.

Is anyone else bothered by that fact that the neighbors are more than a good yell away, in case anything should happen? It'd take an ambulance more than fifteen minutes to get here if Mom, so frail these days, should fall or have a heart attack. But she doesn't care, stubbornly snoring down the hall in her small bedroom. "There's a phone in here if help I should need." Shoshie isn't worried – "Mom, really, we're all right" – asleep in my old bed. The doors are closed, but I can picture them both: Mom, with her arm thrown over the top of her head, sawing wood with her mouth open. Shoshana, making a nest of the covers, bunching them around her shoulders like she's done since she was a little girl.

And Davy and Nate are down the road, sleeping comfortably with their wives in a king-size at that motel on Western Avenue. I'm the only one left uncomfortable and restless in the living room on the lumpy couch. And why? Because I insisted, refusing to take Shoshie's bed away from her. She offered, wanting to make my night easy, but I said no. "What, you think I need help? Some kind of special treatment? Treating me like I'm handicapped. Get out of here! I'm fine."

Shoshie knew, of course, I was only teasing. If Mom hadn't been eavesdropping from the hallway, I would've told her the truth. "You deserve that bed more than I do. Some kind of reward for all the work you've done." Honestly, I couldn't stand it – waiting on Mom like that, keeping track of all the medications. It'd drive me nuts, getting her out of the house to doctor appointments on time. If there's any kind of heaven, Shoshie's already earned her place in it. Who knew she'd turn out to be that kind of daughter? Abe would be proud.

And so would Papa, looking at me with that knowing grin on his face. "What did I tell you?" He'd smooth down his beard. "There's more to Shoshie than you ever knew." The thought of him brings the silence back – a sad quiet in the inky darkness. I press harder into the couch, trying to escape. But the nubby tweed smells like Papa – a faint whiff of tobacco. It must be the remains of those cigarettes he rolled himself. "Better than store-bought." And a little bit of Art Katz, who always drove up from San Francisco with a box of his god-awful cigars.

It's not fair that the smells have lingered all these years – even though the men have left us. I'd trade the stink in a second to have Papa here again. You'd think I'd get used to it – these visits without him. But I have to steel myself each time I walk in the door and feel how much he's gone.

Of course, if he were, all that arguing at dinner tonight wouldn't have happened. Nate and Davy – why did they say things that are better left unsaid? I could've kicked them both for upsetting Mom like that. What's the matter with their eyes? Can't they see she's on her last legs? So why couldn't they've picked something a little more cheery to talk about? And why did I have to defend Papa so quickly? If they were going to get bitter like that, I could've just let them have their say – gotten it over with – instead of making everyone mad.

Damn it! I promised myself I wouldn't do that this visit. Up and down I swore to Padre Guitierrez – come hell or high water, I'd keep my foot out of my mouth. And in just a couple of hours, there it was, the leather between my teeth – like always. Being here makes me forget who I am.

Or takes me back to who I used to be, a fierce and defensive girl. Quick to anger. In an argument, someone who's sure she's right. I thought I'd gotten away from that, grown up to be someone different. But whenever I come home, I act like that girl again. Maybe Papa's beatings affected me too, although I didn't know it. All the hidden fighting in the house – it seeped into my skin.

That sounds too much like Mom, full of fancy insight. Or worse, like Mas, a fool shrink. I don't want to embroider the plain truth or dig into the past to make sense out of my behavior. It's simple. I lost my temper. I won't do it again.

It'll help to hold on to why I'm here: for Mom, for our big project together. If I can just keep focused on the plans for Abe's condos, everything will stay clear. Driving in, I realized that Mom's properties are smaller than I remembered. I was thinking we'd only need one or two lots, but for a development big enough to make a profit, it's going to take more. And yes, it'll change the face of Chapman Lane, but there's no helping it. The pool and tennis courts are needed to attract the right kind of clientele. And look what we'll add to this town – a bit of class, better people and some beauty – built in Abe's memory. Working on this together will bring Mom and I closer than we've ever been.

So I need to stay patient and find the words to convince her. If I can just show her my file with all the pictures, maybe she'll see. These drawings are the best I've ever done – almost professional. Those blueprints and the landscape plans would make Papa proud. He liked to build, to make something out of nothing. Look what he did with the ranch. I'm just taking it one more step.

If I can just keep my grip and hang on to my temper. If I don't let go of myself, things will be fine. It'll help if I can play with numbers. A good game of cards will hold me down. The five of clubs, then six of hearts – an order I can count on. All I need to do is place the numbers in a row.

Chapter 41
LIKE MOTHER, LIKE DAUGHTER

SHOSHANA

I wake with my hands clenched, hearing cards shuffle in the kitchen. I try to hold on to my sleep, but there's the slap of dealing and a pair of muted voices: sounds I remember from growing up in Ithaca. I listen closely, my chest starting to ache.

Fridays, Mom and Dad would stay up late, the two of them talking softly and playing cribbage. Now and again, I'd wake up when they couldn't manage to smother a laugh. "Oh Abe!" I'd hear Mom cry. I'd try to guess who'd just won as they shuffled and dealt another round, but I always fell back asleep too fast. The smell of Dad's pipe and the sound of clinking glasses meant that it was a gin rummy night.

After he died, Mom still kept those Friday evenings, crying and playing solitaire. The two tapers she lit in the monogrammed candlesticks had to burn themselves out before she'd pull away and go to bed.

I wonder what memory drove Mom to the cards tonight. Did she miss Dad too much after all the hard talk at dinner, the bath of family tears?

Of course, maybe it was Grandma who started the game, and Mom who got up to join her. Maybe they decided to celebrate her birthday a little early or indulge in a midnight feast. Whatever it is, there's too much muffled laughter for me not to want to be a part of it. I throw on my bathrobe and hurry down the hallway. "Deal me a hand," I start to say at the kitchen door.

But instead of Grandma playing with Mom at the table, it's Padre Guitierrez. They look up from the furious round of double solitaire that I have interrupted, and she blushes bright red.

"Jeez o'pizzeria," I gasp, letting the wall catch me. I'm stiff, a fence post propped up against Grandma's wallpaper. And like the wood, I feel mute.

"Jeez o' what?" Mom asks, looking over the cards in the middle of the table. She finds a move and slaps down an eight of spades.

"You're playing with a Guardian." I force the words out, feeling silly. She's got eyes. She knows.

"Padre Guitierrez," Mom introduces us as if it's nothing. Her voice is refined, thin and polite. "Have you met?"

The padre smiles, keeping his eyes on the game. They're both acting so normal it makes me want to scream. "He's a ghost, Mom."

She nods, moves a card. Then another. Padre Guitierrez and I watch her make play after play until she shrugs her shoulders. "So, I win."

Win what? The Surprise Award? The Friend of the Guardians statue? Wasn't our Expose-the-Family-Secrets testimonial dinner over a few hours ago?

I feel like Shlima, ready to pull my hair and shout, *What's the world coming to?* I wish Mamale were here, so I could groan with her. *Oy vey! Oy, such a big vey.*

Gitl might pat me on the head. *Why so shocked, bubee? Seeing spirits, maybe it runs in the family.* I imagine her rising out of the floorboards to stand near me. *DNA. That genetics business. It could be blood.*

Maybe so, but this is my mother we're talking. A Republican, much to Grandma's disgust, and member in good standing of the Country Club. President of the Hadassah, as traditional as they come. There's nothing strange or wild in her, like Uncle Mas or Grandma. She's not given to visions – at least as far as I know.

But the Guitierrez is here. Look at the evidence, Gitl insists.

Better yet, look at Mimi, Shlima crows. *So proud.*

She's right. Mom leans back in her chair, done with sorting the two decks of cards into neat piles. A grin takes over her face as she shrugs her shoulders again and looks at me. "Surprise."

It's the pleasure in her eyes that makes me give up, surrender. I throw my hands into the air, then kiss Mom on the top of the head. "Wow," I breathe, pulling up a chair beside her. "Who knew?"

"Who knew about you?" she comments slyly. Then she pats my hand after a moment. "Like mother, like daughter, I guess. But don't tell your grandmother. I wouldn't want her to be upset."

"Upset? She'll be beside herself with happiness."

"Oh no," Mom groans, but she might be hiding a smile. "I was afraid of that."

I close my eyes for a moment, imagining Grandma's pleasure. Instead, I see her as a young mother standing beneath the apple tree. She's keeping an eye on Davy while hanging out the laundry. The Guardians watch from the hill while Shlima and Gitl squabble over the proper way to fold sheets. Grandma trembles, positioning one of Nate's shirts on the line with a clothespin. Unable to trust the magic around her, she stabs another one in place. "All these years," I try to explain to Mom, "in the ghost department, Grandma thought she was alone."

Except for Mae and Uncle Mas, I add silently, but that's not my business to tell. Grandma can decide how much of the story she wants Mom to know.

She looks down at the tabletop suddenly, avoiding my eyes.

"Well, they can be a little scary," I offer, not wanting her to think less of

Grandma. "At least," I nod to Padre Guitierrez, "you sure as hell were to me."

"Be nice," Mom corrects in a tone I recognize from childhood. "You know better than to swear in front of a priest."

It's so absurd that I laugh and the padre laughs with me. Mom joins us, for the first time looking fully at ease.

"Sha! Enough!" She chortles. "We'll wake your grandmother."

"No." I shake my head. "She's up already. I thought she was playing with you."

"Maybe the bathroom?" Mom guesses.

I'm beginning to feel worried. "It's empty. I checked on my way out here. And when I looked in, Grandma wasn't in her room."

"What?" Mom gasps and in two seconds she's up, calling into the living room, "Mom? Where are you?" She runs through the house, checking every space. The walk-in closet in Davy's room. The garage – "Oh my god," she cries. "What if she fell out here?" No matter where we look, Grandma doesn't answer. By the time we put on jackets and go outside to search, I'm feeling too scared to talk. Padre Guitierrez follows us and fades into the shadows by the apple tree, but Grandma isn't sitting near it. The garden is empty, the driveway long and bare.

I walk close to Mom as we hurry down Chapman Lane, drawing on her for comfort. She links her arm with mine. "Don't worry, honey. We'll find her."

Three houses down we see a hunched figure by a pond, hugging her knees. Grandma waves when we get near. "I knew you'd come."

"What are you doing? Trying to catch your death?" Mom scolds, throwing her jacket over Grandma. The fear makes a knife of her voice, hard and biting. "*Oy*, your hands. Cold to the bone. We have to get you in."

And then she stares at Grandma with what Aviva and I call "the look." "I want you to get up, right this minute." Mom's eyebrows come together, and her tone goes shrill. "Don't pull any of your stunts on me."

Unlike Aviva and me, Grandma is bold enough to ignore her. She turns her face up to look at the sky. "Do you know the stars, Shoshie? The names what Grandpa always told me? Orion's belt. The Seven Sisters." Her voice catches for a minute. "Every year, my birthday, he used to bring me here."

"He did not," Mom objects, but, after a moment, she sits down on the ground beside her. "Ach, so wet," she fusses. "You must be soaked."

There's enough moon for me to see Grandma swallow a smile, then take the hand of her protesting daughter. "So *nu*," she says to me, "what's it going to take, *you* should sit?"

I settle on her other side, leaning into a thin shoulder. Mom's right:

Grandma needs as much warmth as she can get. The night has an edge, a cold that cuts under the voices of the frogs and crickets. The stars above us waver in the hands of the wind.

"You and Grandpa always had your own party here for your birthday?" I ask, placing my arm carefully around her waist and hugging her to me. Mom lifts her arm across Grandma's shoulders, holding her tight.

Grandma settles into our touch with a sigh. "At night, yes. Always late, when no one was looking." The lines beside her eyes flare into a corona of wrinkles as she smiles. "He said we should start the year right."

Mom shivers and shakes her head. "Well, I think we should go in, unless you're still hoping Papa will show up for this." She sniffs, sounding insulted or maybe envious. "Even if he came, Shoshie and I would just be in the way."

"God, you're nervy!" I lean forward to tease my mother. She makes a face – it's too dark for me to tell if it's angry or playful – as I ask, "Besides, what makes you think Grandma was talking about sex?"

Mom and Grandma laugh in a big burst, silencing the frogs for a moment. I blush, feeling stupid, when I realize that I've been wrong. "Sex, of course sex," Grandma chuckles, shifting to get up finally. "And he got good at it by the end, too."

"*Sha!* This we don't need to hear," Mom stands and declares, brushing bits of leaves and grass off her bottom.

"No, it's important," Grandma asserts, looking back one last time at the pond. "Shoshie should know – never say a person can't learn."

They giggle, and I feel misplaced, thrown out of my part in the conversation. I feel young, too awkward or inexperienced to understand all of what's been said. The sex part, yes, but that's not the heart of why they're laughing. I stand up, trying to put together the puzzle, as I did listening to the bits of my parents' card games on Friday nights.

It has something to do with the way Mom lifts a shoulder and throws her hair back off her neck, smiling at Grandma. Grandma pats her cheek, like she's a little girl again, and says, "Glad I am, *bubee*, you got my eyes."

I don't need an imaginary Gitl this time to get it. Grandma knows about Padre Guitierrez and Mom's games with him. She can see that Mom feels at home with the possibility of Grandpa coming to the pond tonight as a ghost. But did Mom see him earlier and hear all that he said at dinner? Just how much of this spirit business can my mother do?

I walk behind them on the way home, watching how easily they chat together. Grandma laughs, then turns her head to the side to look up at Mom with a surprised, "No kidding?" She claps her hands together, but I can't tell if it's in delight or sadness. "*Ai yai yai,* my Mimi. So lonely you must've been."

Mom nods, and Grandma pulls in closer toward her. She stumbles on a clump of wild grasses and grabs her arm. Their figures blend in front of me, a damp shadow. As they hurry forward into the darkness, I can only catch bits of their words.

"But why?"

"Crazy."

The O'Dell's retriever starts to howl. "Shut up!" I order it, trying to make sense of the pieces.

"Stubborn."

"No, angry."

"Hard. So hard."

The words float like dandelion fluff ahead of me down the driveway, so faint and insubstantial, that if I don't hurry, they'll be scattered by the wind. For a moment, I imagine reaching to try and snag them. Or at least, running to catch up, so I can hear. But I stop myself. If living in Grandma's company has taught me anything, it's that I know these particular seeds don't belong to me.

I walk more slowly, watching Mom and Grandma enter the circle of the porch light. As they pause at the bottom of the steps, the night stills. No crickets. No barking retriever. I can barely hear the sound of the driveway under my tennis shoes. Grandma nods, and presses her hands into her chest, as if something hurts her. Mom straightens, lengthening the posture she's so proud of, and wipes a tear.

I hear a sigh, a breath that teases the grasses at my feet into a shiver. Goosebumps break out on my arms.

Then Mom's voice: "Shoshie, we're waiting. Hurry up. Don't dawdle."

Grandma spreads her arms in a welcome. "Where's my wolf girl? Come here."

I hurry into the warmth of the house, welcomed into whatever has happened between them. The kitchen is roasting, alive with heat. But Mom fusses, rushing to get Grandma a sweater, wool socks and a blanket. "For goodness sakes, put the kettle on, Shoshie," she orders in an impatient voice. But then she winks, slipping the knife from her words, purposely making them softer. Grandma looks up from where Mom is helping her into her slippers and makes a face. "Do you know who this is?" she asks.

The whole house feels different, as if all the stories that Grandma has told about the ranch are living in the curtains and floorboards. Shlima, Mamale and Gitl are listening to us, wanting to hear this new Mimi talk.

And Mae comes to listen, shimmering in the night air like a bit of fire, a light gleaming in a corner of the kitchen. Art leans against the counter, a solid shadow who wants to hear. And then there are the figures of young

Nate, Mimi with a bow in her head, and Davy holding on to his blue blanket. Grandpa waits in the living room in his easy chair.

But when we settle down with our mugs of tea, I know that the house holds only the three of us. It's the late hour and the eagerness between Mom and Grandma that makes it seem so full. Their words tumble, creating quick pictures of the past, one after the other. They call up names, draw them into the air and laugh. I watch the room quiver, full of wisps that rise like the steam from our mugs. I blink and try to hold on to it all, but it slips away.

The only certainty I understand is this: Mom heard Grandma's spirits when she was young, but she was never able to see them. The voices of her aunts and grandmother scared her, made her feel angry and alone. Even though she knew Grandma heard them too, she didn't have the courage to tell her. Now, she's sorry she didn't speak up. "A whole *meshuggeneh* family we've got. So why should I have been afraid to be nuts too?"

"Not crazy," Grandma shakes her head. "Only people what know from magic." She sips her tea noisily, then looks up. "It's a gift, Mimala, to know how to see."

The Guardians made Mom a gift when they began visiting her last winter. The night my father came back, she knew she'd changed. She could believe the padre when he told her later that Dad had been called by the Guardians when they stood in a circle around her. If all eight of them were united, they had the power to make appear what she needed most.

"Of course, yes. The Circle," Grandma calls, slapping a hand against the table. "How could I forget?" I'm not sure if she means the ritual that Mom saw or the fact that we had all eight of the Guardians here tonight with Grandpa. I take a breath: they'd made a circle around us. Is that why he came?

Mom shakes her head, "What's most important, the padre told me – they hardly ever help the living. The Guardians never do it without asking a price."

Grandma stares at her daughter for a moment, then smiles warmly. "So *nu*, what do you think they want from you?"

Mom tries to laugh. "That I should tell you about our project. Every night, whoever came to visit said the same thing. 'Go home. Rheabie needs to know.'"

"Yes, I need," Grandma nods quietly. But the deep tone of her voice makes me uncertain that she's talking about Mom's mysterious project. She smiles at Mom. "What a pleasure to have such a daughter by my side."

The room becomes quiet, and this time I'm sure that someone is listening. The night feels ancient, the little breeze that makes its way beneath the door wild and cold. "Wina!" I want to call, welcoming her leafy wisdom. I press my hands against the wood of the table. There's something she's waiting for,

I sense, but I don't know what.

So I turn back to Mom, who is able to drink in Grandma's compliment without protesting. Unlike tonight at dinner, she doesn't push it away. She simply smiles, then reaches for another cookie. Staring at the chocolate chips, she declares, "There are advantages, I guess, to looking like a scarecrow. I like eating whatever I want."

"Fine you look," Grandma insists. "Still such a beauty. The best parts of your father you got in your face."

I hesitate, afraid to interrupt their enjoyment of each other. But the skittering of leaves I hear outside and the wind tangling in the apple tree makes me speak. "So," I begin, trying to trace the significance of what Mom has told us, "was it the Guardians who brought Grandpa to us at dinner? I was so busy listening that I didn't see how he came."

Mom looks startled. "Papa was here?"

Grandma nods, looking warm. "Giving me back my life, all what was so confused and twisted." She smiles at me. "You heard, Shoshie? Hard words, but he turned the past around into some kind of sense."

Hurt moves like a wave across Mom's face. "I can't believe I missed him. Too busy arguing. "She puts her cookie down. "Just because I had to be right."

Mom's eyes have gone bleak, pale as a January morning in Ithaca. She curls her shoulders forward and covers her face in her hands. The O'Dell's dog goes at it again. Against the front window, I hear the press of the wind.

"The Guardians gave you to me once," I tell her, surprised at how much I want to comfort her. A rush of tears chokes my throat. But I continue, remembering how the Guardians shimmered around me just before Mom appeared in the garden last October. "I needed you but didn't understand what was going on."

"You needed **me**?" Mom lifts her face. This time she flushes pink with pleasure. What I needed, I realize now, is the complicated woman, with smudged eyes and a trembling mouth, who is sitting in this room. But I'm not sure that I could have seen her then, even if I hadn't gotten frightened. It's hard enough to see who she is now.

"But that's not all." I shake my head, looking at Grandma. A light – something alive and knowing under her skin – shines from her face. "After I went back up north, a group of Guardians in Lydon gave me **you**, Grammy." I lean forward to press her twisted, arthritic fingers. "You didn't know, maybe, that's what sent me home?"

"Home?" she asks. A breeze rattles the porch railing.

"Home," I tell her with a smile.

Chapter 42
THE FAMILY DEBT

RHEABIE

Home – where the wind blows. You can hear it, maybe, through the window? Home – the smell of the gum grove. Grass on the hill. Of course I'm tired, Mimala, and it's late, but I want you should listen. Shoshie, enough with my pills. Stop fussing. There's something more what needs I should say.

Home – more than this house. More than what you've come back to. Listen to the night, my dollies. What do you hear?

A dog, yes, the O'Dell's noisy thing. And right – still those crickets. But *bubee*, there's more – the Guardians are singing. Such a music they're making right out there.

A little song, what comes humming up through the table. Put your hand on it. A tune what blows through the curtains and fills up the air.

All right, so maybe you can't hear the music yet, but I'm telling you, the time is coming. Lovies, the price for circles – bringing back Abe and Jake and all what the Guardians have given – will be here soon. There's a debt the Slominski family owes what needs paying. I'd forgotten until Wina reminded me tonight. All winter, so confused I've been. Tonight I heard again finally. The music, *bubelah*, it's part of the cost.

You don't believe? Well then, look around. Where are Mamale and Shlima and Gitl? You think they could've listened to us talk about them all night and not put in their two cents? Back in Terlitza they are, how they were meant. Satisfied spirits at home they've been for years. But how? And who took them? How come, the minute they left, I could hear the Guardians' song?

Yes, Shoshie, good guess. They went with Mae – the minute she stopped breathing. Once it was clear where the train was going after Mae got sick, they'd gone to her and begged. *Please*, Mamale whispered, appearing by her bed one rainy afternoon.

Please what? Mae asked, waving I should stop with the Chekhov story I'd been reading her.

Rheabie, a little tea maybe Mae needs, Shlima suggested, sounding polite all of a sudden. From the top of the dresser she smiled. *Go. Gey.*

Maybe Rheabie needs, she should hear this, Gitl argued, appearing at the foot of Mae's bed. On the coverlet, she settled. *Bubee*, she patted Mae's knee, *There's a favor we need should ask.*

Mae sighed, then leaned back into her pillows. *So nu?*

If, Mamale began, sounding unsure for the first time. *If it should happen maybe... If the doctors are wrong...*

If from the cancer... Shlima took a breath and then hurried her words. *If you're going to die anyway...*

"*What?*" I screeched. "Nobody's dying here. How can you say such a thing?" Ready I was to throw my book. To yell and scream.

"*Sha!*" Mae spoke to all of us. Such a look in her eyes as she stared at me. "Somebody is dying, but I haven't known how to tell you." The light from the lamp paled her cheeks. "Getting better, I'm not. A happy ending, it's not going to be."

"You don't know!" I argued, stubborn and hopeful. "What, you're a doctor all of sudden? Even that pipsqueak doctor, that Cohen at Mt. Zion, he didn't promise the Angel of Death. I don't want to hear you say such a thing."

Not hearing isn't going to make it any different, Mamale said sharply. Such a comfort she was, yes? My mother, always ready with the sour truth.

Gitl leaned over. *Some things, bubee, can't be changed.*

We don't know! I growled at all of them, even Mae. *The future isn't here yet.*

All right, not here, Mamale gave in. *But knocking on the door. And just in case.* She looked at Mae, her face soft for once. *Would you have it in you to take us home? Like what Mas tried to do.*

"To Terlitza?" Mae laughed. "How could I not? After all your stories, I've always wanted to see that place."

It's not much, Gitl cautioned. *Oh but the trees...*

And such woods, Shlima sighed.

"Full of bullet holes," I reminded her.

The fields! Mamale cooed, as if she was singing some kind of lullaby.

"Muddy. If not under eight feet of snow."

What, you got a lemon in your mouth? my mother asked me. *Shirrup or make nice.*

Neither I could do. What came out my mouth, a scream. "Don't leave!" I called to Mae and my spirits. After all the life what we had known, why was everyone else but me ready it should go away?

"Rheabie, don't," Mae breathed, pulling me to her. So tight, her arms. And the whispers: all what we'd said a thousand times before. "I don't want ... I can't bear ... it breaks my heart ... but *bubee.*" And then the new word. "Enough. I've had enough."

Enough – pretending the scale was wrong, her bones hadn't gotten thinner. Enough – thinking her swollen belly – from the cancer in her liver now – only gas. Enough not keeping food down. So tired. Enough, trapped in her room.

No strength, someplace else she could go.

Oy, how I cried, begging it should be different. All my hopes, all what I'd been working for with the nursing – gone in a second, chased away by the look on Mae's face. Maybe she was wrong, I told myself. Only a nurse – what did she know?

She knew enough not to argue – Mae just held me as the afternoon got longer. No words between us – just looks, little sighs and patting, until it was time I should leave.

And as soon as I tore myself away, my spirits rose up and followed me. Not even out the door of Mae's house and already Shlima began to scold. *Selfish! Thinking only about yourself. Poor Rheabie, all what you're losing in this business. Quit acting like a child. Don't do to Mae what you did to us!*

Do what? I asked, running down the path away from her. Talk about selfish. My sister, she didn't care how I should feel.

Shlima swooped in front of me. *Again you're doing it. Stop with the screaming and crying, like how you brought us out of our graves because you, how could you live, so lost and lonely.* The trees in the gum grove stopped rustling, listening to her. *Taking your clothes off on a winter night in the Ukraine, not caring if you died.*

No, Gitl argued, rising to stand next to me by Art's barn. *We didn't come from death to save Rheabie. This we chose.*

A bad choice, Mamale shook her head, floating above us, *and it's time we should make different. Us you don't need anymore, my daughter. Home we should go.*

"Stop your mouths. *Sha.* I can't take it!" I screamed. "First Mae, then you."

You can take, my mother said, *and that's what's the difference between now and long ago, when you were younger.* She shook her finger in my face. *Live from what Mae taught you. We are not yours to keep. And dolly, neither, I'm sorry to say, is she.*

I looked, *oy* how I looked, at Mamale, a wisp floating in the evening shadows. A light wind what made big and blowy, her black dress. But on her face such a sadness. All what she longed for – Terlitza, its scraggly woods, the smell of the wind come March – from her, this I couldn't hold back.

And Mamale was right. From loving Mae, I'd grown bigger. Even if I wanted different, I didn't need to hang on to the world so tight. So, with all the courage what I could find in me, her ghostly cheek I patted, "It's all right, Mama." Then I walked home, so slowly even the trees I could hear breathing. Each step, first one sad foot, then the other, smack in the heart of the goodbyes, them what should come.

And when finally, after a million years, I got to the kitchen, there you were,

Mimala. Such a soft look that day, when through the screen you saw me. A smile what let me come inside. And there too, Nate and Davy, those good boys, at the table, doing homework. "Hi Mama. "Jake, him what made me sit, rest, "Rheabela, a cup of tea?" That moment, dollies: I thought, maybe yes, maybe true, maybe I can do this. Build from Mae, a life made tender. Keep breathing – in her name – after she should be gone.

But here's the truth, my girls. A secret hope, what I didn't tell anyone – Mae should come back and haunt me. Terlitza she could go – to bring home my spirits, yes – then turn around and come right back. Who knows? A better life we might make together when she should be dead. No Art to bother us. No Jake and his fussing. My sweet Mae I could have all to myself.

It was Mas, him with his ears, what taught me different. One afternoon, my thoughts he heard and some kind of smell, the hope in them, brought him over. Cleaning out Malka's stall, I was. *Oy*, how the boy scared me, sneaking in so quiet and then saying "No."

"No what?" A forkful of hay I'm sorry to say I threw near him.

Mas stepped back. "No, Mae can't come back and be with you."

"Why not?"

"Because of something I learned when I had pneumonia." Mas motioned I should stop, come sit next to him. Interrupt him, I couldn't until he was done.

"When I brought your spirits home, you remember the bonfire in the village afterwards?" he began.

"Yes. So *nu*?" I was impatient, he should get on with it. Bad news I knew that boy had come to say.

"Well, I never told anyone," he said patiently, "but someone was standing in the fire. A Guardian."

Old, she was, that Guardian – older than Wina even. Out of that fire what was burning, she came and took his hand. And then she said, "You have a choice after you die – like everyone else come before you. A Guardian you'll become. So where do you want to be?" Mas told me how she smelled – like leaves, like dampness. A cool wind she was, what he held in his hand. "Choose," that wind said. "A corner of the earth is yours. A place what calls you. From now on, it's your job, you should shield it with your love."

Yes, my *bubelahs*, each and every one of us dies and becomes one day a Guardian. Surprise! The only heaven we get, it's right here. Some joke, yes, on those priests and rabbis? *Oy*, when they die, what a shock!

Like Mas was feeling at the fire, he told me, thinking of Wina and Padre Guitierrez. His powerful Guardians – so full of wisdom, built from magic – were simple. Just spirits of people what loved this place. Grown bigger, yes, but only ordinary. Stretched by wind or the history of trees – more than human, and better, they'd become.

You understand, dollies? Guardians live from a song what comes out of their land. A call, what Mamale and my sisters heard, come all the way from Terlitza. The tune what promised them, trapped in Petaluma, they could grow bigger – this is what was meant. If they got home. If they returned to the place what held them. If they lived from that same song whistling in their hearts.

Guardians keep the bindings of the earth – roots to soil, grass to air, all the blooming and dying. It's them what makes the seeds sprout, a tree fall. An element or season they choose and make it their business. You've seen the oak what lives in Wina, maybe? How about Padre Guitierrez's storms? No? Well, I'm telling you, Mimi, he's got more than cards what keeps him busy. All of them – and *oy*, you only know a smidgen – live and breathe what place they choose to guard.

"But," Mas told me in the barn, "we're talking place, not a person. Even if she wanted, Mae couldn't come back here."

Why not? Because Mimala, you remember maybe, how she loved New York, all that Lower East Side *mishegoss*. So many people crammed together – that's the ground what had hold of her heart.

And besides, even if she chose Chapman Lane, my Mae, she'd be busy. What with all her guarding, the seeding and dying, what time would she have time – never mind interest – for twisting on the hill with me?

Ach, so disappointed I was, but after a ton of tears, washing the hope away, I didn't have it in me to wish Mae any different. What, you think I'd want her to be like Mamale, held back from all what she was meant to be? I'd learned, finally, what it meant for my poor spirits traveling with me to America. So sorry I felt for them, twenty years held in the wrong place. So *nu*, Mamale was right. Finally, I'd grown up enough to want the best for all of them. Loving Mae, it stretched me, full of breath and heart.

And then the end, finally – after a long night of hard breath, rattling struggle. Such work it took for my poor Mae to die. And with me beside her bed, Mamale, Shlima and Gitl, dressed and ready to travel. So nervous they were – sad to leave, maybe – not a word did they say.

Until the very last second, when Mamale I heard calling. From Mae's final breath, the gargling sound what broke my heart, up I looked into the worried face of my mother, *Mae's not strong enough,* she cried, floating just above me, *too worn down from the cancer. The three of us she can't take!*

Gitl sobbed, throwing herself against my shoulder. Poor Shlima, perched on Mae's dressed, started to scream.

And then – never mind how Art wept, how my ghosts tore their hair – the Guardians came, all eight of them, rising up from the floor into the room with us. Around the bed a circle they made, and began to sing. Mae glowed for a minute, something missing for months come back into her body. A shiny light I saw lift up from the sheets. And then above us her ghost was, holding hands out to Mamale and Shlima. Gitl rode to Terlitza, hanging on to Mae's hair. Still the Guardians sang, filling the room with music. Their song, it gave Mae the strength to do what she must.

"Goodbye," I called, watching the best of my life leave me. Such a hole I felt in my chest, a cave without air. So what for me is left? I wondered, touching Mae's face, closing her eyelids. So lost I felt, washing her body, pulling the sheet up around her neck. So alone.

Not remembering Art, him with the bony hands covering his face, crying in the room with me. Not seeing the sun, busy rising, the east window filling with light. Nothing but just bleak woods, Terlitza after the pogrom, the smell of burning – that's what filled me. Each death I'd never mourned come back to hurt me. Every bit of courage, what held my heart together, broke apart.

All right, I thought, so maybe it's me what can die now. Who wants this world? There's nothing left.

There's something. Wina stepped forward, from the foot of Mae's bed to shake me from my sadness. The tree what lived in her looked at me with knowing eyes. *Your mother asked we should make you a gift,* she said, sounding like leaves talking in the gum grove. Her hand, some kind of blessing maybe, she put on my head.

Yes, I thought. Now I can die.

But no dying, dollies. Instead, aliveness. *Oy vey,* so disappointed I was. Then amazed.

There, by the bed, whole world, it turned wavy. All what was solid in Mae's room, filled it got with light. So I could see – through the walls of the house, through the curtain on the window. Wood and cloth melted – the sun I watched touch the day outside. Saw a breeze move through the yard, its hungry fingers brushing everything. So sharp my eyes, the grass I saw shake.

And then the oaks at the top of the hill, magic it seemed, how they stepped closer. Between leaves, a woodpecker did his business on a trunk. And below me in the rose bushes, little feet I saw – a sow bug walking. The yellow mustard – what Art had forgotten to weed along the driveway – such sucking it made, roots digging deep. For a minute, each and every sound I heard, what lived in the earth's big belly. And then, up from the ground, slowly, *oy,* such a song I heard.

A beautiful music what went straight inside my body. Such singing! A thousand voices – every bird, each weed. Tied me, it did, to the lane, like the rope what linked me to Mamale all those years ago I slept in her belly.

Or maybe, the mother I was now, and Chapman Lane it turned and kicked inside of me.

Understand? No? Listen, *bubee*, it's easy. A magic Wina made, so one of them I could be. Yes, it's Guardian eyes what she gave to me. Imagine! The first and only living member, what shouldn't be, of that special group.

This, the clever gift, promised from Mamale. She knew my grief, how I'd wail for Mae, wanting I should follow. No matter what kind of brave lived in me, the Angel of Death I'd want, he should raise his hand. But instead, sadness, tears AND a singing. Each time I wanted I should stop breathing, the garden, it spoke to me. Asking for seeds, asking for manure – it was planting time already, so *nu*, I should hurry up and feed its hunger. It wouldn't let I should turn my back on the earth what needed me. So my loneliness for Mae, for Mamale, Shlima and Gitl – eventually it turned over. Became the Lane's voice, each breath I took a piece of home.

A rundown house, yes Mimi, hardly big enough to dance in. Malka's old field, the yard – you know from gardening, Shoshie, such an awkward piece of land. But mine: the apple tree, roses what I planted in Mae's name, each year the tomatoes. Even the old chicken sheds, tired and useless, what long ago I should've torn down. But this I couldn't do, feeling Chapman Lane living so much inside me. The whole of it – for better, for worse – held right here in my hands.

Each bird. Each grass. Even a worm, inching the compost. And the ground, with every touch I feel it breathe. And *oy*, do I want to guard it – every bean seed, trying to push out a root, it should suck water. Each ant, busy carrying eggs when from rain or watering, the nest it gets wet. In my fingers, every life taking hold by the soil. The dying too, the shriveling and turning over. Breaking down, becoming something else – this I know.

And it's mine to pass on, the family debt, an inheritance. This gift from Mamale, I don't want with me it should die. And the Guardians don't, either. There's a danger coming, they say, something what will hurt us. A living person we need, should fight in our name.

Understand I didn't until now, so I'm asking, my two girls what got eyes to see, you both so full of magic. After I die, you'll stay here maybe, feel the song? So much the Guardians have done for you – making circles, giving visions. Do you have it in your heart, you should do right by them? From love, from a sense of home, from family. I'm only asking. Do you want? Do you feel big enough? Chapman Lane, can you hold it in your hands?

Chapter 43
The Birthday Gift

Mimi

I consider Mom's request for a hot minute when she finally consents to go to bed at 4:00 a.m. – but "No," I shake my head as soon as I hit the covers. It's too wild, as farfetched as any of the crazy stories she used to make up for Shoshie when she was small. Baba Yaga. Her Cossack battles. Listen, who in their right mind can believe this one? The Guardians taking care of the land and wanting one of us to help – it can't be true.

They exist, of course. But a Slominski debt, all this owing business? "Come on, Mom," I want to say.

But then I sound smart-assed and mouthy, as bad as Aviva and Shoshie when they were teenagers. Why is it that every time I visit this damn place, I lose my good sense and turn young?

Well, I'm not looking for a fountain of youth or to live side by side with any magic. "I'm sorry, Mama," I say to the wall just before I fall asleep. I can still smell Papa, his no-nonsense ways surrounding me. The feeling comforts. "Become a living guardian – no."

But the darn question is there as soon as I wake up – 11:00 already. The big birthday party is only two hours away, and I feel like hell. I don't know why I'm even considering moving here, except for the way the three of us look when we straggle into the kitchen. It helps that I'm not the only one with baggy eyes and a bleached face. And all right, so I like it that we're goofy enough to make jokes about it. Aviva and I could never do this, as much as we're alike. We'd both growl, snapping at Beth, instead of chuckling while we wait for the coffee to brew. This easy feeling reminds me, I realize with a lurch, of family Saturday mornings when the kids were small. When Shoshie lifts her mug as she reads the paper, I see Abe.

But once we get to the park where we're having Mom's picnic, the idea of moving here becomes impossible. Petaluma is scrubby as usual, nothing polished or pretty. It hasn't changed a bit – not the harsh light or the promise of fog later, an edge under the sunshine, beginning to chill the breeze. The scraggly oaks make me long for big trees, the quiet shade of maples. Everything's so open and exposed here. I settle my sun hat tighter onto my head and long for the sheltered quiet of my backyard. As I hurry to set out the food before all the guests arrive, I wonder: what would it mean to become a Guardian of this place? Would I have to love it? I can't imagine finding anything here I'd want to protect.

Except for the peace I feel between Mari and Davy. In between greeting old family friends, they glance shyly at each other as if they woke up this morning and made unexpected love. When Davy finishes hugging old Luba Blumberg, he places a hand on the small of Mari's back and guides her to the food. The way she smiles up at him, leaning into his shoulder as they wait for their grilled hotdogs, reminds me of how they were after the war when they first fell in love. The two most wounded ones from our old crowd had finally found each other. And they were bold, the way they touched and nuzzled in public – even though some folks called Davy a Jap lover. "Yes," he agreed, nuzzling Mari. They were shameless, not caring what anyone thought.

"You're just jealous," Abe teased, "because you won't let me kiss you like that with your parents looking."

He was right, no matter how much I argued against him. And we had a good time, making up for what we wouldn't do in public in the bedroom at home.

If I became a living Guardian, I'd protect that old memory and the way Davy smiles at his wife over a mound of potato salad. I'd protect how Nate grins and pats the picnic bench where he's eating with Carol. "Hey, sis." He holds up his bottle of root beer. "Come here."

My brother looks more at ease than I ever feel in this place. He pats my arm. "You seem full of big thoughts today. Are you okay?" When I nod yes, there's nothing in his satisfied look that hints at the way we argued last night about Papa. "You've done a helluva job with this party." He points with his bottle. "Look at Mama. So damned pleased."

She's become the queen of the afternoon, her folding chair the center of a big group of laughing people. There are so many, I can't make them all out. But they make a buzz of noise, a whir that fills the park like a swarm of insects. It's all I hear, especially now that they're whooping at someone's joke.

"Rob," Nate informs me. "Telling a dirty story."

"In front of Mama and Luba?" I dig my hands into the picnic bench. "How do you know?"

"Easy," he laughs. "I know the punch line. It's the latest from Washington – I told Rob last night."

"But the old ladies…" I start to protest.

"Ah, Mimi," he says, kissing my cheek. "Relax. From dirty stories, they both know. Everything's going to be okay."

Everything's okay, at least, with my older brother, who leans against our picnic table, humming the song that Luba's niece Heather is playing on her guitar. The group around Mama stops talking. When it's time for the chorus, they belt it out. Nate gets up. "Got to join them. Haven't heard that much

Russian in years."

The song's memories don't seem to bother him, like they do me, bringing up lonely evenings when Mom ran off to the Yiddish chorus. And who was it, stuck at home with the pot roast to clean up? All those dishes, slapped into the sink by my angry hands. "Unfair!" I've railed all these years. She should've stayed and washed them. I was a teenager. Wasn't it my time to date and have fun? But what kind of fun did she have as a girl, fleeing a *pogrom*? Then the ranch, all three of us such a handful on top of her ghosts. Mom had so many ties pulling at her that I never knew.

Does it make a difference now that I know more of the story? More important – can I give her this one last thing that she wants, finally making her proud?

Nate stops his walk away from me and looks back. "You coming, doll?"

I smile at his request. "In a minute," I promise, glad to see his eagerness, the loose way he's holding himself, the ease in his stride.

If I do what Mom wants, it will be for him, for Davy, to guard who the boys are becoming. It'll be for Shoshie and Aviva, to make easier whatever they need to bloom. But honestly, isn't there a better way than jailing myself here in Petaluma? If I built Abe's apartment building, turning Chapman Lane into some place with a little class, I'd make us all a mint.

The singers have moved on to sixties songs, old union ditties and protests. Off-key and higher than all the rest, I can hear Mom howling. "We shall not be moved."

And that's true. She might not be moved – to sell some land, to build the complex. All her cockamamie Sierra Club ideas – it might be the last thing she has in mind. I don't know how that song she hears – the *mishegoss* she told us last night about her garden – will affect things. But damn it, she needs to listen to reason. I've thought it out, worked every angle. It's the best thing for everyone involved.

Mom leans back in her chair and fans herself with her hat – tired already. Imagine – singing one song and she's lost her breath. I'm glad Shoshie's giving Mom something to drink. Better she should tell her to stop. Just rest. She doesn't have a lot of time left to make nice.

The bottom line, I realize: I want to make nice with Mom before she goes, working on the apartment together. Building for the future. Making something tangible from what she would call "the truth what lives in the heart."

"So what's your truth?" I imagine Mom asking.

"Abe," I'd tell her. He's the only truth I've ever known.

She loved him too. And she'd want to be part of any tribute to him. She always told me, "that Abe, he's like another son." With all the ways he took care of us, even after death, surely we owe him a monument that's physical. If Mom's right and he's really become a Guardian, this is something he could touch. And maybe, by touching it myself, I'd be holding him again. He's the only song I want in my hands.

But I also don't want to disappoint Mom, watching her bend to blow out the candles on her cake. I can guess the wish she's making – "please let Mimi or Shoshie follow after me" – and God help me if I'm the one to prevent it from coming true. Shoshie could do it, yes, but she's so young and unsettled. No husband or kids. What can she know about from protect?

I shake my head, then stop because Mas is watching. He comes to help me clean up one of the tables, full of packages of hot dog buns and bowls of macaroni salad and baked beans. "You don't have to do this."

Like always, I'm not sure what he means – is he hungry for more watermelon or Jell-O? Then he smiles at me. "You have to understand – what Rheabie wants is not an obligation. She's asking you to do this out of love."

That's the problem, I know, as tears come into my eyes. It's hard to admit how very much I feel for her. We've had so many years of sniping and fighting. There have been all those times when I've given in and yelled. But I can't scream anymore, because of how frail she looks, her hat held on by loose elastic. When I see how slack her arm has become, without the firmness that I loved in it, my bones shake, as if the ground is moving. I hate California earthquakes. I never know where to stand.

"Under a doorway," Abe used to say, so I picture the entrance to his apartment building. My feet anchor between the walls I'm going to build in his name.

But my sense of being jarred and rattled lasts the rest of the party, no matter how many times I think about the complex. I can't shake the feeling until the evening, when Shoshie and I lounge across Mom's rumpled bed. "This is great," she sighs, handing me a bottle of fancy cream, one of Mom's presents from Luba. "So *nu?*" Mom asks, propped up against the headboard. "You think it'll take my wrinkles away?"

"What do you want to do that for?" I tease, rubbing a dollop into her cheek. "They're beautiful and you earned them. Be proud."

Mom blushes and the warmth in her face settles me for the first time today. I step out from Abe's doorway. "Let me tell you about my project," I ask.

"*Mazel tov,*" Mom winks. "So long we've been waiting. This whole visit – never mind the party, the family dinner – for this, I've been holding my breath."

That's true, the way Mom struggles sometimes, but Dr. Kendall said not to worry about it. Nothing serious – a little anxiety, small panic attacks. "Just don't tax her," he urged this afternoon. "Take it easy."

I'll try, if only she'll let me. If only the butterflies in my stomach go away. So what am I so nervous for all of a sudden? Why do I beg her, "Promise, Mama. Don't interrupt until I'm done?"

I refuse to get the building plans until she agrees. "On your honor?" I ask. She nods, but a little absently. I have to be sure, or I might set her off, like Dr. Kendall warned. Besides, if she won't let me talk straight through, I'll never be able to tell it all. "Cross your heart?" I demand, like we used to say when I was small.

"And hope to die," she finishes the vow.

"I didn't mean that," I hurry to correct, laughing as if she's made some kind of joke instead of telling the plain truth. "Hold your horses. That part you should maybe postpone for a while."

Mom's smile, so warm but tired, sends me scurrying for my folder. She stares as I lay out all the drawings on the bed.

"It's named for Daddy," Shoshie points to the sign in front of the complex.

"Sha," Mom orders. "We promised. So Mimala, talk."

I hold my breath, then begin to speak as if I'm talking to the Temple Board, presenting a year-end report of Hadassah projects: fund-raising for the youth league, collecting for the tree-planting near Haifa. The frown on Mom's face is just like Harvey Rothbloom's, the Temple president, the day we proposed sending a bar mitzvah class to Jerusalem so they could become men in a temple near the Wailing Wall.

"Here?" Mom asks, sputtering just like Harvey did, "on Chapman Lane you're talking? A big apartment complex you want to build?"

I nod. "Not just any apartment. In Abe's name. A monument to honor him."

Mom tries hard to stay silent, but a mean look comes into her eyes. "What? That ugly stone you put on his grave – it's not big enough?"

"You said you'd listen," I remind her, making sure none of the edge I'm feeling moves into my voice.

She frowns, then looks down at her hands. "*Nu?* So talk."

I take a breath. Maybe I can still convince her. "This is for the family. To make money so Nate can retire early. So Davy and Mari can do something with their house."

"How do you know they want anything done?" Mom interrupts again, pulling at her fingers.

Why can't she see? I remember convincing the board, but it took logic, a slow procession of facts. "I want to do this for Aviva, to help with college for the kids. For Shoshie." My rebellious daughter sits up straighter on the bed. Mom doesn't understand how much Shoshie's sacrificed. She'll need help later when Mom is gone. "Taking care of you isn't a career. It's not going to help her get set for life."

"I don't need to get set." Shoshie sounds sixteen again, stubborn and ugly, as she rubs Mom's shoulders. They're united against me, like Viva and Shoshie used to be. "I know how to make my way."

I clench my hand, trying to remember that this is not a teenager who pouts in front of me. But the way Shoshie lifts her chin and waits with a sneer on her face brings back all the old arguments. "Waitressing in some dive is not a job to be proud of, young lady. We didn't spend all that money on your college so you would end up like this."

Doesn't Shoshie remember how she left me for Berkeley the fall after Abe died because he would've wanted it? I cut my teeth on the silence in the house that first winter because we'd hurt his memory if she didn't follow his dream. All those long Sunday nights waiting for her to call home. "How's it going, honey? How're your grades?'"

An impatient sigh. Silence. "Grades don't matter."

"Did you fail another test?"

And then crying or yelling. "Why don't you ever ask about me?"

She didn't understand. I **was** asking. At eighteen, what kid ever sees the good in what her mother is trying to say? But she should know better by now, and so should her grandmother. The two them are staring at me, leaning against the headboard. The same frown marks each stubborn face.

"Shoshie has nothing to be ashamed," Mom defends. "Feeding the people, she is. Like your father. A job with honor."

Papa is the key. I take a breath again, try to slow down. "Papa liked to build. He'd be excited. I'm doing what he did with the ranch – making something better out of what we've got here."

Mom flips through the drawings, her arthritic fingers scraping at my plans. "What kind of better? Tennis courts? Swimming pools?" She looks disgusted. "So much concrete, paving over. So the land can't breathe." Then Mom's eyes go wide. "Ach," she cries. "Like Gitl told me." She points. "You! You're the danger. From mine own family. Finally I understand."

I don't, but I hate the way she's looking at me, as if I've become an enemy. As if we're back to how it's always been. "I'm not a danger," I insist, tears flooding my throat. "I only want to do something for everyone. With you. The two of us working together. Mama, listen to me. I want we should be like mother and daughter, making something for Abe."

Now she starts to cry. "And to do this, you'd take away what my mother made for me? Her last gift? A danger, this. Hurt my land, you can't."

"It's not yours!" I shout. "Abe got you that land. All that money you've been buying with, it came right out of his bad heart." She looks frightened, so I try to sound quieter. If I thought it would help, I'd go down on my knees to beg. "I'm asking you to do this, Mama, for me. For him. For the rest of the family. Put us first for once. Don't do what you've always done."

The room goes still while she considers. I hold my breath, hoping she'll finally understand. "So," she nods at last, no longer teary. "A test, we're talking. I'm dying, so you need to know how much you matter? You want I should make a choice between you and my ghosts? Betray the Guardians, so you're sure I care?"

"No!" She's got it wrong – as usual. Something as simple as love, and my mother makes like it smells bad. "I'm your daughter. I'm asking you should help me. Help me do for others. Why is that so hard?"

Mom shakes her head, as if she's sorry. "*Oy*, Mimala, so much you don't see. The land is family too."

She's nuts, pure and simple. "Not flesh and blood. Not like me," I shout. But it does no good. I can tell from the way her face has turned hard, as plain and ugly as the hills behind the ranch. Mom won't move. I suck a long breath down to my belly. The plans I drew, all for nothing. Those evenings with Padre Guitierrez – wasted time. What a fool I was to think she'd listen. When in her life did she ever do anything for me? "You're so selfish!" The words come out in a whoosh. "Your whole life – thinking only about yourself."

Mom shakes her head, as if she's going to argue. I don't give her a chance. "You took in Davy and Nate and ignored me. Neglected the three of us, so busy with your ghosts. Then Mae – leaving us when times were bad, when we most needed you. Now you're doing it again."

All my years in this house have risen up and are standing like soldiers behind me. Every argument we've ever had is crowding the air out of this room.

"So what do you need?" she asks, as stern as I've ever seen her. Like some medieval general, she's thrown down her standard. Our usual battle has begun.

Damn it, I don't want to do this. I'm too tired. Mom, I beg silently, can't we just quit? Two late nights in a row – my back hurts, and my feet are killing me. The old accusations refuse to fill my head. Listen, I want to tell her, this visit was supposed to be different from all the others. I promised Padre Guitierrez I'd find another way. I close my eyes and picture the two of us, playing cards in the safety of my kitchen. So much laughter while we planned this trip. And he kept repeating the same advice in that soft Spanish accent of his. "Tell the truth."

I try it. "What do I need? You," I say, the words coming hard, but I force them. "How many times do I have to tell you? The project – us together. Out of love. Planning. For Abe. Filling our days." It doesn't make any sense, but I feel as if a new wind has rushed through my body, filling the hollow spaces.

There's no muscle or bone for it to cling to, just wide, empty space.

I hear Shoshie say something in that wild emptiness, but I can't hear because she's so far away. I seem to be east of her, no longer tired, standing on the edge of a windy plain. "What?"

"This can't be for Daddy," she repeats across the expanse of grasses. "Mom, listen. He's not here."

"Of course he's not here." I don't know why she's telling me the obvious. "We have to build it first before he'll come."

She shakes her head. "It doesn't work that way," and I don't know why she sounds so sure. But the empty plain is quiet, so I lean toward her and listen. "Petaluma isn't Dad's place. If he's anywhere, he's back in his garden at home. No matter what you do here, he won't move."

"But he'd love this complex," I insist. "It's just what he wanted when we got old."

"What you want," Mom corrects, but there's nothing nasty in her tone. "A pretty place to hold you. What you deserve."

I don't want her to turn this around, like she always does. "This isn't about me," I correct, hoping I sound soft. "It's for Abe. What he'd like."

"Not now," Shoshie contradicts gently, "not since he's become a Guardian." Then she laughs a little. "You know what Dad's like this time of year. He's too busy taking care of his roses. He's got all those tulips to help bloom."

"That's ridiculous." But true. I wipe my eyes and look for a Kleenex.

Mom hands me one, patting my arm. "Listen to your daughter." I want to shake off her fingers, but can't move them. Such warmth comes from her touch, pressing hard into my skin.

Shoshie smiles at Mom, then turns to me. "If you want to build for Daddy, you have to do it in Ithaca. A community garden. Something with plants."

Mom moves her hand finally. I shiver, relieved, then find I miss the touch. "I don't like gardens."

"No?" Shoshie picks up the plans. "Look at this. Daddy would love what you've done. You've got the touch, Mom. An eye for color. This is a damn good design."

So many nights looking over Abe's garden books, reading about landscape planning, the principles of the color wheel. Making careful lists of perennials. Their culture and requirements. Thinking texture, bloom cycle, the shape of the plants.

"Yes," Mom nods. "This garden – a celebration of Abe. You made – not for who he was, but the Guardian what he's become." She peers at the plans for a long minute, then stares up at me. "The biggest inheritance what I have to give you, Mimala – not money, not land – this lesson. Clinging to the dead, it's not something we get – this I learned finally. So much they change shape after they leave us. Let them go and make your own life."

"I don't have one," I admit. The wind inside begins to rise again, whipping the grasses on the plain, whispering Abe's name.

Mom pats my hand, "Like me, my daughter. After Mae died. After your papa. The same loneliness. But you," she shakes her head, "such a better fighter. A life for yourself, this you can do."

"Why don't you do more of this?" Shoshie suggests. "Landscaping. Working with plants. Doing designs for your friends."

"But I don't know enough." These plans were fun, but take them seriously? What if I'm no good? What if I'm just wasting my time?

"So study," Mom shrugs. "You've got the brains for it. More important, dolly, for this you've got the love." Love of plants? Love of Abe? I'm not sure what she means, until Mom winks. "Between you and me, a little word of warning. They come back, the dead, when you're doing for yourself, full of gladness. A reminder of pleasure they want, when your hands are full of dirt."

"Sex, you mean?" Shoshie asks. "From being in the garden?"

"Don't think so small, *bubee.*" Mom grins at me, and I understand her finally, remembering the night the Guardians brought Abe back. Shoshie's too young to get it yet. But to prepare for when she's older, Mom tries to explain. "Bigger than sex. We're talking love."

"You'll help me?" I ask, barely believing it. I imagine going back to school, getting a degree, maybe starting my own business. The thought makes me shudder. With fear? Excitement? Or maybe I should try this community garden *mishegoss*. I'll need to investigate exactly how those things work.

"Of course, help," Mom answers, "for you, the new life you're making. Whatever you need – a little money, advice. Interest. My own flesh and blood, how could I not?"

I need to make sure she understands. "But, not here. Not in Petaluma. This living Guardian thing I just can't do." She nods, but I can't bear it if she's disappointed. "I wanted to try it for you, Mama, because you asked. Because it's so important. But I can't. I just don't belong."

"I know, dolly. A little foolishness of mine, a mother wanting her daughter." She brushes tears from her cheeks. "So many years I've missed, you and me, side by side."

"You have? Even with all our fighting?" It's hard to take in how she looks at me. Those eyes, her dark eyes.

She nods. "*Meshugge,* yes? But the truth, always. Underneath the squabbles, I knew between us lived some kind of love."

"The birds," Shoshie nods, looking wise, but I don't know what she's talking about. It doesn't matter. What counts is the open way she smiles and how Mom pulls up from the pillows to pat my hand. "Ithaca, it's your place now, Mimala, built from all what you and Abe loved. So don't worry, *bubee*. Besides, Shoshie wants – this place, it's grown in her, become home. This afternoon she told me. So you go back east and start studying, *shayne maydele*. So proud you'll do me. It's all right."

Chapter 44
WHERE THERE'S A WILL...

RHEABIE

But it's not all right, Rheabie. Wake up now. There's danger.

What wake? What danger? You got some nerve, Wina. Four in the morning, we're talking. A woman's got a right to rest.

Not while there's still a danger.

No. Danger, I did already: broke my hip, fooled with my kidneys, made peace with Jake, sent Mimala home. All the things what you warned me. They're done.

I wasn't warning you about those things.

Ach, stop already. Warning, of course, about all those things you were. What else? Listen, we did them, this long bad year and now – good luck, goodbye – they're finished. The last, the worst – but it's over. Packed up happy, Mimi was, taking her *farfufket* plans with her. For Abe, she won't dare build on this land. You heard how it was, our conversation. Difficult and angry. Then something new. Like a peach pit, Mimi broke open. So much softness, the seed curled inside.

No.

Yes! I saw the way her face split. All what was hidden in her, it came pouring out. And maybe you noticed how already, how busy she is with the blooming? The call we got yesterday, only two days home – classes she'll take at the university. Already, a community garden, she's found. And that laughing voice, what I hadn't heard in her for years. Only a little sharpness at the end – "Are you taking your medicine, Mom? Are you paying Shoshie a salary?" – the knife of her fear.

And what knife do you hold? Why are you so afraid, talking at me and not listening? Piling up words one on top of each other so you can't hear. I'm speaking about the danger, the one still here in this room.

Not here. Not ever. Relax. It's just you and me.

Yes, with so many years between us. Do you think I don't know you? You're like one of the saplings I guard, coming into wisdom. It's coming time for you to leaf out. But instead, you're holding the leaves in. What is it? Why are you afraid?

Because you're going to tell me – the danger, I'm dying.

Are you surprised? You didn't know?

Of course I know, but I don't want. Not when, finally, in the family, something good is growing. If I should leave now, so much I won't see: Davy coming back into himself, Mimi's adventures. Exactly what retirement might do to my good Nate. And who's Shoshie going to become now that she's taken her life in her hands, chosen she should move here? Even the garden. A woman wants to know: how much applesauce from the tree this year? Those purple beans, so odd, will they really grow?

So yes, it's hard to leave, even knowing what's ahead, becoming a Guardian. All these years, looking forward. But now? All right, so yes, scared in my bones, I've been all winter. Not listening. Each time the Angel of Death, he has the *chutzpah* to come close, the very thought curls my hair.

And the fear makes a danger. Look in the mirror. I'm not talking about dying. Something is wrong for the living. A threat. It's right here.

No one's here. Look for yourself. Just me. Only me.

Yes.

What? You're telling me – the threat I am? Me, making danger?

Never! How could you think such a thing? *Vey iz mir*, I'm like Jake now, a hurt to all what I love? Maybe like Mimi, making bad by the land? Such a curse, an insult. Where are your eyes?

The dream.

About the land, yes, what Mimi wanted to do with it. Paving and building. So nothing could breathe. But I made sure – her building won't happen. Her and her plans I sent home.

And there's one more thing to do to make it safe, a matter for the living. Only you can cure the danger you've made.

Listen, I'm telling you, I haven't made any! Please. It's late. I'm tired. I need you should explain, for once in your long, long life, what you mean.

You don't need me. If you'd quit shouting and think, you'd find you already know.

What I know – it hurts to breathe. Mine friend, the enemy, the one what squeezes my chest, he's in the room.

So see who he is. Look at him like you saw Mimi the other night.

What I saw was a girl, hungry for the love of her mother. A girl – never mind she's almost sixty – what didn't have a taste yet of her own life.

Yes?

All right, like me, so many years ago. Under Mamale, Shlima and Gitl's shadow. Just like me, afraid to take a breath. Holding too tight. Not willing she should let go.

And to let go now? What are you holding?

You. This house. My garden.

Yes, you're beginning to understand. From the moment your mother gave you the gift of living as a guardian, you've had a task. And you've done it well, but now that time is ending. There's one last thing. You need to open up your hand. Look in the mirror. See the danger and be a Guardian. Give it love.

You want I should give love to a danger?

Yes. To whatever hurts the land. We make circles. For you. Mimi. Shoshie. We watch the threat, keep it company. Try to understand. Then we come and circle, nourishing the root of the need. All these years, you've wanted to know what makes our magic. The only thing we do, my sapling, is act from love. Think back to all the times we came to you or Mas or your spirits. Think what you did for Mimi the other night.

Listened past what that poor child, she was saying. Finally, I heard the hunger what lived in her eyes.

Can you hear the hunger in your own? A woman afraid to die won't make plans for the future. You have one last task. Protect the land.

What? Only a will, you're talking? The big threat – a simple piece of paper? False as a marriage license. Ach, go on.

This is for the living. For the land.

No. Jake and I, we never liked wills. Bringing the law into personal business. Courts. Lawyers. Socialist, it's not. Besides, the *kinder* know from what I want. What's to worry? Anything happens, Shoshie will make right.

Mimi thought you'd want her apartment building. You need to do better than that.

All right, so maybe you've got a point, but now she knows better. That girl, I straightened out. So enough. What you want – it's not necessary. Besides, against a principle you want I should go?

No. Against your fear. One last time, you need to stop grabbing.

I'm grabbing? What?

Holding tight to what's not yours anymore. It's time. Pass on the land you're guarding. Let Shoshie take up the hard task.

And then what? I should do what you want and poof? I'm dead? But so much I've been looking forward to, in the summer, by the garden. After all the *tsuris* this long winter, you don't think don't I deserve so much?

It's not up to me to decide. But tell me, what do you want?

A little time, after I should get this will business done and over. A season or two, I should enjoy before what comes next. So maybe I could get a little snippet, what happens at the end of the story. Well, not the end, but the beginning – of the life the *kinder* should make next. Only a whiff, I want, a chance to see what it means, the future. Are you big enough, you can give me that?

I can only hold you – an act of love, no matter what happens. I thought you understood. There's no boss, no one in charge. Only your body knows when you'll become a full Guardian. I can't promise you any time.

Then understand, at least – what hurts, all the regrets, the holding. Maybe, for you too many years it's been, but in me, still something what wants to bite at life. So tasty, even when it's bitter. An odd flavor maybe, here at the end, but like a hard candy in some forgotten pocket – a little dusty, flecked with old Kleenex – still, in my mouth I put it. I want I should suck.

Trust me, then, old friend. The tasting doesn't stop, even after the body has ended. Make a will, Rheabie, and no matter what happens, you'll feast on the wind.

Chapter 45
ENTERING THE BREEZE

SHOSHANA

The wind comes up on a hot Thursday afternoon in September, twisting down the hill behind the ranch and billowing its grasses. It heaves and gusts against the apple tree, making its branches creak. I look up at a loud gust from my chair on the porch, holding tight to the newspaper. The breeze fills my tee shirt and pulls at my skin, getting me up.

It's time to check the water on the cucumbers. I move the hose to the tomatoes. The squash I need to gather for supper hide under wide, yellowing leaves. Once they're picked, I look up at the sun to try and guess: four o'clock maybe? Warmth teases my shoulders, and I smile at the wind singing through the purple beans.

If I could read the breeze, I'd know that Grandma is dying in her bed, instead of napping. The clear cast to the air, the rustle of grass and rose bush, is not simply weather, but the ranch reaching up its arms to say goodbye. The two sagging chickens sheds, the red petunias in a pot on the porch steps and the dozen jars of homemade applesauce cry out to hold her. They know that, at this very moment, she is reeling from a stroke and laboring hard.

I don't feel it. I see only a tidy kitchen brightened by the marigolds on the table when I come in from the garden. I look at the big clock – 4:45 – and worry that it's late. Heather and Luba are due for dinner soon, and it's time to get started. I whistle down the hallway, my signal to Grandma that she needs to get up.

"Grammy?" I call when she doesn't stir after a few minutes. I wait, then listen to my feet making sharp sounds as they walk down the hardwood floor. "Are you all right?" I ask, standing in her doorway. "Do you want to help cook?"

A gust fills her bedroom, ruffling the curtains and fanning her will, a sheath of papers, well-thumbed and bent at the corners, that rests on her bedside table. Grandpa's picture on her dresser moves a little and falls. I don't notice that until afterwards, because all I see is that she's turned on her side and is struggling. The odd sound of her breath, a long inhale that gargles, makes me gasp.

Grandma's face is pinched in a grimace as if she is screaming. Her eyes have gone milky, the lids half closed. But they move under the skin – to the right, then left – as if she is searching for something. The breeze lifts a fringe of hair off her forehead. She relaxes her mouth, then draws it up again.

After her birthday, she made me promise that if she got sick, I wouldn't call Dr. Kendall or anything close to an ambulance. Mom nodded with me. "I'll be here too, and we'll keep you safe." But now, alone, it's hard not to look at the phone or to imagine how it would feel if my fingers were dialing. Where's Uncle Mas? How come Mom isn't with me? Couldn't *Jikan Fujin* or Wina have given us any warning about this?

What's to warn? I imagine Grandma saying, *There is only the doing. Afraid of this, I've been, but look at me. Bad, it's not. So come dolly, sit. Stay with me.*

I count the seconds between her breaths, sitting on the bed beside her and holding her tired body. Two, three, four. The curtains lift up, stretch out, fall flat. Seven, eight. Finally, she breathes again.

"Grammy, I'm afraid. I don't know what to do now."

I wish she could pat my hand. *Ach bubee, yes, you do.*

I touch her face, fingering the hollows of her eyes, tracing her cheekbones. I watch one of my tears catch in the maze of wrinkles that ripple across her skin. Her chest rises and falls, the gaps between breaths getting longer.

Then the room stills, and I clutch at Grandma's arm, squeezing it tight. "Don't," I beg. "Not now. Not yet."

Shlima appears in the air above us. She is thinner than I imagined, a stick in a long black dress. *Shoshanala, finally. Such a pleasure to meet you.*

Mamale whisks in through the window, a broad woman in a rustle of silk. The red scarf that covers her hair brightens the room. She looks me over and nods. *A worthy granddaughter.* Then she waves her arm. *Gey. We have a business now.*

I feel Gitl's hand covering mine for a moment, a wisp of coolness. She whispers in my ear. *Dolly, it's time you should get out of the way.*

Grandma frowns, her eyebrows drawn together. "I'm sorry, but I'm not leaving," I declare loudly. I peer through their filmy bodies to watch Grandma's face.

Another moment of quiet and then her breath changes, getting bigger. She wheezes and gasps. The air heaves into her lungs and out again, moving quickly. Her shoulders rock up and down with every huff. And there is no time between breaths, the rhythm quick and jerky. She's laboring, and I'm frantic that there's nothing I can do to give her ease.

What did you expect? I hear her pant. *Bubee, it's work, to come in and out of life.*

And yes, the work is beautiful, making my ribs stretch while every bone in my body rattles. Mamale, Shlima and Gitl float in circles above her while the house trembles, listening as she breathes. Grandma becomes the one still spot on a rippling, twisting blanket. I'm so shaken by the movement, it takes me a moment to realize that her breathing has stopped.

Stopped. And from her chest comes a rattle. Wet and full of water, the sound floods her lungs, throat, mouth.

She gurgles. Gurgles again. Then, nothing. The ranch holds itself quiet and waits, but Grandma is gone.

As I start to howl, like the wolf she always saw in me, I can feel her all around me. She lifts up to join her mother and sisters and becomes something close to heat. She's a drift of flame, a wild blaze that shimmers. She glitters in the air while I cry out, *Grammy! Don't leave.*

She laughs. *My Shoshanala. Oy, such a wonder.* I feel a touch of fire down my face. *The taste of the wind. So big, so very big.*

And then Wina comes, rising out of the floorboards to stand in front of me. I am crying so hard that I barely feel her touch when she puts a hand on my head.

Epilogue
HEARING THE WIND

SEPTEMBER 1982

A year later, the breeze still ruffles the branches of the old apple tree. I feel leaves strain against the gust, then pull back. One twig falls, shocked to be torn from bark, to twist in the embrace of the wind that holds it. I lift my palm, fingers out stretched, and manage a catch.

Thank you, Grandma.

The dahlias I planted last spring bow under her touch, ruffle as she runs her fingers over their blossoms. Heather's wind chime, the one she made me for Chanukah, sings when Grandma breathes. She wafts around me, blowing the bangs out of my eyes, puffing my skirt with her billows. I know I shouldn't, but I fling my arms out to hold her and laugh.

"Shoshie, come in out of the wind," Mom calls from the kitchen. "Your hair needs combing." She fusses over me as if I'm ten again. "Uncle Nate and Aunt Carol just called from the hotel. Viva's scared the kids will get dirty if we don't hurry. It's time to leave."

Grandma follows us, a little gust tearing at the red flowers of the bottlebrush that line the cemetery. She bends the grasses that cluster at our feet, making them shiver in the afternoon light. A windy caress rims the bowl of tomatoes and zucchini that I place at the base of her new gravestone. When Uncle Davy sets down a jar of marigolds from the garden, she ripples their leaves.

Mom stops professionally assessing the landscaping to say a little prayer, but Grandma lifts her words so we can't quite hear them. Bad enough we buried her, instead of an ecological cremation, but now we have to throw in some religion as part of the unveiling? *Feh!* I hear her snort. *This is a battle you should've won, Shoshanala.* I shake my head, looking over the small group of family and friends gathered here. *All right yes, I understand – keeping the family peace you were.* I nod and she quiets, ruffling only the edge of Hannah's stiff petticoat. Uncle Nate steps forward and begins a speech.

"I hope Mama approves of the wording on the stone." He winks at Uncle Davy and smiles at Mom. Maybe he's remembering all the arguments we had this winter, the endless phone conversations discussing their different ideas. I tug on Heather's hand, thanking her for getting impatient and scribbling out a compromise late one rainy night. "There," she offered. "Something simple. Close to all that she was."

Uncle Nate runs a hand through his hair. "I'd hope to announce the final plans for the park today, but the Nature Conservancy, the county and I are still negotiating. You know bureaucrats. Or at least, I do, since I used to be one." He grins at the mention of his retirement, then sighs. "They like the idea of turning her property into a living-history ranch and don't even mind Shoshie running it." Heather nudges my shoulder, looking proud. "The tearing down of any new houses, keeping only what was here in the twenties, doesn't bother them a bit. And I have to tell you – I like the idea of Chapman Lane cleaned out, back to the way I knew it. But," he takes a long breath. "we're stuck on the damn chickens. I keep telling them that's one of the conditions of her will – no ifs, ands or buts – but they're worried about keeping them. They don't want the smell."

The old timers chuckle. *So what's a ranch without a stink?* Grandma laughs with them. Uncle Mas snorts, swallows a grin and winks at me across the crowd.

"So we're still fighting, being stubborn, like Mama would want. But so help me, if it's the last thing I do, I promise to make Slominski Ranch come to be."

Luba lets out a whoop and the rest of the group joins her. Grandma cheers with them, rattling a breeze through the trees.

Then Mom steps forward and lifts the cloth covering Grandma's stone, and the wind breathes over it. The gust lingers, drying the tears on my cheeks, tracing the chiseled words.

A Woman of Heart

Rheabie Melnick Slominski
1902-1981

Dayenu
It was Enough

I feel the roots of the trees in the gum grove shift, drawing up water. I hear the echo of Mae's voice in a finch that shifts through the leaves. Grandpa hums, a song coaxed from the threads of dandelion thistle. Grandma's life, the long winding thread of it, throbs in my hands.